CONNECTIONS
(CONEXIONES)

By

Tony Lavely

All Maps by Tommi Salama

tommisalama@gmail.com

This is a work of fiction. Names, characters, places, and incidents are either products of the author's imagination or used fictitiously. Any resemblance to actual events, locales, or persons, living or dead, is entirely coincidental.

Edition 150511.4

Previously

Beckie Sverdupe and Ian Jamse are introduced in *Mercenaries: A Love Story*, the story of their meeting, Ian's invitation to Beckie to join his mercenary group, and then, his proposal of marriage to her. In the second volume, *Freedom Does Matter*, Beckie demonstrates her desire to have the team move away from direct combat types of contracts, favoring negotiations and protection offerings instead. The results are not uniformly positive, but London is saved.

Amy Rose Ardan enters the story during *Freedom Does Matter*, where her nascent relationship with Abby Rochambeau, an older team member, is exposed and put on indefinite hold: Abby is sent to assist the team setting up campaign security for a Peruvian presidential candidate. Meanwhile, fifteen-year-old Amy continues her home schooling. As *Freedom Does Matter* ends, Beckie and Ian return to the Nest; coincidently, Amy disappears on her sailboat.

TABLE OF CONTENTS

THE NEST

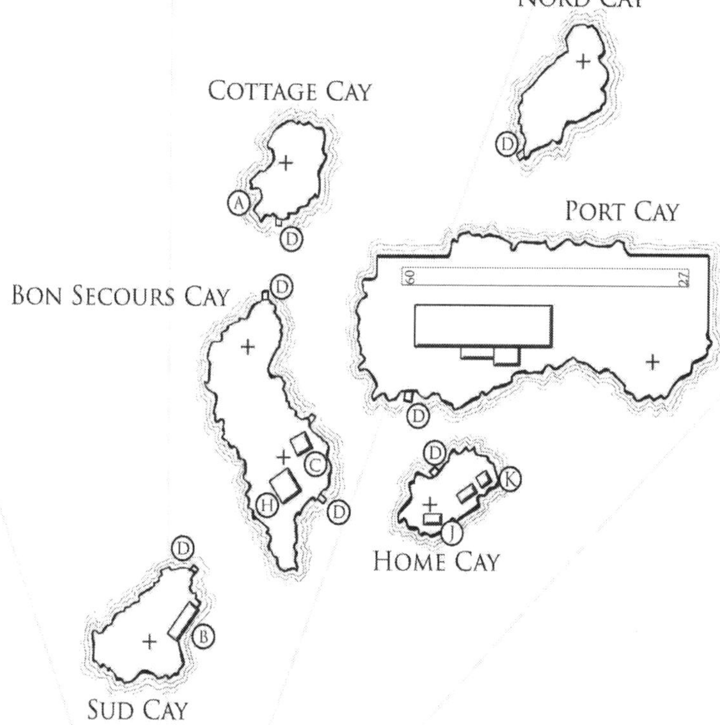

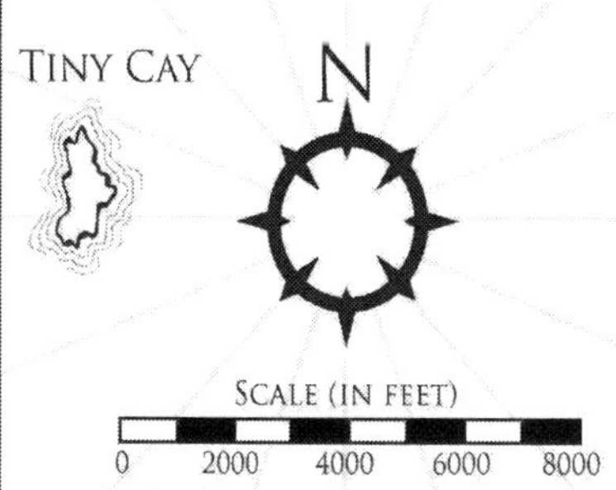

LEGEND

A - ANCHORAGE
B - DEEP DRAFT DOCKING
C - SECURITY AND BASE OPERATIONS
D - INTER-ISLAND DOCK
H - HOSPITAL
J - IAN JAMSE'S HOME
K - KEVIN DEVEEL'S HOME
\+ - HIGH POINT

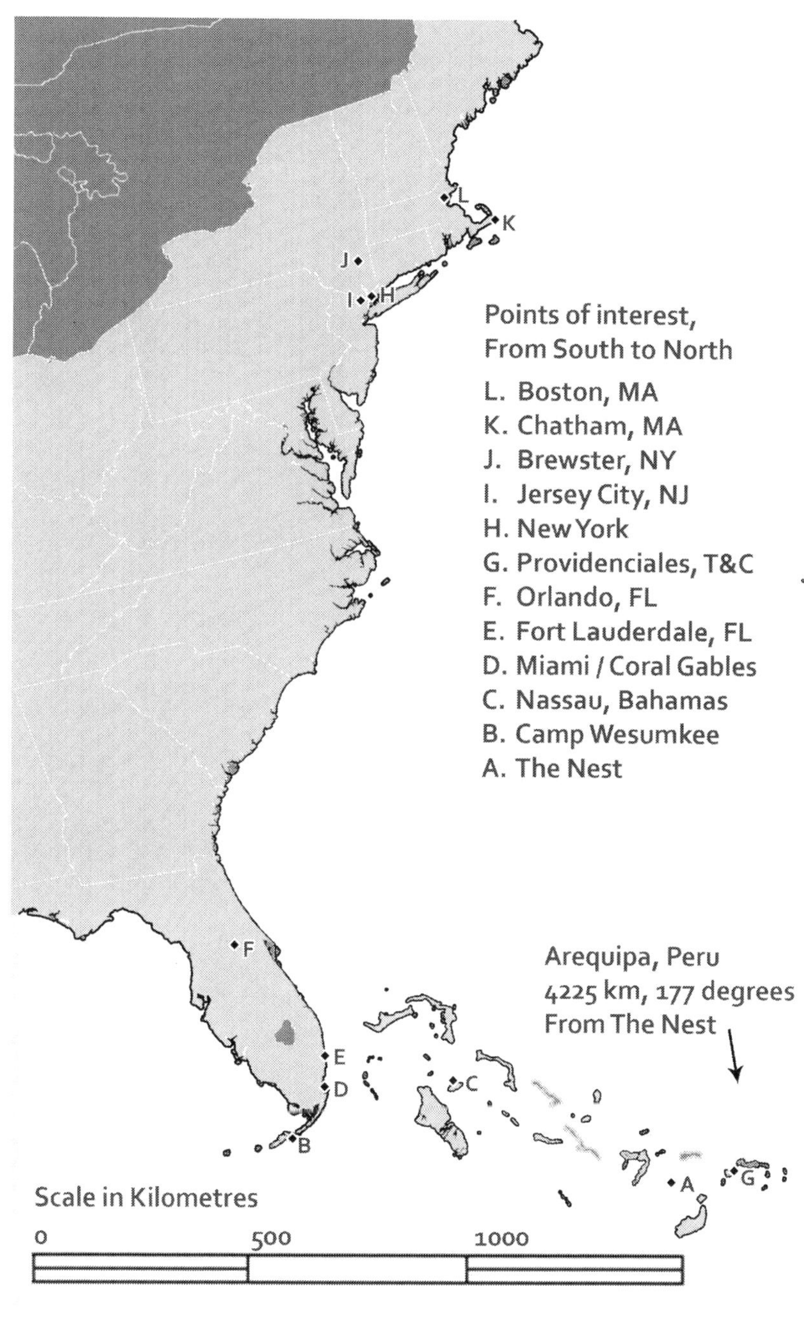
L
K
J
I
H
Points of interest,
From South to North
L. Boston, MA
K. Chatham, MA
J. Brewster, NY
I. Jersey City, NJ
H. New York
G. Providenciales, T&C
F. Orlando, FL
E. Fort Lauderdale, FL
D. Miami / Coral Gables
C. Nassau, Bahamas
B. Camp Wesumkee
A. The Nest
F
E
D
C
B
A
G
Arequipa, Peru
4225 km, 177 degrees
From The Nest
Scale in Kilometres
0
500
1000

Chapter One
New York

PIERO SALVADORE'S FELLOW NEWARK-BOUND passengers clogged the jetway, slowing him even more than his misgivings. During the trek to the terminal, his phone signaled a new message from his boss, Mateo Huamán. "I can't make it to pick you up," he'd written. "Meet the limo outside Baggage Claim. We'll talk later." Piero sighed. He still had no idea why he'd been invited to attend the conference at the United Nations.

During the limo ride into New York City, Piero concocted reason after reason for Huamán's sudden command to join him. None made any sense. As Peru's Minister of the interior, Huamán's role was understandable. As Huamán's sub-Minister, Piero might provide background, he supposed, but then thought, We did all that before he left last week. And he would never have forgotten so much that a phone call wouldn't suffice!

When Huamán greeted him at the hotel, the tension in the man's face and carriage soothed Piero not at all. While the conference, a symposium on natural resources and their allocation on a supranational level, is important, he thought, it could not cause such angst.

Nothing reduced the mystery during dinner, except Huamán told Piero they had an appointment at nine that evening; they would leave the hotel a half-hour before.

Though New York was experiencing an unseasonably cold October, Huamán chose to walk. Striding alongside Huamán, Piero noticed the evening traffic—taxis and police cars, mostly—and the leafless trees along the curb. When Huamán spoke, however, the scenery faded away.

"I'm sure you remember the meetings we held with Nayra on Jaime's behalf?"

Piero was shocked into silence. After a few paces, Huamán tapped his sleeve. "Piero?"

"Jaime's campaign financing violations? Of course. How could I forget? But what… He's out of prison, now, and out of politics."

"Yes. It is not he you should recall. Instead, the video recordings he made for—"

Piero tripped over a smooth section of sidewalk. "The video…"

"Yes. While they would not impact you, as sub-Minister, so much, Nayra and I… we might have…"

"Yes." Piero looked around, expecting to see Peruvian staffers surveilling them. "What of it? And is it safe to discuss, even here?"

"I think so. I hope so." Huamán continued walking, his arms first swinging in cadence, then clasped behind his back. "What of it? On my arrival, a… gangster, I suppose, introduced himself as I walked near the UN. He called himself Donato Talos, and eventually told me he had the original video Jaime made of our meetings."

Piero recovered from his shock enough to say, "What? How?"

"Talos would not say how the video came to him. He wants…" Huamán paused as they passed a young couple. "He wants a substantial amount, in gold he said, to return it. No other party could provide both interest and funds, he said."

Piero sneered. "I can only imagine he has not looked very hard."

"Perhaps. Or I was his first target. In any event, for all our sakes, I will purchase his package, and give the video to Nayra." Piero said nothing. "Before you ask, I have done all the research possible to be assured he has what he claims, and the payment will finish the story. The gold is at the hotel."

Piero mumbled something that might be confused as assent, but his mind roiled. Finally, he could speak again. "So, I'm not here for the conference at all."

"True." He stopped to face Piero, the clouds of their breaths billowing before vanishing in the breeze. "I need your help making the exchanges. There will be no risk, I'm sure."

As he stepped off again, Piero smiled in mock agreement. I doubt Nayra Mamani is the best repository for that evidence.

After a few more moments of conversation to agree on their plan, Huamán slowed, consulting a scrap of paper. Piero noticed the dark wood facing of a bar, tall silvered letters proudly, incongruously, announcing its name, The Quiet Pub. Huamán tipped his head at the glass door.

When they entered, a tired looking barmaid listened as Huamán murmured his name, then pointed to a table where two men waited. Glasses and a large chrome pitcher stood before them. As Huamán led the way, the two stood and with a single curt wave, the shorter man invited them to the table.

"Thank you, Mateo. First names will do," the man said.

"Good evening, Donato. My… friend is Piero." Huamán sat across the table from Donato.

"Please. Donny is fine." He faced Piero. "A pleasure, I'm sure."

Piero nodded. Both of the men impressed him. No, he admitted, the unnamed man impressed him. Donny terrified him. Donny's eyes were cold; emotionless. At least, hints of feeling flitted across the other man's face. And the rose tattoo on Donny's neck.

Huamán began directly: "The recording? When may I see it?" Looking at Donny, Piero cringed inwardly, wondering about the wisdom of starting with a demand.

"In good time, señor, in good time. Perhaps Piero can deliver the payment tomorrow morning to León?" He inclined his head toward the second man. "Then, after we validate the weight, you and I can meet tomorrow evening for the exchange."

"But how will I be sure—"

"You doubt my word? Come, come. You have seen the screenshots; how would I make them without the original? What in the Virgin's good name would I do with the videos if not turn them over to you? They have no value outside your tiny world."

Piero agreed. However, inside Peru the videos could trigger a bidding war. Or worse. *¡Dios!* I might be entangled in that war!

However, Huamán had instructed him to observe; he remained silent. He looked once again at Donny and quivered. Silence would serve him well.

Piero remained focused on Donny while Huamán continued to protest. Donny was calm, without evident emotion, but definite in his position. He sipped from a wine glass, but Piero didn't believe it held wine. As Donny repeated himself, a small smile crossed his face. An emotion: he enjoys this.

Huamán tapped his shoulder; together, the two men rose. As Huamán made their goodbyes, Piero turned to León. "At my hotel?" Piero glanced at Huamán to see a brief acknowledgement.

"*Sí*. Your room?"

"Fifteen thirty-two. Ten o'clock?"

León nodded.

At the appointed hour, Piero had the gold, in a wooden crate stenciled 'Machine Tools,' ready for León. By his watch, the knock was a minute late, but since Huamán had said, "I'll see you at the U.N. at twelve-thirty," he felt unhurried.

He opened the door, then fell back as a short, black-haired girl stumbled into his arms. In reflex, he caught her and held her up as he realized first, she was nearly nude, and second, Donny and León had followed her in.

León tossed aside the wrap the girl must have worn; Donny strolled around the room's perimeter to the chair at the desk. He waved at the girl. "Enjoy. She's a distraction for you while we validate the package."

Piero couldn't speak. He stammered, but his protest was unintelligible. He held the girl away, observing, before she hugged herself to him again. "But…" She was attractive, perhaps twenty or a year older. Her breasts, not large, quivered minutely as she moved. He wondered if she was Andean; her color and facial structure argued she might be.

She reached to place her lips against his ear. "Please, do not refuse," she whispered. "We will both suffer, believe me."

He pushed her away but she fought him to crush her lips against his mouth, cutting off his questions but also, he shamefully admitted, causing a reaction she took advantage of, grinding her hips against him. After a minute of the vertical foreplay, she released his mouth and took his hand. With a smile, she pulled him out of the suite's sitting room into the bedroom.

"Wait," Donny said with a smile. "The package?"

Before he kicked the door closed, Piero pointed to the wooden crate.

Behind the door, Piero asked only why they would both suffer. "I for not being attractive to you," she said. "You for paying attention to what Jefe does, rather than me."

"And the penalty?" Surely he wouldn't—

"For you, I guess it would depend on what the box contains and his expectation. For me, at least a beating, perhaps worse."

"I must be at the U.N. by noon."

She glanced behind her at the clock. "Jefe said he needed less than an hour, so…"

"So?"

"So, not much foreplay!"

She laughed as she drew him to the bed; she fell on her back, dragging him down atop her.

Piero didn't have his pants on when Donny threw open the door. "Camila, out." After the girl scampered through the door, Donny pushed it closed. Piero tried to swallow but his throat was suddenly dry and constricted. He gasped, trying to breathe. Donny didn't seem to notice.

Maybe he has that effect on everyone.

"Everything's fine," Donny said. "We'll take care of the package."

A single nod was all Piero could manage.

Donny smiled and went to the armchair by the window. "Now. While señor Huamán has been a profitable acquaintance, I hope to meet someone. Perhaps someone like yourself, who might bring me an advantage in dealings I plan."

Piero managed to force two words from his tight throat. "Dealings, señor?"

Donny laughed as he turned the chair and dropped into it. "Relax, Salvadore. Piero. Breathe. Pull your pants up. I will not kill or even injure one whose collaboration I wish to gain."

Piero nodded. He rolled off the bed away from Donny, then pointed to the bathroom. He felt marginally better when he returned to sit on the end of the bed across from Donny. "Thank you." He turned to check the time. "We have a few moments, señor Talos. What help do you think I can provide you?"

"Nothing of great import." He paused just long enough to worry Piero. "Simply put: I have a need for a reliable source of cocaine in bulk."

Piero smiled tentatively. Smuggling cocaine out of Peru met one of his personal goals: every kilo shipped into the northern hemisphere was a kilo not distributed in Peru. He leaned back on his hands. Sara can always use more money. And that *finca* we've been looking at… But… He looked up at Donny, sitting, still patient, a humorless smile twisting his lips. His eyes… He could have killed her, Piero knew in his heart. And probably me, too.

He nodded, a small motion, then said, "The girl—"

Donny stopped him with a gesture. "She's a distraction. You won't see her again…" His eyes opened wide. "… unless you wish to?" Piero didn't dare answer that. He couldn't guess how either a yes or a no would be interpreted. "Do you wish to see her again? If not her, another? Similar? Different? Older? Younger—"

"No! Yes. Yes, I would like to see her again." Which seals my fate, undoubtedly, but protects her. But Sara… It's done now, no matter what.

Donny was already at the door. "León, send Camila back in here." He turned back to Piero. "She's available while you are in New York. If you wish to take her to Peru, that can be arranged, but I won't do that until we speak again. Have a good day, señor." He patted Camila on the butt as she came through the door, then Piero heard the front door to the suite close.

"We weren't *that* good, Piero." She dropped her wrap over the chair. "But practice will help. Shall we try for a more… Hmm. A more relaxed experience?"

"No. I must meet… for lunch. Please stay here; we will talk when I return. Order yourself lunch or anything you wish." He glanced at her bare body. "Perhaps some clothing for dinner?"

Once she nodded, he verified the crate was gone and left.

Later that evening, as Talos and Huamán began their meeting, Jolene Rochambeau walked out of the Dag Hammarskjöld Library at the United Nations. She wrapped her scarf tight and pulled her coat together as she hurried to the gate on 1st Avenue.

New York spread out in all its nighttime glory. The wind cut through her coat and slacks; she shivered. Traffic was still heavy though rush hour had passed. With a snort of disgust, she rejected the buses lined up along the avenue and walked west along 42nd Street. She frequently did the mile walk to Times Square, but not often when her breath clouded before her.

After a stop in MacDonalds for a bag of dinner, she strode toward the subway station, where she could catch the number one train to 116th Street, and Columbia University.

Just before she reached a small park, the sound of a scuffle ahead stopped her before she stepped into the light from a streetlamp. She scanned the area, but saw no one. Most particularly, she saw no police.

She sidled up to the corner of the building and peered into the open space.

About fifteen feet away, two men were struggling beside a scrawny tree. For a moment, she watched them. Just as she decided to cross the street to avoid the unpleasantness, light glinted off something in the shorter man's hand. By the time she'd recognized the knife, it had fallen three, four, five times.

Transfixed, she watched the wounded man slump against the tree. The attacker knelt beside him and began to rifle his pockets. The light gave her a good view of his face and the black rose tattoo on his neck. Her paralysis faded, though not her panic, and she looked around, hoping to see someone, anyone.

Thank God! she thought as one of New York's normally ubiquitous blue and white police cars drifted toward her. She ran to the cruiser's side. The officer stopped short and was out of the car in an instant. Breathless, she just pointed to the man lying against the tree.

The attacker had noticed the activity and was running. The officer told her, "Stay here!" He and his partner hollered "Stop, Police!" as they took off.

Piero escorted Camila back to the hotel after a late dinner; in his room, he was preparing for another pleasant interlude when several sharp raps on the door destroyed his mood.

He glanced at the clock; at quarter to midnight, it was far too early for Huamán to return… Unless there was a problem! Heart in his mouth, he pushed Camila to the bedroom and closed her in. He surveyed the room for any incriminating objects. Another impatient blow on the door just as he reached for the handle made him wonder why Huamán was so anxious.

Finding a uniformed policeman and a second man in a rumpled suit was a relief only for a second. "May we come in? Only be a couple of minutes."

Dazed, Piero just nodded and held the door for them. As he closed it, he gestured to the chairs. "Have a seat," though his experience with police at home suggested they'd continue to stand.

They did. "You are..." The man in the suit referred to a scrap of paper he slid from his notepad. "Mr. Piero Salvadore? Sub-Minister of the Interior from Peru? Do you have some identification?"

What? Piero nodded, dumbstruck. The officer's surly voice was not unfamiliar to Piero, accustomed to dealing with his police forces at home. A little unsteadily, he retrieved his coat and dug his passport from the pocket. He handed it to the man.

"Thanks." After a long look flipping the pages, the man returned the document. "Sorry, Mr. Salvadore. It's been a long day, and it's not getting any shorter. I'm Detective O'Keefe; this is Officer James. I have the unpleasant duty to inform you of the death of your countryman, Mr..." He looked down at the paper once more; while Piero could guess what the detective's next words would be, he reached for the chair and as O'Keefe said, "Mr. Mateo Huamán," he fell into it.

"What... how... What happened? An accident?"

"No. It looks like he was set upon by a mugger, a common thief, and fought back." The detective shook his head sadly. "He was stabbed. We apprehended the killer before he got away." He slipped a pen from his shirt pocket. "It was about ten-thirty this evening. There was a witness." He clicked the pen, ready to write. "Do you know why Mr. Huamán would have been out walking at that hour?"

Piero wasn't so dazed that he answered immediately. He dropped his head to his hands and thought. No reason to get involved. All my problems may be swept away. "He had an appointment earlier in the evening; something personal which we did not discuss. Also, he may have wished to take a walk; that would not be unusual for him."

"Do you know who he was meeting?"

Piero shook his head.

"Okay. If you think of anything that might help us, here's my card. Call anytime. They'll get me the message. Thanks. And my sympathies on the death of your friend."

The news had taken the steam out of Piero's ardor; he sent Camila to the sitting room while he called Sara. Then he called his new superior, Peru's President, who asked him to stay no longer than necessary to help with the investigation, and then bring Huamán's body home.

Camila had been surprisingly adept in helping press the night's events to the back of Piero's memory. "Of course I will stay with you until you tell me otherwise. But I must call..."

"Call" meant a lawyer. Her look of surprise when her call was answered at two-thirty in the dark morning, not by voice mail but a live voice, could not have been faked. As she replaced the phone, she said, "He will meet us tomorrow evening in the lobby of the Pennsylvania Hotel. Everything will be set then."

In the plane, escorting Huamán's coffin, Piero reflected on the meeting with Frank Pella. Frank's boss, Talos' lawyer, was too busy trying to keep Talos out of jail to meet in person, but Frank reminded Piero of his agreement with Donny. Camila would continue to "be available," he said. "She can arrive in Lima in a week.

"Either I," Frank continued, "or someone will accompany her, to make sure the proper arrangements are in place."

Piero had swallowed deeply. He was certain that "proper arrangements" had nothing to do with a place for Camila to live. In fact, Piero knew even if he dismissed the girl the "arrangements" would survive. The thin envelope Frank had handed him settled that. He waited until Camila slept to use a leftover dinner knife to slit the top. A typed piece of paper slid out; he read: "Call this number when you have set up an account to receive your compensation." A ten digit number followed. He tore the number out of the page and slipped it in his wallet, then burned the paper.

Ten days later, Piero drove to Arequipa's Rodríguez Ballón airport to meet Camila's flight. His home was near Arequipa, and he owned through family connections a town house in the city's Cayma District. He'd spent the week furnishing it for Camila's use.

In the terminal, Camila hurried as soon as she saw Piero, but not so much as to leave a tall heavy-set man behind. As Piero watched him huff to a stop beside the woman, he thought, this is more than overweight. He will die if he does nothing.

Camila was speaking. "… Samuel Goldfarb. He could not meet you in New York, but—"

"We can talk about these things when we are settled," Goldfarb said.

Piero nodded and led them to his car.

Goldfarb asked Piero to find him a "good hotel" for the next two or three days. Piero decided to put him up in the Libertador Arequipa; the manager and he had a comfortable arrangement, and it was one of the best hotels in the city. Goldfarb voiced his approval as Piero approached the entrance.

"Shall we talk here, Mr. Salvadore, or have you another place in mind?"

"We can use the room we take for you. Unless you have concerns?"

With a shake of his head, Goldfarb levered himself out of the car and stood, looking around the park while he caught his breath. "Beautiful. What season is it, here?"

Piero smiled. "We are in *la primavera.*"

"Spring," Camila said softly. Goldfarb nodded as Piero flagged a porter for Goldfarb's bags, then led the way into the building.

In the room, Camila said, "Shall I go down to the bar, or—"

"Not on my account," Goldfarb said. "You've heard it all before." He chuckled. "And you are my messenger. You can make sure I don't leave anything of import out. Piero, are you comfortable in English? Sadly, my Spanish was never—"

"English will be fine." Piero glanced at his watch. "I have a meeting in ninety minutes, so…"

"Of course. To cases, then. Mr. Talos was impressed by you when you met. He wishes to confirm the arrangement you and he agreed."

He gave Piero a look Piero could only consider questioning: one brow up, the other down, and a half smile on his lips. Having accepted Camila, and sent my bank number away, I'm in, no matter what. "I believe I can confirm our arrangement, unless something has changed?"

"Well, Mr. Talos is incarcerated and between the three of us, with that woman's testimony he's not likely to be free any time soon. However, between Frank, León and myself, his organization will continue, and may even prevail upon the witness." He walked to the sofa. "I must sit. Camila, could you order us some drinks and perhaps snacks? That's a good girl."

"Are you to describe what Mr. Talos requires?"

Goldfarb shook his head violently. "Of course not. But anyone who claims to speak for us, or makes a request on our behalf, will have bona fides that will be clear."

Piero also took a seat. "And what is your bona fide, Mr. Goldfarb?"

The man waved his arm at Camila. "She is."

Chapter Two
Piero visits Goldfarb

Arequipa, Peru

NEARLY TWO YEARS LATER, IN the middle of August, Piero and Camila discussed the directive she had delivered from the lawyer Goldfarb. Piero himself was to acquire and deliver to New York counterfeit $100 bills in the amount of two and a half million dollars.

He considered refusing. While the quality and availability of counterfeit dollars made Peru an excellent source for Goldfarb, Piero said, "Why should I take this chance? Goldfarb would have me documented as a smuggler. What could he then force me to do?" While the payments from facilitating the cocaine smuggling operations were generous, and he surely enjoyed fondling Camila, were they worth this risk?

"Oof!" The next evening, Piero stretched out face down on the dry grass behind his Arequipa finca. Laughing, he watched the soccer ball careen into the makeshift goal. His son had made a scoring shot under Piero's outstretched arm, and the boy and his sister, both excellent junior soccer players, were celebrating their victory.

"You three! Inside now, for dinner!" Sara, his wife and their mother, called from the back door.

Piero rolled over and spit a few bits of straw from his mouth. The Peruvian high desert in August, he thought. Lovely. He raised himself. "You heard *Mamá*; let's get going. You can gloat over dessert."

With shouts of pleasure, the children ran toward the house.

Inside, washed and seated at the head of the table, Piero felt more like Minister of the Interior. At least until the children shouted in unison: "Mamá, we got the last goal!"

Sara looked across the table at Piero, a smile curving her lips. "Is that why you were sprawled on the grass?" Her smile faded; Piero didn't like her new expression. "We need to talk later."

"I am to work tonight."

"*Before* you leave."

He agreed, keeping his reluctance to himself.

After dessert, the children retired to their schoolwork. In the living room, Piero and Sara shared the sofa. He sipped his *pisco* and waited patiently for her to break the silence.

Sara's brows furrowed. "I understand Nayra Mamani will join the Presidential campaign against us. She has augmented her staff by contracting a campaign manager. And—"

"We expected her, and planned for it." He paused, his glass half-way to his lips. Goldfarb's demand… perhaps I *can* use that.

"So you wish to challenge her as well as the others?"

"Of course! I have the backing." He sipped, gazing at her over his glass while rethinking his last statement. "She's just another fish, as they say. Still, I will bring it up at the meeting." He set his glass down and stood. "The biggest impact will be financial. She has good support, there."

"Does it change your plans?"

Piero considered her question. "It may. I will see. I'll return late, I fear. *Te quiero*."

In spite of his brazen words to Sara, the threat Mamani posed to his campaign was sufficient to reconsider Goldfarb's demand. I can do this, he thought. Two suitcases, not even large ones, and under diplomatic seal, especially if I enter through Miami.

So, how may I take advantage of this situation? A moment's thought brought a recollection. Huamán's videos would be an excellent weapon…

Inside the home in Arequipa's Cayma district where he'd installed Camila, he kissed her more hurriedly than he'd intended, and took a welcome drink from the glass she offered. No time to waste, he thought, and plunged into his decision. "I will bring the currency to Goldfarb as his message instructed. He should make sure the payment has been transferred."

"I thought you feared him having so much control?"

He finished his drink. "Times and circumstances change." Pulling her close, he opened her blouse. "Beautiful as usual…" His voice trailed off as he kissed his way down her throat to her chest.

The trip to deliver the fake bills offered the chance to take Sara and the children, not only to New York, but Orlando as well. His position as Minister made arranging the trip easy if not convenient. He would visit the UN for a half-day and Goldfarb the next. Meanwhile, the family would spend a couple of days touring and then, on the return home, they would stop at Disney World. Piero admitted his children were more excited than Sara, but she was willing.

New York

In New York, Piero had the limo driver drop him at Goldfarb's office in Jersey City. He hurried through the glass door and entered Goldfarb's office.

"Señor Goldfarb, how nice to see you again." He dropped the two cases beside him. "I believe you are expecting these?"

"Yes, thank you. Relax. Colleen will arrange anything you'd like; I'll be back in a few minutes."

Colleen smiled. A professional woman of perhaps forty with a well-toned figure, she brought a light lunch with a small glass of *Macchu Pisco.*

Piero touched the glass of the Peruvian wine. "Thank you very much for this; it brings my country here." He smiled knowingly. "Did Mr. Goldfarb betray my weakness?"

Her grin spread quickly. "Actually, Camila. I hope she did not speak out of turn?"

"Of course not." He raised his glass in a mock salute. "Do you have a paper?"

"Just a moment."

She returned in a moment with copies of the *New York Times*, the *Post* and the *Daily News*. With a courteous "Thank you," Piero opened the *Times*.

He hadn't finished the first section before Goldfarb strolled into the conference room. "Very satisfactory," he said. "As promised, those goods are now on the way to Saint Louis for distribution."

"Good," Piero said. "Now, we have business to discuss." Goldfarb's eyes opened wide. My tone gives him pause. Excellent. "First, I would betray your hospitality if I didn't thank Colleen and you for the lunch and newspapers." Goldfarb relaxed and Piero smiled. The smile faded into a forbidding expression. "I have made the delivery. I will *not* do this again. In fact, beginning now I alone will control the delivery of product from Peru." Piero paused to let the lawyer think. "You must decide if you can afford to create a new network to replace mine. If I fall, it does as well."

Goldfarb cleared his throat.

My work this past year will now pay its dividends, Piero thought as he smiled, the smile that had surprised many of his countrymen when he'd discovered a new gold seam, or smuggling route or most recently, a new safe house for his counterfeiters. "Before you fret, señor, I make a proposition. You are concerned for the income stream from my products." He waited; the lawyer sipped before nodding agreement. "However…" Piero brought his dealing-with-miscreants voice into play. "… I am now interested in the video recordings Talos was to have handed to señor Huamán two years ago. Remember those? So. I can supply a viable, inexhaustible source of revenue—until the US enacts reasonable drug laws, at least—if you and Talos will give me the videos.

"For me, for other Peruvians, the videos lose value as time passes. The next elections may depend on them, if I can employ them to my benefit.

"I am sure my proposal is clear to you. I must have the recordings before the elections. You must have my product. Can we agree?"

"We can," Goldfarb said. "However, Mr. Talos remains adamant the video cassettes cannot be retrieved whilst he remains incarcerated."

Piero smiled again. "Then it will be in your interest to solve that problem."

Chapter Three
Missing

A Calm Day

BECKIE SVERDUPE CURLED UP BESIDE Ian Jamse, her fiancé and mentor, on the Gulfstream's sofa. The pilot had assured them nothing would interfere with the short hop from Nassau to their home. Home, she reflected. The Nest. Wonderful! Seven Out Islands in the Bahamas that Ian had purchased as home base, not only for him, but for his mercenary team.

She wriggled in pleasure, rubbing her cheek against his chest. The drone of the engines, the heat of Ian's skin and the beating of his heart lulled her, though she'd already napped through the trip from London to Nassau.

The Nest. It is aptly named, Go Shen thought as he dropped into his comfortable desk chair. As security director, it is my task to keep it safe.

Although, he admitted with a smile, this Tuesday in early September hasn't been much of a challenge! He opened his laptop to check for messages. According to Ian, the flight from Nassau would arrive on time; he and Beckie would soon deplane on Port Cay. Shen glanced at the clock and thought, Yes, I should hear it landing any time now.

Ten minutes later, he did, and checked his monitors to make sure everything was in order. With a smile, Shen joined—in a virtual sense—the small crowd greeting the couple. Not every business trip gets *that* welcome, he thought. Won't take me long to straighten up here; I can get Ian's final update on Reverend Billy's arrest.

Before Shen finished, however, his phone rang. When he answered, the front desk person said, "Doctor Ardan is out here; she'd like to see you."

"Send her back." Doctor Millie Ardan, trauma specialist, ran the Nest's hospital for Ian, in addition to traveling with teams going into situations where injuries were likely. Before he'd decided he had no idea why she'd visit him rather than Ian, she rapped the door frame and entered. In green scrubs, she held her head high but tipped slightly. "Thanks, Shen. I came by to see if Amy's been in touch. *Guppy*'s not in the anchorage and it's getting late. I expected her way before now."

He regarded her with what must have been a completely stupefied expression, based on her next words: "You remember my daughter?" Her mouth quirked up in a twisted grin. "Fifteen years old? So tall?" She held her hand a little above her own head. "Long brown hair? Sailing an old white Contessa 26?"

"Sorry. Of course I remember Amy. *Guppy* too. My expression reflected my surprise, nothing more." He consulted his computer. "The morning watch's log noted she left the anchorage before six, but nothing since. Sit down, please." He tapped the keyboard and looked again. "No, nothing. It's not all that late, though. Didn't she leave a note or something?"

"No, which isn't unusual. But she always calls when she's later than I expect. We talked yesterday, and today after lunch, we'd planned to begin her junior year courses." She shook her head. "I'm worried, Shen. What could have happened?"

"Does she have a sat phone?"

Millie shook her head. "I tried her cell, but it went right to voice mail."

He nodded and worked the computer's keyboard again. "Yes. Unless she's close to an island, there'd be no coverage." He gazed at the display for a moment before spinning the computer to face the doctor. "Here's the twenty-five mile radar image, with an hour's tracking data. I can't see any of these targets being her."

"Do we have earlier data? Could we see her leaving?"

"Hang on, I'll check. But don't get your hopes up." He picked up his phone. "Unless there's something suspicious, we only keep an hour or so of this data." He talked for a minute, confirming the display on his computer represented all the data they had. "Sorry."

She caught her breath. "What else can we do, Shen? She must be in trouble. I'm certain she'd have contacted us if she could. You didn't see her yesterday. She was excited about starting the new material, and my promise to take her to Disney if she did well."

"I'll ask if Jean-Luc is available to search—"

"Thanks. While you do that, I'll talk to Ian, and Beckie." Millie rose and headed to the door. "Amy was emailing back and forth with her; maybe she knows something."

"They're at Ian's. I'll meet you there after I see about Jean-Luc."

As he walked her to the dock, he wondered about Amy. Disappearing didn't feel like something she'd do; it didn't fit her personality. But, getting entangled amorously with Abby Rochambeau didn't seem to fit her either. I don't know, he thought, and his worries slipped to his own adopted daughter, approaching the age of independence. With a sigh, he continued toward the airfield office on Port Cay to find Jean-Luc.

THE CALM DISSIPATES

Inside Ian Jamse's home, Beckie Sverdupe sipped her glass of champagne. She stepped aside to the lanai railing and looked over her friends, all there to welcome her and Ian back from their week in London tying up loose ends. The railing caught her at the waist; at five foot nothing and a smidge under a hundred pounds, she didn't worry about it holding her safe from the four foot drop to the beach.

Their trip had been successful, if turning a miscreant over to the police for what would likely be a long, long time should be called successful. September had just begun. In the US, Labor Day had been yesterday; in the Bahamas, it had been another Monday.

The flute in her right hand, she reached back with her left to pull her chestnut ponytail around to trail over her bust down to her belly. She finished the wine and placed the glass carefully on the rail. Her lips curved upward as she observed their guests.

Ian stood nearer the slider into the house. Beckie didn't see what he'd noticed; her attention was fully taken by him. His tan slacks matched her shorts; they had both chosen white polo shirts. His ice blue eyes contrasted with her bright green irises, flashing now with pleasure. She could feel her love flowing across the ten feet between them. He rubbed his short blond hair. No, it looks white this afternoon. She really enjoyed running her fingers through it, almost as much as tucking her head under his chin and cuddling him.

Her heart beat harder, and she clenched her jaws to calm herself. Don't need that here, she thought with a giggle, what would the kids think? Ian turned to step into the house; with a moué of disappointment, she walked toward Shalin and Kevin deVeel, their special friends.

Across the lanai, Millie had collared Ian; she was upset about something. Before Beckie could decide she needed to join them, they approached her. The upset on Millie's face had morphed into something else: her jaw trembled, her eyes were slitted and her brow was furrowed.

Beckie's heart jumped. Why is she scared? Who… Her mind leapt to the teammate injured in the last operation. "Elena? Is she—"

Ian touched her arm. "Ms Rios is fine. It is—"

"Amy! Amy's disappeared!"

Damn! Beckie thought. That's the last thing we need. "Calm down, Millie. I heard what you said, but what?"

Ian took Millie's arm and led her to the sofa. Beckie accompanied them, taking a seat next to the distraught woman.

Go Shen hurried across the lanai to them. "Talking about Amy?" When Ian nodded and both Millie and Beckie turned to him, he said, "I told Millie most of this, but… She sailed out of the anchorage before six this morning. Waved to the camera like she always does. We thought nothing of it. We've had no signals from her, and there are no reported weather issues for, well, anywhere within her range in *Guppy*."

"There's nothing, Ian. I'm afraid…" Millie's lower lip was quivering, she had pulled her arms tight to her torso; Beckie grasped her around the shoulders and hugged tight.

"Right," Shen said. "Specifically, no maydays. Jean-Luc and a crew are taking the copter, but with night coming on, they'll only be able to search a little while."

"Does it seem early to send Jean-Luc?" Ian asked, looking at his watch. "She's been out less than twelve hours."

"Millie convinced me." Shen snapped a glance to the woman.

She pulled herself up and glared at Ian while reviewing the reasons she'd earlier given Shen.

"Very well," Ian said to both the doctor and Shen. "Advise him to communicate anything needed to advance the search."

Shen pulled a chair over and sat. "He's got radar, and Amy had the reflector and the masthead antenna; *Guppy* should show up bright and clear."

"So he's actually looking… for… debris…" Millie broke down, sobbing into her hands.

The others at Beckie and Ian's impromptu welcoming party, attracted by Millie's cry, had been listening, but in the silence broken only by the woman's sobs, drifted away. Kevin stayed, but Shalin helped nudge the others along.

Beckie mouthed "Thank you," to her as they slipped through the door. "Is that true, Shen, that they are looking for… if she sank?"

"They're using radar and the big binoculars, looking for anything out of the ordinary. Including," he murmured, "a debris field. But if she capsized, it's far more likely the mast is in the water, but the hull isn't submerged." He rose. "I can't help find her here. If you want information thirty seconds earlier than I can call, the conference room is available." He walked around the sofa and took Millie's hands. "I'm sorry I don't have any good information for you."

Ian gazed at Beckie; his eyebrows were raised and his head canted slightly even before he spoke. "There was no hint of Ms Ardan doing anything unexpected?"

Millie stared at Ian, but said nothing.

Beckie clutched her tight again. "Not a word. You both know we talked, and exchanged e-mails while you and I were in London, but nothing to suggest this is more than Amy taking a day sail." She looked at Millie. "You're right; she was excited about the stuff you were gonna start in her classes."

"I know," Millie said, though her voice was breaking. "We talked about it all weekend, and I thought… I thought with Abby gone, she was ready to begin the year eleven lessons."

"Ah," Ian said. "Abby. The elephant in the room, perhaps."

"No, I don't think so," Millie rejoined. "Amy was okay with her leaving and already planning a reunion for when she got back."

Beckie sighed and gripped Ian's hand. "Let's go over to Shen's conference room to wait." She took Millie's hand.

About ten, Jean-Luc returned with his eyesore crew. "Nothing but water. We circled the Nest in a spiral out to about fifty miles, then a grid from west to east. A few boats, but none like Amy's."

At first light, Beckie joined the crew when Jean-Luc again lifted off to search. Shen advised the Coast Guard of Amy's failure to return or report, but without better information, they too were left to make wide area searches, searching for anything unusual.

By sunset, Beckie's eyes were aching; she was ready to soak her head in drops. The rest of the crew felt the same, she was sure: grateful to be back at the Nest, worried sick over not having seen anything that hinted at Amy's fate.

"I'm not ready to hold a memorial!" she snapped at Ian when he tried to ask how she felt. "You listened to the same boring radio traffic I did; you know there's nothing!" He straightened; his face paled and his mouth dropped open. She buried her face in her hands and apologized. "I love you, guy." She pulled him close for a kiss, then looked into his face. "I'm so worried about her. Is there anything else we can do?"

"Let us talk with Shen. He's been in contact with the Coast Guard. Perhaps they have a new bit of…" He sighed. "I doubt it, having listened to them all day also."

Hand-in-hand, they made their way to Shen's office. Beckie said, "I've gotta wash my face," as she turned off to the ladies room. Inside, she found Millie, crying over the sink. Beckie spent a few minutes attempting to comfort the doctor before taking her along to the conference room.

She filled two cups of coffee and set one before Millie. Just as she raised her cup to her lips, Shen ran into the room.

"She's ok!"

Beckie cheered with the others, but quickly realized Shen hadn't finished. "Where is she?"

Shen's voice was now rife with hesitation. "This morning, she cleared Customs at Caicos Marina, Providenciales, in the Turks and Caicos. She probably arrived last night. The Customs officer said she told him she was headed to Blue Hills to visit friends."

Millie almost dropped her coffee. "She doesn't know anyone—"

"I guessed as much because at Providenciales International Airport, there's video of her getting on a plane to Miami. Her ticket was booked in the name of Amy Rochambeau and the passport she used matched."

Beckie fell back in her chair and let the voices flow over her. Well, what the hell? she thought. This came up over the weekend? While Ian and I were flying back?

By the time Beckie tuned back in, Millie was stomping out the door. While she appeared to be happy Amy wasn't dead, Beckie saw no guarantee most of Millie's relief wasn't because she'd now be able to kill the girl herself.

The others, Ian included, came to rapid agreement Amy was a simple runaway, chasing Abby. Beckie shook her head. A runaway doesn't fit Amy's personality, but with love involved… Who knows? she thought, recalling the conversations she'd had with the girl about her relationship with the older team member.

Ian looked at his partner; Kevin deVeel reached for his phone. His brief conversation with Barbara Saunders in Peru provided one bit of news: Abby was working incommunicado in Arequipa, so Barbara wouldn't be able to ask her about Amy until she checked in, "Unless you want me to interrupt the surveillance?" she asked.

"No," Kevin replied. "Not for what we know now. But Abby should call either Ian or me once she reports in. We'd like to ask about the passport Amy used."

Beckie stood and touched Ian's shoulder. "Nothing more to be done here, is there?"

"I believe not," he replied.

Quietly, they left the conference room. Out on the crushed shell walkway to the dock, Beckie took Ian's hand. "I'm sorry."

"Whatever for?"

"Thinking I had an inkling of what was going on in her head."

"That blame is shared among many people, most closer to the girl than you. We were some distance away."

"I know. Just, it seems like something should have given it away. I spent time with her; she's not that good at hiding things. She's pretty open, in fact, so I'm at a loss."

He handed her into the skiff and motored across the channel. On the way, she smiled at him in the half-light of the setting sun, then looked at her phone. "Well, tomorrow I should head to Miami. University started classes last week, so I'm behind already."

CHAPTER FOUR STARRING AMY

AT EIGHT FORTY-FIVE THE Saturday after Amy'd disappeared, Beckie skipped down the steps of the air taxi from Miami. School was out for the weekend, and with Tropical Storm Eight brewing off the coast of South America, it might be out for a week. Maybe Amy's back. That'd make it a great weekend, she thought.

Until Maurice Boynton, Ian's factotum, opened the door for her. His face, his body sagged before he straightened. She could tell he had no smile to greet her. He nodded his head toward the slider opening on the lanai. "Bad news, I'm afraid," he said. "Ian did not sleep well last night... No one slept well. I'm not sure this was a good time to visit."

"Why?" When the man didn't answer, she said, "Don't act like Ian, please."

"No, no. It's simply... You'll see." He sighed and turned away.

Beckie looked after him, completely befuddled. She shook her head and went to the lanai.

All conversation stopped when she stepped through the sliding door. She met each face in turn: Kevin. Millie. Shen. Ian.

Ignoring the message of the taut faces, she went to Ian and kissed his cheek. "Hello, love." She looked him in the eye. "What the hell have I walked into?"

Faces turned away; gazes fell to the owner's hands. She snorted and pulled the last chair out. Dropping into it, she looked, first at Ian, then focused on Millie. "If you're here, this is about Amy. What?"

The silence held a moment more until Shen, still staring at his hands, said, "Amy was not the runaway we wrote her off as." Beckie leaned against the table. Shen glanced over at her. "She *is* not a runaway. She's being… tortured, somewhere."

"Augh!" Beckie slammed a fist on the table, but then counted three slow breaths. "What happened? When—"

Ian touched her hand. "Shen intercepted a message addressed to Ms. Rochambeau. Do you have it there?" As he gestured toward Shen's laptop, Beckie realized he was as angry as she. Boynton's words made more sense, now.

"Yes." Shen opened his computer, typed a few commands and spun it so the display faced Beckie. She spent a moment reading the short message:

> `Jolene, you haven't answered any of your mail. That's very naughty of you, and we need to find an adequate punishment. While we consider what that should be, enjoy the show at our favorite file-sharing site. You know what to do to free this girl and make us go away forever. If your memory needs jogged, just watch it again. I'm sure something will occur to you.`

"'Naughty?' Who even talks like that anymore?" She read it again. "Jolene? Does that mean… Abby?" Shen nodded. Back to the note. What's this mean? She read aloud: "'You know what to do to…'" Her voice rose to signal her confusion. "What girl?" Silence followed, except for a choked sob from Millie. So, it's Amy. Must be. Even as she said, "What's the link to?" she slammed her finger on the touchpad. Got to stay calm, she thought, as she sucked on her knuckle.

However, when the video player opened, any calm Beckie'd pressed on herself evaporated like dew on sun-baked pavement.

The small image was too clearly a woman spread-eagled on a platform, and a man having brutal intercourse with her. Unbelieving, she expanded the window to fill the screen and clicked the start button again.

Beckie sucked in her breath and forgot to exhale. In the expanded picture, Amy Rose's features showed through the bruises, cuts and blood. Her lips were split, as were her left eyebrow and cheek.

The shock of seeing Amy's beaten face was overcome by the horror of her rape. Damn! Those guys are so dead! Her breath whooshed out and she grabbed at her ponytail, yanking it around to cover her chest. Someone touched her arm; she jerked away before seeing Ian's hand.

She blinked tears away and tuned out the assault; it would have been boring if not for Amy being there and the brutality the men displayed. But she didn't turn it off. After the window closed, she looked up. The others had been discussing ways to track Amy, to find her now.

"There's something there," Beckie said. "Something familiar. Not sure what. I need to think."

While Beckie pondered the background scenery in the video, she listened with half an ear as Barbara reported Abby had requested leave, then left before receiving authorization. A few minutes later, Kevin phoned Derek to ask about Abby's history. Derek's not particularly informative, "Pure as the driven snow, isn't that what they say?" brought her head up, but not for long as he went on about Abby's vetting at Columbia University and at the U.N.

Until Derek's voice rang out: "Ah! Wait a mo." She heard keys clattering as he apparently typed at full speed. "I sent a link to you, Shen. If that's not what we're looking for, it's buried deeper than anything I know about. You can ask Elena about 'er training, but… No, that's it."

The Internet was not speed of light fast, but the laptop, still facing Beckie, dinged before anyone had time to react. Shen took it and typed. His eyes got large, and he rotated the computer so the others could also see.

"Columbia Student Star Witness in Murder Trial," the headline read.

Beckie felt her heart jump again as she read the *New York Times* story. "I don't understand," she said. "According to the story, this guy's been convicted and is in jail."

Ian looked up. "If we believe the *Times*, the whole case turned on Ms Rochambeau's testimony. Were her testimony to be discredited or recanted, the defense would argue the conviction should be dismissed. Were she to recant, it is likely the court would agree with the defense."

"So, the defense snatched Amy to force Abby to… to recant?" Beckie sucked her lip between her teeth. "But they're lawyers, they can't do… that," she said, waving at Shen's laptop.

"It isn't likely," Kevin agreed, "but we don't know anything about the killer, either."

"Indeed. Kevin, please see what you can learn about…"

When Ian stopped and looked at Beckie, she read, "Donato Talos. The one in jail, you mean?"

"Yes. Kevin?"

"On my way. Keep in touch." He turned to leave. "Oops, sorry," he said to Elena Rios, who bounced off his hip as she attempted to enter.

"It's okay. But you might want to hear this."

Ian nodded, and Kevin followed Elena back in.

"I was ready to go through Amy's room." Elena dipped her head to Millie, who nodded. "Right in the middle of her desk, this was lying face up." She dropped a pink envelope on the glass table. They all scowled at the addressee written in Amy's neat hand. Elena nudged the envelope toward Beckie.

Beckie reached out but her hand moved as if the envelope were a scorpion. She used a fingertip to pull it close. As she stared, her indecision frustrated her, and she ripped the flap open to grab the folded paper inside.

She read silently until she heard a cough. When she looked up, she felt her cheeks warm. "Sorry." She looked back at the letter.

"'Hi, Beckie!'" she read. "'I don't expect you'll ever read this unless I tell you about it first, but just in case. Mom'll never look in my room, so something'll have to really be wrong for you to see it, in which case, I want you to know what's happened.'" Beckie glanced at Millie, who nodded slowly, though the muscles at the sides of her jaws were clenched. Beckie decided not to ask about that, now at least.

"'I got a little package from Abby the other day, but it said wait to open it, so I tucked it away in my underwear drawer. Then early today, Monday, I got an email from Abby.

"'She said she was able to take a week off, and if I wanted to join her, I should open the package. If I didn't, or couldn't, just leave the package alone. Ha-ha! You know I wasn't going to pass up the chance!

"'You were flying, I guess, so I couldn't talk to you. I ripped the package open and in it was a passport with my picture in it, and Amy Rochambeau's name. She's eighteen, or I am, I guess, with it! Inside the passport, there's a plane ticket from Providenciales, that's in the Turks and Caicos you know. She said she remembered when I told her about sailing there a couple years ago. My butt's still sore—'"

"Not as sore—" Millie slapped her hand over her mouth. "God, that was stupid! Forgive me."

"Millie, if you would rather—"

"No, Ian, what I'd rather is that Amy was here beside us, not being raped and tortured in some shack somewhere." She rose and walked to the rail overlooking the ocean. Her voice was clear in spite of facing away. "Forgive my outbursts and then forget them. I'll do my best to help us, no matter what you think that is." She faced Ian. "As long as I am informed."

Ian nodded, first to Millie, then to Beckie.

"'My butt's still sore from that ha-ha!

"'The ticket is from Providenciales to Miami, where she's gonna send a limo to pick me up! A big white one, she said!

"'This will be such fun! I can't wait!

"'Anyway, I expect I'll be back in about a week, and then we can laugh about this letter before I burn it ha-ha.

"'Hope you and Mr. Jamse work your thing out. Thanks for helping Shalin with Alisha; I really like both of them.'"

Beckie's voice was more ragged than she wanted, but she finished. "'Your friend.' She ends with her initials and a smiley." She swiped a tear away.

"Kinda scary hearing that, knowing what we know now," Kevin said after a minute's silence. "I'm sorry, Millie." At the door, he stopped. "Shen, someone's got a lot better access than they should, if they can get a picture good enough for a passport, and get a package into our deliveries."

"That's for sure." Shen smacked his forehead. "That damn boat!" Beckie stared at him. He looked around. "Let me do some work knowing what we do now." He focused on Ian. "There isn't any reason to think Abby was involved in any way? Not that it would answer anything but the photo," he finished.

"I am unwilling to dismiss the possibility completely, but it is the last thing we should spend time on." His wave halted Shen at the door. When he spoke, his voice was so taut, Beckie turned to him. "Kevin and I will meet with you in the morning. Be prepared to discuss our security lapses."

Beckie felt her jaw drop. This bothers him. Even more than I expected! I don't know… "I'm going to take a walk," she said. "There's something in that video. I need to think. Want to walk along with me, Millie?"

The doctor spun around, wide-eyed, mouth open. "What? No, I'd better get back to the hospital. I'll be in touch." She fixed Beckie, and then Ian, with a glare softened only slightly by the tears wetting her cheeks.

Beckie took Millie's arm and walked to the door with her. She turned back into the space, now dominated by Ian's tense posture. "Ian, I'll see you in a half hour unless something clicks first."

His smile was one of the thinnest she'd ever seen.

The half hour on the beach provided no enlightenment; Beckie returned to the house to find the lanai and kitchen both empty.

Well, where could he be? A slight noise from the bedrooms gave her the clue; she walked to Ian's door and rapped, but gently.

In a moment, he'd opened the door and invited her in, and through to the balcony lanai looking out over the beach and water to the south. When she reached the railing, she turned and caught his hands in hers.

"Something even bigger than Amy's bothering you, Ian. Please tell me."

He retrieved one hand and scrubbed it through his hair. The side where Millie'd shaved him to work on his skull still showed, even though none of his white-blond hair was long.

He sighed and reached for her, to embrace her. She forced herself to listen to his soft-spoken words rather than the pounding of either of their hearts.

"Do you remember the papers you signed for Rou when you agreed to join us?"

Whoa! What's that about? "Not really. I mean, I looked at them, but honestly? She said I had to sign them, and you said they wouldn't be used to toss me out, so… I signed them." She kissed his chest through his shirt. "Dad looked at them, too. He didn't see anything to worry over. Why?"

"They contained a two-way promise: from you-to-me, as you would have expected, and from me-to-you."

"And the you-to-me part bothers you now, right? Actually, the you-to-Millie and her family part." She straightened without releasing him. "Let's go to the Bright Room; use the sofa there."

He allowed her to lead to the room on the eastern end of the house. He and Boynton had created a sort of escape there. While it did have a couch and a bed, it also had several reading chairs, a few thousand books, an easel with blank canvases, oils and watercolors, a game table with a supply of board games, a guitar and to complete the picture, an antique harpsichord that Pieter kept in tune.

Beckie found it too… too enticing, usually, to spend much time there. Sleep would end early; the sun shining in the morning gave the room its name. Still, for this, it was perfect. She and Ian were still under Millie's orders about sex, or rather, no sex, so cuddling and talking would have to fill the bill.

She pushed him to sit, then lay down with her head on his thigh. Looking up, she said, "I hope to hell you're not going to try and hold yourself responsible for a teenage girl's attempt to find love and freedom all at the same time. No matter how it worked out."

"No. Of course, that is a major concern. However, beyond Amy Rose's… abuse lies an even greater problem. Where we… Me, Kevin, Shen, Millie and possibly others have failed Amy Rose… We allowed the tools to be given her, enabling her brief flight into a hell she neither intended nor deserves. That is my concern."

"Shen does really good work, you know that."

"Of course he does. Still, he may have erred. If so, we need to understand how, to prevent similar attempts."

He gently urged her to her knees, their faces approximately level. "Whether you or they read them or not, I have made promises to every team member: to protect them and those they involve with us; to heal them at need, and to release them when they determine that is the proper course for them. Amy Rose's abduction is a dereliction of that promise." The ice blue of his eyes splintered her. "I must ensure that not only she is recovered safely, but that it cannot recur."

Beckie touched his lips as he finished and whispered, "*We* must ensure that. You're not alone, love." She crushed herself against him. "It's the team's promise to us, for us."

"Thank you, love, for reminding me. I would ask you to join us in the morning…"

She leaned away so he could see her smile. "I'd be superfluous. You can sort things through without my stumbling around." She twisted to sit across his lap, their arms encircling each other. While kissing along his jaw, she said, "I'll keep Millie occupied, and try to remember what it was in that video."

Chapter Five
Rescue

TUESDAY, BECKIE WAS BACK AT school, or rather, she was in Coral Gables, in her off-campus apartment, lying in bed listening to the Noon News. Tropical storm Hanna was now projected to graze Florida's west coast after washing over Key West tonight. School had not closed after all.

She stretched and sat up. Might as well get moving. As she went about showering, dressing and collecting herself, she thought over the couple of days since she'd discovered Amy was being raped and tortured. Through her walks on the beach and her talks with Ian and Kevin, nothing had revealed whatever it was in the video that tickled her memory.

Without interesting tidbits to contemplate, her mind drifted to the news broadcast. She'd been to Key West, once, for an evening—

That's it! Camp We-something. That astronomy class last February. The Winter… Winter Star Party! Camp Wesumkee!

She grabbed her phone and called Ian. No answer! Where is he? She ran out of her room and down the hall to her roommate's room.

She hit the door with her fist. "Sandy! You in there?"

The door flew open and Sandy Daniels looked out. "What the hell,

Beckie?" Sandy wore a towel; her shoulder length hair was dripping down her arms and face. "I was—"

"Washing your hair, yeah. Sorry. The Hummer's still downstairs, right? I need to borrow it. Please?"

"Sure. Why?" Sandy opened a small case on her desk and flipped a set of keys to Beckie.

"I need to drive down the Keys. With the storm, I figured my Miata might not be the best car."

Sandy laughed and closed the door. Beckie heard "Be careful." Suddenly the door opened again. "Take Greg along. You're not big enough to fight any storm by yourself." Her face clouded over. "I'd go, too, but I have that interview…" She swung the door closed again.

Beckie took a step back to lean against the wall, considering the option. Sandy's brother Greg, their upstairs roommate, offered height and weight, and familiarity with the Hummer. She'd been in it once when Sandy had suggested they beach it for a day last spring.

Then, could she put Greg at risk the way she'd done to Haleef a month ago; at risk first from the storm, and second, from whoever was holding Amy?

She straightened and jogged up to the second floor where Greg and his significant other, Marla, shared space. As soon as Greg heard Beckie's review of Amy's situation, he jumped up from his desk and pulled on his jeans. Beckie and Marla giggled together as they watched him dash around the room.

"You bring him back safe, hear?" Marla was the daughter of a Cuban immigrant; she took no prisoners when they played the occasional game of D&D or even Monopoly. Beckie didn't want to disappoint her.

"Don't worry about us," Greg said as he dragged his shoe on. "Let's go, Beckie. The H1 is plenty heavy, but still…"

She nodded. "Thanks for loaning him out, Marla! Want to drive, Greg?"

"No, I hate it. I'll ride. Maybe sleep a little. It'll be a couple hours, I guess."

Ten minutes later Beckie'd changed into camos and removed her Ruger LCR from the safe. She had ensconced herself in the Hummer's cab after they pulled the seat all the way forward. Her feet now reached the pedals, and she reviewed her wide open viewpoint. The revolver went in the close-at-hand storage bin. "Hope I don't need it," she said to Greg.

He'd taken the back seat; he could almost stretch his six foot height across the width without bending his knees.

The GPS knew Camp Wesumkee and gave a toll-laden path estimated to take two and a half hours. Beckie thought the 120 mile trip might take a little longer today. She wanted to get to Florida City before Monroe County closed access to the Keys.

As she headed to the Florida Turnpike south, Greg pointed out they had fuel to drive about three hundred miles. That's a margin, Beckie thought. Not comfortable, but greater than zero.

"I wonder if the sat phone..." She took it out and dialed. "Ian, I love you! I think I know where Amy is... On a key, in a Girl Scout camp. It's Camp Wesum-something. On Scout Key... Next to Spanish Harbor Key. About sixty miles before Key West..."

"How—"

"You'll never believe... Last February? When I couldn't come home that weekend? The Winter Star Party? No? Never mind then. I recognized the inside of the chickee they were filming in. I'm on the way..."

"Take care."

"Of course I'll be careful. Greg Daniels is with me, so I'll have to take care of him too." He grinned and made some wild gesticulations. She laughed. "He says he'll watch out for me..."

"Leave the satellite phone on; we will track the beacon. As soon as I can arrange it."

"Okay, see you soon..."

"As soon as may be. I love you."

"Love you, too!" She found an elastic strap around one of the sun visors and slid the phone under it. She checked to make sure it was on and folded the visor into place. "Ian says he'll try and figure out how to get here. If he can, he'll follow the phone…" She pointed to the visor. "… to find us."

"Where is he?"

"He didn't say. If he's at home, he's in the Bahamas."

Florida City had a warning about dangerous conditions expected on the Overseas Highway, especially near Key West, but no check points. Beckie glanced in the mirror to see Greg still sleeping.

An hour later, she stopped in Layton, looking through the huge windshield at the black wall of storms ahead. In the back seat, Greg held up his phone. "Weather Channel says Hanna picked up speed toward Key West. They expect her to make landfall about eight tonight."

"Thanks," Beckie said. A gust of wind shook the heavy vehicle. "Huh. I better focus on driving. GPS says we still have thirty-five miles to go. I doubt we're gonna make real good time."

"Yeah. Looks to be a small storm, but intense. Storm force winds are maybe fifty miles from the center."

"I'm more interested in the storm surge. We're about ten feet above the water, here, and the camp is lower still."

"Won't they pack up and leave?"

"Don't know. They haven't displayed super-intelligence so far. It's why I wanted to get there fast."

The Hummer lumbered along. The increasing wind forced her to drop the speed; she was uncomfortable over twenty now. As she arrived in Marathon, police were shepherding traffic out north, but while the officer looked at the vehicle and shook his head, he made no move to stop them. Occasionally they had seen vehicles headed north, but now, with wind-blown spray almost solid, Seven Mile Bridge was empty.

"Smart people," Greg said, perhaps reading her thoughts. "Getting nasty. Tell me again why this is a good idea."

Beckie's fists tightened on the wheel. "It's not," she said. "You know that. Except there's this fifteen year old girl—"

"I know. Just talking to hear myself. Don't worry."

"I'll turn around right now; take you back to Marathon. But I gotta —"

"Shut up! I'm in, dammit. Just 'cause I'm scared to death… Shut up and drive."

Me, too, Beckie thought.

The clock in the dash read five thirty when they passed the sign for Scout Key. Beckie assumed it was there; she didn't see it. But Greg called out "Eight-tenths of a mile, on the left."

"I remember the left. Trees on both sides and a gate."

Like they had been on the other keys, the trees bent before the wind. Leaves, fronds and twigs flew across the road. Grateful for the automatic transmission, Beckie was barely moving. The daylight had failed, and the glare of the headlights off the rain made them nearly useless.

"There! Is that the turn-off?"

Beckie turned across the highway and narrowly missed a clump of trees. The buffeting wasn't as bad in the lee of the trees, and Beckie could see the gate swinging in the wind. The faded Stop sign was hanging upside down and shaking back and forth.

This is really stupid, she thought. The water already covered the key to where they were stopped. "How much water are we good for?"

"I don't know the limit. We've had it up to the seats." He patted the cushion. "The snorkel helps."

"So as long as we're just sitting in water, it'll keep going?"

"For a while, anyway. We only forded streams and small rivers." He gaped out the window at the waves being driven at them. "Nothing like this."

"I'll buy you a new one," she muttered. "If…" She backed away from the trees and headed toward the gate. It slammed against the side as she drove by.

Greg wriggled his way to the front seat. "Which way? And how far between where we're headed and the ocean?"

"Do you have the locator still on your phone?" She inched further away from the gate as he tapped. When he shook his head with an expressionless face, she glanced at the trees and began a turn to the right.

"It wasn't more than a few hundred feet to the chickees. There are ten or so of them, grouped down here."

The wind slowed, and the light improved a little. Beckie increased the speed to a crawl, which raised a bow wave. Greg opened the door and peered out. "Not quite two feet deep."

They passed the bathhouse keeping it between them and the ocean. The light faded as the wind regained its former strength, but before it went all gray again, Beckie saw the first group of chickees. "There!" She pointed but Greg was nodding already.

"I don't see any cars or trucks."

"Maybe a boat?"

"No, but the trees over there blocked my view. And then the wind." He looked out again, but this time when he opened the door, a wave of water overflowed the sill. "It's a little deeper."

"So I see." She stopped. "The first group of chickees ought to be right over there." She pointed toward the ocean, where she could see shadows that might be the little huts. The sides were flapping in and out.

Greg spent a moment looking at them. "What are they? Chickees?"

"Little thatched roof huts that sleep six. They are raised a foot or so and the sides are open, except they have screens and shades. That's what's blowing around."

"You think someone could be in there?"

"They shot the video in one of them. I'm sure." She hoped her doubt wasn't as obvious to him as it was to her.

Greg tipped his head at the storage bin. "You taking the gun?"

Beckie surveyed the area. "No. I doubt anyone's here and it'll get sand and water in the works. You know where it is if we need it." She opened her door and climbed down.

"Wait a minute! If I can't do anything else, I can keep you from falling. I'll be right around."

In a second, he'd splashed around the front of the truck and taken her hand. Holding tight, they worked their way to the little semi-circle of five buildings. With a look, they separated and while Greg took the eastern most one, Beckie waded toward the opposite end.

"Ow! Damn it. Watch out for the shades, the bottoms are weighted!"

When Beckie looked, Greg was rubbing blood from his forehead. "Are you okay?"

"Yeah, it's only my pride hurt."

Beckie opened the screen door and looked in. The beds were pushed against the corner posts; debris bobbed in the water.

Greg was waiting at the center chickee when Beckie waded out of the fourth one. "Nothing." They slogged back to the Hummer.

As Beckie hiked herself into the cab, a gust of wind caught the door and slammed it closed on her ankle. "Oww!" She pulled her leg in and kneaded it.

"Let me look," Greg said. "Sandy had a broken ankle once."

"No. The bone's not sticking out; I'll be fine." She twisted her face into a semblance of a grin. "I won't need that foot till I have to walk again."

"I think the water's gotten deeper. Want me to drive?"

"No, it'll be fine." She drove another four minutes, two-hundred fifty-feet into a second group of five huts. The wind had increased, and the water was still rising. The dash clock said six forty-five. Dark was nearly complete. She looked around. "We'll go together this time. Let's start there, away from the ocean. Those two are blocked from either the road or the water."

He nodded and dropped down into the water. When he got to Beckie's door, she allowed him to catch her and let her down gently. The water was up to her hips; the waves soaked her to her neck. She looked to see Greg was wet to his belly. She shook her head. "Let's go before we get washed off our feet."

On her first step, her ankle gave way, and she pitched into the flood. She opened her mouth to scream, but it filled with water so full of sand it felt like a mouthful of rock candy, except salty. Greg tried to stop her fall, but only extended her arm; she fell sideways. He didn't let go, however, and before the water filled her ears, he had her up, supporting her.

"Thanks," she muttered after spitting out the brackish water-sand mixture. “Guess I better lean on you.”

“You oughta stay here.”

“No! This is— I can’t let you go alone. I’ll be okay, now I know what to expect.”

After the first few steps, the pain became commonplace, and she didn’t lean on him as much.

Beckie was sure the first hut they approached was the one; the sound of the wind through it made a moan she was sure signaled Amy’s death knell. The slamming and swinging of the shades was worse than any of the ones they’d already examined.

But it was empty.

With a glance around, Beckie led the way to the neighboring hut. The wind threw her into the door, then when she yanked on it, a squall ripped it from her hands and threw it against the corner of the chickee. The hinges failed and the door took flight. She didn’t wait to see where it landed, but fell inside, pulling Greg behind her.

Even though the chickee was elevated, her head went under water when she fell. She wrenched herself into a sitting position. She shook her head violently, like a wet dog, but her pony tail, compacted by the water, came around and smacked her cheek and jaw. Startled, she gasped for breath and then gagged. Even with the wind storming through and knee-deep water, the inside of the hut smelled like an open sewer. She breathed through her mouth. “You okay?”

He nodded.

She attempted a survey. The Hummer’s headlights shone dully when the wind threw the shades back, but they couldn’t dispel the gloom inside. This hut was like the others: Beds were piled against the far wall. One of them had fallen through the screen siding; it hung, half in, half out. Suddenly, she felt a hand; Greg pointed. “There.”

Beckie strained to see in the murky dark. One bed hadn’t moved and there was something atop it. She crawled in the water toward the bed. She wondered why it was rocking until she realized it was trying to float. The water covered the thin pad of a mattress; waves washed over a nude female body.

"Greg?" Beckie turned to look for him. Where did he go? What happened?

Beckie returned to the body, unsure whether she wanted it to be Amy or not. A splash behind her brought her around, fists up ready to kill.

"Greg! What the fuck?"

He held a flashlight, one of the big black metal kind, and two sheathed knives. He handed a knife to Beckie. "She's tied, hand and foot. With the wet rope, we'll have to cut them off her." He waded to where the girl's feet disappeared in the water and bent down.

Knife in hand, Beckie stood and scrambled to the other end of the frame. Hands shaking, she turned the girl's head. It was Amy, terribly battered. Oh, God! Is she… Amy's mouth fell into the water and her breath bubbled. She's alive! Beckie's heart started again. I better get her head up. And outta here! Keeping Amy's head above the water, she cut the bonds. A splash over the wind interrupted her; she almost dropped her knife.

Greg was pulling himself up. "Stepped on…" He held an empty bottle, looking at it before tossing it across the small room. The wind threw it back at him and he swatted it out the hut's open back side. "Nutrition drink. Guess she hasn't eaten much."

Beckie looked at Amy's body, comparing it to what she recalled from a month ago. Her ribs showed and her cheeks were hollowing. On her face and breasts especially, bruises and cuts showed dark against the pale white skin. For a second, Beckie was torn between cursing, retching and crying, but quickly pressed those useless reactions back. We gotta get her out before we can do anything to fix her!

Rather than risk cutting Amy's wrist, she cut the binding at the bed frame. Amy's body moved. Greg lifted the girl's right leg out of the water to clear the way for him to duck down to free the left. Beckie saw the bloom of light through the sand and debris filled water as Greg hacked with the knife.

Watching Amy's chest rise and fall however weakly, she opted to wait before cutting the ties at Amy's wrists, not wanting to have Greg yank and pull unexpectedly. He had to make one trip to breathe, but soon, sooner than Beckie'd feared, Amy was floating away from the bed.

"Hold her while I cut these ropes," she said.

"Yeah. Here, use this knife; it's sharper. Just go slow. Cut lengthwise instead of straight across."

She did and with the sharper knife, soon had Amy free of those fetters, too. She looked again at Amy's face, trying to find a light of consciousness, but while her eyes were wide and flicking back and forth, there was no other reaction. Beckie looked at Greg, but he shook his head and shrugged. "I wouldn't much want to come back, either."

Beckie nodded. "Yeah. Okay. The next thing is to get her into—"

The chickee rocked sharply, violently. Greg's eyes were wide, as wide as Beckie's, she was sure. Her back had been to the front wall of the hut, her butt into the wind. Greg was speechless, mouth hanging open.

She rotated like she was on a turntable, slowly creaking, to see… The hut rocked again, but not quite as violently. After grabbing Amy to prevent her drifting away, she turned to see the bow of a boat reaching to brush her back.

She ducked away, attempting to leap over Amy and the bed, and tripped herself. She avoided landing on Amy, but cracked an elbow and knee on the bed frame. Again she popped her head clear of the water but this time, Greg reached out his hand.

"Who—"

"No idea," she responded, though she was sure it didn't sound like that as she spat water with the words. The boat rose on a wave and lifted the building again. This time both she and Greg went down.

When Beckie got clear of the water this time, she heard the boat's engine in the brief lull. As suddenly, the wind returned, howling through the trees and the structure. Before either of them got to their feet, the chickee fell off whatever had passed for its foundation; the floor now rose from back to front and the boat had room to pitch.

A shadow stood in the ruined doorway. Beckie ducked down to avoid the beam from the intruder's light, then shoved Amy's body to Greg.

On her hands and knees, with her head almost in the fetid water, Beckie sloshed toward the door. The knife in her hand wasn't the comfort she wanted, but she kept a tight hold on it. If Greg keeps his attention, I can maybe hamstring this guy. Why the fuck are they coming back? The question slowed her.

A flash of light from behind her: Greg had responded to the intruder's light by directing his beam in the invader's face, hoping, she thought, to blind him while she attacked.

Water cascading from her clothes and hair, she jumped up to attack.

"Ian!" The knife skittered off his arm slicing open his sleeve. "Fuck! I almost killed you!"

He hugged her tight. She felt the body armor under his shirt. "I would forgive you. Amy Rose?"

Beckie was shaking in his arms. The unrelenting noise, the cold of the water in every crack and crevasse of her body, the terror that Amy, in spite of her eyes moving, was in fact dead because she hadn't arrived soon enough, the fear she'd attacked Ian! She loosed a hand to point toward Greg. "Greg has her. I don't… She's… alive. But, I don't know… if she'll make it! I couldn't save her."

She heard him speak, but not the words. As he lifted her, she saw two more shapes push by, hurrying toward Greg and Amy.

Beckie gathered herself to wave as she called, "It's ok, Greg!" She heard splashing from his direction.

"Sorry, Ian. I'm still thinking about Wu Ting." She shook her head, splashing water across his face. "Sorry." A half-hearted grin forced its way to her face. She reached up to wipe the excess water away, but he caught her hand.

The look in his eyes disconcerted her for a second, until she read respect and gratitude there. "You never could control Ms Wu's fate. Tonight, however, you have recovered a team member for us. Thank you." He brushed a kiss over her cold lips.

"If she lives. Now we need to crush everyone who took her!"

"Not tonight, I fear."

"No, not tonight." She turned to look at Amy. "Who's there?" She pushed away toward the figures.

Ian pulled her back. "Kevin and Millie. Daniel will assist as needed." He pointed at the doorway. "We would be in the way." He relaxed his hug and started toward the door. "You came in the Hummer?"

She touched Dan's arm as she passed him. "Thanks, Dan." She pulled Ian's head down to talk in his ear. "Yeah. It's Sandy's. If they don't need me, I gotta take it back."

"Hmm. And Mr. Daniels?"

"Well, we're not gonna leave him."

"No, of course not."

They had reached the Hummer, still running. The water was almost to the fenders, but Beckie found it solidly planted when she leaned against the door. She cast a baleful look at the Archangel 440 still nosing the chickee. "Is that boat safe enough?" She giggled. "Must be, you got here."

"It is sufficient." Four shapes went by, the first holding Amy, wrapped in a silver blanket. Beckie recognized Millie alongside the girl, holding her hand.

Greg stopped in front of them, followed by Kevin.

"How'll we get the Hummer out?"

Beckie straightened. "I'll drive it," she said, "soon as I warm up a little."

Ian pulled her body against his. "Thank you, Mr. Daniels. She and I will return the Hummer. Kevin, Mr. Daniels will return with you on the boat. With the same number of people returning in the truck, the authorities may have fewer questions. Assuming they noticed."

"Okay. Let's get moving then." Kevin looked toward the stern and the swim platform. "Dan's got Amy aboard. Millie will work on her all the way."

"She's… she's still… bre—"

"Breathing? Yeah, I felt her twitching when I handed her to Dan. Enough to say she's alive." He patted Beckie's cheek. "You two are some kind of saviors, you know." He put his arm around Greg's shoulder and walked him to the boat.

Ian opened the Hummer's door, but Beckie looked him in the eye, hoping the determination she felt carried to him. "I can make it. I drove the damn thing down here and I'm used to the way it handles under water." She removed his hand from her arm and walked around the front to the driver's side door. It opened as she put a foot on the rail and heaved herself up.

Beside them, the boat backed its bow out of the chickee and slowly made its way toward the ocean. In seconds, it was gone, hidden behind the scud and the breaking waves.

"Good journey," Beckie wished aloud.

Chapter Six
Amy Healing

THE WEEKEND AFTER AMY'S RESCUE, Beckie took the air taxi home to the Nest. After Ian, her first stop was the hospital to see Amy. Millie was like a mother panther, watching over an injured cub. She even snarled at Beckie before catching herself.

"Sorry, it's just—"

"No need to apologize. How is she?"

Millie brightened, giving Beckie a small smile. "Physically, she's healing."

"And?"

The smile washed away. "Mentally, I'm not sure how she's doing. She'll hardly talk to me. Or anyone. She's skittish, and the orderlies report she's not sleeping very well."

Beckie said nothing, just gave her a sympathetic look.

"But you're not here to see me, right? Ian said you were bruised but —"

"All 'own goals,' as they say in soccer. Falling, tripping, swimming in sand-infested water. But I was careful to take care of my ribs," she said with a laugh.

"Good. We have enough patients."

"So can I see her?" Beckie looked into Millie's face until the woman returned her gaze. "Alone?"

Millie gave her a weary look before her hand went up to rub her forehead. "If you want no one to hear, you should take her down to the beach."

"I'll do that."

Amy's hug of greeting seemed honest enough to Beckie, but before she said anything else, she hustled Amy into a wheelchair and rolled her out of the building. In the sunlight, Beckie studied the girl. She looks… Damn! Big dark circles under her eyes. Body's almost limp. Her face, washed out, like she hasn't had any sleep. And what did I expect? I still flash back…

Go Shen hurried out of the security building as they went by, interrupting Beckie's memories of Thailand. "Hi, Beckie, Amy. How are you? And where are you headed?"

Guess which of those questions is more important to him, Beckie thought with a grin. "We're pretty much fine, I guess. Just headed to the beach on the west side." She pointed up the path beside the building. "We wanted some privacy, but we'll stay close to one of your cameras."

He smiled and went back in.

Beckie pushed the chair until they reached the sand.

"I can walk." Amy stood and took a few steps. "It's like Mr. Jamse was; Mom's just… overprotective, I think they call it."

Beckie stared agape at the girl. Does she still think she has too much protection?

Amy started slowly down the beach to the water's edge. Beckie caught her as she kicked her hospital slippers off and continued into the small waves. "What was it like?" Amy asked as she splashed.

"I was terrified." She grabbed Amy's arm and pulled her into a fierce hug. "Now come up here and sit so we can talk."

"Why were you— Oh, the storm."

"No. Fuck the storm. It was not being sure I was right, and putting Greg in danger. Then it was I was right and you looked so… so damn dead I couldn't stand it! I 'bout fell over when Kevin told me he'd felt you moving. I wanted to come and grab you myself, but… But I took his word for it." She sat in front of Amy, interleaving their legs so they could hold hands. "Then I was scared they'd injured you so… so you'd die anyway. Or be permanently, you know, messed up."

"I was so mad at you. Mom, too, and Mr. Jamse, but I'd left *you* the note. I thought sure you'd read it and figure out… Well, I really expected Mom to come leaping out of the sky to take me home. I wasn't hoping for more than a day or two with Abby before…" She bent over to stare at the sand next to Beckie's foot. "That was the second stupidest thing, I guess. Thinking Abby would actually send a message like that."

"They were playing on your hope, not your sense."

"Yeah. That's what they mean by experience, huh?" She looked up. "How'd you find me, anyway?"

"You'll listen to your teachers when you hear. I was in that same camp, in one of those chickees, last February. My Physics instructor made arrangements for some of the class to spend a weekend at the Winter Star Party, where amateur astronomers get together and… look at stars, believe it or not.

"While I was watching the video, something bothered me—"

"Yeah, Mom said you watched the whole thing. She was impressed."

"I actually watched you only about a minute. Long enough to be sure it was you." She shuddered. "Rape porn doesn't do it for me. I watched the background, trying to remember what was tickling my mind." She sighed. "Sorry. It didn't come back till I heard the news about Hurricane Hanna hitting Key West. After the star-gazing ended, we went there for dinner before heading back to school."

Amy reached for Beckie's hand. In a barely audible voice, she said, "I don't know how to… to act. To—"

Her whisper was cut off when Beckie hugged her.

After a bit, Amy gave a humorless laugh. "You know the absolute worst part?" she whispered. "They wouldn't even take me with them when the storm came. Just left me… Like you and Mom…" Beckie stiffened at the charge, but before she could protest, Amy continued,

"Yeah, I know it's not the same at all. But…" She sniffled as more tears rolled down her cheeks. "But it wasn't different, either, from where I was… in my mind." Beckie met her eyes. "Can you understand that? No one came to get me, and they left me to… to drown."

"Yeah. I get it. I'm sorry."

"The past couple of days, I've been taking myself to the courtyard since I can go there alone. I see Mom watching me from inside, frowning and shaking her head. She's blaming me, I know she is. For—"

"No!" I have to make sure she understands. "What happened wasn't your fault! Your mom is worried about you, not passing judgment."

Amy burrowed her face into Beckie's neck and shuddered.

"Can you believe me?" Beckie asked. "This is important."

Amy nodded in her arms, but said nothing. Do I push it?

Beckie didn't notice time passing until water soaked her shorts; the tide was coming in. She used her fun-filled voice to say, "Do you need *more* saline soaking?"

Amy shot up. "What?" Beckie ducked the loose fist swung at her arm. "No! No, thank you." Amy laughed so hard she fell over into the sea foam. She lay, gasping for breath, until Beckie pulled her up.

While clouds lined the horizon, the sun was comfortable as they dripped dry. Amy sobered quickly, pulling Beckie to sit above the high tide mark. I guess she's not ready to head back yet.

"I feel really stupid, no matter—"

"Why do you feel stupid?" Beckie retorted. "Believe me, there's no call for that. Just because you made a… hormone driven mistake, probably, it doesn't mean you're stupid. I'm here to tell you people make mistakes every day. I'll bet you even make some from now on."

"For a while, I thought I should just kill myself, you know." Beckie hugged her again, pulling her across to wipe her eyes. "That everyone'd be better off… That *I'd* be better off."

"You decided to stick it out, though."

"Yeah." She choked on a sob. "Maybe more 'cause I was scared…"

Beckie wasn't sure where to take that. Telling the girl death was part of the human condition and shouldn't raise fear didn't seem like today's best therapy. At the end of the day, she thought, it doesn't matter. She's holding off.

"I want to go."

Coming as Amy shook, holding back more weeping, Beckie was sure she didn't mean back to the hospital. "You know that's not possible. And it's a really bad idea."

Amy sat up so quickly she banged her head against Beckie's. "Sorry." Her face flushed and she took a deep breath before demanding, "Why is it even a little bit of a bad idea, let alone a really bad one? How do I get that time back? My… virginity back?" She pounded the sand between her legs but then used the fist to knuckle tears away. "It's supposed to be so special, and I can't give it away to the person I want to, if I ever do. They took that, along with everything else." She collapsed in Beckie's lap.

Beckie reached deep inside herself, trying to answer Amy.

"How does Meili deal with it?"

A question Beckie could begin to answer. "Meili saw her friend being murdered. Being rescued before she, too, was murdered was a big offset to being raped. Sorta put it in perspective, if I can say that about rape. That was the impression I had when we talked about it." Beckie was cradling Amy's head, stroking her hair. "Even though she didn't have her family to go back to, she had me for a while, and the Go's since then. She feels wanted, and important because of it." She spent a minute rubbing Amy's tear tracks away. "I don't think she dwells on it, but she'd be willing to talk to you, if you think it would help. But make sure Xia's there; I'm pretty sure Meili's English isn't up to that conversation."

Amy wriggled around so her face was in Beckie's belly.

"Another thought: you've never made love with anyone, have you?"

Amy's eyes snapped open, but rather than allow her to protest, Beckie hurried to say, "Think about it. The physical act of penetration is just that: someone using force to overpower, to take what you refuse to give. That's not making love. At least, to me it's not. It shouldn't be to you, either."

"Yeah, I understand. Just…" She closed her eyes.

"I believe your chance will come, if I can keep you alive—"

"What's that mean? You can keep me alive? I..." Amy spluttered a couple more seconds.

Beckie wondered if she should duck from the girl's flashing eyes. "I guess your mom didn't tell you. Ian and I talked... I asked to take your safety as my job."

"But... Why?"

"How could I not? You've helped me, you're one of the team, you're a girl who's been abused... I could go on and on—"

"But... but—"

Beckie laughed, making sure it wasn't a making-fun-of kind of laugh. "Stop the sputtering and get over it. Rou won't give you the papers to sign till you're eighteen, but you can read Ian's promise to you. You're one of the team, and the team leaves *no* one behind!"

Amy's eyes were wide; her body stiff. "I guess I thought that... that phrase meant something else. Like in combat?"

"Of course! But what you've been through, that's not combat? Nothing I've heard about rape makes it better than combat. Worse, in fact! But, I have to stop thinking about you that way."

"What way is that?"

"As a girl who's been abused. You—"

"I'm a survivor, damn it!"

"Damn straight you are! And I'm glad of it."

As she spoke, she squeezed Amy, then rolled her off her lap with an authoritative push. "While you think about all that, we should go back. While I'm sure your mom is watching with Shen—"

Amy's face went flat, unresponsive.

"Okay, tell me about it."

"I don't wanna."

"Whoa." Beckie giggled. "Listen to you: 'I don' wanna.' Sounds like one of Shalin's kids. Have you been practicing?"

"No, damn it! I just... She's all the time around. I can hardly go to the head alone." She glanced over, forehead furrowing. "How'd you spring me, anyway? I never asked you that."

"I asked, politely. More politely than she expected, probably. You might try it."

"I tried everything. Polite, snippy, bitchy, rude! Nothing worked. She—"

"Com'on. She's scared to death, girl! You came within a gnat's eyelash of being dead with not one fucking friend or anyone to… to even be with you!"

"Whoa! Sensitive much?"

Teeth bared, Beckie spun and swung open handed at her, but pulled the blow halfway round. "Yes!" She caught her breath. "It's the same problem Ian and I have: worrying about each other till we can't do anything."

Amy was still leaning back. Guess she's not sure I won't swing again. "From Mom, it doesn't come across that way, like it does for you two."

"She hasn't had much practice, probably. She thought you were safe till Shen showed us the video."

"The video? Oh…" Beckie nodded. "Did anyone here *not* see it?"

Good, Beckie thought, she's angry. "No one saw it that wasn't going to work on getting you back. Your mom, Ian, me, Mr. Shen, Kevin, Elena. It's not something we wanted to distribute." She leaned back on her hands. "Ian and Shen believe Abby's seen it too."

"Yeah, Mr. Jamse told me that when he told me she'd taken leave. He sounded, I don't know, disappointed?"

"Yeah, he is. We could help her, whatever's going on. Now, she's out there alone, kinda like you, and while we're looking…

"You know, you've maybe not thought it through. What do you think would have happened if you'd decided not to sail off to Providenciales?"

"It would have all fallen apart. That's what Abby said… My God. Abby didn't say that, did she?"

"No. But you're right. *That* scheme would have fallen apart. Shen has just spent several thousand dollars adding cams along the beaches where you run. Ian's pretty sure that, had you taken the sensible course, they would have grabbed you off Bon Secours, and nothing else would have been different."

"There would have been a long boat ride instead of one in the limo, I guess."

She's reacting well. "Yeah. Not that you would have enjoyed it any more."

She reached for Amy's hand, but the girl shied away. Maybe she's not reacting so well. Amy's eyes were wide and she gasped. "They might still be coming? No! No, I will—"

"Relax. Amy! Stop it!" Amy was almost hyperventilating, gasping, swaying back and forth. "Listen to me! Listen. It's why I talked to Ian. It's why you're always with someone. It's why Mr. Go added the cameras. No one's gonna be able to sneak up and grab you."

Amy was calming, slowly. She wasn't gasping now, but her eyes were still wide; Beckie could see whites all around. I gotta be careful here. "It'll be tough for a while, thinking everyone's sticking to you closer than… your underwear." That worked, Beckie thought as Amy snickered, a weak giggle. "Until we figure out who they are and stop them, in the shower's the only place you'll be alone. And that's only if there's no windows in the bathroom!"

"This is sure payback, isn't it?" Beckie's confusion made it to her face; Amy said, "Wanting to be independent, not needing protection. Really, wanting to be left alone to do what I wanted. Those guys didn't need to go that far to teach me a lesson."

Beckie only nodded.

By noon, the girls had done their conversation to death. Beckie led Amy back to the wheelchair and drove her to the dock facing Ian's home.

"I'm going to take the chance your mom won't mind me keeping you as long as I don't lose you. Maurice has a great lunch planned and you can listen to me and Ian try to figure out what's next. Just listen, okay?"

After the boat ride, they walked the path to Ian's home. He and Maurice were in the kitchen building a crab salad. "That looks great!" Beckie said.

"Or perhaps you are starving," Ian rejoined. "Have you eaten yet today?"

"Well…" She admitted defeat when her stomach rumbled. "I invited Amy, okay?" She peered into the bowl. "Looks like plenty there."

"Ms Arden is more than welcome." Ian lifted Amy's hand and brushed his lips against her fingers. "It is a pleasure to see you up and about, Amy Rose."

Her head bowed, she said, "Believe me, Mr. Jamse, it's a pleasure to be out and about."

Maurice had set down his utensils and was holding a chair. Beckie nodded to him and pushed Amy to sit.

The small talk bored Beckie after she'd finished her helping of the delicious salad. "Have we heard anything… about anything?" she asked.

Amy sat forward, fork frozen over her plate. "Any word about Abby?"

"No. I suspect she has travelled to the United States, but without being noticed by Mr. Go's informants."

"You wouldn't…" She looked into her plate and then glared at him. "You're not trying to protect me, are you?"

"I am unsure of your meaning—"

"I'm not." Beckie turned to face Amy. "Of course he's trying to protect you! Remember what we talked about? But that doesn't mean he'll lie to you, or tell you things that aren't true. We do expect you'll have the sense to allow us to protect you. We *need* you to have that sense." She faced Ian. "She's afraid you're not telling her what we know, for fear she'll run off to rescue Abby."

"I gathered that as you were chastising her," Ian said with a wry smile. He looked at Amy. "Please look at me, Amy Rose." He waited until she raised her head and gazed at him. "I will give you any information I have regarding Ms Rochambeau as long as I deem it safe for you, her and the team to do so. Before Rebecca's… tirade, I might have withheld information I felt you had no need to share, but watching you… I will tell you what I know."

"Thanks, Ian," overlapped Amy's "Thank you, Mr. Jamse."

"I confirm today I have no additional information to share with you." He looked around. "Do we have any calmatives, Boynton? I fear Rebecca is somewhat… stressed, shall we say?"

"Huh? No, I'm not… well, maybe a little."

"This is the least strong elixir we have," Boynton said as he poured a measure of champagne into a fresh flute of orange juice. "Would you like one also, Miss Amy?"

"Mom'll have a fit, so yes, please!"

"You may detect just the slightest hint of… rebellion? I think rebellion, yes." Beckie grinned. "I haven't teased that out of her, yet." She raised the glass to Boynton. "This hits the spot, Maurice. Thank you. And you, love." She clasped Ian's hand.

Chapter Seven
The Nest

Abby's Package

BOYNTON MET BECKIE AND IAN as they came through the front door. They'd spent two days at a conference investigating rising ocean levels; with no good news about the Nest's future, Beckie was ready for a long shower and some relaxation with Ian. Maybe not so relaxing, at first anyway!

The look on Boynton's face pushed all that aside. No relaxation yet, she grumbled to herself. Boynton led them to the lanai, where on the table a Fed-Ex envelope lay, festooned with official stamps. Sure, Beckie thought, it *looks* innocent enough.

Neither sat. Ian poked the package around so they could read the label: J.A. Rochambeau, with her box number at the Nest.

"Shen brought it over this morning when it arrived. It was dispatched in Georgetown, Grand Cayman last Monday," Boynton said, pointing to the label's date. "As it was self-addressed, he thought you should decide if we should open it."

"Self-addressed?" Beckie looked at the neat script, but she'd never seen Abby's handwriting.

"Shen and Derek agree; it is written in her hand."

Beckie looked at Ian, who had a disconsolate look. "What are we waiting for?"

"Nothing." He sighed and scrubbed his hand through his short blond hair. "But I am concerned over the penchant both she and Amy Rose seem to share: leaving important information to be discovered late in the game, perhaps too late. Pfaugh!" He snatched the envelope from the table and ripped the sealed end open.

He peered inside, then tipped the contents, an opened foil snack package, a folded paper and an envelope, onto the glass table top. Beckie picked up the chips wrapper, saying "What…" followed by "Oh," as she pulled Abby's salt- and crumb-covered passport out. Boynton handed her a napkin as Ian tore the smaller envelope apart.

While Ian studied the envelope's content, Beckie picked up the loose piece of paper and read: "The enclosed passport has been found, but not the owner, so we are returning it to the owner's home."

Ian still hadn't finished with his letter. "Relax, Ian," Beckie said with a smile as she placed a hand on his arm. "What's it say?"

"I am unsure." He handed the single sheet of paper to her.

She scanned the seven words twice before handing it to Boynton.

"Dewey, Cheatum and Howe?"

Beckie giggled. "She must have a lawyer friend. It's a derisive term for a law firm. Confirmed by the 'JD' after. Read it aloud: Do we cheat 'em? And how!" She glanced at the paper again. "But it's crossed out? Except for the JD."

"Indicating perhaps Ms Rochambeau did not recall the name of the firm, only the principal. Samuel…"

"Goldfarb," Beckie finished. "Okay, who's he?"

"Samuel Goldfarb was the defense attorney at the trial Derek apprised us of," Boynton said. "The one at which Ms Rochambeau testified." When she gave him a questioning look, he said, "I researched the case, hoping to expand on the *Times* article. Goldfarb's name figures prominently in the contemporaneous media reports. As did his potential linkages with not only Donato Talos, but other unsavory characters. His training in criminal law and racketeering was money well spent."

"Well done," Ian said. "Possibly a viable connection." He sighed and looked into Beckie's eyes. "Promise me you will write notes with more clarity, should you find it necessary. Is Ms Rochambeau going to visit Goldfarb? Does she believe he is a person we should investigate? How might he be connected to Ms Ardan's ordeal?"

"Well, given Abby's not here to explain herself, let's do what she expected us to do when she wrote this."

"What would that be, Rebecca?"

"I think Abby's sent you this because she depends on you to help her. Now, what she might view as help is problematic." Both Ian and Boynton smiled. Well, Boynton smirked. "Yeah, I know," Beckie continued, "easy for me to say. But she's smart enough to realize going alone is foolish when the team's ready to help for nothing but the asking.

"However, Abby's nothing if not proud. Could be Amy'd have some insight, you know. And we promised to keep her up to date."

"Millie would have to know as well. How will you dissuade Ms Ardan from attempting to join us?"

"By saying 'No!' as forcefully and as often as I need to. I have no interest in putting her at risk. Millie will back us up. And—"

"I notice you keep saying 'us.' What about your school?"

Beckie could feel the blood rushing to her face. She looked down at the passport lying on the napkin. "Ah. School. I forgot... They..." She forced a neutral expression to her face and body before looking up. "I got a call from the Dean of Students. She believes I would be better off leaving this semester and returning when I can apply my talents to attending class more often."

"You've been thrown out," Boynton said with that little smile of his, as if he'd known it all along.

"In words of one syllable, yeah." She looked at her hands, writhing as she twisted them together. "Until January."

"Do you believe you will be able to put our work aside in January?"

"I can't answer that, Ian. Will something come up I can help with?

Maybe Shalin and Kevin's kids'll be stolen? All I can say is I'll try."

"Your parents… This violates the spirit of our implicit agreement with them."

Beckie shoved the chair back; she reached to catch it, but missed. Crying, she ran to the railing overlooking the ocean and vaulted over. When she hit the sand four feet below, she thought, Damn, that was stupid. Ankle still hurts. She took a deep breath and ran to the ocean.

Why'd he have to bring the parents into this? That's not fair! I can't control what happens, only how I react to it. She ran into the low surf until she had to swim, then she swam another few yards. Not getting any smarter, am I? Weighed down by the wet jeans and shirt, she wriggled out of them and, holding the bundle on her chest, did a one-handed backstroke back to the beach. The waves helped, allowing her to awkwardly surf until she hit her head on the compacted sand.

She threw the clothes over her head and turned to swim out. I need to work… No, damn it! I need to apologize to Ian. This acting like a baby; it won't work. It doesn't even make me feel better!

She flipped over and headed toward the beach. She tossed her head to clear the salt water from her eyes and nose. A tall form stood in the shallows. Well, yeah, you didn't think he'd let you stay out here alone, did you?

She swam to knee-deep water and stood in front of him. "I'm sorry, Ian. That was so completely uncalled for… I wouldn't blame you if you threw me out again. I wouldn't like it, but I deserve it, this time."

"Never. Would you like these?" He was holding her dripping clothes.

She waded to him, took the bundle and pitched it further up the beach. "Too cold in these wet things." She unhooked her bra, then shoved her panties down.

Ian looked a moment. "Surely you will be chilly."

She felt a shiver, but it wasn't the cold. She held out her hands to him. "Surely you will warm me."

He removed his shirt and pulled it around her shoulders as she hugged herself to his warm bare chest.

Amy's Message

In the bright sunlight of morning, Beckie led Ian to the kitchen, where, as she was coming to expect, the coffee maker chimed as she reached for a pair of cups.

As they enjoyed the Jamaican Blue Mountain, she said, "You know, I was right. Abby does have a lawyer friend." Ian said nothing; rather, he gave her an inquisitive look. "That newspaper article Derek sent us. Not only did it mention Goldfarb, but Abby's lawyer, too, an Eilís O'Bannon… though why she needed an attorney is another question."

"According to everything I could find," Boynton said, "anyone dealing with Talos would be well advised to bring their own legal team."

"Ah. Well, I noticed it then, but forgot it till now. I'll call her later; see if she knows anything. But now…" She pulled her phone out and scrolled to Amy's number. She slid it across the table. Ian looked quickly, then nodded.

She punched Talk. "Amy? You ready for the day? I'll be over in ten minutes, so get outta the PJ's!"

Thirty minutes later, she led Amy to the table on the lanai. Boynton was just setting pastries and fresh coffee to the side. "Or would you prefer tea, Miss Amy?" She shook her head and he left.

Ian entered as Boynton disappeared. "Good morning, Amy Rose. How are you today?"

"Fine, except hungry for one of those rolls and jealous—" She clapped a hand over her mouth, red flowing up her cheeks.

"Jealous?"

Beckie laughed, and it set Amy off. "Yeah! It's just so obvious that you guys… well… You know," she finished weakly.

"Amy," Beckie heard Millie from just off the lanai, announcing her arrival, "intellectually, you know couples… enjoy themselves."

"Yeah, Mom, but Beckie *so* enjoys it!"

"And it's polite not to mention it in public. That aside, why are we invited to interrupt the love birds this beautiful morning?"

Beckie glanced at Ian, who nodded back. That wonderful smile, God, I love him!

"Com'on here to the table," she said. "We got this from Abby." She pointed to the envelope. "Actually, I guess it came yesterday morning, but we opened it last night. By the time we got to where we could call you, it was too late, so…"

Amy was wiping crumbs from the passport from her fingers while Millie read the note about the passport. Amy picked up the envelope with Ian's name and looked at him. When he nodded, she slid the paper from within and read it.

"Jesus, this is just like her!"

"Amy, there's no call for—"

"Sorry, Mom." She handed the note over.

"What does this mean?"

^"We were hoping for a reading from Amy."

Amy's glance snapped to Beckie, then she picked up the paper again. "Well, she does like to talk in codes. But, I don't think I've heard this, exactly…"

"Dewey Cheatum and Howe is a derogatory way to refer to a law firm—"

"Oh, I get it. That's good! And the JD? Not juvenile delinquent, I guess?"

"Juris Doctor. A law degree, if we didn't get the first reference. And the guy's name is from the trial Ian told you about. The defense attorney."

"So…" Amy took the note to the railing Beckie had vaulted. She looks more stable than me, though. Beckie glanced around; everyone, even Boynton, was intent on the girl in shorts and hip-length robe leaning against the deck rail. She was as oblivious to her audience. Her eyes scanned back and forth over the words. She lifted the paper to her face, breathing in any scent it might have had left. After a minute, she folded the note and wiped her eye. "I don't know what I can tell you." Her voice caught twice as she spoke.

"Well, I don't want to put words in your mouth, so... Why did she send this, addressed to Ian?"

"Oh! To tell him what she was doing. Going after this guy..." She looked at the note again. "... Goldfarb. And telling Mr. Jamse it'd be okay if he helped out." She lifted her gaze to Ian. "That's why she sent it to you." Once again, she wiped her overflowing eyes. "She thinks a lot of you, you know. Everyone, really, but you and Mr. Hamilton are top of her list." She walked back to the table. "May I keep this?" she said, not extending the hand with the note. "Please?"

"Of course. We are confident there is no secret ink message."

"So, if we went after her—"

Amy's voice stopped her. "Can I—"

The chorus of "No's" was deafening, even to Beckie.

"Com'on, Amy." She pulled the girl's hand down from her face where she was covering her tears and led her outside. Back on the beach, she put an arm around Amy's shoulders, but didn't resist when Amy turned to hug her with everything she had. "We talked about this, remember? You're not healed, yet, and you're still fifteen, and—"

"And, and, and!" she cried into Beckie's neck. "I just... She wouldn't be in this mess if... if I hadn't been so stupid!"

"I thought we punched this ticket already. You're not stupid, and neither is Abby. You got fooled by some guy who gave you a pretty good reason to believe what he was selling. Like I said, they wouldn't have stopped there, even if you'd talked to your mom, or me or Shalin. Or even Abby."

"But... I feel so helpless."

"Com'on, walk with me. Let's wade along the water, okay?"

Beckie started with her arm around Amy's shoulder, but in a few yards, shifted to holding her hand. A quick glance back showed her Ian was following at a respectable distance. She held Amy to a slow pace, drifting in and out of the waves.

She looked at Amy, who was looking out to sea. The girl's eyes were wide and her face looked drawn. As she asked "What?" she followed Amy's gaze.

"Nothing," Amy said. "Trying to... I don't know, exactly. Just thinking about Abby."

"Yeah." She looked back again; this time Ian waved toward the dock. "Let's see what Ian has in mind."

Ian was waiting as they approached the dock. As they came up on it, suddenly Amy fell to her knees and dropped back to sit cross-legged. Her elbows hit her knees and her face landed in her hands.

"Okay, girl, what's the matter now?" Beckie said as she waved Ian to a walk.

"I am so stupid!" Amy screamed into her hands. "I know how..." She took Beckie's hand and helped pull herself up. "Abby's private email. I've known all along. And a number that used to be good for texting, too," although Beckie could see more doubt as Amy said that.

"And what will you send?" Ian said.

"To tell her I'm okay and with you guys, and safe. Even if I can't go."

"You know you can't go. We've had that conversation."

Amy's head drooped and she shoved her hands into the pockets of the short robe she was wearing. "Yeah, I know. But..." Her head came up and her eyes flashed. "... I still *want* to come and help."

"Letting Abby know you're safe will help. Maybe she'll even come back."

Amy looked out over the ocean to the east. "No," she finally said. "Not till she's done. But it'll help if she knows I'm safe. And if she expects Mr. Jamse to help."

Ian had landed the skiff and walked with them to the security office. As Beckie looked around to see who was there, Amy said, "I'll need my phone." Millie dug in her pocket and slid a cell phone across the table. Amy glanced at it and said, "No, sorry. My iPhone." She looked across at her mother with a look of shock before putting her head on her arms, sobbing quietly. "It's probably still on *Guppy*, waiting for me. In Providen—"

"*Guppy's* in the anchorage," Kevin said. "I asked a couple of the guys to sail her back, rather than running up a humongous bill before you remembered her."

As he finished, Amy landed a huge hug. "Oh, thank you so much, Mr. deVeel! I can't thank—"

"Don't mention it. This hug makes it all worthwhile. Now pull yourself back together and wait while I ask… Where did you leave the phone? No one saw it."

"It's in the forward cuddy, along with my passport and a folder of cash. In case the marina needed more," she said. She stood to allow Kevin to straighten, and she pulled her robe closed. "7-23-14, for the lock."

Elena was standing by the door; she nodded and left. While they waited, Amy composed a message using Shen's laptop. When she'd finished, she turned to Beckie. "Can we talk?"

With a nod, Beckie led her to the restroom where she'd earlier found Millie. "What is it?"

"We had a joke, Abby and I, the next time she'd see me…" Beckie was amazed at the color in Amy's face. That's not a blush, it's a conflagration! "She'd see me… naked." Amy spun to face the sink, unaware or uncaring Beckie could see her face in the mirror. She still glowed bright. "If you take a picture of me… to attach, you know, to the message… then… then she'll know it's really me, and I'm really ok."

"Oh. Oh." Beckie stammered a few more times before grabbing Amy's shoulder and spinning her around. "Oh!" Amy's robe was once again undone, revealing her chest, bare. "Now I understand what Kevin meant," Beckie said with a giggle as she pulled the robe closed. "Do you think it would be enough just to snap your boobs? Not your whole body?"

"Yeah! Yeah, that would be fine. I'm sure Abby'll get the message."

In another fifteen minutes, Elena had returned bringing Amy's phone, passport and cash. "Thanks, Ms Rios," she said before sliding the cash across to her mother, mumbling, "For our vacation… I hope…" and handed the phone to Beckie. In the restroom, Beckie took the photo and Amy rewrote her message to Abby. She clicked send, and then sent a text message to Abby's phone: "U have mail."

Chapter Eight
Following Abby's Signal

Brewster

THE LINK BETWEEN GOLDFARB, TALOS and Abby had been clarified—slightly—during Beckie's conversation with Eilís O'Bannon, Abby's lawyer. While most of what Eilís told her was recapitulation, hearing it live from one who'd lived through it made it more real.

Once Amy's message had been sent and Abby's response cheered, Beckie felt like she'd spent the rest of the day flying, with Westchester County Airport the final destination. Ian guessed New York would be a good jumping-off point; Jean-Luc had already filed the documents for the flight. After Beckie's conversation with Eilís, Shen had no difficulty tracking Abby's return text message to Chatham, Massachusetts, specifically to Eilís' home. Abby's phone was again trackable and Eilís had shared Abby's destination: Talos' home in Brewster, New York.

By eight, they'd landed at Westchester and rented a black Escalade. As Kevin started the engine, Ian said, "To review: Our sole brief is to find and support Ms Rochambeau. I expect we shall return in short order.

"We have reviewed the map of the area. Beyond that, we have no sitrep other than the building, according to Ms O'Bannon, was Talos' home prior to his incarceration and his men may be securing it. If possible, refrain from gunplay, but take care."

Kevin drove out of the airport lot as Elena set the GPS for Talos' address. Beckie and Ian shared the back seat with Millie and her medical kit.

After forty minutes on the rain-swept roads, the GPS proclaimed "Your destination is on the left." Kevin drove a few more seconds until he reached a wide spot, a boat-launching ramp, from which they could deploy.

Beckie got out of the SUV; Ian and Kevin followed. Elena delayed to check the radios with Millie, who would stay with the vehicle unless someone was injured. They'd stopped just past the house; once the team moved off, Millie planned to move to a parking lot away from the lake.

When Elena joined them and Millie'd driven away, they surveyed the area. Across the road, the lake was black in the night. Trees lined both sides of the one-lane road. Steady rain splashed in puddles on the cracked asphalt; it was getting heavier. Beckie hunched up the collar of her black shirt, which was rapidly absorbing the water that didn't run down her back between her shoulder blades. She shrugged and stepped off behind Ian, leading the way through the woods. For a couple steps, she heard Kevin or Elena behind her, but after that, nothing but drops on leaves. The wind was still.

Beckie stepped carefully, placing her boots where Ian had set his. The half mile that would have taken ten minutes at a reasonable pace took forty-five, between Ian's checks and watching so carefully where she stepped. Ian held out his hand and pointed through a scraggly bush.

The house had two windows on the first floor lit, and one on the second. There was no sound except the rain. Beckie looked around, but saw nothing she didn't expect. Ian reached around her to point to Kevin, sending him off to the left. Elena didn't wait, but turned to the right.

Understanding her role—stay back, don't take the point and help where needed—Beckie leaned against a tree where she had a better view of the field between the team and the house. After a minute spent scrutinizing, she turned her attention to the woods to the left and then the right.

Well, Abby's supposed to be here. She tapped Ian and signed, "I'm backing up a little so I can talk to Millie." He agreed, and she walked back about fifty feet. She pressed the mike. "Millie, has anyone said where Abby's phone is now?"

While she waited, she heard Kevin's voice, "I think Abby beat us here. Just found a guy all tied up out of the way back here. Nothing else."

Millie was quiet so long Beckie was ready to do another radio check. but then she heard, "Her phone's about two hundred feet from yours. Been moving slowly toward the house, Shen says."

"Cool, thanks."

Millie said, "Hundred seventy-five feet."

At the edge of the trees, Beckie dropped to her knee to see if she could backlight anyone against the lights in the windows. "There!" she whispered into the mike. She felt Ian kneel beside her and sight along her arm. He nodded.

As Beckie watched, she saw another figure and then a third. Faintly, she could hear a tussle, so soft that if she hadn't been watching it, she'd never have noticed. They all disappeared. She rubbed rain from her eyes, and one of the shadows rose and glanced toward the house, then back at the woods.

What the fuck? Beckie watched as the figure—she thought it was Abby, but what she was doing made no sense—ran across the front of the house. Beckie heard a woman's scream, no words, just a visceral ululation. God, that's awful! Beckie pushed up to stand so she could see better. Before she could, Ian grabbed her shirt and yanked her to the ground beside him.

ThwiPOP!

She smelled the humus her nose had shoved aside as she recalled the sound of a passing bullet. You never hear the kill-shot, she remembered, and shuddered. Two more POPs, the second so close it could have been an echo, and a scuffle. Ian was up and running. Beckie jumped to follow but she fell; her feet couldn't find purchase in the leaves and loose soil.

Cursing under her breath, she fought her way up and, keeping low, ran after him, scrubbing dirt and leaves from her face.

"Millie, to me! Quick but quiet!" scratched in her ear as she reached Ian, kneeling beside a figure. "Kevin, check the other person!" He pointed to a darker shadow. "Elena, patrol!" He caught Beckie, keeping himself between her and whoever was on the ground.

In her ear, Kevin's voice continued, "This one's no problem. Lena, watch the drive. I'll focus on the house."

"It is Ms Rochambeau," Ian said. "I fear we are too late."

Beckie forced her way around him to look for herself. The bullet had taken Abby at the base of the throat and the blood puddled under her told Beckie Ian was right. She reached out to touch Abby's cheek, to wipe the splash of blood away before the rain did.

Very gently, she leaned down to kiss the woman's lips. "Goodbye, girl. Safe landings." She rose and took four or five steps away before the reaction hit; bent over, hands on thighs, she retched, dry heaving for a few seconds before catching her breath. She wiped her mouth, then cried as Ian led her to the treeline.

Millie made little noise as she ran out of the trees. "Who? Where?"

Ian took her to Abby's body. Beckie watched, hoping against hope what she'd seen was not as bad as she knew it was. She watched as Millie touched, listened, lifted and felt some more, but in a minute, the doctor looked up at Ian, shook her head and made the sign of the cross.

Fuck! Beckie leaned against the nearest tree and cursed steadily for a minute.

Ten minutes later, all five huddled around Abby's body.

"First," Ian said, "situation report?"

Elena tipped her head to Kevin, who said, "We went around the house and down the drive. No one moving."

"Very well. We shall move Ms Rochambeau's body to the car. What did you find in your survey?"

Millie had been walking the grassy field in front of the house. She dropped a dark, wet duffle bag at her feet. "This is Abby's; it was up near the two bodies, where she started from. There are three more bodies, two there…" She pointed toward a boulder to the left. "… and one up closer to the house. A knife was used for the first two. The other body is the guy she fired on to protect Ian and Beckie, according to Elena."

Elena looked in that direction. "I saw her begin to sprint with that ungodly yell. I didn't see the shooter till then. He was behind that rock till she startled him, so he missed the shot at you guys. He fired at her at the same time she fired on him. Both their shots went home."

Beckie fell to her back, letting the rain wash the tears from her face. She felt Ian's hand grip hers and she held tight until her muscles began to cramp. If I believe in God, this means Ian and I are here to do something.

"There's a shed over there," Kevin said. "And a body behind it; knife again. Except for a few wooden crates, the shed's empty. There's blood on the door step and inside on the floor. Not enough for a slit throat. That was outside."

Millie bobbed her head. "Abby has a gash down her leg from the hip. Clean, like a knife. If she got in a scrap with that guy, that could explain it and the blood."

Kevin nodded. "The house seems to be empty," he continued. "With three shots fired, I'd think someone would have looked out the window."

"The sound wouldn't carry very well in the rain," Elena said.

"Yeah, but still. The two back there…" He hooked his thumb over his shoulder as he pulled a miniature radio out of his pocket. "… had walkie-talkies. No one's hollering for them."

"Hmm. Very well. Rebecca, you have Ms Rochambeau's weapon?" When Beckie held it up, he continued, "Millie, please bring the car. Kevin, please stay with Rebecca, guarding the area she does not. Elena, with me. We will investigate the house." He looked around. "Millie, please operate without lights once you leave the paved road."

Millie returned in a half hour. Nothing had challenged either Beckie or Kevin; they had set up one on either side of Abby looking across her at the hemisphere before them. Kevin stood when they heard the car and Beckie used her small flash to signal.

Millie got out and pushed the key fob to open the rear hatch. She rummaged for a few seconds, then walked over carrying a large flat piece of plastic. “I hate to use a body bag, but there’s no other way to get her to the plane without ruining the car in a way the police will want to understand.”

Beckie was glad to have physical activity to occupy her mind. They worked Abby’s body into the bag and then into the Escalade’s cargo area.

“That really sucks,” Beckie said.

Both Millie and Kevin simply nodded.

Beckie’s phone reported midnight before Elena and Ian walked down the slight hill to them. He looked in the rear of the SUV and inclined his head. No smiles tonight, Beckie thought. “Kevin, if you will assist me? We discovered two gold bars in the shed. Ms Rochambeau may have smeared her blood on their container; whether or not, her initials are scratched into both of them.

“Millie, there will be no difficulty in moving closer.” He rubbed his eyes. “Once the gold is aboard, we will return to the airport and then the Nest.”

“We’re going to take it?” Beckie said.

“Indeed. Until we understand better what has happened. I am interested due to Ms Rochambeau marking her claim. Also, the markings on the container suggest it originated in Peru. With the bodies here, the police will soon be involved; they will have sufficient confusion to sort through.”

While Ian, Kevin and Millie collected the “machine tools” in their wooden case, Beckie caught Elena’s arm and together, they did one more survey of the grounds. “Didn’t Kev say there was another body back of the shed?”

“Yeah. Why?”

“Three of these guys were in the video… raping Amy.”

When they returned to the SUV, Beckie’d confirmed the four dead bodies were four of the five men she’d watched. The man they found alive and bound; he hadn’t been the fifth man in the show. Elena updated the others as Millie drove off the property.

On the plane, Millie had finally succumbed to her emotions. Beckie wanted to huddle in Ian's arms, but sitting with Millie seemed to be… "It's what I *should* do," she told him. He kissed her in agreement.

During their conversation, Millie had exclaimed, "Amy! How am I…"

Beckie rolled her head back for a second, then wondered who was speaking the next words she heard, "I'll talk to her, Millie." And the voice was familiar. It was hers, she realized. Why did I say that?

At Customs, Ian declared the gold, which he valued as ballast, and since the inspector knew them all, the examination was cursory; Abby could have been sleeping with the covers pulled up.

A Conversation with Amy

At six in the morning, Jean-Luc flared the Gulfstream and landed at the Nest. Beckie was standing behind Jean-Luc and saw Amy and Shalin standing at the pad where they expected Jean-Luc to park the plane.

"Wait here," she told the others. "I'll take Amy away. Millie, are you going to call for the ambulance?"

Still white-faced, Millie nodded. "When it's clear."

Beckie walked forward to the stairs and when the plane stopped, she released the latch and let them drop. God, this will *really* suck.

She ran down the steps and over to hug Amy in a crash. She guessed Shalin could tell from looking at her face; the woman's face was stark and pale. "Kevin's waiting aboard," she said softly, pleased at the change in Shalin's expression. "Amy, come walk with me."

Amy fought Beckie's arm, but Beckie'd been expecting something. She was better trained at restraining prisoners and such; holding Amy wasn't easy, but she could do it.

"What happened? Is Mom okay? Is Abby aboard, too?" She pushed her face into Beckie's. "What the fuck happened!"

"Hold on, please." They reached the rocks making up the seawall, protecting the runway. Beckie picked out a big one and dragged Amy there. Once they were sitting, she made sure both her arms were around the girl. "Your mom's aboard. She's ok. Abby… Abby's ab… aboard too," she managed to choke out. She looked at Amy. The girl wasn't breathing, her mouth and eyes wide open. "Abby… didn't—"

"Didn't what, damn it?"

"She didn't make it, Amy. She's dead."

She grabbed Amy hard as the girl convulsed, trying to get away. For minutes, they struggled, Amy trying to get free, crying great wracking sobs Beckie was sure were audible over the whole Nest. Even after Amy gave up fighting, Beckie clutched her, wanting her to know someone was there for her.

Fifteen minutes after she'd given up fighting with Beckie, Amy turned back. "Okay. I'm okay now." The skittish look in her eye and the tinny sound of her voice gave Beckie some doubt, but she was communicating. "Can I see her?"

"In a little while. She's being taken to the hospital, but yeah, once that's settled…"

"What happened?"

Beckie spent the next half hour describing the trip and everything she'd seen and heard. "She died instantly. No pain. Attacking."

"She said she was afraid of being caught and shot in the back of the head." She shuddered for the tenth or twelfth time Beckie remembered. "God, Beckie, what do I do? How do I remember her? How do I honor the feelings I have for her?"

Beckie crushed Amy's head to her chest. "You live the best life you can. She removed all the… those… men, so—"

Amy sat straight up. "She was after *them*?"

Beckie nodded. "If she hadn't been, I would have."

Amy grabbed Beckie's black shirt and pulled her up to her face as she shouted, "Fuck! You know better than that! You told me better than that! If she'd just left it, come back here… Fuck!" She let go the shirt, grabbed her hair and pulled. "If she'd just come home…" She collapsed.

I've got nothing to say to that, since she's right. Beckie stroked Amy's hair and allowed her to cry.

This time when she said, "I'm okay, really," Amy sounded better. While her voice was hoarse, the tinny note was gone and the eyes were still, not roving like they had been. She looked up into Beckie's eyes. "So, I guess that's what they mean by 'two graves.'"

"Huh?"

"'When you seek revenge, first dig two graves.'"

"Uh. No. Well, yeah, that's what it says, but no… We think Abby had gotten that… the revenge part, done and over. Protecting the team… protecting Ian, that's what she was doing. I told you I heard the bullet go over our heads."

"Oh. Yeah." Amy looked back down, at her hands, twisting like they wanted to get away, too. "What's gonna happen?"

Maybe we can keep her sane after all. "We talked about that coming back. None of us were sure if she was religious at all, so…"

Amy shook her head. "Nope. Confirmed atheist. She'd be really upset at a service."

"We'll have a little memorial, then, before or after we bu… the funeral."

"That would work. Make sure there's wine. She liked wine, white wine or Champagne; we should have it for everyone."

"And Eilís O'Bannon, her lawyer, when we talked to her, she wants to come, too, since Abby had no family anyone knows about."

"Her lawyer?"

"They spent the weekend before Abby… went to New York. I guess they've been friends since forever. Since Abby was like five, anyway. Same schools, everything. So, *really* close."

"Oh." Amy put her head back down. "Well, I didn't think I was… her only…" She choked back sobs; Beckie squeezed her shoulders until the girl regained control "Anyway… Will Derek, Mr. Hamilton come, too?"

"I think he and Emily are already on their way. Why?"

Amy looked up, then stood and walked to the next stone to look out over the blue water. "I want to ask him what it was Abby was going to bring to the team… Maybe I could… learn that… take that…"

Beckie nodded. "I'm sure he'd be happy to talk with you."

Amy stepped back to offer her hand. "Let's go. I want to see Abby before…"

Beckie took Amy's hand and stood. As they started toward the dock, she used her phone to warn Millie.

Chapter Nine
Sailing, Dinner and Secrets

BECKIE RAN DOWN THE DOCK to *Guppy*. Amy had been given time off her studies and permitted to go for a sail—if accompanied. Beckie'd answered her call instantly.

"Unbend the bow line," Amy called from the cockpit aft. "I've got the stern line ready when you are."

Beckie glanced at Amy, then guessed 'unbend' meant untie; she looked for a rope. In another second, she had untied it.

"Throw it aboard and run down here to hop on."

After Beckie had clambered aboard, she caught the PFD Amy tossed her. "Okay, first, put that on," Amy instructed in a firm tone.

"We hav'ta use life jackets?"

"Uh… Yeah. Why would you not?"

"No reason, I guess. I never thought about it. Makes sense."

"Even more if the boom comes around and knocks you overboard, believe me. Ask me how I know." Beckie snickered as she struggled into the PFD—she still thought of it as a life jacket—then watched as Amy started the engine and took Guppy out of the anchorage.

"We've got light winds today, out of the east, as usual. So… We'll sail northwest a little, then tack back and circle the island. You ever sail before?"

"Never. I hope I'm not gonna hav'ta do that hanging off the mast thing."

Amy laughed so hard she fell back against the rail. When she could talk again, she shook her head. "No, that's for heavy weather or racing." She shut the engine off. "Stay back there for a second while I get the sails up and we can be…" She sang, "Sailing, sailing, over the bounding main."

Beckie stayed clear and watched as Amy ran the sails up, first the jib, and then the mainsail. She set them to catch the air and then dropped onto the cushioned seat next to the tiller.

Beckie watched as Amy set a course of 310; the two girls carried on a conversation while observing the boat sail itself single-handedly.

"So this is what you did, sailing to Providenciales?"

"Yeah, except I was headed east instead of northwest. And the wind was heavier, so I was going faster. *Guppy* is great, but she's not so good beating to windward. Heading into the wind," she answered Beckie's confused look. She raised herself to sweep the horizon. "We'll be able to see that in a bit."

"Why?"

"Cause the wind is keeping out of the east, and we'll have to go back to get home."

Beckie nodded. The explanation made sense, though she hadn't figured how Amy could sail back into the wind. More to learn, she thought. She inched up to eventually sit on the rail on the right side of the cockpit. The additional height gave her an impression of solitude she hadn't felt since sitting in the 737 flying to Egypt. The water here replaced the clouds there in limiting her worldview.

"Mom finally remembered Abby's duffle she brought back… with her."

"Oh, yeah. I remember. We looked through it. Decided you should have it."

Amy nodded. After a moment of silence, she said, "There was a note to me, in there."

Beckie froze. She remembered the four-inch-square cream-colored envelope. She wasn't sure she wanted to continue this conversation by asking what Abby had said to Amy in the hours before she ran into a speeding bullet.

Amy decided for her, reaching under her preserver and shirt and withdrawing an oft-folded piece of paper. "You can read it…"

Beckie dropped off the boat's rail to sit on the bench. I do not want to drop this overboard! She was even more sure of that when she took the note; it was damp and warm. She's been keeping it against her skin. Maybe we'd be better off framing it and putting it in her room? Amy's eyes followed the paper as Beckie unfolded it. I won't suggest that just yet.

She scanned the single page, written in the same clear hand the envelope and Ian's note had been. Okay. Nothing new here, except Abby feeling, what's the word? Prescient, I guess. She read it again, more closely.

When she looked up, Amy was staring at her. "Did you see her?"

"Huh?"

"When she was shot? Did you see her?"

"Not when she was hit. Ian slammed me down before… just as she started to run."

"Did she look like… like…"

Beckie couldn't guess what the girl was trying to force out. "Like what? She was taking an offensive stance. She was advancing; doing what she had to to draw the shooter's attention to her."

"That. Drawing his attention. Did she look like she thought she… she would die? Like she was suiciding?"

Beckie lolled for a second in shock, glad she had dropped off the rail. Then she sat up and swung her legs under the tiller so she faced Amy. She focused on the girl while she lined the words up in her head. "No," she began carefully, quiet while strong. "Abby was not running to get herself killed. She was putting herself in danger, yes, but survival was her intent."

"It's just… she sounded so… worried. And then, giving everything over to me..."

"If we have a chance, everyone putting themselves at risk does the same thing, I think." She reached out to grab Amy's thigh. The girl didn't pick up her hand. "I think she wanted you to know she was thinking about you. Especially after a weekend with Eilís."

"Eilís said—"

"None of my business. That's why I went down the beach while you guys were talking."

"I know. Thanks for that. But this... I want you to know. Eilís told me she never had Abby's interest, at least... for... lovemaking, I guess she meant."

Amy was staring up at the sails, so Beckie laid a finger along her chin. When the girl dropped her head to look into her eyes, Beckie said nothing, just held out her arms. Amy slid forward on the cushion and accepted the embrace.

After a couple minutes of silent communion, Amy sat up straight. She glanced at Beckie's bare arms and legs and grinned. "As captain, I order you below to get some lotion from the port-side locker. You'll be burnt, otherwise."

"Aye, Cap'n! But first." She handed Amy the letter before going below.

Amy stayed in her seat while Beckie applied the suntan lotion to her exposed skin. Finished, she handed the bottle over. "Your turn." She smiled as she waited for Amy to relinquish the cushion. Beckie then minded the tiller while Amy spread sunscreen on her arms and legs, then restowed the lotion.

When Amy took the tiller again, Beckie hiked herself up to sit on the rail, looking around. "I can't see the Nest," was her first reaction. Immediately, she wanted to take back the whiny tone her unease had imbued the words with.

"Don't worry; it's still there." Amy glanced at the speed gauge on the cabin bulkhead. "We're doing about 4 knots, so we've gone below the horizon from them." She looked up the mast, then back at Beckie. Her grin was huge. "If you want to climb up there—"

Beckie snorted. "No way!"

Amy laughed. "The reflector on top of the mast is still in Mr. Go's radar's range, so he knows where we are. If he's watching."

"I'm pretty sure he's watching. And if you see a helicopter… that'll be Ian, making sure we're okay, too!"

Amy laughed again, then straightened herself and scanned the horizon again. "Okay, nothing but water. Sit back down while I come to a southerly course. Actually, a little east of south will bring us west of the Nest."

Beckie kept her head down as Amy spent a couple of minutes bringing *Guppy* to the new heading. When everything settled, Beckie climbed back up to sit on the rail, watching the waves and a meandering dolphin.

There's a glint over there… "Hey, Amy, what's that?" She pointed toward the bit of reflected sunlight.

"That's a good reason to call home," she said after a concentrated stare. She picked up her phone. "Hi, Mom. Can you tell Mr. Go or Mr. Jamse we've got a power boat coming up on us? I can't tell how fast, she just showed up. We're about five miles out and tacking to head back. Yeah, we'll be careful. Love you."

Everything came together in the next ten minutes. The intruder came up but not quite to them, because by then, Jean-Luc had the helicopter over their heads. Beckie and Amy watched, awestruck, as Jean-Luc made a pass over the boat and someone aboard the boat fired a shot at the copter.

As the man at the wheel put his gun down and spun the wheel, Jean-Luc responded with an overflight that just cleared the boat's Bimini top and blew it on its beam. A second man screamed in fear as he tumbled over the transom. The man at the wheel apparently didn't notice; he'd thrown the throttles to full power and headed back the way he came. The man in the water was not so well off; he'd disobeyed the first rule of boating and had no life jacket. As Beckie watched, she was pretty sure he couldn't swim, either.

Amy was bringing *Guppy* about to intercept him, but she hadn't lowered any sails. Beckie's phone buzzed; as she reached for it, Amy shouted over the copter's noise, "We're gonna go right by him; I don't want him aboard with us. Throw him a life ring as we go by."

Beckie nodded and pushed the accept icon. Jean-Luc's voice almost exploded out of the speakers. "Don't pick him up!"

"We're not. Just gonna throw him a life preserver." She held it up and shook it.

"*Bien.* Mr. Jamse wishes to speak with him. He and Kevin are coming. I'll stay on station until they arrive."

"Cool. Thanks! And thanks for running him off."

Amy was touching up her course; the man was attempting to tread water about thirty feet ahead. It was a matter of seconds before *Guppy* passed by, close enough to splash him with her little bow wave, but not close enough to hit him. Beckie marveled at Amy's control; she'd placed the boat within five feet of the man, who was in the water on Beckie's side of the boat.

As *Guppy* swept by, Beckie dropped the ring directly in front of the man, who seized it as if it was his last hope. Once he'd clutched it to his chest, he screamed something at Beckie, but between the sound of the boat in the water, and the chopper overhead, she couldn't make it out.

In another five minutes, Beckie could no longer see him, but Jean-Luc assured her he was still afloat. Since she'd brought *Guppy* back to a course to the Nest, Amy had focused on the tiller, making what looked to Beckie like minute adjustments having little or no effect. Both girls looked up as Ian and Kevin went by in one of the team's powerboats; they exchanged waves and Beckie watched as they drove on to where Jean-Luc was holding station.

Beckie looked at Amy again; she was back playing with the wind vane thing that was steering. "Okay, girl. Leave that damn thing alone for a second. Com'ere and tell me what's wrong."

The look of disgust on Amy's face was surely intended to tell her she should know exactly what was wrong, but she made one more tweak and then came around the end of the tiller to sit between Beckie's legs. "They were after me, weren't they?" She put her forehead on Beckie's knee and cried softly.

"Only in passing. If you were the easiest target, then sure. But, without Abby, who would they pressure to get you released? I'm pretty sure if they were after us, it'd be me, 'cause then they'd think, you know, Ian would be willing to… bend over backwards."

Amy looked up, wiping her eyes. "I'm so silly. But, I don't know if it makes me feel better or worse that I'm not a big target anymore."

Beckie pulled her closer, so her head lay back against Beckie's belly. "You got your phone? You should call your mom."

Ian waved as he and Kevin shot by, headed back to the Nest. Beckie couldn't see where the man was being held, but since Jean-Luc had waggled his rotor at them, she was sure he wasn't in the water.

After the three hour return to the Nest, Beckie helped, as much as she could, tying up *Guppy* and straightening up while Amy furled the sails more neatly than she'd done just outside the anchorage. They went to Go Shen's office. "He's got a place to hold the guy, so that's where they'll be."

As they hurried along the walkway from the dock, Ian came out of the building. Beckie ran to him and they greeted each other with a kiss. Amy stood, one eye on them, the other on her watch. Beckie could just see her out of the corner of her eye and guessed what she was doing; she held Ian lip to lip until Amy cleared her throat. Based on his embarrassed laugh and repentant look to Amy, Ian had also guessed what both Beckie and Amy were attempting.

Beckie pulled Amy into their hug. "She needs love, Ian."

He squeezed both of them tight. "She has it, Rebecca. She has it."

Beckie saw Kevin appear from the security building, but waited until he'd approached to greet him.

"What did you learn from that guy, anyway? He didn't bite down on his cyanide tooth, I hope."

Ian laughed. "No, though he may have wished he could do so." He turned serious and spoke to Amy. "Amy Rose, you are invited to dinner, since Kevin wishes to dine with his family. Call your mother, please, and invite her as well. Tell her I've taken a demanding sort of turn, and you fear for your sanity if she fails to appear."

Beckie was still hugging him, but laughing so hard the hug was to keep her from falling down. Amy had stepped back; her wide eyes and slack jaw gave her surprise away until she grinned and pulled out her phone.

Forty minutes later, showered and in clean clothes, Beckie and Amy joined Millie and Ian on the lanai.

After Boynton had stuffed them with a wonderful cedar plank salmon, Beckie felt her head nodding and asked Ian once again, "The guy you dragged out of the water; what'd he say anyway?"

"His name is Flores," Ian said. "I believe he works for the lawyer Goldfarb, and he seems to have been attempting to enforce Goldfarb's comment about compensation."

"'Comment about compensation?'" Amy said. "What's that about?"

Mr. Jamse inclined his head toward Beckie.

"This morning, before you called, I had an email from Eilís. I don't have it here, but best I recall—check me, Ian, if I miss something—she said she'd received an unsigned message she thought was from Goldfarb. He wanted, compensation, she guessed, for the dead men, but more, he wanted the gold back. He said the package we're looking for wasn't there, and we could negotiate for it after compensation had been agreed."

"Wait, what?" Amy spluttered. "They tried to kill— They killed Abby!"

"In their view," Mr. Jamse said, "their loses were greater, especially since… Since we took Ms Rochambeau's body with us, they may be unaware of her death. But the reference is to the gold, I am certain. No matter how competent the men she terminated, hired guns are available."

"Is that like you, then? Hiring guns?"

He looked at her. Beckie thought, This is an interesting test of our relationship, too, almost as important as when I went into Billy's building alone. "No, Amy Rose," he finally said. "We do of course have men, and women too, who fall into that category, but generally, that is not their main qualification.

"I think you realize Rebecca does not fall into that group. Nor did Ms Rochambeau. Indeed, if your own plans come to fruition, you would not be a 'hired gun,' either." Amy nodded. "None of our critical team members would be so classified."

"So, the fact it was us was incidental?"

"Indeed. They were seeking a 'target of opportunity,' as he described it. Talos' organization has been watching both the Nest and the airport at Fort Lauderdale for several days, seeking to intercept one of us alone. *Guppy* was the first boat out of the Nest since they began looking at us, and as you know, since Ms Rochambeau's memorial, we have been hanging fire."

"So, where's the package, then?"

"Either he does not know, or fears his employers more than he does his captors."

"Okay," Amy said. "What's this 'package' we're looking for?"

Beckie's face lit up like Christmas. "See, Ian, I told you she'd get it!" His smile was full as he nodded to her. "We have no idea," Beckie continued. "But with the link to Peru—"

"What link is that?"

"Ah," Beckie said. "Sorry, Millie. You haven't been as involved. The murder Abby witnessed, committed by Talos, was of a Peruvian government official…"

"Mateo Huamán, Minister of the Interior, at the time," Boynton said.

"Thanks. The police called it a mugging, but Talos… Well, he didn't seem like someone who'd be involved in a mugging except from a great distance. More a boss, you know? And the box the gold was in came from Peru, too. So, being curious, Ian and I called Barbara this morning, to see if her contacts had any different information."

"And?"

"Haven't heard back, yet."

Beckie glanced out over the channel toward the security building. "Are you going to send him back? Flores?"

"Eventually. I doubt he will register a complaint. Monsieur Fereré made a most enlightening video."

"I'll say!" Amy said. "The prop wash when he overflew the boat gave me a scare, on *Guppy*."

While Boynton refilled their coffee cups, Doctor Ardan finally spoke up. "Ian, you spoke as if… Amy's role later on, when she graduates, was a… *fait accompli*?"

"At present, subject to all the vagaries of fate between now and then, it is." Beckie was watching Amy, who had a twisted grin on her face, along with wide eyes, as if she was saying I told you so while at the same time thinking, It can't be. Beckie remembered the same feeling when Ian had invited her to join his team, over two years ago, now. "Of course, at the time, she must still wish to join us. I am confident she will complete the courses of study you and Derek set her." He reached to take Beckie's hand. "I have been reassured by Rebecca's exploits… once I manage to overcome my fear of them. I see no reason Amy Rose should be less effective."

Beckie sat forward a little, without removing Ian's hand. "I don't think you need to worry about her starting field work just yet."

"But I already helped Abby! And Mr. Hamilton asked me to look at some things for him."

"Do you have reservations, Millie?"

Beckie watched Amy's face drop and her eyes fill. Then the girl turned to her mother. "Please don't answer that, now at least. I need to gain a little more maturity before I face *that* disappointment."

Millie reached to grab Amy's shoulder. "Don't worry. I already told you, whatever works for you is okay with me. I'll be here to support you, just like I do for all our team members. I make stupid comments at times, or inappropriate ones, but never doubt I love you and want the best for you." She turned to Beckie. "Ian mentioned O'Bannon's offer to use her house; I'm sure we can find a couple of weeks, if I can't go to

Chatham myself. But I won't be so easy to convince if you want to take her... to South America, for instance."

Beckie did an internal fist pump. Millie hadn't ruled out taking Amy on the job! But the payoff... We've got to see a massive benefit before we can even suggest that. Beckie looked at Ian, who was not quite as happy, implying he'd intuited her desire to indoctrinate Amy sooner rather than later. That's okay, she thought. We can talk about that... after they leave.

Discretion suggested she change the subject. "If we let Goldfarb junior go, can we follow him? Could we get any useful information that way?"

Ian looked out at the ocean, probably weighing the idea, Beckie thought. "It is problematic at best. I did consider allowing Ms O'Bannon to mediate his return—if he has any value to them—and see what advantage we might gain. But I had not thought of... just releasing him. We shall see."

In the silence that followed, Amy twisted and wriggled, then sat up. "Uh, Beckie, we need to talk..." She looked around the table. "No. I have something... I... I need to show you." She stood. "I'll be right back."

"Want me to go with you?" Beckie said.

Ian drew everyone's attention. "Please. Either you, or I, or Shen. She should not be out alone." He sighed as Amy's face tightened. "I know you are not a child, Amy Rose. That is not my rationale. Please permit Rebecca to escort you."

Amy's nod was spare at best.

The two girls made a quick—and quiet!—trip Bon Secours Cay, to the Ardan home.

She still hasn't said a word. Ian musta gotten to her. As they entered Amy's bedroom, Beckie hugged the girl around the shoulders. With a resigned look, she shrugged off Beckie's arm and opened the top drawer of her dresser, then dug to the back of the explosion of underwear. Beckie glanced around the room; for all their recent association, she'd never seen this space Amy called hers.

She caught sight of a leather belt lying on the bed; it had no closure or buckle. As she reached to pick it up—to examine it—Amy said, "It was Abby's. With these." She knelt in the closet entry, grabbing something. Beckie nodded when she saw one of the team's black duffles. Amy opened a side pocket and gingerly removed two ceramic knives. Beckie gaped at them for a second before she realized that together, they'd make a buckle for the belt she was holding. "Yeah. With these, I can wear it. Pieter—Mr. Nijs—showed me about cleaning the blades and he sent me to Ms Rios for how to use them—"

Beckie chuckled. "If she's teaching you weapons, you can probably call her Elena. And him Pieter."

"Yeah, I suppose. Anyway, they're ceramic. Like glass, I guess, so really sharp. And breakable, if I'm not careful." She slid the two blades into the sheath of the belt and draped it around her hips. "See?"

"Cool," Beckie said with a smile. "But—"

"Yeah. They aren't what we came for." Amy handed over the package she'd dragged out of her dresser. "This is what you and Mr. Jamse need to see. It was in Abby's bag, too."

"Hmm. Okay." After a glance in the dark, Beckie handed it back. "You hang on to it till we get there. Wouldn't want to drop it overboard."

Beckie led Amy through the slider; they both settled at the table. Dropping the manila envelope on the glass tabletop, Amy looked at Ian, then Beckie, then said, "This was in Abby's duffle Mom gave me yesterday. I looked, but… I'm worried 'cause I can't understand why she'd have anything from Peru… But I'm sure she wasn't working against… against you, Mr. Jamse." Her own whisper was barely audible by the time she finished.

"I agree," he said. "I also wonder how it came into her possession. Thank you for bringing it to light." He picked it up and gazed into her eyes. "May I?"

"Yeah. Didn't make much sense to me."

Ian smiled as he spilled the cassette, key and white envelope on the table. "I understand your confusion." He used a clean spoon to push the items around, peering closely. "Boynton, would you ask Shen to bring his print kit?" His eyes came up to meet Amy's. "Did you handle them?"

Amy faced the table, staring through the table top. "Not much." She raised her head. "But yes. I'm sorry. I wasn't thinking about prints or stuff."

Beckie touched Amy's arm as Ian said, "No matter. We will allow Shen to test. He may require your prints."

Her hand touched Beckie's on her arm. "Thanks. Just, I don't understand, you know?"

The others around the table nodded.

The conversation before Shen arrived didn't add to Beckie's knowledge; none of the others seemed pleased, either. Twenty minutes had passed before Boynton stood and left the lanai, returning in moments with both of the Go's, Mr. and Mrs.

As Shen unpacked his kit, Rou took in the scene with a smile. "My two most favorite… boundary extenders, along with their wonderful mentors." She looked again. "On the table, a fine example of a safe deposit box key. I must ask why—" Their confusion surprised her. "What? It's obviously not a door key, and that design is one of the Mosler Company's. From here, at least."

"I guess that makes sense, given this envelope." Beckie pointed at the white packet.

"But why would anyone keep a safe deposit key and envelope together?" Amy asked.

"Largely because no one remembers their box number without it," Rou said. She turned to Ian. "When you asked Shen to work his magic, I came along to thank you. I'd never seen a Good Delivery bar before except in pictures, and now there are two of them in the vault."

"A what?" Amy asked.

"I believe Rou refers to the two gold bars we recovered from Brewster." Ian looked at the woman, his eyebrows raised and lips slightly quirked.

"Yes. Of course. Together, they represent a million dollars, more or less. Accepted for bullion transactions worldwide. So, thank you for the opportunity."

Beckie listened as the Chinese woman continued: She had done a survey in spite of the bars' markings; they had both assayed at 997 fine. One was exactly twelve kilos, the other thirteen grams less. In addition to the foundry mark and serial number, a stamp had been placed on the side of both bars. "And of course, Abby's initials." She smiled at Amy. "I don't believe that's enough to add them to her estate, unfortunately."

As she finished, Boynton slipped away, then returned with Else Meyer. The blonde German-born woman smiled as she set her case on the table and dropped her slight frame into the empty chair. "Ah, Else," Shen said, "how are you? I'm almost finished with the cassette." He took a series of photos of the dust-covered surfaces while Else made a face. "It won't be that bad," he said, "I'll clean it off."

"Never mind," she said with an expression Beckie took as midway between a smirk and a grimace. "I'll do it."

After a thorough cleaning, Else loaded the tape in the player and pushed Play.

"Buenos días, señor Talos."

"Y a usted, señor Huamán. ¿Cóm—"

The recording ended abruptly.

"That's it?" Beckie felt nothing but disappointment.

Else allowed the tape to run to the end before popping the cassette out of the player. "I'm afraid so. Sounds like a teaser, identifying the speakers. Even with no training in Spanish, I can tell it's been cut off mid-word."

"That's right," Amy said. "'Good day,' and 'You, too.' And the guys' names, of course."

Beckie stood. "You speak Spanish?"

"A little. Mostly from the nurses and staff."

"Cool," Beckie said. "Well then, the interesting part of the conversation is gonna be what follows."

"I agree," Boynton said. "However, even this snippet would present difficulty for Mr. Talos. One of the defense's claim, neither proven nor refuted at trial, was that Talos and Huamán hadn't met before the fatal encounter."

"Hmm," Beckie murmured. "And this tape came from Peru to Talos' attorney in the middle of August. Who? And why?"

Shen packed his gear. "I've got what I can. I'll check the partials against Amy's prints first, and then the 'big database in the sky.' It'll be a couple of hours, so I'll talk to you tomorrow."

Else set the cassette on the table in front of Ian. "Anything else I can help with?"

"Not for now. Thank you."

As Else quit the lanai, Beckie said, "Well, love, should we send the cassette to Eilís and have her drop it on the prosecutors in New York?"

Ian paused, pursing his lips. Beckie grinned—internally—before he said, "We should advise Ms O'Bannon of its existence and wait to see what develops. At present, I believe there is little risk of Talos' release. She can inform us if that changes."

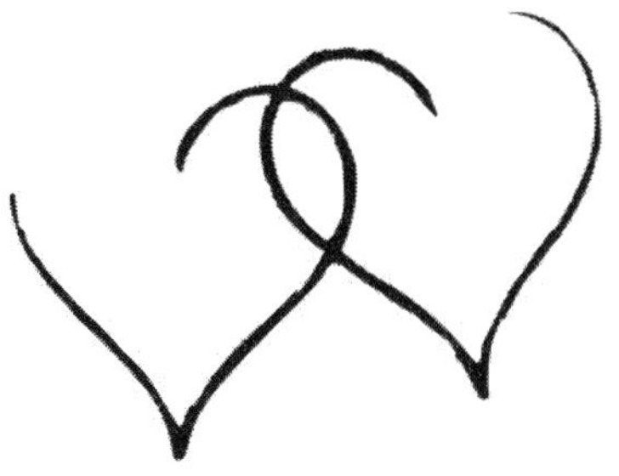

Chapter Ten
Peru

Barbara Visits Mamani

BARBARA SAUNDERS TUGGED ON THE peasant scarf she wore against the sun. Her olive complexion didn't burn often, but at 3800 meters, the sun was bright and the atmosphere thin. It had taken her a couple of weeks to adapt, as it had the rest of her team.

The call the day before had surprised... Well, no, she admitted, very little Ian and Beckie did *surprised* her, but still, their request had been unexpected: "Ask Mamani about Mateo Huamán's death." She walked into the house where Nayra Mamani had established her headquarters. The receptionist gave her a salute of recognition and opened the door. She returned his smile and entered.

At the desk, Philip Gomez, Mamani's campaign manager and Barbara's primary contact, wiped his face with a limp handkerchief and greeted her before waving her into the main office. He directed her to the chair standing in front of the uncluttered desk.

Mamani entered from a side door to Barbara's left. As usual, her black hair was plaited and coiled atop her head. Her suit was a dark blue, with a white collar. Her scarf was loosely tied about her neck; its bright colors evoked the jungle: deep greens, brilliant reds and yellows on a field of warm dark brown.

She shook hands as Barbara said, "Good morning. Thank you for agreeing to meet so quickly."

"I can always make time for those who help me."

Barbara nodded. "First, we are nearly finished arranging security for your campaign. I will deliver the final report next week.

"Second... Mr. Ian Jamse, my principal, has an off-topic question he requests me to pose to you." She waited until the politician nodded. "Is there anything you might tell us about the death of Mateo Huamán?"

Mamani didn't answer immediately. Instead, she walked to the window and gazed out for a minute. Then she seated herself behind her desk and finally looked Barbara in the eye. "Forgive me. Would you like tea or coffee? Anything? I will have tea, so don't think it an imposition."

"Then yes, tea, please."

The server brought a small table holding a lovely china tea service to place beside Barbara. All grace and composure, he poured the tea and slid the cup and saucer to her.

She lifted the cup and sipped. "Mmm. Very good." With a full smile, she said, "Thank you so much. The hotel has a..." She tried to think of a diplomatic phrase. "The hotel has a more limited selection, I fear."

"Of course. These leaves are selected for me." Mamani sipped her own. "Now. Your question. It raises a delicate matter. Providing an answer means I must trust Mr. Jamse with... It would not be too much to say my life."

Barbara winced. Well, there goes the idea there's nothing to discover. I wonder how they guessed—

"I had hoped..." Mamani sighed. "But no, it is not to be." She stood and came around the desk. "I have a few minutes before my next meeting. Let's take a short walk."

Barbara followed the woman through a side door and into the garden she had seen from the office. She stepped into the brisk air and surveyed the area.

Walls bounded the space; the plantings were separated by grassy strips a meter wide. The red flowers of the *k'antu* bushes almost glowed in the light. Barbara hadn't appreciated them through the glass.

"This is lovely," she said, still following the woman.

"It is. One of my father's gifts to me and to the family." Mamani stopped at the foot of a large tree. "This tree… My father built this garden for it, to protect it where it couldn't otherwise grow. A monument to his legacy."

While Barbara nodded politely, Mamani hadn't addressed Ian's question.

"May I ask… What… Why has this question arisen?"

"You may ask, but I have no answer," Barbara said. "He called yesterday with the request, and Philip arranged our meeting. I can ask—"

Mamani raised her hand, palm out, then said softly. "Can you tell Mr. Jamse I would meet with him? I would hear the genesis of his question before imparting answers. You may tell him I do have answers, although they may not sit well with him."

Why might Mamani's answers not 'sit well' with Ian? And how would she keep focused on their primary task: creating a safe environment within which Mamani could campaign for President?

The woman's soliloquy had ended a few seconds earlier; Barbara swallowed her surprise as she realized the woman was looking at her, a query on her face. "I beg your pardon, senõra. I was woolgathering."

She smiled and took Barbara's elbow. "You are forgiven." She started them toward the building. "I wondered if you had any questions."

"No. I will discuss your request with Mr. Jamse this afternoon. Also, I assume either I or Mr. Quinn can meet with you should something arise, or if we have news."

She smiled, but Barbara saw little pleasure in the expression. "Of course. I hope for an early response," she said as she opened the door for Barbara. Inside, she glanced around. "Twenty-four kilos of gold may also be part of my answer. Should he be able to visit."

Well, twenty-four kilos of gold intrigued Barbara, as it would Ian. If they collected on it, it would about double the fee for this job. If, recalling Kevin's oft-repeated mantra, their expenses weren't high. But what would earning the gold entail?

Beckie and Ian Visit Mamani

Friday afternoon, Beckie accompanied Amy to the gym for an hour-long workout, then dropped her at the Ardan's home. Back in her room, she showered, dressed, then went to the lanai, thinking to check her email, then read.

Ian had taken his usual chair; with his eyes closed, he might be resting. Well, I won't interrupt him.

Just as the thought passed, Ian's phone rang and smiling at her, he sat up to answer it. Boynton came through the slider as Ian said, "Hello again, Ms Saunders."

Beckie listened as Barbara responded, "I asked Mamani about Huamán… It was interesting." She repeated their conversation.

"She has answers to Ian's questions," Beckie asked, "but won't talk about them until he answers some for her? Is that right?"

"That's it."

"She's not sure how Ian'll react? And she's offering a bunch of gold? Maybe?"

"Right again. You're doing good, Beckie." Barbara's laugh proved contagious.

Beckie grinned, then gave Ian a serious look. "I can't imagine why we'd be concerned about the answers, no matter what they are. Let's go, see for ourselves."

When Ian didn't speak, Boynton said, "That might have the best return."

Jamse nodded. "I agree. Can you ask Jannike for assistance scheduling the trip?"

Beckie stretched as she followed Ian through Arequipa's Rodriquez Ballon Airport. They'd entered Peru in Lima and Beckie hoped the trip that had started at two that morning was finally done. Though clean and neat, the terminal appeared dark compared to the bright sunshine outside. Through the glass doors she saw Barbara and Rich and hurried to catch up with Ian.

She returned Barbara's smile with one of her own and greeted both of them. While Ian exchanged news with Barbara, Beckie looked around. The cloud-covered volcanic peak of El Misti loomed above the barren cone.

Rich took her elbow. "With the miniature cars we rented," he said, "you get to ride with me; Ian will go with Barbara. If that's okay?"

"Yeah, but I thought the roads here are really bad?"

"Some are worse than others, but today, we'll be fine. Paved, at least. You'll see."

"Okay, I guess. Where are we headed? And what about Mathilde and her copilot?"

"They've got rooms in the hotel. We're going up another four hours or so, to Mamani's headquarters. Her home, actually. It's on the way to Juliaca and Lake Titicaca, but not that far." He chuckled at Beckie's groan. "Barbara didn't tell you, eh?" With a wave, he drew her attention to the vista around them. "This is lovely Arequipa," he said before opening the door. He pointed at the peak to the east. "Someone on the plane probably mentioned the volcano. El Misti."

"Yeah. Mathilde needed something to talk about, so avoiding the volcano became a topic." She laughed. "It's not that far away, I guess. So Mamani couldn't come here to greet Ian?"

"No, even on Sunday, she had meetings. We think she wanted to meet Ian there. She's not expecting you, though."

"Last minute hanger-on. I was curious to know what's going on here, and Ian thought it wouldn't be a long trip. Down and back, so to speak."

"Well, I hope you'll at least stay overnight."

"Have to. Mathilde's used up her hours for today. Anything special planned?"

"Just, Sue and Willie will join us there."

"How about the altitude? Mathilde had the plane at about ten thousand feet, getting us used to it, but—"

"That's higher than here, but her HQ is about thirty-eight hundred meters. Over twelve thousand feet. We've got water for you. Based on our experience, as long as you get back here tonight, there won't be any problems."

With a nod, Beckie buckled her seat belt.

Rich took a right turn out of the airport. Beckie sat back and watched the scenery. The road was two-lane, paved. The businesses lining the road were set back about twenty-five feet. Wow! Beckie thought. I'll keep my opinions to myself, but it looks really run down. Except for no sand, it could be any small town in Egypt. Replacing the sand was a ubiquitous white dust. Away from the city, the dust seemed less prevalent, but she still saw few green plants. Lots of trucks, not many people.

"Will it be like this the whole way?"

"Pretty much. This road is paved all the way till maybe the last half hour." He paused to pass a heavily laden truck. "Have to watch out for rocks in the road. Or maybe boulders is a better description. And the trucks and buses. Drivers here… Well."

"I see," Beckie said as she watched two on-coming trucks, one passing the other, leaving barely enough room on the shoulder for Rich to squeeze by.

"See? No problem."

"Take as long as you need. I'm in no hurry!"

In Barbara and Rich's office, Barbara said, "I'm pretty sure our report on the security plan won't come up today; we'll deliver it Wednesday,"

"Are there difficulties?" Ian asked.

"None. This meeting is to answer your questions, according to Philip."

"Philip?" Beckie said.

"Philip Gomez. Her campaign manager. You'll meet him."

Sue and Willie joined them as Barbara finished, but they had no news. After Barbara spent ten minutes describing Mamani's home and its grounds, Ian suggested they head to the palace.

"Mamani won't see us all," Barbara said.

"Rebecca will come with you and I. Rich, can you remain here with Susan and Willie?"

"Sure. Take Willie's SUV; it's a little bigger."

Inside the office, the receptionist smiled at Barbara; however, his gaze became hard as he stared at Ian. It softened, but only slightly, when he turned to Beckie. Barbara handed him their documents; as he perused them, his face relaxed, and he waved them on.

The man in the outer office welcomed them in a way that made Beckie wonder about his sincerity. About five feet eight, he was definitely portly. Must weigh two hundred pounds. He's too happy to see us. That little heh-heh laugh all the time. And ugh! He sweats way too much. But when Barbara introduced him, "Meet Philip Gomez, Mamani's campaign manager. He's the boss," Beckie thought, Oops! Better keep those thoughts to myself.

Gomez used his phone and then led them into the main office, directing Barbara to the seat directly before the desk, and asking Beckie and Ian to use chairs to the side.

The side door opened and Mamani looked through. "Well…" The note in her voice matched her raised eyebrows. "… this is an unexpected pleasure!" She entered and walked to Ian. "I assume you are Mr. Ian Jamse. Barbara I know, but…"

"This is Rebecca Sverdupe, in training to undertake my duties. I wish her to be cognizant of all our important clients and their requirements."

Mamani offered Beckie her hand. Beckie rose and shook it with vigor. "It is a pleasure, señora. Thank you for seeing us on a Sunday, and for allowing us to work with you."

"Believe me, Rebecca, the pleasure is mine. Or so I hope." She faced Barbara and greeted her. "I would rather invite you to a more comfortable room. If you will?" She directed them through the side door.

The space Beckie walked into was about the same size as the office. Windows on two walls, directly ahead and to the right, gave on the garden Barbara had described; Beckie agreed, it was lovely. The ceiling was twelve feet high; the walls, where they weren't covered by photographs, paintings or framed documents, were stark white. A second doorway was set into the wall to the left, about halfway down.

Two sofas stood away from the walls, at opposite edges of a hand-worked rug. Matching chairs filled the open ends and low tables could be reached from either the sofas or the chairs. I wonder how close these designs are to the Navajo, Beckie mused. She put the thought aside and allowed Ian to direct her to the sofa looking away from the garden. The seat was comfortable, soft without allowing them to sink in and make rising difficult.

As they all settled themselves, Mamani exclaimed, "I am sorry! Barbara told me you arrived directly from your flight. Would you like to freshen up? Or refreshments? Barbara enjoyed the tea I offer."

"For me," Beckie said, "I'm fine. I changed into this…" She plucked at her skirt. "… before we landed. Tea would be magnificent though."

"Tea or coffee, as you find convenient," Ian said.

"Coffee then. You will join Rebecca and I, Barbara?"

While the refreshments were being prepared, Beckie stood and walked the room's perimeter, examining the framed images one by one.

"Most are my family. We are prolific," Mamani said with a laugh. "The letters are land transfer documents, mostly, proving our ownership of this, our home and finca. Ranch, or estate, you would say."

"Very nice. Who is this?" She pointed to a portrait, a yard square, of a boy of perhaps thirteen or so, dressed in what Beckie thought was native garb.

Mamani didn't approach. "My father, years ago."

Fortunately, the refreshments arrived in the next moment; Beckie took her seat and waited while the server did his work.

Once everyone was settled, Ian said, "Señora Mamani, I thank you for allowing us to talk with you about your compatriot, Mateo Huamán."

Mamani sipped her tea; Beckie did likewise, enjoying the light scent of freshly mown hay.

"I must request your discretion," Mamani said, "with anything I tell you. Barbara asked only about his death. What is your interest?"

"His name arose twice in our investigation of a team member's kidnapping." He explained the little they knew and suspected, based on the news reports and the research Boynton had done.

"So," Beckie said, "I thought it unbelievable this Talos would be involved in a street crime… an ordinary mugging. When we heard the audio tape of Huamán and Talos, it seemed even less likely. Hence, our question to you about his death. What actually happened?"

"Why me?"

"To be honest…" Beckie shot a glance at Ian, who smiled his quiet smile. "… you came to mind first because Barbara was already working with you. We would have asked her to query others had you had no information. Or interest." She smiled. "Now, I hope you have something to gain from talking with us."

"Hmm." Mamani sipped her tea. "Well, while it is long and dry, especially for those who did not live through it… I will attempt…" She sighed. "Very well. The story must begin several years ago. Our political group was briefly enamored of… improving the operation of one of the government's departments."

"Which department, señora?" Ian asked.

The woman didn't respond at once. Her drawn lips and flared nostrils; is she angry with him, or is she just scared of telling us? Whichever, Beckie thought, this is hard for her.

Mamani stood and began pacing, first slowly then more rapidly. She stopped at the end of the sofa. "The Ministry of Justice and Human Rights," she said curtly, then returned to her pacing.

A small smile curved Ian's lips. "That Ministry has a storied history of… corruption, or it may be more politic to say, take-over attempts."

Mamani stopped short and gaped at him for a second before responding, "True, I suppose. However, earlier attempts were not… recorded." She took her seat. "One of our group…" She stopped, her face twisted, but Beckie didn't see anger or hatred there, just confusion and fear.

"I don't understand, señora." Out of the corner of her eye Beckie saw both Barbara and Ian nod in agreement.

Mamani sighed. "Five of us planned to force the Minister to overlook some egregious violations of the then campaign financing regulations. Myself, obviously. Mateo Huamán, Minister of the Interior. Piero Salvadore, Deputy Minister of the Interior and two others, one of whom has since died and the other... The other, Jaime Lobera, used video equipment to record our meetings."

"You didn't know... or... You thought to control him?" Once the words were out, Beckie feared her disbelief was too clear. Her next question—How could that happen?—she kept to herself.

Mamani's lip twisted. "I can understand your surprise. Jaime was to record the meetings as a protection for all of us. If each of us had the same video... In any event, when he was arrested, due to the campaign financing violations I mentioned, we were dismayed for him, and then for ourselves, thinking he would use the recording to... improve his own position. However, he did not, and Mateo discovered the reason when he visited him after the trial." She sipped her tea. "He could not because the cassettes had disappeared during the investigation."

Beckie sat back as Barbara said, "And no one—"

"No one knows who purloined the videos, correct," Mamani said. "After several attempts to trace them, we agreed they must have been taken in an attempt to help our friend." Her telephone rang once, but she continued, "Like the others, I hoped they had been destroyed, though deep down, I feared otherwise."

As Beckie nodded, thinking, I can understand the hope... and the reality, Mamani lifted the phone and listened. "Good," she said into it. "Bring him in, please." She replaced the handset and said, "Because your question dealt with Mateo's death, I asked Piero Salvadore, our Minister of the Interior, to join us, and he has just arrived."

The door opened, and Philip showed a moderately tall Hispanic man in. In his suit, he appeared a well-groomed fit man; his black hair was neatly trimmed, but Beckie was surprised, his eyes were downcast, almost apologetic.

"Welcome, Piero. Thank you for making time."

"How can I help? I only have a few minutes, so…"

"Of course. First, this is Ian Jamse, Rebecca Sverdupe and Barbara Saunders, all of Ian Jamse, LLC, who are assisting with campaign security."

Piero approached and shook hands with each of them. Beckie used a firm grip and was surprised to find it too strong. She relaxed and gave him a smile. As he moved to a chair, he said, "Our security people have reported you have also provided them valuable insights, so I'm glad to meet you. Even though we…" He nodded to Mamani. "… oppose each other, we both wish the election to be fair and safe for all."

Mamani gave them a wry smile. "We were discussing Jaime's videos… As I mentioned to you, Mr. Jamse is curious about the circumstances of Mateo Huamán's death."

"Do you believe the videos are related to his death?" Piero asked.

"I'm afraid we have no real idea," Beckie said. "His name came up in a different investigation, so we thought to examine it further. Hopefully you can assist us."

"I don't know how much I can help, but… Let me tell you what I recall.

"About two years ago, Mateo, then Minister and my superior, called me to meet him in New York, at a symposium at the United Nations. While I was unaware at the time, he intended me to help with an… exchange he had arranged."

"We have already talked about the videos," Mamani said.

"Very well. I assume, since our mutual fates rest with them…"

Ian sat up even straighter. "Be assured, Minister Salvador, we will divulge nothing we hear here."

"I must accept that, if Nayra has described the video's content as we understand it." He sighed. He's not all that comfortable, Beckie mused. I wonder why. Piero continued, "So, the exchange he had arranged… Well, the night I arrived, we met with two men, Donato Talos and his man, León, in a bar. Eventually, we agreed León would come the next day to my hotel room, where we had placed the gold. I would deliver the gold to him, and then, later in the evening, Talos and Mateo would meet so he could receive the videos from Talos.

"The only thing that changed from the arrangement… Talos joined León when they came for the gold. And of course, he and Mateo apparently disagreed about something, and Mateo died of a stab wound inflicted by Talos.

"The next day, the police told us a woman had seen the fight, and she would testify. They also reported neither of them had any video recordings.

"Talos' attorney confirmed that, but suggested neither the arrest nor the witness would greatly inconvenience either Talos or us. However, he also told us while Talos was incarcerated, no one had access to either the gold we had paid or the videos.

"I believe that is all I can share with you."

Mamani had been walking back and forth while listening to Piero.

"The attorney's name? Do you recall it?" Beckie asked.

"What? Yes, yes of course. Goldfarb. Samuel Goldfarb." He looked at his watch. "Unless there is something else…" He stood and went to the door.

"Thank you Minister," Beckie said, echoed by Mamani.

He waved and went through the door.

When Beckie turned back, Barbara's face was pale; she'd never seen such a sallow color. "Barbara? What's the matter?"

Barbara snapped around to gawk at Beckie. "That witness he talked about… That was Abby?"

"According to the reports we have read, yes," Ian replied.

"In Abby's notes… I put this in the reports but didn't flag it; it seemed to have no bearing on the contract work… She had heard stories of counterfeiting dollars, smuggling them into the US."

"Any details?"

Barbara twisted her lips into a wry smile. "None. Well… No. You know I assigned her to the undercover work in Arequipa, working with the opposition teams to ferret out any rumors of violence or disruptions. She reported every week, but this had been logged for the third, just after her last report." Barbara took a tablet computer from her bag and tapped the screen. "Right… She hadn't heard any names, but the informant told her 'high-ranking government official.'"

"Did she record the informant's name?"

Barbara shook her head. "SOP, here."

Ian nodded.

Beckie pulled her ponytail around to play with. "That's interesting… I suppose it could play into her—" Ian's touch stopped her short. "Anyway, right now I don't see any possible connection." She sipped the cold end of her tea. "Let's return to the video. How would you have verified it?"

"Talos provided convincing excerpts when he made the initial contact. Mateo and I were both in the meetings; we agreed the images he showed Mateo were from our video." She paused. "I hope this answers your questions, as I have no more to tell."

"One question, señora. Why did you think it better we met you here?"

She smiled. "Aside from showing off a little of my beautiful country, you mean? Simply for security. As the Minister said, my words to you would be as bad as the videos if overheard. Here," she said, waving a hand to indicate the house, "I have some control. I could not afford the time to travel to you. That is all." Her brows rose and her lips quirked into an inquisitive line. "You have an interesting expression, Mr. Jamse."

"I am sorting through the facts you have added. You have made an excellent beginning," Ian said. "I can confirm some of your story, in that I believe your gold is now in our possession. Two bars in a wooden case marked machine tools, is that correct?" She nodded, mouth now open. "They appear to bear identification; I will ask that photographs be sent so you may verify if they are the same bars."

"Thank you. How did they come to your possession?"

Ian described Abby's conflict in Brewster. He paused when he finished. "You may have answered a question which has bothered me since then: why has a million dollars worth of gold laid gathering dust for two years."

"Oh? How is that?"

"If Talos' man did take the gold, Talos may have instructed him to place it in the shed, rather than pointing him to a secure but secret resting place. He, Talos, was then arrested before he could recover it. The crate had been opened, but the gold would not have been obvious in a casual examination."

"I understand." Mamani said. "However… The video cassettes have not appeared?" Both Beckie and Ian shook their heads. "If they should surface during the campaign…" She shook her head. "Should you be willing… I would offer the gold as your fee for returning the videos to me." Wow! Being President… or not being arrested, at least, must mean a lot.

Philip had been moving anxiously; Mamani glanced at her watch. "Unfortunately, my next appointment is near. Please forgive me."

Ian was focusing on something; Beckie didn't know what. Could it be he's thinking about the attack? Or Eilís's message? She faced the woman and replied, "I understand. If we have more questions, will you have time tomorrow morning?"

Mamani glanced at Gomez, who opened his notebook. "You have twenty minutes available at 8:15 tomorrow."

"That will be fine," Ian said. "Thank you."

During dinner, Ian agreed with Beckie that they had no reason to believe the counterfeiting and smuggling operations in Abby's notes related to her death, and Goldfarb's mysterious 'package' could be the videos Mamani sought. "But we should not discuss either of those here," he said. She pouted a moment before leaning forward into what she considered the off-topic conversation: Barbara and Rich's security work.

OJT

On Monday morning, Beckie and Ian curled up in the Gulfstream as Mathilde flew back to the Nest. So as not to waste the time, Beckie asked about Flores, and if Ian had decided.

"While the chances of gaining information are remote, they are not infinitesimal." He took his phone and as Beckie watched, asked Elena Rios and Beth Stadd to shepherd Flores to the mainland, and then monitor his onward travels.

Beckie spent a couple of hours the next day, Tuesday, in the gym with Amy as the girl worked on rebuilding her strength and endurance, then as she and Ian shared a tasty conch salad with Boynton, she brought up what she considered a tender subject.

"I want to head over to Miami, to the university; meet with the Dean about January and make sure nothing will interfere from their end."

Ian's smile was worth all the angst she'd had about the topic. "I heartily agree. We shall endeavor to keep things clear at this end."

"I know we will. How about tomorrow? Anything planned?"

He paused a moment before answering. "I would prefer Thursday. Ms Rios reports Flores has taken a hotel room in Fort Lauderdale for the night. She believes he has booked a flight in the morning."

"Well, I have no interest in running into him. I'll make an appointment for Thursday."

"Do you expect a problem?"

She laughed, a short chuckle devoid of humor. "No, Maurice. But even one of my tender years learns when the lesson's been beaten in enough." She stood and captured Ian's hand in hers. "Com'on. Let's walk the beach for a few minutes."

The appointment with the Dean went as Beckie hoped. She would be permitted to return in January with the usual caveats. For her part, Beckie nodded soberly and promised to put maximal effort into attending every class and completing every assignment. Just like last year, she thought. The Dean offered Beckie her best stern smile.

On her return, Beckie was pleased to have Ian to herself, especially when, after her progress report about the meeting with the Dean, he invited her for a different course of education.

"If you can make the time, I would like you to spend a few days with me in Peru working with Barbara and her team. It will give you background in how to organize and run this type of job."

Her happiness grew as the night went on.

Arrangements took until the next afternoon; Beckie was neither surprised nor pleased when Mathilde again scheduled a two AM departure. Neither she nor Ian were happy about Barbara requesting Millie: "Sue wants her help dealing with a funny bug some of the locals have been coming down with."

"Better than 'lead poisoning,'" Millie reminded them.

The first two days they spent as Mamani's guests, acclimatizing to the almost thirteen thousand foot altitude and getting a better sense of the possible security problems Barbara had identified. None seemed insurmountable.

Ian split Beckie's training between Barbara describing their proposal for Mamani's security, and Rich explaining how they'd integrated Willie and Sue's field observations. Beckie told Ian Wednesday evening, "It's kinda like being back in school. High school," she emended. When he chuckled and asked why, "There's not much room for originality; everything's kinda by the numbers, if you know what I mean." She paused, snuggling close. "That's not bad; people have been doing this a while, and they know what works and what doesn't. The trick will be to remember it. I hope I can learn by example, so when I experience it, it'll be familiar."

"Indeed."

On the Sunday, Mamani had invited them, and Barbara, too, for an early dinner in Arequipa, since she had meetings planned there and in Lima that week, and Beckie planned to follow Willie into the undercover work he'd taken up from Abby. That would also be in Arequipa, so the arrangement made sense. Before sending her off with Willie, Ian told her the rapport she was building with Mamani might serve them well.

Willie decided disguise and being unobtrusive would form the basis of Beckie's lessons. Monday was disguise. He sent her out on Tuesday to do nothing but observe. Wednesday, her instructions were to disappear in the crowds where Ian and Barbara were working and track them. "True," he'd said, "they won't be looking for you, but…"

He admitted she'd done him one better when they met for dinner. She'd spent three hours on his assignment, but then scampered through a restroom with multiple exits and gleefully trailed him.

"I'm not happy about that," he said once she'd regaled him with a report of his own movements. His smile gave the lie to his words.

Thursday, they met Ian for lunch. Beckie thought she'd have some fun telling him what he'd been doing the day before before they decided the next steps. Willie joined with her laughing at Ian's expression. Willie even had the grace to grin when Beckie then recounted her trailing of him.

However, as Willie chuckled, Ian's expression became somber. "I hope you will keep in mind a unilateral change of an operational plan may not always have benign consequences."

She cuddled against his side. "I know. I'll be careful."

While Beckie and Willie dug into the spicy *Adobo* at the *picantería* Willie had suggested, she complained briefly about the modern features. "Can't get away from TV, even here," she moaned, turning her back on the bar. However, in the middle of Ian's review of Barbara's concerns about rising and increasingly aggressive disputes between the supporters of the several Presidential election candidates, Willie directed their attention to the screen. Lotta good it does, Beckie thought, since I don't speak Spanish. A moderately tall dark-haired man was addressing a group while a voice-over covered anything the man might have said.

"That's Mamani's main competition," Willie said. "Piero Salvadore, current Minister of the Interior."

"I thought I recognized him; we met him, remember?" Beckie said.

Willie nodded as Ian asked, "What is his platform?"

"All the usual things." He waved at the TV. "This ad focuses on his work to improve Peru by directing law enforcement efforts toward major crimes rather than what are generally considered minor infractions. I'd have to hear it again to say exactly what that means, but I suspect consensual prostitution and possession of small quantities of drugs for personal use would be top of the list." He drank some of his beer. "He's already lowered the prison population that way."

Ian leaned back in his chair. "How is his popularity compared with Mamani?"

"Would that matter, Ian?"

"No, love. I am merely curious."

Willie smirked at their interaction; Beckie made a face at him as he continued, "He's less popular overall than she. Even though he lives in Arequipa, his strength is closer to Lima, and in the mountains."

"That's where the violence Barbara was talking about is," Beckie said. "Is he, or his people, inciting any of that?"

"There's no evidence, which doesn't prove it either way. Should I move that way?"

"While it seems a good idea," Beckie said, "I think Barbara and Rich need to be part of that decision."

"I agree," Ian said. "We shall table that idea until the weekend when we meet with them."

"Kinda funny." Beckie waved at the television. "He's a lot more self-assured than he was in Mamani's office."

"What do you mean?" Willie asked. "Wouldn't he be ready for a TV taping?"

"I suppose, but that confidence is so different from when he talked to us. Why would he be so nervous meeting security contractors?"

"Can you ascribe it to anything?"

"I can't, but it makes me wonder."

With the coffee, Ian smiled and Beckie relaxed. Her phone buzzed, the signal for an appointment. "Look, it's time for lunch with you!" She curled up next to him and tapped the phone. "Hey, mail works, too."

"Civilization. Grand, is it not?"

"Depends," she mused, scrolling through the messages from school. "Usual stuff from Lissa, she and Mike are in the new apartment. We'll have to go out and visit, soon. Mom and Dad are headed to Canada for the vacation they've never had." She gave a snort of humor. "Amy!"

"What?"

She read the screen. "I think she misses me. As a confidant, anyway, for all I wouldn't let her come with us. She's likely just tense about Shalin acting as guardian, with Millie and me here. And she's worried about the key and the tape."

"Has anything occurred to justify her concern?"

Beckie scrolled back. "Nothing I've seen. Probably she's just interested. I am, too, now I think of it." She fell silent, sucking her lip in to worry it with her teeth. Before the men responded, she said, "I've learned a lot in the past two weeks, and since Mathilde needs to get back..."

"Indeed. So you will trust me to live through the next few days while you return to dispel Amy Rose's worries?"

"Yeah." She reached up to kiss his cheek. "I will. I'm sure Barbara and Willie will get on famously without me."

Willie smiled across the table at her. "We'll not have nearly the fun we would have, though."

"Thanks... I think."

Ian touched her arm. "Call Boynton and let him know to expect you. I will continue your training later."

She kissed him again, ignoring Willie's soft "Woo-hoo!"

At the airport, she said, "You be careful, hear? I'll be upset if something happens to you, and you know what happened the last time." She smirked up into his face.

"I shall. You do likewise."

Chapter Eleven
Infiltration

THE FIRST SATURDAY IN OCTOBER, Silvio Flores tapped on the door of Frankie Pella's apartment. Lightly; he wasn't sure he wanted to be heard after Frankie had dumped him over the stern and ran away. Leaving me to—

"It's about time you got back." Frankie's overwhelmingly cheerful voice burst through as the door opened. "Hey, everything okay? I could see they'd pick you up, no problem, and I knew you'd get out smooth. Get you ass in here and have a beer. Or whatever. If I got it, it's yours."

Silvio mumbled a hello as he slipped by the larger man. He hit everything I could complain about, he thought as he opened a Dos Equis. At least the beer's cold. "*Hola*, Frankie. Your trip back easy enough?"

Frankie spent five minutes going over his return. "Biggest problem was making sure the helicopter turned back before I headed to Matthew Town. Didn't want to lead him there."

"That's for sure. Thanks for the beer. Nice and cold."

Frankie waved the comment away. "Now you're here, we'll meet Goldfarb and another couple guys." He grabbed a jacket. "Finish up; he's waitin.'"

Silvio shared the taxi with Frankie, regretting he'd taken a shower earlier in the day; Frankie hadn't, and this Toyota was no limo where you could get away from a fellow passenger.

The ride ended at the Marriott at Newark International Airport. "We goin' somewhere, Frankie?"

"Naw. Not us. New guy's here for a quick indoctrination and then back to Fort Lauderdale."

"So, what do we do?"

"Hang tight for a minute, till we're outta the cab." When the driver stopped, Frankie added, "Pay the guy off and let him go. I'll be inside the door to the left."

"But..." Frankie was already out of earshot. Silvio quashed his question about getting back to the city and dug out his wallet.

Inside the lobby, Frankie had taken a chair out of the way. Silvio hurried over, wondering if he should ask for the cab fare. A look at Frankie's face and he decided the money wasn't enough to worry about. Frankie gestured that he should pull one of the low chairs closer; when he did, the man smiled and handed him an envelope.

"You get the easy job. When we get in the room, and Goldfarb tells you, just show the guy the photos in there, one at a time, until he agrees." Frankie smiled. "I figure two or three is all it'll take. Go ahead, you can look, too, if you want."

Silvio slid the photos out, but only looked at the top one: a Hispanic woman, perhaps thirty or more. She would have been attractive if not for the look of terror on her face. Silvio recognized the man holding a gun to the head of a small boy; Juan, he thought the name was. The barrel was crushing the boy's ear. Silvio couldn't see his face. With a forced smile, he reinserted the photos. "Lead with the best. Should work."

"Oh, they get better. Questions?"

"What's he going to do?"

"He's going to work for those assholes who ran me off."

"For that Jamse guy? How'll that happen?"

"Better we don't know all that." He glanced at his watch. "Let's go."

They rode the elevator to the third floor. Frankie paced the hallway until he found the room; when he knocked, there was a brief pause before it opened.

Goldfarb greeted them.

Silvio stopped short, the sight of Goldfarb's face was horrifying. "What happened to you, Sam?"

"Ah, yes." He brushed the fresh scars on his cheek. "You haven't seen me since… since I was attacked. By the woman you and Frankie were to recover last week. Not only attractive, she is capable with her knives. A warning to you, when you meet her. Her name is Jolene Rochambeau. You may not injure her until after she speaks in court."

"Why?"

"She holds Donato Talos' freedom in one hand and his balls in the other. You do remember Donato?"

Silvio felt weak; he dropped onto the luggage bench beside him. My father… She is the one… at the trial. Damn her!

Goldfarb smiled when Silvio looked up. "But that's neither here nor there, tonight. Now, please meet Estevez. Paulo Estevez."

A dark Hispanic man stood behind Goldfarb. He was an inch or so taller than Goldfarb, and a little heavier than the lawyer's 150 pounds. Goldfarb's workouts and conditioning had left him in better condition than drink and perhaps drugs had left Estevez. The man waved, much more tentatively than Silvio expected. He returned it. How did he connect with the woman in the photo, Silvio wondered.

Frankie stepped around Goldfarb to sit on the bed, close to Estevez. Silvio now noticed two other men on the far side of the bed, but he didn't recognize them.

Goldfarb took command once more. "Before you two arrived, I described the job's requirements for señor Estevez. He is minded to decline. I hope you will prevail on him. Bring him to his good senses, so to speak." He nodded to Silvio.

There's nothing to say. Silvio's heart fell as he stood, trod slowly past Goldfarb and stopped in front of Estevez. He placed his hand on Estevez' chest and pushed him to sit on the bed. He handed Estevez the envelope.

Estevez needed to look at more of the photos than Silvio had guessed. However, he didn't look at them all before shoving them back, tearing the envelope. Silvio retrieved the package and handed it to Frankie, who declined. "You hold it for now."

Goldfarb had pulled Estevez close to the dresser, behind the flat-screen TV that blocked Silvio's view. He heard Estevez's voice, even weaker than his wave had been. "Very well. I will perform to the best of my ability. Please, hurt them no more."

"You get clean for the next week, before your interview with Shen Go, and get the job, then do as we ask, they will be fine. Wonderful, even. They will enjoy their vacation." Silvio heard the pause before Goldfarb continued. "But if you fail, their vacation will not be pleasant."

Goldfarb walked toward the door. Before he left, he took the envelope from Silvio. "Frankie. Take señor Estevez back to Fort Lauderdale and stay with him until the interview. Report when necessary. Good to see you again, Silvio. I'll be in touch." Silvio's heart dropped the rest of the way to the floor when Goldfarb turned back to say, "Keep Thanksgiving week free. We're having a get-together."

Finally, he was gone, and in a blink, everyone else was, too. Silvio found his own cab back to the city.

Chapter Twelve
Between Chatham and Brewster

EXCEPT FOR TAKING ALMOST TWELVE hours, Beckie's trip home was fraught with nothing more critical than boredom. After almost two weeks at twelve thousand feet, she could almost chew on the thicker air, even in the airplanes, and landing gave her a welcome feeling of strength and vitality.

The good feeling persisted through greeting Shalin and Amy at the foot of the air taxi's stairway. She passed on the well-wishes to them both, then after they walked Shalin back to her house, Beckie took Amy's hand and allowed her to lead. They ended on the lanai at Ian's home.

"Good morning, Maurice," Beckie said, but he seemed to be… concerned? "Don't worry, I didn't bring any coco leaves home," she added with a grin.

"Thank you, Mistress Rebecca," Boynton replied, in what she recognized as his 'stiff-upper-lip' tone of voice.

"Why?" Amy said. "What's so special about them?"

"You've heard of cocaine?" Beckie said. "Remember that joke song, *No Cocaine in Cancun*? Comes from the coco plant, and in Peru, they use it to make a tea that's excellent at relieving altitude sickness."

"But, we wouldn't—"

"Right!" Beckie chuckled. "But I wouldn't want to take a drug test for the next couple days."

Amy laughed. When they picked up their coffee cups together, she snickered before saying, "How long are we going to wait before checking that stuff out?"

"'That stuff'?"

"Com'on, Beckie. You know—"

"The key and the tape you found?" Amy bounced on her chair agreeing, to Boynton's amusement. "Well, what do we know about them?"

"We know the bank the key is for…"

"Yeah. And?"

"That's all, I guess. All we *know*, anyway. We think…" Beckie gave her a pointed stare; Amy started again. "*I* think there's a longer tape somewhere, between those two guys, because why would anyone have mailed that lawyer the short one if there wasn't? And it might be in that bank." Boynton's small nod caught Beckie's eye; she found it comforting.

"Anything else?"

"If I remember, Mr. Jamse found the gold in the shed?" She paused and Beckie tipped her head in agreement. "They looked around, but when I talked to Elena, they didn't spend a lot of time."

"Yeah, with all the bodies… We didn't want to be there if the police showed up, for sure. Did Elena have any suggestions?"

"No. It was just they rushed, more than she thought anything was missed."

"Hmm." Beckie picked up her phone. Once she'd connected and greeted Ian, she placed the phone on the table so Amy and Boynton could also hear, then spent a couple minutes explaining Amy's worries. "I was thinking of going up to New York and seeing if I could open the safe deposit box. And, you, Kevin and Elena all vaguely remembered other things in that shed. Maybe I could… Maybe I could get in and look around."

"I am… I would not like for you to be alone."

"Well, there are a few ways around that, but really, I don't think there'd be a problem."

"We thought that in London, if you recall."

"Well... Here's a thought, I'll start in Boston, with Eilís O'Bannon, and we'll head for the bank. If we can get in, we'll see where it takes us. I can hold off on Brewster, for now."

"What does Ms O'Bannon offer?"

"Abby left her car there, and she may be better positioned to get us through the bank."

No one spoke until Ian did. "Ah, yes." Resignation dripped from each word. "Very well. Keep in touch."

Beckie snatched up the phone and promised, making sure Ian understood her sole wish was to get into his arms again.

Amy intervened after they thanked Boynton and were making their way back to Shalin's home.

"I think," the girl said, "the car is actually mine, right?"

Beckie nodded, guessing where this line of questioning would lead and trying to decide which result would serve them best.

"So-o-o..."

"Yeah." Beckie stopped and pulled Amy around to gaze into her eyes. "Leaving aside the question of how we'd get you through Immigration without a parent or guardian, what's the benefit? How does you being there advance the cause?"

"Oh." Amy was silent, looking at her feet first, then the sea, then Beckie's hair, blowing in the breeze. "I really wanted to see where... where it happened..."

Beckie pulled the girl into a hug as she whispered, "Let me think about that."

After dropping Amy at Shalin's home, Beckie joined Willie and Boynton; they spent almost two hours on Skype with Ian and Millie. The conversation was not all about Amy; after Willie updated other jobs, Ian told them the situation in Peru, though fluid, was no worse than when she had left. What interested Beckie the most, however: Ian expected no change in the near term.

Millie was conflicted about her daughter, at least until her phone rang and she slipped out of the Ian-Beckie-Willie conversation to answer. When she returned, her position had firmed.

"Beckie, if you can keep Amy safe, then I'll give you the same authorization I give Shalin when I'm away. She's up to date on her school work, so I'll let you decide."

Beckie caught her breath. Wow! That's a surprise, she thought. "I'm… Thanks, Millie. I'm not sure yet, but… that will make it easier." It clicked in her head. "And I'll bet you're off the hook now, no matter what I say, right?"

Millie laughed as she nodded.

Ian's voice tightened as he said, "May I have a minute alone with you, Rebecca?"

"Sure, just a second." As she looked around, Willie and Boynton were already stepping through the slider. "Okay. Though I am on the lanai…"

"That will be fine." She heard his sigh. "This trip; what is the benefit?"

"You mean Amy? She—"

"No, if you go, with Millie here, I agree Amy Rose should go also. But what is the benefit of *your* trip?"

"Well, geez, it seems perfectly clear to me, Ian. First, we keep the team safe. Next, we make money by helping our client. That *is* what you were telling me before?"

"Yes, that is. What I am struggling with is… Well, first, Amy Rose would be safer if you both remained at the Nest."

"I guess. But how much safer? Unless Shen's going to hire a bunch of security guys? But with Abby dead, I don't see that Amy's gonna be that big a draw." She stopped as his probable real concern flooded her mind. "You're not thinking I'd be at greater risk with Abby dead, are you? Odds of that seem pretty long… No one knows me from anyone." She suppressed a giggle. "You'd be at higher risk, since O'Bannon's been using your name."

"I concur, though with little pleasure. How do you plan to profit—"

He stopped short.

Did he figure it out?

"The shed does not contain the videos."

"Yeah, that'd be too easy. But how many places could they be? I think you hit it when you said Talos got arrested before he could put the gold away… and get the videos. Makes sense it'd be close to where we found the gold, then." She caught her breath, hoping Ian would agree. Or at least, allow the possibility.

After a couple moments, Ian laughed. "Very well. Look for anything we can apply to either Talos or Goldfarb as recompense for their attacks on us. Again I say, be careful and keep in touch."

"We will. I love you."

As the sun disappeared behind Sud Cay, Beckie walked over to the deVeel's home. Shalin happily invited her to share their dinner; as she ate, Beckie explained she would take Amy north with her in the morning, to visit Eilís O'Bannon in Boston, and then a short trek to New York.

Before turning in, Beckie talked to Dan, still watching the terminal at Fort Lauderdale, hoping, she thought, he'd find the man who'd hassled them three weeks before. All was quiet, and he'd buy them breakfast before their flight. By nine that night, she was dreaming about Ian.

Saturday morning, the air taxi arrived to ferry them to Fort Lauderdale, where they would enter the US and meet Dan for coffee and muffins. Then they'd proceed to Boston, where Eilís was waiting with open arms if the phone conversation Beckie'd had with her was to be believed.

So it was. Beckie led Amy out of the concourse into the expanse of Logan Airport's Terminal C where the younger girl's height advantage allowed her to spot Eilís first. The woman was running from the foot of the huge escalator toward them. With the meeting and greeting done, Eilís brought them to her car.

"We'll stop at my place, then head down to the Cape, to Chatham.

You'll be able to leave from there Monday morning."

"Sounds wonderful," Beckie said. "But it also sounds like it's screwing up your weekend—"

"Believe me, it's not. I had nothing planned for today or tomorrow; and I needed to get down there anyway. You guys can help clean up." She paused. Beckie looked at her; the pause was unexpected. "I think there are a few things Jo left, too, besides the car." She brightened. "Since the title's in her 'work' name, I suppose we'll need to practice some to get the signature right. But that'll be the easiest way to do it."

"Uh-huh," Beckie said, not happy about forging names but not seeing any better way to transfer the title to Amy, either.

"Where will you keep it?" Eilís asked.

"For now, since the kid's too young to drive, and even on Bon Secours, there's no room, or road either, we'll dump it at my place in Coral Gables. If that's okay with you, kid?"

Amy continued the face she'd been making through Beckie's speech, evoking laughter from Eilís. "I suppose. I don't think there's any gas at home, either."

Beckie nodded. "Yeah. Just AV gas at the hangar. Well, except for the boats."

"That'll be a fun drive," Eilís said as she drove into the tunnel headed toward the city. "Boston to Miami."

"Yeah. Maybe we'll stop in Orlando."

"Ooo!"

"Or maybe not!" Beckie said with a laugh. "Depends on how you behave."

"I didn't think that letter meant you had to *act* like Mom."

Eilís drove into the parking garage and found her spot. Thirty minutes to freshen up after the four hour flight and they were on the way again. Saturday afternoon traffic was moderate for an October weekend; in less than two hours, Eilís parked next to a red and blue MINI.

Beckie opened the door and got out. She glanced at her phone as Amy stretched beside her; it was just after four. The sun was headed down over the houses to the left.

"This way," Eilís called. Beckie pushed Amy ahead of her, but then stopped as she finally noticed the house, a saltbox cape. While she couldn't call it a mansion, it was a beautiful example of traditional architecture, with classic weathered-to-grey shingles and white trim. Facing the ocean, the front stood two stories high while the back dropped almost to the ground. This has gotta be a million dollars sitting here! "My god, that's beautiful! And big! Does the whole town stay here in storms or something?"

Eilís laughed before saying, "No, and it's not really that big. Not big enough to get lost in, that's for sure." She laughed again, then used the key pad to open the red painted door.

"I'm going to walk on the beach for a couple minutes," Amy said once she reached the crest of the ridge the house topped.

Behind her, Beckie shrugged and followed her as far as the end of the grassy area. Eilís came up behind her and held a can of soda over her shoulder before sitting beside her. Beckie took a long drink and thanked her.

"So it's the MINI that's now Amy's?"

"Yeah, once we work over the title." Eilís drank from her glass. "I had a local kid drive it over to the nearest dealer and have it checked out. Seems to be in fine shape."

"Good. I can garage it until Amy needs it. How old is it?"

"Four or five years old."

They sat in companionable silence until Amy, jeans soaked well up her legs, ran back up to them. Laughing, they headed into the house.

Inside, Eilís pointed toward the back, across from the kitchen. "Bathroom," she said. "Get out of the wet clothes. I'll throw a robe in for you."

While Eilís directed Amy, then sought a robe, Beckie looked around.

There were few pieces of furniture downstairs. The floor plan could have been as traditional as the exterior design, but Beckie didn't know. The whole downstairs was open, except in the center where a staircase wrapped around an exposed brick chimney. To the left of the entry door, there was a bed, ready for use.

To the right, a pair of side chairs were arrayed behind a leather sofa, guarding the window in that wall. Under the window in the front wall a low table stood.

Farther back, behind the living room, she could see professional appliances: a stove, refrigerator, microwave oven as well as cabinets set into the low wall. Skylights in the ceiling recovered the illumination lost to the roofline.

Beckie shook her head and headed out the door. "I'll bring in our bags."

When she came back in, Eilís pointed to the bed immediately off the front door. "You guys get that room. I'll take the upstairs." When Beckie protested, Eilís laughed. "Hey, whatever. But the upstairs has only one single bed. The whole rest of it is storage. Not too comfortable for sleeping."

She lugged the bags over to the bed and tossed them atop it. "Well… Thanks, Lin—"

Amy came running around the fireplace, shouting. "You gotta see this bathroom. It's immense! And the tub… I've seen smaller pools! Com'on!"

As Amy grabbed Beckie's hand, Eilís laughed. "I've seen it. You go ahead."

Amy's robe flared as she spun, first to grin back to Eilís, then around to pull Beckie with her. Lots of well-tanned leg, there, Beckie thought as she allowed herself to be dragged through the kitchen and into the bath. Together, they giggled and marveled over the marble shower and fittings and the eight foot square hot tub. Oooing and aahing done, they returned to the kitchen.

"I ordered pizza. We have beer or wine… or soda," Eilís said, looking at Amy, who instantly scowled back.

"I think she could have a mimosa as long as she's not driving," Beckie said. "It'll give me more leverage." She grinned as Amy turned the force of her scowl on her.

"Excellent! Pizza will be here in a half hour." She waved them back to the front room. Amy dropped to sit on the sofa. Beckie took her place beside the girl. When they had settled, Eilís handed them both tumblers full of orange juice and champagne, then sat on the coffee table in front of them. "Now," she said, "why are you really visiting me?"

Beckie felt a slight blush creep up her neck and cheeks. "Am I that obvious?"

"Not at all." Beckie wasn't reassured. "But since Amy can't even drive the car, and the holiday was last weekend, and we don't get much foliage down here…"

Beckie threw her arms up in mock dismay. "Okay, okay." She pulled Amy close, put her arm about the girl's shoulders. "There are a couple or three things. What about that guy in the catch and release program? Ian said you would maybe broker something, if you could."

"Ah, yes. Silvio Flores. He slipped back into the woodwork and hasn't been seen since. Goldfarb professed no knowledge of him, though he offered to make sure he landed safely." Eilís had an interesting look on her face.

"Would it do any good to ask Goldfarb about him?"

"Probably not, but it would remind him we're still out and about, so to speak. I can do that on Monday."

"Good. Next. Somewhere in her travels, Abby, Jolene, came across a safe deposit box key. It's for World Commerce Bank, in New York. What trouble will we cause trying to open it?"

Amy had grabbed Beckie's arm. "It's World Bank of Commerce."

Beckie turned and nodded once she'd heard Amy out. "Right. So that's another thing. And finally, we were going to look over the place in Brewster. On the phone, you said it was up for sale, right? Maybe I could be looking to buy…"

Eilís stood, glass in hand. "You ready for another?"

"When the pizza comes. For her, too." She tipped her head in Amy's direction. She didn't need to look to see the scowl renewed.

Instead, Amy wiggled out from under Beckie's arm and trailed Eilís into the kitchen. Beckie smiled.

Before Eilís finished, Beckie noticed lights on the street, followed by a rap at the door. "Pizza's here," she called as she went to the door.

"Put them on the sideboard," Eilís called back. "Oh, wait, here's the…"

Beckie finished paying and with a "Thank you," closed the door.

"You didn't have to do that. You guys are the guests."

"Big deal. I'll take it out of Amy's inheritance if you insist." She came up behind Amy and tried to smack her rear end. "Well," Beckie said, disappointed, "with the robe, that doesn't work at all." She noticed Amy's incredulous look. "What? You thought I wouldn't see you guzzling from that bottle?"

"It was empty!" Amy looked at Eilís.

"It was, nearly. Not enough for another mimosa."

"Then, the padding of the robe is justified. But next time, there will be no next time. Drinking out of the bottle isn't good even in college. Com'on, let's eat before the pizza gets cold."

As Beckie picked up the last piece she planned to eat, a double rap on the side door warned them just before the lock snicked and the door swung open. A tall man… No, he's a teen, Beckie realized as she surveyed him, a good-looking one, too. Wearing jeans, sneakers and a windbreaker, the newcomer was not quite six feet tall, she judged, and thin. Windblown brown hair didn't look long enough to reach his shoulders; his eyes were dark, and questioning until they lit on Eilís.

"Ms O'Bannon, hi! I thought you weren't coming down this weekend, otherwise I would have waited."

"And if it hadn't been me, but a robber, what the heck do you think you would have walked into?" She stared at him until he dropped his gaze to carefully examine the floor at his feet. "This young man, trying out for unarmed neighborhood watchman of the year, is Dylan Rees. He's been our neighbor since Mom bought the place, and as he implied, he does his best to look out for it while I'm up in town." She walked over and clapped him on the back. "Okay, Dylan, that's enough pouting. Head up and meet Beckie Sverdupe and Amy Ardan."

Amy smiled, though Beckie could see the embarrassment on her face. She clutched Beckie's arm as she made an excuse and whispered, "Where are my clothes? I can't sit here in this."

"Excuse us," Beckie said before leading Amy to their bedroom. She stood guard in the open archway while Amy dug through her bag. Beckie smiled internally but otherwise refused to acknowledge Any's little gasps of dismay, but instead said over her shoulder, "The pizza's almost gone."

After another few seconds of rustling and muttered curses—at least, Beckie was pretty sure they were curses. If it'd been her, they would have been—Amy spun her by the shoulder, obviously wanting approval of her choice. She'd donned short blue shorts and a red tee shirt, both more at home in the warmth of the Bahamas. "Well, you look fine…" She smirked as she noticed Amy'd dispensed with her bra. "… though I'd guess any walks on the beach will be *very* short," she said as she pushed the girl back into the living room.

Beckie smirked again at the changes in Dylan's expression as he noticed Amy, now unpadded by the terry robe. Once he'd gone from curious through interested to what looked like Wow! when his eye caught her chest and her flimsy shirt, Beckie took his arm and walked him to stand beside the girl. He blushed quite prettily when he realized his ogling had been noticed and mumbled something to Amy that might have been an apology, based on her cheeks' rapid coloring.

Eilís was grinning like a madwoman, but after exchanging a glance with Beckie, she waved toward the sofa and chairs. The four spent several minutes in greeting and exchanging information they were comfortable with; Dylan had more to share than the girls. Beckie sat back, enjoying watching the Amy-Dylan dynamic ebb and flow. She wondered if Eilís intended them to meet, but the continuing conversation didn't support that. The boy had arrived home from a basketball game and noticed the lights on. Beckie discreetly shook her head; what *had* he been thinking?

By ten o'clock, the seating arrangements had shifted slightly, leaving Dylan on the table, his knees and Amy's occasionally touching, still casting surreptitious glances at her legs and… and other things, Beckie thought with a grin. While she was still beside Amy on the couch, Eilís had pulled a tall stool in from the kitchen and was comfortable there.

Beckie felt only minor disappointment that no further discussion of her goals had been possible, except she and Eilís agreed there was no point in leaving the next day, Sunday. Even Monday was doubtful if they wanted Eilís to find assistance in New York.

Dylan offered to take Amy and Beckie to the nearest mall, in Hyannis, to shop for more appropriate clothes. Beckie was sure he'd included her as camouflage, or perhaps in the hope she'd refuse, but she couldn't do that. As sure as she was Dylan was not acting for Big Evil in any way, she still couldn't allow the girl to be that far out of sight.

After the third time Amy yawned, Beckie pulled her up while Eilís showed Dylan the door. "We'll be here tomorrow," she told him.

"You think he's… interested? Dylan?"

They were tucked into the big bed just off the front door, a pillow between them. Beckie laughed, not a guffaw which would embarrass Amy, but a meek little chuckle type of laugh. It was enough for Amy. "I mean, in me?" Beckie killed her humor; she recalled too vividly how she'd felt when Ian sent her home. Amy seemed not to notice. "I'm not sure… I mean, like, what do I do?"

Beckie reached to caress Amy's cheek. "Just relax. Be yourself."

"And, you're not gonna let me outta your sight anyway, are you?"

"We are joined at the hip. Be glad I'm a girl, so we can go to the ladies together. And we can't take him back with us, so consider the commuting that'll be involved."

Amy rolled over to lie on her back and blew out her breath. "Eilís is kinda funny, you know."

"Yeah, but we need her help."

"You think she had Dylan…"

"What? Show up for you?" Beckie rolled her head over to watch Amy nodding. "No. He wandered in out of the goodness of his heart. And maybe a bit of lust for Eilís…" Amy gasped, but shared no other reaction. "And found you and me here. My signals were pretty clear. While he's cute, I'm not in the market. Leaving you as an unknown. A pleasant, attractive unknown."

"You think he and Eilís—"

"I have no idea. But he seemed familiar with everything. Just like a friend of the family would be." Beckie sighed. "That should be at the bottom of your list of things to worry about. Sleep. We have to talk to Eilís in the morning before Dylan gets here."

Amy lay still, feigning sleep until Beckie's breathing steadied. She slipped out of the bed and padded to the window in the east-facing wall. Lights from a boat—fisherman?—were visible and she could faintly hear the waves, a long way away.

Don't hide, she told herself. You're not sleeping because you're… you're guilty! I did come on to him pretty quick. Like you and Abby did, too. She blushed and ran her hand over her belly, trying to recapture the feeling. Doesn't work, she thought. He's really nice. Com'on, girl! You met him what, three hours ago? He's good-looking; he's a guy. He acts interested in me. That might be 'cause you pointed your boobs at him! She blushed. I did, didn't I? Well… She straightened her night-shirt. Abby wouldn't mind, I'm sure. I'll see what he's like tomorrow.

Back in the bed, she snuggled up to Beckie's back; her pillow'd gone somewhere and she wasn't interested in finding it.

Beckie blinked twice before holding her hand in front of her eyes. The sun was glaring off the smooth water and staring in through the immense window in the front wall. She tried to bury her head, only to find Amy in the way. They were again spooned the way she'd described to Ian. She elected not to breathe on Amy's neck the way Ian had hers. Discretion: the better part of valor, she rationalized.

After a few moments, she gently unravelled herself and sat on the edge of the bed. Amy's clothes from the beach yesterday were neatly laid across the foot; Eilís must already be up. A trip to the bathroom was in order.

In fifteen minutes, Beckie perched atop a tall stool at the counter dividing the kitchen and the empty space Eilís said was allocated for the dining room, "If I ever buy a dining room set." They had agreed on coffee and Eilís was scrambling eggs while chuckling with Beckie about Dylan and Amy. "I promise, I was completely floored when he walked through the door like he owned the place! Never did I expect that."

"It did make me wonder—"

"Nope. Never. I love him dearly, but… No."

Beckie relaxed. While Eilís' reaction was quick, it didn't seem to be faked. And the woman was still speaking. "I lay awake a while last night thinking about your other two things. While you guys are off shopping today, I'll call a couple of people I know in the city. I think with the right accompaniment, the bank will roll over unless they think something's going on. The house in Brewster is more interesting."

Beckie put down her coffee. "Why's that?"

Before Eilís could answer, Amy leaned around the wall hiding the central staircase. "Hey. You think I can go for a run on the beach?"

"Sure," Eilís said. "Jo used to do it every morning, rain or shine. Well, rain, anyway. That's all we had."

Beckie stood and wriggled her toes. "You don't mind if I tag along? How far are you planning to go?"

"Way out there, it looks like the tide is out, so the sand will be good. Maybe two, two and a half miles and then back. Okay?"

"Drive up to the lookout across from the light. Park and run from there. Head south." Eilís pointed to the right. "It's a bar and with the tide out, it should be okay. Just watch if the tide's coming in. On the way back, keep an eye on the light."

"Okay. What time is Dylan coming?"

"Mall opens at noon today, so he'll be here about eleven unless he's got a game. Or church." She picked up her coffee. "Are you like Jo, eat after you run?"

Amy nodded. "You ready?"

Beckie looked into her cup. "Coffee's gone, so, yeah."

Seventy-five minutes later, Amy led Beckie back through the front door.

"How far'd you get?"

"I made the full five miles—by time, anyway, and Beckie, what?" she said, while looking at her.

"A little over two miles. I was walking just so I could see miss fleet-foot's dust."

"No dust out there. Just like home. Tide was coming in, so I turned tail."

"Breakfast is coming up. Pick your coffee."

Eilís told them she'd picked out a couple contacts to call in the morning, trying to advance Beckie's agenda. The three of them sat at the table and called the real estate broker who had listed Talos' Brewster home for sale. The woman told them it was still available, at the bargain price of seven hundred thousand, furnishings included. It was originally built in the 1880's, though it had been 'freshened' within the past ten years. The lot was just under ten acres and included access to the lake Beckie recalled seeing that night.

"I'd very much like to see it," Beckie said. "I will be in town both Wednesday and Thursday. Can we meet?"

"Of course."

The woman paused, rather longer than Beckie expected. "Yes?"

"I hope it's not a problem, but our agency requires a credit check..."

"That will not be a problem, but I'm not going to give you the information over the phone. We'll arrange that on Wednesday."

With that, the woman was more than happy to set aside time Wednesday, continuing to Thursday if needed. Beckie smiled. Everything should go so easily.

Beckie allowed Dylan to drive to the mall—keeping his hands busy, she thought smugly. Eilís had laughed and said she had things she could do in the quiet; they could take her Jaguar. Amy asked Beckie to take the MINI, saying "I can get a little feel for it, then." At the mall, Amy and

Beckie both purchased warmer clothes; Amy and Dylan continued the getting-to-know-you dance.

Eilís called her friends in New York on Monday morning; Goldfarb would return Eilís' call in the afternoon, his office promised. Monday afternoon, Beckie and Amy packed up the MINI; at ten Tuesday morning, once Eilís completed the follow-up calls, they headed toward New York. Beckie expected to arrive between five and six; they could relax that evening, then, in the morning, ride the train to Grand Central Station to meet Eilís' first contact outside the bank. No matter what happened at the bank, they'd take the train back and find the real estate office.

In the bank, both Beckie and Amy wore thin gloves. The box attendant had barely minor angst about Amy's request, but the box had been noted with a bearer notation; Amy had only to sign. She did so, using the signature she'd practiced to complete the bill of sale for the MINI, the signature Abby had affected on her departure from Peru.

The box was a disappointment, at least to the women peering into it. It contained three photos and another mini-cassette. Amy slipped the key and the cassette into her backpack and Beckie used Amy's phone to copy the photos, though she didn't see what bearing they could have on the problem.

The trip back to Brewster captivated Amy almost as much as being in the city. And we didn't even go outside the building! The trip in had been early; she'd paid minimal attention to the rail car, to the sights outside the window, even to the idea her phone connected to the internet. After her nerves at the bank, fearing they'd be stopped or arrested, she felt alive, free. A little colorful foliage graced the valley through which the train traveled. "Thanks."

"What?"

"For not treating me like the country mouse. I feel really overwhelmed. It wasn't overwhelming at your place."

Beckie grinned at her. "Mom and Dad are pretty much in the country. Believe me, you're doing fine!"

Back in Brewster, it wasn't time to meet Rosa Simmons, the real estate lady Beckie'd spoken to Sunday; after a stop at the shipping center to FedEx the cassette to Shen, she set the GPS to Talos' home's address. In the daylight, it didn't look near as forbidding as it had that night.

She drove into the driveway and stopped. Even before getting out, she had to catch her breath. So much had happened, with so little benefit. With a glance at Amy, she opened the door and stepped out.

Amy ran around the front of the car before Beckie decided her next move. "Where was it?" Amy whispered.

Beckie didn't trust herself to speak; she took the girl by the hand and walked, first to the tree line to get her bearings, and then to the spot where Abby had fallen.

The rain had washed all traces of Abby away, and the grass had recovered from the light crushing.

"Can we… can we mark it?"

Beckie looked at Amy. Silent tears were streaming down her cheeks. She reached out and pulled the girl into her arms. "If we come to an agreement to purchase it, yeah. Eilís said we could even put a deed restriction so it has to stay, no matter what." After a few minutes, Beckie lifted Amy by the elbow. As they walked across the front of the house, Beckie asked, "You gonna be okay when we come back? You could stay at the hotel."

"No! No, I'll be okay." She scrubbed her cheeks with the palms of her hands. "See?"

"Yeah," Beckie said with a chuckle. "We'll wash up at the hotel before." She stopped at the head of the drive. "Hang here for a second. I'm gonna check out the shed for a second."

"Not the house?"

"No, it's gotta be locked. The shed, maybe not."

She ran across the side yard to the small outbuilding. It was finished in the same white siding as the house, with matching shingles on the roof. The front boasted a small double-hung window alongside the door. The roof was extended to cover a porch; on the ground just off the left end, a chair lay on its side.

Slipping her gloves back on, she replaced the chair, then glanced through the window. There was nothing to see except another window in the center of the back wall. The door had no lock; she peered into the opening. Several dark stains in front of three wooden crates caught her eye.

"Beckie!" Amy's voice was anxious, but not panic-struck. "It's time." Beckie used her phone to record the interior, then trotted back to the car. Amy had sidled toward it already. Beckie handed her the phone, then started the car and headed off to the village center and the real estate office.

Beckie followed the agent through the front door. Even with the sidelights and reasonably sized windows, the house's interior was dark. And it smelled musty. "We haven't had many prospects," Rosa Simmons said as she pulled curtains open. All three of them studied the living room. Beckie didn't know what to make of the decorations; it looked like an explosion in a chintz warehouse, all flowers and leaves and… It took her breath away. "I've talked to the owners about opening it up once in a while, too."

Beckie made a noncommittal grunt and continued into the kitchen. Except for the big lighted island, this is a farm kitchen, she thought, looking at the black iron stove and the other appliances, done in an incongruous stainless steel. "I guess this was updated fairly recently?"

The woman flipped pages in her notebook. "It was, about eight years ago. But they liked the old stove."

“It almost looks like a wood stove, converted to gas,” Beckie said.

Amy closed the refrigerator. “Is someone living here?”

“No, why?”

“There’s stuff in there.” She tipped her head toward the fridge. “Beer, rolls and deli stuff. Looked fresh, but…”

“I didn’t think… But of course, the owners could have someone staying here. For security.”

Beckie nodded. She’d have to be more careful than she would have anyway. She wandered behind the agent as she led them through the upstairs, as dark as the downstairs had been, thinking of how to make her approach and what good could come of it. In her talk with Ian after dinner last night, she’d hinted at her plans, nascent though they were, and he hadn’t tried to dissuade her. She’d sent him the pictures of the shed’s interior and he and Kevin had agreed: as far as they recalled, except for the gold they’d removed, it was unchanged.

They came back down. Outside, the sun had fallen behind the trees and hill; the yard was getting dark. “I wanted to look through the basement,” Beckie said, “and then traipse around the property, but it’s getting late. Can we come by in the morning?”

The woman rustled her papers, then looked at her phone. “I can meet you here at nine, but after we look at the basement, I’ll leave you. You’ll be able to traipse about by yourself, I’m sure.” She stopped at the foot of the outside steps. “What’s your impression so far?”

“Positive, but uncertain. It needs work.” And I’m not gonna tell you I’d buy it no matter what.

The woman nodded. “That’s fair. I’ll talk with the owner tonight.”

“Make—”

“Don’t worry. I do have to tell them when we show it.”

“I know. And I recall you work for them, not me.” Beckie patted the woman’s forearm. “Which won’t be a problem, I’m sure.”

The woman nodded, a trifle uncertainly. Amy walked around them to cross the lawn, stopping where she had earlier. Beckie followed slowly, giving her time.

"God, Ian! You should have seen it! So different from your parents' place, or mine. All flowers and… and the contrast between the upholstery and the darkness of the tables and woodwork. No real lights, either. I can't imagine who would have wanted to live there."

"Are you persuaded not to continue, then?"

"Not really. I'll look some more tomorrow, and decide then. If I make an offer and it's accepted, we'd have a base to work from here, and the team can use it for, I don't know, vacations? Lots to do in New York, and it's not far from Boston, either. Or Montreal and Québec."

They talked a little while longer about how she would investigate the land around the house before the conversation turned to sweet nothings and Amy walked out.

The basement was damp, and the smell more musty than the upstairs had been. There were three bare bulbs, one on a switch at the top of the stairs, and two with short, frayed strings hanging from little chains. Overhead, the floor joists were exposed, dark and cobweb laden. It'll take weeks to get this place clean, Beckie thought, as she worked her way along the wall under the front of the house.

Amy, on the other hand, was keeping well away from the walls and the lally columns supporting the joists. "Bugs!" she'd explained. "We don't have basements at home; now I see why!"

"We don't have basements at home because they'd flood at low tide," Beckie said, giggling at the thought. "Stay there, then."

Beckie continued to explore the recesses behind the two utility tubs, the old washer—still with a wringer—and the furnace, itself a huge asbestos-covered beast lurking at the right end of the space. The big ducts growing out of the chamber at its top spread across the ceiling before vanishing into it, like tentacles in a bad anime. Beside it, toward the rear of the house, several sheets of plywood leaned against the wall. From the look of them, they hadn't been moved since the wall had been whitewashed. Beckie called up the stairs to the agent, "Does all this stuff go with the house, too?"

"Yes," Simmons hollered back. "They'll take it away for an additional ten grand, I think she said."

"No, for ten grand, I'll do it myself." Beckie stomped around another minute, then looked for Amy.

The girl was crouching beside the sheets of plywood, silently waving Beckie over. When she approached, Amy stood and tipped the wood away from the wall. A metal hatch had been set in the wall about a foot from the floor. Perhaps a foot and a half wide, and two in height, it boasted a large lever handle. Amy reached around to push the lever. "Easy to turn," she whispered.

Beckie nodded. She noticed the hatch swung freely into a dark opening beyond the wall. "Good work," she murmured. "Close it up, now."

Amy looked a little disappointed, but pulled the door closed and replaced the plywood. Beckie gave her a little shoulder hug before pushing her up the steps.

"Thanks for letting me in," she said to Simmons.

"No problem. Oh, one thing the owner asked me to remind you, the painting over the sofa in the front room is not included in the sale. They will have it picked up in the next day or two." She led the way to point it out. "Maybe they didn't think they'd have someone actually interested in the place."

Beckie smiled. When she looked at the painting, she was sure the abstract oil didn't appeal to her. "I have to say…" She waved her hand, first at the painting and then at the rest of the room. "… it doesn't enhance the rest of the decor. Seems out of place, I think. Anything else they want to keep?"

"Nope. I checked once again when we talked."

"Okay," Beckie said. "I think we'll take a walk over the land, now. I doubt you'll need to stick around."

The agent started toward the front door, but Beckie opened the door from the kitchen to the rear of the house, and looked out over the back yard. Simmons came back and exited with her. "The property goes into the trees a ways. Don't get lost."

Beckie held up her GPS. "I'll be fine, thanks."

"Right. I'll get back to work. Please call me later, when you're ready to talk."

As the woman walked around to the front, Beckie unlocked the back door and pulled it closed, making sure the slam was loud enough to be heard. She caught Amy's arm, walking her off the lawn and into the sparse forest north of the house. When she heard the car's tires leave the gravel drive, she stopped. "I'm going to walk a big circle around back of the house and come out past the shed." She pointed. "You want to stay here, or come with?"

Amy shook her head and pointed to her sneakers. "They're okay for running, but not much for hiking. I'll stay here." Her eyebrows dropped as she pointed back at the house. "What about the…"

"I left the door unlocked, so I can come back later and see if there's anything interesting. But now, I want her to get back to work and not come back to find us inside."

"Yeah, that would suck."

"If you stay here, keep watch. Send me a text if *any*thing happens, right?"

She laughed as Amy agreed, then stepped off.

Leaves crunched nicely beneath Beckie's feet; the first rain in a week was predicted for tonight through tomorrow. She took her time. She was glad she'd donned her jacket; the air was chilly. The car had said the temperature was forty-two degrees when they'd driven up, but even with the thickening clouds she thought it might be a little warmer by now. A light breeze ruffled her hair, and she unconsciously twisted it into a rope and looped a scrunchie around it before tucking it down the back of her coat.

It took less than an hour to circumnavigate the property. The GPS told her when she was nearing the property line, and kept her on track with the house out of sight to her left. She broke into a partially cleared section and saw the shed a little way off to her right. Amy was sitting on the right fender of the car looking at something, probably her phone.

Beckie decided to check out the shed again before following the property line further. On the porch, she opened the door and stepped in. The dust was thick. The windows were dirty, not so dirty light didn't come through, but dirty. She'd already guessed the stains on the floor were blood, and further, Abby's, from the gash on her leg. She flaked a bit off, then wiped the finger on her jeans. Her nose wrinkled. While the inside didn't smell musty like the house did, there was no freshness in it, either.

She remembered the three small wooden crates lying about a third of the way from the left end, kind of behind the door. She swung the door through its full arc; it cleared the closest crate by a little more than a hand's width. She pushed the door closed and studied the boxes. There were a few marks, stamps, on the sides; she captured them in a photo for later analysis. She dropped the phone into her pocket and went outside.

Amy didn't turn from her phone and everything appeared calm, so Beckie canceled her wave and turned toward the house.

After fifteen silent seconds of listening during which she reviewed the floor plan, she cracked open the back door. She spent a second scanning the kitchen, but then hurried to the door hiding the stairs to the basement. Once she'd pulled it to, she rushed down the steps to the cement floor, and then to the plywood stacked against the wall.

She took a moment to decide how to move the sheets to allow access to the hatch. She hadn't turned the lights on; in the dim light from the small, high, dirty windows, the opening behind the hatch was a black pit.

A check of her phone's battery icon and she thanked her lucky stars for remembering to plug it in last night after talking to Ian. She scrolled to the flashlight app and lit it up. Her first look down hinted the shaft was deep; the bottom was dark and dim. A steel ladder had been set in the outside of the basement wall. The shaft was perhaps two feet square; when she stepped through to stand on the rung below the opening, Beckie couldn't stretch even one arm out, not even diagonally. However, keeping her arms tucked in, she fit with room to spare.

She lit the stairs down once more, then killed the flashlight and, one careful, tentative step at a time, she crawled into the ground.

One,
Two,
Three…

After twelve, her foot hit dirt. It wasn't soft squishy dirt, and the smell of the dark wasn't damp, or wet. Beckie reached out with her hands, then, since she found no boundary but the ladder, she grabbed her phone. The light showed a well-built tunnel, with metal walls and ceiling. Rusty metal, so she thought it was probably iron.

The light from the phone faded after only fifteen feet, so she couldn't make a good decision without moving. The tunnel led away from the house, but she remembered nothing, no place where the tunnel might end. In the shed? Maybe… I guess. No hatches had been evident in the ground outside. While the tunnel was dry, standing still provided no other information.

She flashed the light once more and began the trek away from the ladder, one step at a time.

A minute took her forty steps. The second minute she didn't count; those steps went a little faster. The phone showed a corner ten feet ahead, not a sharp corner, but a turn nonetheless.

Four feet before the corner, in the wall to her left, she found a doorframe with an iron door.

At first push, it seemed immobile, but as she threw her weight against it, it creaked and moved a smidge. Four more blows and while she held her aching shoulder, the door had swung far enough she could wriggle through the opening.

The space was six or eight feet square and as high as the tunnel, which meant her hair brushed the rusty plate above. The floor here was iron, too. A safe of the type Beckie remembered from cowboy movies stood at the wall away from her. Other than that, the room was empty. Beckie shut off all the questions the safe provoked and after checking her gloves, tried the handle. She wasn't even disappointed when it remained unmoving.

However, the location… Not exactly *in* the house, but clearly an adjunct to it. She leaned against the unmoving door and contemplated. This seems like a good reason to make an offer. They're asking seven hundred. I'll talk to Ian about offering six-fifty.

Returning to the tunnel, she carefully traversed it to the far end, a second vertical shaft. When she climbed the fifteen steps on that ladder, she found a wooden door. Lifting it proved the shed was the terminus. She stuck her head out for a second before dropping the lid and engaging the latch to secure it. In two minutes, she'd returned to the basement.

As she pushed the plywood back over the hatch, her phone made the aggrieved chirp it reserved for a delayed text message. As her heart pounded, she swiped the icon.

Amy'd sent a single word. "Help"

Beckie ran up the basement stairs, but rather than breaking into an unknown scene, she lay her head against the door and listened. Unfortunately, her pounding heart made more noise in her ears than anything external; she eased the door open a crack until she could see… nothing!

She squirmed around the door and snuck to the dining room, where she recalled a window with a view of the driveway.

An SUV had been parked behind the MINI; three men stood, looking around. Amy lay on the gravel drive, and Beckie's heart stopped for a second before again pounding. As it did, she felt her face flush and her fists tighten. You idiot! You've really screwed up! You saw the food… and Simmons said… And now 'cause you didn't think it through, Amy's lying out there in the dirt. Again! She deserves better! So you better get your butt in gear and protect the hell outta her. If you can't do that, send her home where someone will!

Her internal diatribe hadn't taken very long; she swallowed her anger and stared out the window. From her vantage point, she guessed the men at the car might have plans, too.

One of them had knelt beside Amy, his hand at her neck. The second stood beside them; the third man held a pistol in one hand and a phone in the other. Inside, Beckie couldn't hear his voice, but when he dropped the phone in his pocket, all three scanned the quadrant centered on the shed.

The man with the gun trotted to the shed and looked in, then trotted back. The other two picked Amy up and carried her toward the house.

Beckie raced to the kitchen and threw herself into one of the large pantries, the one with a louvered door. At least, she'd know if one of them headed toward her.

The front door opened, then slammed shut. Must have gone to the living room, she thought when no one appeared in the kitchen.

Muffled voices kept her still for minutes. The fact none of them were Amy's bothered and frustrated her more and more. The sound of the front door again opening and slamming closed arrested her hand's motion toward the handle.

This is stupid! None of them have come back here. Beckie reached again, grasping the door knob and turning it. She stole into the dining room as someone clomped down the stairs from the second floor. All the action must be here, she thought as she pressed her back into the wall beside the built-in cupboard. The footsteps from the stairs tramped into the front room; again, she could hear them talking, but not what was being said. Outside, a sedan had been added to the MINI and the SUV.

She snuck along the wall, careful not to touch anything that might be loose or squeaky. Finally she got to the archway leading to the entry, and beyond it, the front room. She stepped across the arch and flattened herself behind the conveniently placed grandfather clock. Have to be careful, she thought, as she looked through the glass panels which made up the clock's sides and front. Long as they don't see me move…

Through the glass and the foyer, she saw Amy lying not particularly gracefully on the ugly chintz sofa under the painting. One leg trailed off to the floor. While she had a thin trace of blood running from the corner of her mouth, all her clothes were in place, and the blood seemed to be from a split lip. Beckie sagged in relief watching the girl's chest rise and fall.

A short but well-fed, swarthy man Beckie hadn't seen outside walked by Amy, speaking to people out of sight. A Hispanic accent underlaid his voice. "… the phone you said there were two. What happened to the other one?"

The responding voice was faint and apologetic. "I was guessing 'cause she hollered. And she's too young. But I never saw anyone else."

"Right. Just her."

"Jesus! You jackasses get the hell out of here! Give me the key, then get out; let me figure out what to do."

The three men who Beckie'd seen outside trooped out, looking neither left nor right as they slunk out the entry door. As Beckie watched the man bend over and check Amy's pulse, she heard the SUV start and drive away. Apparently satisfied with her heartbeat, he brushed his hand across Amy's cheek. Before he turned back, Beckie slipped across the archway and returned to the kitchen.

There, she caught her breath, then thought, He doesn't know I'm here. Or look all that fit. Maybe… She edged her way to the door into the front room. The man was standing with his back to her, looking out the window at the drive or the road. Amy was out of sight behind the sofa back. Beckie slip-slid across the pine floor to stand behind the man. She judged the distance between them.

She took a deep breath. "Hey! What you doing here?"

The man spun and tripped himself on the loose throw rug. As he caught his balance, Beckie swung her open hand, slapping him as hard as she could. The heel of her hand caught him where she wanted, at the point of his jaw, and her fingers smacked his ear. Before he recovered, she shoved him to lie awkwardly on the sofa, then leapt to land on his thighs, driving her thumbs into his eye sockets. Don't want to push so hard they come out! Yet!

"Be still!" she shouted as she stuck her middle fingers in his ears for leverage. "Don't move! If you can hear me, say yes."

He tried to nod, but she shouted "Stop!" More quietly, she said, "Don't… fucking… move. Speak. I know you can."

"Yes," he gasped. "What… what do you want? What are you doing? My eyes—"

"Your eyes will be fine as long as you don't move. Must I repeat that?"

"No!" A muscle in his cheek twitched.

"Okay. What are you doing here? My friend. What did she do to aggravate you?"

"Nothing."

"Then why is she out cold with a split lip and whatever else? I don't have a lot of patience. Let's start with who you are."

"Talos. Emidio—"

"Talos?" Beckie almost let go. But wait… Wrong name! It was… Don… Don something. "Like I said, who is… Emidio?"

"Yes."

I better watch out he doesn't hyperventilate.

"My brother is Donato Talos. This is his home. His man told me someone was on the property."

"On the property, looking at it, thinking to make an offer. But you attacked my friend! Why?"

She heard a rustle behind her, then a thud. "Amy, that you? How you feeling?"

"Hunhh." A groan was stifled. "Lemme get up… So… my head hurts, my face hurts… but I've got all my clothes on…"

"For which our guest, Mr. Talos, can be grateful."

Amy appeared in the corner of Beckie's eye. The girl gasped. "What are you doing?"

She didn't turn her head, but answered quickly to allay Amy's fear. "Keeping him still until he answers my questions. As long as he wants vision for the rest of his life."

"I do! I didn't attack you!"

"I'm looking around," Beckie said softly. "I don't see anyone else here. The guys who were here left meek as you please when you gave the order. You might forgive me for thinking you tell them what to do."

"I do, I do. But I don't order them."

"As I said, it looked very much like you do. Remember this? 'You jackasses get the hell out of here!' Tell me what you were doing if not ordering them."

Amy moved beside her. Beckie said, "What…" as the girl loosed her belt. In a few seconds, her actions meant something: she'd slipped Abby's ceramic blades out of the sheaths in the belt and held one out to Beckie.

"No. Come around behind the sofa and hold both of them against his throat. Emidio, assuming you'd like your eyes back…"

"Yes," he croaked.

"My friend will place her knives at your throat. Her knives are *very* sharp. As long as you don't move, they won't hurt you because, unlike your buddies, she's not a killer. Will you stay still for me?"

"Yes. Yes, of course!"

Beckie nodded to Amy, who laid the blades just under his jaw, the way Elena had taught her. Beckie nodded again. "I'm gonna let go your eyes now. I know you'll want to rub them, but move only one hand. *Don't* move your head. One at a time. Don't move!"

She backed her left hand away from his face. Slowly, he moved his hand to rub his eyelid and cheek.

"Put that hand down and I'll let go the other one."

In two minutes, Emidio was sitting still. His eyes were tearing up but Beckie was sure he wasn't crying. She was half-sitting, half-standing next to him. Amy was still standing behind him holding the blades. He was pressing his head back, away from the knives.

"Now, explain in small words just why your buddies attacked two women who are planning to make an offer to buy this place."

He started to shake his head, but Beckie's hand stopped him. He breathed deeply, then said, "Because they are idiots! There has been… trouble… here, so they took it on themselves to watch. Protection, I suppose." She noticed the wet spot on his trousers. "I mean you no harm. Please…"

"Alright." She put her hand on his forehead and pushed him away from the knives. When Amy came back around the end of the sofa, she handed Beckie one of the blades and continued to the second sofa. Beckie released Emidio and waved the blade in front of his face. "This is one of the knives, just so you know." She stood and stared at him while she waved to get Amy's attention. "Call Ms Simmons and ask her to meet us here. I want to see how much Emidio has been making up. Don't tell her that, though. Tell her... Tell her I need one more piece of information before I decide."

Amy took Beckie's phone and scurried out of the room. The call took no time at all; Simmons would finish another meeting and come over.

The atmosphere in the room was tense for the forty-five minutes it took Simmons to return. Amy wanted to shout at Beckie, scream at her, but the look on her face while she stared Emidio down scared her.

I'll... Crying's not the answer, now. But I hav'ta understand why...

Beckie met Rosa Simmons at the door. "Thanks. I'm sorry to interrupt you again, but I need some help." She walked the woman toward the front room. "I'm hoping you can intro—"

The real estate woman was standing flat-footed, mouth open, gaping. Like I feel, Amy commiserated. Simmons rallied to say, "Emidio! What are you doing here?"

"I guess that answers that question," Beckie said. "Do you know him —"

"Of course! This is Emidio Talos, a friend and neighbor. Why?"

Beckie took Simmons' arm and gently directed her to the sofa. She dropped down next to Emidio as Beckie turned and handed the knife to Amy. "Don't put them away yet," she whispered.

Amy wanted to scream, Why? Are we going to kill both of them?

Simmons had recovered her composure enough to ask Beckie, "What was the question between you and your decision?"

"Bear with me," Beckie said. "It may take more than one. Can you vouch for Emidio Talos?"

"Of course! I have known him for years."

"What does Emidio share with his brother?"

Simmons eyebrows rose. "With his… With Donato? Nothing I know of except a love of fine food. What does Donato have to do with this? This is not his property."

"Oh," Beckie said. "I had understood… from I guess older property records, he was still listed."

Emidio was leaning back, once again sighing in relief. I wish I was.

"No," Simmons said. "His wife, Maria Talos, is sole owner. We have the powers of attorney and the deed transfer documents. We would not have accepted the property for sale, otherwise. Since Donato is…"

Her "unavailable" overlapped Emidio's "He's in jail."

Beckie stared at him before focusing on Simmons. "So," Beckie continued, "am I to understand you would not expect Emidio and his brother to work together?"

Simmons snapped her head around to stare at Emidio, who immediately shook his head. "I would not. Even on family matters, they didn't speak." She faced Beckie. "Why?"

Beckie shrugged. "Being paranoid and without current information, I feared he meant to stop the sale." She sat next to Amy. "Nothing more. Thank you.

"I am prepared to make a firm offer of six hundred fifty thousand dollars for the house and its contents, the shed and its contents, and the land as you described the property limits earlier."

"How much of a deposit can you give me?"

"Give me the bank information; I will have seven hundred thousand transferred today. That should cover it all including the incidentals. I'll expect the excess at closing."

"You… you are paying cash?"

Beckie nodded, a little surprised. "Surely this is acceptable? And not all that uncommon?"

"Yes, yes."

Amy thought, She's not as good at lying as Beckie, as the woman's skittish eyes and fingers betrayed her.

"I'll call now, if you have…" Beckie took the card with the bank's information and stood. "I'll be back directly. Please stay," she said to Emidio. "I have a few more questions you may be able to help with. Amy, please watch them."

So I can kill them?

While Beckie was gone, the three sat, stolid, until Simmons and Emidio began a conversation which sounded more like neighborhood news than anything Amy was interested in.

On-line banking was great, but this transaction the bank wanted to discuss. Beckie gave them all the information they needed, and thanked them. As she wandered about outside answering questions designed to trick her into revealing she was not in fact the depositor she claimed to be, she ended up next to the privet hedge lining the drive. She followed it a little way toward the road before checking the time and then taking long strides to the house.

"Very well," she told Simmons. "The money should be in your escrow account before five today. Set up the lawyers and all once the owner approves, if you will."

Simmons nodded and said good-bye. "Call me, Emidio. We'll have lunch." Emidio gave her a weak wave of agreement.

"Now, Emidio, why did you show up here? Are you opposed to the sale?"

"I told you, Frankie called me." The tic was back in full force, and his breathing was speeding up.

"Calm down. I really can't put that together in any sensible way. Frankie works for who?"

"Samuel Goldfarb. Donato's attorney."

Beckie stifled her gasp. "His attorney?" Emidio nodded. "What's *his* interest?"

The man shrank back into himself, almost cowering. "There was a… a fight here about a month ago. Donato lost several men."

"If you're not working with him, why'd he tell you this?"

He paled even more. "I asked. There were reports—"

Beckie snorted involuntarily. Yeah, I guess there were. When "lost" means dead. "Sorry. Why were you talking to Goldfarb? Or even know him?"

The silence loomed; Beckie waited. She wouldn't put easy words in his mouth. Or more likely, the wrong words.

Emidio rubbed his face; his breathing sped up again as his eyes opened. He stared at Amy, sitting on the sofa across from him. When Beckie cleared her throat, his attention snapped to her, as if he'd forgotten her. "I do not deal with Donato, especially while he is…"

Yeah. Always nice to be abandoned by your family in prison. Of course, I suppose he might deserve it, too. "So you talk to his lawyer rather than him?"

"Exactly."

"What else did he say?"

The man was shaking. Beckie thought about trying to relax him, but decided it'd be quicker this way. "What else?"

He looked up at her. Not gonna respond to that look.

"I was foolish," he said.

Beckie still didn't react. "Goldfarb had… severe injuries to his… face," Emidio continued. "They appeared to be knife wounds…"

"And you asked him to explain?"

"I asked, yes… And he told me of a girl… He said the girl had knives… She killed people." So *that's* the reason he's scared of Amy. He threw his head back against the cushion, away from them. "Please!" His exclamation came in a whisper. "I never… hurt you…"

"Relax," Beckie said. She turned to look at Amy and mouthed "Abby." Amy nodded, though her face was tight with both shock and fear. "I'm gonna get some water," Beckie said. "I don't think he'll…" She waved at Emidio, still goggling at Amy.

In less than a minute, she was back. The tableau was unchanged. She offered a glass to Emidio before saying to Amy, "Go get yourself a drink, okay?" Amy stood a little shakily; she stumbled once on her way to the kitchen. Beckie addressed Emidio again. "Tell me more about the girl and what she had to do with… with anything."

"Goldfarb said she is the same girl who testified against Donato. That she could get him off. She visited him early in September, but he got nowhere. They tracked her to a motel near New Haven, but before he could speak, she'd killed his two… guards." He straightened a little, but shied away as Amy returned with a glass. "Anyway, she killed them and attacked him, cutting his face. He wouldn't say any more about that. He did say he believed she orchestrated the attack here."

"So that's her. Why were you and Goldfarb so lovey-dovey?"

He shrank back away. "I hoped to… I need to have Donato free."

"Why do you want him free? If what Rosa Simmons said is correct?"

"It is. But… he has something, Donato, that my mother and sister wish returned."

"He stole the family jewels, huh?"

Emidio looked at her, eyes wide, eyebrows cocked.

"He took something away that has value to… Never mind. What was it?"

Emidio wiggled on the sofa. "He… May I stand?"

Beckie stood before nodding. She watched him stay well clear of Amy, who still held Abby's knives in view. "Okay, what did he take?"

"A family Bible."

"A what!" Beckie blurted. "For this much trouble, it must have been printed by Gutenberg."

Behind her, Amy gasped, but Emidio just stared for a moment. "No," he finally said. "It is a simple King James. However, within it are family heirlooms."

"Oh. That makes better sense. Are the 'heirlooms' intrinsically valuable, or just to the family?"

"Both."

Beckie nodded. "What are the chances it's here, in this house?"

He gave her a bright smile she didn't think was too fake. "It is not here. We have investigated, and Donato told our mother it was not."

"But he didn't say where it was?"

Emidio nodded in agreement, but with a frown. "He refuses to speak with her again while… Until he is released from prison."

Beckie returned what she hoped would be a sympathetic smile. "So, that's why you want him free, huh?" He bowed his head. "Well, if the sale goes through and I find it later, I'll return it. I don't need it." He nodded and sat again. "I think we should all get out of here."

Beckie exchanged phone numbers with Emidio, then walked with him to the door.

Amy shrank into the corner of the sofa while Beckie walked Emidio to the door. When she returned, Amy hadn't moved, trying to decide how to bring her concerns… Yes, damn it! I'm scared.

Before Beckie'd crossed the room, Amy stood. As she refastened her belt, she said, "Let's go back to the hotel. We need to talk." Good! Amy thought, staring at Beckie. That's another uncertain smile she's got. I wish I knew how to tell her how much she scares me! And how much I hate it!

Now anxious to be out of the dark, musty place, Amy helped by peering though the windows for unfriendly activity. Outside, she watched Beckie lock the back door and test it. She waited in the car while Beckie spent another couple of minutes checking the car, "for tracking devices we don't want."

In the hotel, Amy trailed Beckie to the desk where she asked for the use of an empty room. "I'm a little worried," Beckie said, "after the shit this afternoon someone could have bugged our room. I should have brought some electronics, but who'd have thought this trip would need that?" She took the chair against the back wall. "Okay. What's on your mind?"

Amy walked to the window and stared at the iron-grey clouds above the parking lot. "Is it s'posed to rain? Kinda looks like it."

Beckie joined her, checking her phone. "Sixty percent chance of rain. Now…"

"I'm gonna take a walk." Amy took small steps toward the door. "We'll talk when I get back." We'll see if she'll let me go.

"Change into something that looks different… And wear my leather duster over it."

Beckie watched Amy stomp off toward their room through the not-quite-closed door. Not gonna leave her alone… Even though that's what she wants. And maybe needs… well, to think she's alone, anyway.

Once the girl had disappeared behind the landscaping, Beckie slipped out of the room and headed to the lobby, where the view from the large windows allowed her to see the front of the building Amy would have entered. As a bonus, the windows also overlooked the parking area, and the MINI.

The wait for Amy to reappear wasn't as long as she feared; the girl walked out with the leather coat over her shoulders. At the car, Amy flipped the coat off and over the front of the car, then stretched and ran.

Beckie watched her until the bushes hid her, but then in a couple of minutes, Amy's fuchsia South Beach sweatshirt shone through the branches as she followed the parking lot in front of the upper buildings.

The next half hour was boring. Beckie used her phone to check e-mail while keeping an eye on the bright shirt flashing through the landscaping. She clicked off the phone when Amy stopped and then did a cool down.

Then, Amy grabbed the coat and bent down to retrieve, something. The keys! Dammit! I left the keys in the pocket. What… Before Beckie could vocalize the objection, Amy'd started the car and turned onto the road fronting the motel, off to who knew where!

Well, this is why I wanted to link her phone. If she even has it!

The next half hour was equally boring, but also thrilled Beckie with the fear—not that she was stuck here, she could get out with no difficulty —the fear Amy would end up in deep trouble, not least from the police, who would ignore the car's registration in her name in favor of her lack of a valid driving license.

I don't want to call her… and if she has her phone, what would it ringing while she's driving do? I'll give her a few more minutes, she thought, once she'd asked at the desk about rental car availability. "No more than three miles up the road; shall I call them for you? I think they'll drop off…"

Beckie'd waved off the offer for the time being, and plopped herself in a comfy chair facing the window.

Before she could work herself into another dither, the MINI rolled around the turn and made the left into the parking lot. Amy didn't open the door, though, and Beckie couldn't see what she was doing. Finally the girl cracked open the door and Beckie watched as she swept the parking lot with her gaze before running to the room.

Well, what was all that about? Better get back where she expects me.

Amy's short trip ended back in the parking lot, uneventful. Heaving a sigh of relief, she took the key from the ignition. Before she opened the door, motion off to her right took her attention; she shrank down in the seat to scrutinize the scene.

That's the SUV with those guys in it! She convinced herself it was the same one once the driver turned toward her, checking on-coming traffic. She slid even further into the footwell, peeking over the door. When the SUV drove off, she opened the door and ran for their room.

Inside, she backed up against the door gasping for breath. When she finally calmed enough to move, she stepped into the bathroom and saw herself in the mirror. She felt, first her lip, then behind her eye where the skin was puffy. Her mind slowed, allowing her to pick ideas out. Still tender, but not bleeding. Headache's almost gone. She fluffed her hair. I can fix this. She rummaged in her bag.

In three minutes, she tossed eight to ten inches of brunette hair in the trash can and spent more than a minute staring one-eyed through the peephole. Heart again pounding, she cracked the door and looked more. She ducked behind the door before realizing the people coming along the hallway were a mother and her two pre-teen children, making their way to a room further along.

Amy made a fist and slammed it into the door. Since that did no good, she knuckled incipient tears from her eyes and stepped through the door. The man passing by shied out of her path and continued on his way. She paused a second to allow her heart to slow again, then found the room where she'd left Beckie.

She knocked after again checking in both directions; tapped so softly she knew no one could hear. Even me, she thought as she tried again.

After a fifteen minute wait, Beckie took a deep breath and forced calm on herself. She was scrolling through her contacts when she heard a faint knock at the door. Amy was visible through the peephole. Show time, Beck; make it good.

When the door began to move, Amy shoved it open, spun away from Beckie's grasp, and rushed in to stop against the wall about halfway to the window.

Beckie swallowed her heart as soon as she confirmed no blood or obvious injuries. "Something happen out there?"

"Did you know this place backs up to Talos' property?"

"I knew it was close; we left the Escalade over at that restaurant." She waved in an indeterminate direction, mostly along the building's axis. "Why?"

"I thought I saw one of them… The guys you said what's his name sent off."

"Here, or over there?"

"Here. I hid before he noticed." She threw keys on the table next to Beckie's computer. "I took the car down the road." As Beckie stared at her, she continued, "I filled up the gas and got a shake at the Red Rooster. Pretty good."

"No use… Maybe I should spank you?"

"Why?"

"Disobeying the law?"

"I don't think so. Not after you tried to put that guy's eyes out. Don't talk to me about fucking laws and stuff!"

"What?"

Amy rattled around the room before throwing her coat across a chair and sitting on the floor with her back to the wall and her legs out straight. She snatched the ball cap off her head and flipped it toward the chair with her coat, then let her head fall so her chin rested on her chest.

Astounded, Beckie let herself drop to the floor, sitting cross-legged by Amy's knee. She reached out to touch Amy's hair, chopped off short, shorter than Abby's had been.

"What? What's going on, Amy?" She tried to lift the girl's chin, but Amy was having none of it. "What'd you do to your hair?"

Amy unfolded in a snap motion; before Beckie could blink, Amy was on her hands and knees, in another second she was standing. "What the fuck do you think I did?" Beckie'd never heard anger and emotion in Amy's voice like this before; she sat, a statue. "I cut it off! Maybe no one can tell I'm a girl, now. Or weak. Or law abiding. Or in love with a girl who kills people. Or abuses or tortures them. Or…" She collapsed on the floor, shaking and crying, much quieter than her ranting had been.

The spell broken, Beckie popped to her feet and knelt by Amy. "I can't lift you, girl, you're gonna hav'ta help me," she whispered in Amy's ear.

As she grasped Amy's shoulders, the girl rolled over and struck out blindly with both hands and feet. "Get offa me! Leave me alone. Killers!" She threw herself away, ending up against the wall with her face against the baseboard.

Beckie rocked back on her heels, rubbing her cheek where one of

Amy's blows had found its target. Well, she thought, *that's* a change. She got up and found a chair, and waited until Amy's breathing became regular again.

Amy rolled over onto her back just before Beckie ran out of patience. "I give up, Beckie." She dropped an arm over her eyes. "I just give up."

"Not gonna let you off that easily," Beckie said. "Talk to me."

"Or what? You'll stick your thumbs in my eyes? Or take my knives to hold at my throat? What?"

"Okay. None of those things. But…" She rose and walked the few steps to stand beside the girl. She licked her lips, squatted down and grabbed Amy's bra between her breasts. Before Amy could react, Beckie dead lifted her from the floor, pinning her against the wall in preference to dropping her.

"What the fuck are you doing?" Amy scrambled to get her feet beneath her.

"Now, will you talk to me?"

"What are you gonna say? That's it's okay when we do it? That Abby should've—"

"Stop!" Beckie took a deep breath, forcing her hands to her sides instead of raising them. "Just stop. Since you don't want to talk, how about listen?"

"No, you listen! I don't know how to get over Abby's death, especially when she dies to… to exact revenge because I was stupid. Two stupids don't make a smart any more than two rights make a wrong." She stopped to breathe and pull her clothes back into position. Beckie was smiling at her. "You know what I mean. There's no place to sit here; let's go back to the room."

In the room, Amy sheered off to the bathroom while Beckie dropped her computer and the duster beside the desk. She sat on the end of the bed waiting until Amy reappeared.

"Sit on the sofa," Beckie said with a wave at the piece of furniture. Amy dropped the sweatshirt she'd been wearing and threw herself down. "Go ahead," Beckie said. "I'm ready."

Amy rolled onto her belly, folding her arms under her head. "I miss the hell out of Abby. I know, you thought maybe Dylan would... fill in for her? Something like that? He's nice, but honestly? He's not gonna be very much more available than Abby, is he?"

"Abby and Dylan aren't the problem, though, are they?"

Amy nodded her head, which Beckie understood to mean she agreed.

"So," Beckie said, "I disappointed you big time today, I guess. I'm sorry for that, but not for doing what I thought was the best thing to protect you. And me."

"But..." Amy was talking into her arm; it muffled her voice. "But he was just another guy... no threat, no... no guts, even. He pissed his pants, you scared him so bad! How can that be the right thing to do, the right way to act? I understood Abby killing those guys. I cried about it, not just because she didn't come back, but because she couldn't find a different way to protect... me. And herself, too. But I kinda understood it, you know?" She rolled her head to peek over her wrist into Beckie's eyes. "But what you did was just so... I can't even find the word!"

"Egregious, probably."

"Egre... What's that?"

"Outstandingly bad, shocking."

"Yeah. Yeah, that's it exactly." She dropped her eyes to stare at the cushion. "How could you do that?"

"Today was action in an abundance of caution. I saw two guys beating up on you while a third waves a gun around. While I'm waiting for a chance, a new guy shows up. Soon as he does, he's ordering those three around. You missed that part.

"I wasn't going to take the chance he wasn't what he seemed to be. You were lying on the couch, out cold. Maybe you didn't notice..." When she held her hand over her head, Amy stifled a grin. "... but I'm not such a big person. Since I didn't have a weapon, I acted to give us the best chance of surviving with no more injuries. I won't apologize for that."

"But..."

Beckie slid off the bed and sat beside Amy on the sofa. "Budge over," she said with a light-hearted note in her voice. "No buts." She rubbed Amy's back through her tee shirt. "Elena and Sam gave a lot of their summer last year to teach me. I'm willing to use that to protect you. To protect the team." She leaned over and kissed the back of Amy's neck.

"Why me?"

"You're my sister."

"Oh."

"Trust me."

Several silent moments later, Beckie's phone rang, the generic ring tone. She reached for it, and after a glance, answered.

"Your offer has been accepted," Rosa Simmons said. "The funds have been received and the closing can be scheduled a week from today, on the thirtieth."

"That sounds excellent. Thanks very much. It's been an interesting pleasure."

"So," Beckie said as she turned back to face Amy, "can we agree I'll do what I have to to protect you?"

Amy pulled herself into a seated position and reached out to pull Beckie close. "I don't know, if I'm honest." She burrowed her head into Beckie's neck. "Will I hav'ta…"

Beckie reared back and took Amy's chin in her hand. "Is that what this is about? You're worried you're gonna hav'ta become all this great killer?"

She dropped her gaze to stare at her legs. "It came to mind that… when I asked Mr. Jamse if I could fill Abby's place… that I didn't realize what I was asking him. I don't think—"

Beckie clutched the girl tight. "Of all the things kids pick to worry about…" She kissed Amy's forehead. "You'll never have to do anything you don't want to." She rubbed Amy's back again as she continued, "Of course, you know that's not true. You'll have to do things that… But nothing like Abby did. Or even like I did." She gently pressed Amy back against the sofa. "Look at me," she said, watching Amy's eyes dart around the room, but finally locking with hers. "I don't like what I did, but I didn't see an alternative that was even equally attractive. Thinking back, I still don't.

"No matter what you decide to do, even if you decide to live in a convent, you'll face decisions. Even if it's just the decision to let someone else run your life so you don't have to. Not all the options will be neat and clean, and worse, you won't be able to see what each of the choices will… what the unintended consequences will be, once you've made a choice."

Amy blinked. "I gotta get up."

Beckie moved to make it easier. Did she even listen?

Amy closed the bathroom door behind her. Beckie went back to the foot of the bed. I should probably take her back to the Nest. Just, I'm not sure anyone there will listen and help her when she gets into one of these funks. She laughed to herself. Not real big on psychology, are we? Maybe… For whatever reason, I'm not liking the idea of staying here for a week with nothing to do.

She picked up her phone and scrolled to find Eilís' number. "Hey, it's going fine," she responded to the woman's greeting. "You think I can come back and stay, maybe down in Chatham? I've got a week before the closing can be scheduled, and—"

"Of course. You'll have to replace the wine you drink, but otherwise, the place'd just be empty."

"I don't think that'll be such a problem. Can you come down?"

"Nope, too much to do up here. Will that be a problem? You could stay in town, at the Dev—"

"No, too close to masses of people, there. We'll be fine."

"Still got the girl, then?"

"For now."

"Dylan'll be happy. I think he was entranced."

Beckie laughed out loud. "He's what, sixteen, seventeen? Boobs and legs'll do that!"

"Yeah, I know." Beckie heard a voice in the background. "Gotta go.

Code's the same. Call me when you get there, okay?"

"Be tomorrow afternoon. Thanks!"

Amy was in bra and panties rooting through her duffle. "Who was that?"

As the girl pulled a pair of khaki pants up, Beckie said, "Eilís. I think it would be… stupid to stick around here for a week. So, unless you want me to take you back to the Nest…"

Amy froze, one arm in her shirt sleeve. Then, she dropped to the floor in front of Beckie. Her face was white, eyes wide until she squeezed them shut so hard her whole face wrinkled. "I…" Beckie watched her force calm, the muscles in her throat working, up and down as she swallowed. "Would you do that?" She opened her eyes, but looked down for a second before peering up. "I know I'm a pain in the ass, and useless, too, but…"

Beckie swallowed hard herself, then grabbed Amy's hands and pulled her up to sit on the bed. "I guess that week in Florida hurt your self-confidence as much as anything," she murmured. "Sometimes you're the old Amy, bright and full of… piss and vinegar. But sometimes, all that washes away in the fear… in the loss of control those assholes whipped into you.

"You are neither a PITA nor useless. Well, not all the time, anyway," she said, hoping to get a positive reaction. None. "I asked in case you *wanted* to go back. If I wanted to rid of you, I wouldn't ask."

"I just… I'm really scared, Beckie. Sometimes, it all comes back… Not even the rapes so much, but being ignored. Like I wasn't even there. And when they left… They thought I was, like, trash they didn't even have to clean up." She shuddered, a body-wracking tremor. "Just left me to drown."

Before Amy finished, Beckie had hugged her, so the last words squeezed out against her shoulder. Not that it mattered; Beckie knew what the girl was going through—she Beckie still had nightmares where Werner had avoided her attack and… And that was two years ago. This will be with Amy a long time. We'll just have to keep reinforcing her confidence.

Amy's head lifted. "You saved me then and you're doing it again. Why?" Her question was more than a little plaintive.

"Because you're worth it, sister. Because you're worth it. I'll be right pissed if you give up now." She kissed Amy's cheek. "Now, put on the shirt, please, and think about if you'd be better off at the Nest." Amy stood up and finished buttoning while Beckie went on, "It would be safer, but maybe not as interesting…"

"I'd… I'd like to stay with you, please."

"Okay. But put a little more oomph into that, okay? You're not some weak little kitten, being carted about before being dropped off at an SPCA. You'll have to work." Beckie grinned as Amy zipped up her pants. "I'm depending on you to get us safely through Disney after the closing, okay?"

Beckie was sure Amy's squeals could be heard out on the highway.

The rain the clouds had promised was delayed; it arrived in the small hours of the morning. When Beckie awoke, the dark grey clouds didn't hide the steady showers being blown into her face by the gusty wind from the northwest. A quick check of her email—no changes from the news of the day before—and she pulled Amy's foot to get the girl motivated without opening the door and window to allow the 45 degree air to bluster through.

The four hour trip took closer to six, due to Friday traffic and the rain, following them to the coast, Amy joked. Unfortunately, that was about the only thing Amy said during the trip. Every time Beckie stole a glance from the road, Amy was curled up with earbuds in and eyes closed. Occasional shifts in position implied she wasn't sleeping.

While Amy was using the bathroom at a rest stop, Beckie used her phone to search out and make an appointment for Amy at a spa three miles from the Chatham house. *I'll drop her off for the two hours and go unload the car. Maybe cleaning up the do will help… along with the massage.*

Several shocked looks greeted Amy when Beckie shoved her though the door of the Oasis/Spa. "I don't want to see a boy cut on her when I get back. And…" Beckie caught Amy's wrist so she'd listen. "… don't leave this building. I'm depending on you."

On the way back to collect Amy, Beckie decided pizza would cover their dinner requirements, since she recalled what Amy wanted last time. She placed the order.

At the spa, Amy had a styled look that belied its hacked beginnings. She was also as tight and stiff as a cooked noodle. Beckie grinned as the girl practically flowed out the door and into the car. "That was three hundred bucks well spent," she said, checking the directions to the pizza place.

"My God! I could do that every day. Well, not the cut, but the massage!" She twisted around the shifter to hug Beckie, who gently guided her back so she could drive.

"The cut's not bad, though. The… blue streak. That's an eye-opener."

Amy pushed at the bangs in front. "Yeah," she said with a grin. "I really liked that. I wanted orange, but we agreed the blue would look better." Beckie cringed at the thought of orange, but Amy, busy sleeking the sides, didn't notice. "I guess I was really sloppy when I started cutting —"

"I'm not sure 'cutting' is the right word…"

"Guess not," Amy agreed with a grin. "Anyway, Kara and I spent like twenty minutes looking at 'tomboy' cuts. She said I hadn't left quite enough to do any of the longer styles." She swung the visor down and examined herself in the mirror. "I can shove it around anyway I want. Part it on either side, make it tousled or smooth. Cover the blue or make it stand out."

"Well, it looks a lot better than it did. Your mom'll have a cow, though, with it all short, but," continuing over Amy's mutterings, "she'll get over it. And the color, too." At a stop sign, she turned to examine the style again. "Yep, looks nice. The test'll be Dylan, acting as a stand-in for every boy in the world." She laughed aloud at Amy's blush.

Back in the house, Beckie laid out the pizza while Amy poured herself a soda and Beckie a glass of wine. Once they'd finished the pizza, Beckie leaned back in her chair.

"You chopped off your hair to… to avoid looking like a girl? Or to try and disguise Amy Rose?"

Amy stood and brought back the cold wine bottle. As she poured, Beckie said, "Stop. That's enough."

"It's only half full."

"Good. That's like three of Maurice's mimosas. Or Eilís.' Your inhibitions are free enough." She took her own glass and walked to the front room, where she curled up on the sofa. She patted the cushion next to her.

As she joined her, Amy sipped the wine. "Guess I'll just make it last." Beckie nodded. "Okay. I was in a fit over… over those guys again, so some of it was to not look like a girl."

"You're smart enough to know—"

"Yeah. The boobs give it away," she said with a little snarl. "So I guess mostly it was so I wouldn't look like me. I guess that was kinda stupid, too."

"No. The guys we're dealing with don't seem bright enough to notice the other similarities between a girl with longish hair and the same girl with blue streaks in her short hair."

They talked until half past seven, when Amy got up to sort out her gear and then, together, they planned to call Millie for some homework assignments Amy could complete while waiting.

A double rap on the door interrupted them. Beckie waved Amy back into the bedroom while she went to the side door. When she used the peephole, Dylan's smiling face shone back at her in the light from the porch lamp.

"Dylan, how are you? We didn't expect you at all."

"No problem. I saw the light on and… wondered what was going on."

"Well, at least you didn't barge right in on the robbery," Beckie said with a laugh.

He twisted a little, staring down at the floor as he acknowledged her.

Amy bounded in. Beckie almost laughed out loud; Amy had brushed her hair to emphasize joyful rowdiness, it looked like, with the blue highlight out in front. With the tighter shirt she'd donned, not only was she attractive, she was all girl. This is the Amy I know and love, Beckie thought. I might take him back as her therapy-guy.

It took a second for Dylan to focus on Amy's hair; Beckie watched the smile spread from his mouth to his eyes, and overtake his whole body.

"Wow! I love your hair, Amy, it looks so… It's really great!"

Amy, already relaxed from the massage and the wine, about melted as Dylan approached and took her hands. She gave him a chaste hug. Together, they looked at Beckie. She grinned back. "You can pretend I'm not here as long as you keep your hands in sight. All four of them," she clarified. "Soda in the fridge. You can have the couch." She waved into the front room. "I'll sit here and compose some emails."

They hadn't waited for her to finish; on the sofa, they were deep in discussion in words too soft to be heard.

Beckie was nearly finished when she heard a little "Eeep!" from Amy. When she turned to look, Amy was turned halfway round from Dylan. Her hands were over her face and she was shaking. Beckie wasn't close enough to tell if she was laughing or crying.

A look at Dylan and she was pretty sure Amy was crying. He was sitting up straight, eyes open wide in a look of shock. Or maybe terror, Beckie thought.

By this time, she was most of the way to the sofa. With a questioning glance at Dylan, she sat next to Amy, a little sideways with their knees touching. Dylan shook his head and raised his hands. "I don't know," he said. "We were just…"

Beckie looked at Amy, who must have felt the stare. She dropped her hands to reveal slight tear tracks on her cheeks. She knuckled her eyes.

"It's my fault," she whispered. She reached back and grabbed Dylan by the shoulder to pull him over against her chest. "I just got… scared, I guess."

Beckie caught Dylan's eye—hard to do with him crushed to Amy's shirt—and said, "Remember, I said 'hands in sight'?" He nodded. Bet they both liked that more than I wanted. "I wasn't just talking. She's working through some… some bad memories. You brought some of them back, I think." She looked first at Amy and then Dylan. "Not the worst ones, since she didn't swing at you."

He picked his head up and gaped at Beckie. "I didn't… Really, it wasn't like that."

"It was from where she saw it. Or felt it."

"Sorry."

Beckie flashed with momentary anger. "Don't fucking apologize to me! She's the one you scared, apologize to her."

"If I can get a word in," Amy said. "It's okay. I told you, it's my fault, not Dylan's." She giggled and pulled his head back to her. With a kiss on the top of his head, she let go and allowed him to straighten himself.

"Maybe so, but—"

"I learned *that* lesson," he said. "Thanks for the… reminder about who's important."

Beckie gave him a smile, then stood. "No problem. And now, I think it's time for some rest." She offered Dylan her hand. "We'll be here for a few days, lying low, so to speak, so—"

"I can come back, then?"

Beckie glanced down at Amy, vigorously nodding. "I think so. If you behave as well—"

"Do you run?" Amy said. "I go out every morning for a couple miles on the beach."

"That'd be fun. What time?"

"How about half past six?" Beckie said, ignoring Amy's horrified look.

"That's fine," he said. "Give me time to plan some… plans." His grin was a little sheepish, but he turned to offer his hand to Amy.

She rose into a loose embrace with him until Beckie tapped his shoulder. "I never thought I'd be my mom so young," she said with a laugh.

With the door shut and locked, Amy grabbed Beckie's arm and dragged her to the sofa. "While I appreciate you were worried about me, I'm not—"

"Anytime someone makes you squeal in discomfort… or cry, I'll step in. Just a good thing he looked so… worried and upset."

"Or what? Thumbs in the eyes again?"

"Damn it, Amy! No. The thumbs just keep him still. Hurting you would… It'd be hard to hold back, then."

Amy stared for a second, then focused on her hands, writhing in her lap. "This is still protecting me, isn't it?"

Beckie pulled the girl into a hug. "Of course it is, like it or not. Not only me, either. I'd rather embarrass you a tiny bit than have you go through… Florida ever again." She brushed her lips across Amy's cheek. "For what it's worth, I think I've got Dylan on our side."

"If he shows up ever again."

"I'm pretty sure you don't have to worry about that. Let's hit the sack."

Clouds stopped the sun from shining in Beckie's eyes, but they had no such effect on her phone, set to go off at six-fifteen. She expected Dylan to show even if Amy didn't, so she threw the covers off and pushed Amy off the far side.

The chill breeze through the open window motivated both of them into their running togs.

"Are you coming with me?" Amy looked slightly discouraged as the clock showed six thirty-one.

"I'm watching Dylan come up the drive, so I'll do what I did the first time, walk behind you. Not close."

"He's here? Ooo!" Amy reached for the door knob just as they heard a knock.

Amy enjoyed the whole rest of the day, once she'd vanquished her embarrassment of the evening during the run. Nothing like holding hands and being able to harass Beckie in her role of substitute mom. She felt far better when Dylan's hands wandered, though he was scrupulously careful. How do I tell him it wasn't that he touched me, it was I didn't expect it. By the time he left, she hadn't figured out a way to do that. She glowed when he promised to return.

Sunday morning dawned chilly but bright. Under the voluminous down comforter, Beckie rolled over only half-awake to get away from the light and into what she thought—hoped—was Ian. No… When she opened her eyes, blue hair made it apparent she was not sharing with Ian. For a few moments, the girls snuggled, but before the sun rose enough to shadow them, Beckie threw back the covers and headed for the bathroom.

The smell of bacon seeped under the door and kicked her appetite into high gear. As she entered the kitchen, she said, "Thought we were going to run this morning?" When she looked, Amy was still in the longish tee shirt she'd worn to bed. "And those long bare legs, aren't they cold?"

"I closed the window. You were in the bathroom."

"And you're hoping Dylan comes over early, right?"

Amy had the grace to blush as she pressed the shirt against her body, looking at the floor. "Not… not exactly… but…"

"But you'd try to survive the embarrassment," Beckie said with a laugh. "Get in there and put something over… Get dressed!"

On the way, Amy turned back. "I thought we'd run after breakfast. I was hungry, and…" She disappeared behind the bathroom door.

Beckie laughed and cracked eggs into a bowl.

Eilís' Jaguar was in the parking place when they returned from the run. She was sitting in the kitchen with a cup of coffee. Greetings complete, she said, "Update on the Goldfarb front. He told me Flores got back to New York with minimal problems." She shook her head. "Drunks and idiots, I guess."

"Huh? What's that mean?"

Eilís handed Beckie a mug of coffee and pointed Amy toward the hot chocolate. She sat and looked at the two girls. "God protects…" Beckie nodded. "You remember when we sent him back. No one would acknowledge him?" Beckie nodded. "Well, Goldfarb is now willing to remember him. He's one of Donato's kids. The younger one. Like I said, he's working for Goldfarb." She drank from her cup. "But that's not the interesting news." She got up and walked to the sink, rinsing her cup and placing it in the dishwasher. She leaned against the counter. "While he would have been happy to abscond with you two—either one of you—he had been sent to get Jo. Abby."

Beckie froze, her cup between the table and her mouth.

"But…" Amy spluttered.

"It's a good thing I was on the phone and not a teleconference. Or in his office. I think I managed to cover my shock."

Beckie had set her drink down. "Of course. Just like Ian said, there'd be no way for him to know, would there? We said nothing about it, and since she had no family…"

"I didn't tell anyone," Eilís confirmed. "No reason to."

"So, why?" Amy asked. "Why's he looking for… for Abby?"

"Same reason they took you… Donato still thinks she can free him by recanting her testimony. Right, Eilís?"

Eilís returned to her chair. "We didn't discuss it, but… almost certainly, that's where Donato's head's at. Or maybe, some of his family —"

"Not his brother! I'm sure of that… Well, as sure as I can be. We met him, in Brewster."

"You did? Emidio? How?"

"Tell you later. As a story, it deserves a drink, and I'm not ready, yet."

Eilís gave her a look she then transferred to Amy, who blushed and paid a great deal of attention to the inside of her mug. "Well trained, I guess. Anyway, as I was about to say, possibly some of his family or his troops who may still want him out."

"Any reason to think they know anyone who worked with Abby? Like…" She turned to look at Amy.

Eilís followed her eyes. "Not that I know of."

"But they do know," Amy protested. "They found me, didn't they?" She buried her face in her hands. "So, if they know about me, and the Nest, they know about the team. They have to!"

"Knowing who the team is isn't the same as knowing who the members of the team are," Beckie said. "I could guess they don't know anyone's name besides you and Abby. Unless they were coming to snatch you off the island, there'd be no reason."

Amy looked up. "That note I got. It had Mr. Go's name on it."

"We can check, but if I remember, he's the one with all the contacts with the government. He'd be the exception."

"I can tell you for sure Goldfarb never mentioned anyone's name except Jolene. Abby."

Beckie took her cup to the dishwasher. Staring out the side window, she said, "Since Flores came back with nothing, are they still looking?"

"Flores isn't, according to Goldfarb. While he didn't say, I had the impression they were cooling their jets, at least for now." Eilís leaned toward Beckie and whispered, "He also said Abby… terminated, I guess, five of Donato's men, and injured a couple more."

"There were five of them on the tape. The four I saw matched." Beckie stood up and walked to the fridge. "What's for lunch, anyway?" She ignored Amy's quick gasp.

Mid-afternoon Sunday, Dylan knocked on the door. A few minutes later, Millie returned Beckie's call to discuss an assignment list for Amy. Dylan wasn't able to disguise his smirk in time to prevent Amy smacking his arm, but when the call was over, he said, "Why doesn't she… Sorry…" He turned to Amy. "Why don't *you* come with me tomorrow? To my school?"

Amy gave him a look, then transferred it to Beckie. "What do you think, Mom?"

"Let me think about it… Okay, but there are conditions.

"Dylan should check tomorrow that a visitor is actually okay with them. Then, you could go on Tuesday, as long as you will always stay together… Girls' room breaks excepted." She fixed Dylan with a stern look. "I'm telling you both this, so you can't play one off against the other. If plans change, you will let me know first. No looking for forgiveness instead of permission, understand?"

Tuesday morning, Dylan arrived at seven to collect Amy. He agreed that, as a guest, her jeans and Oxford shirt would be okay. Beckie called Ian once she'd finished her first coffee; it was time for an update, both ways.

The situation in Peru was "fluid," he said. When she asked what that meant, he said it was difficult to explain, but safe. Mamani was hosting meetings in Lima while the team, except Willie, was still at her base, working with the local security forces. Willie remained undercover with the group he had infiltrated.

Elena hadn't finished translating the tape, but even what she had done would have been devastating to Talos' attempts to have his sentence reduced. What does it say? Beckie wondered. When she asked, Ian agreed they'd discuss it when they were next together, which would be Thanksgiving. Beckie added the little information Eilís had provided about Flores and the detail he'd been after Abby. Then, after a weighty pause even Ian remarked on, she described her failure to pay attention in Talos' kitchen, and the result: Amy's getting beaten-up.

"Amy Rose has recovered, correct?" When she made a noise of assent, wondering where he would go, he continued, "There is nothing I can add, Rebecca, beyond take care. You have identified the cause and lived the result. She holds no grudge?"

"Not exactly, but some of my… techniques, I guess, upset her. We can talk about that Thanksgiving, too, but I think we're okay, now."

Additional mutual exhortations for care ended that call. A few more minutes with the phone and she'd checked in with Boynton, Shalin and Shen; the Nest would be there when they returned.

The situation in Brewster hadn't changed at all, especially since Beckie'd left. Based on Rosa Simmons' updates, the closing would occur as scheduled.

Last call for today, she thought, as she scrolled to Sandy's number and tapped Call. "Hola!" she responded to her University of Miami roommate. "We'll be headed your way in about a week."

"Oh, so you're still alive? What are you doing about classes?"

"I'll explain when I get there. Tell Greg Amy's coming after we stop in Orlando for a couple of days. So I'm hoping you didn't rent my room!"

Sandy laughed. "Not likely."

"Cool. Oh, yeah. Will it be a problem to leave another car there?"

"Not for me. Greg and Marla won't care, either. Plenty of room down there. You buy another one to keep your Miata company? They won't have little ones, you know."

It was Beckie's turn to laugh. "No. We'll explain when we get there, too. Oh, before I forget again, all three of you are coming to the Nest for Thanksgiving. No excuses, hear!"

"That sounds great. I'll let the lovers know they'll have to be satisfied with the beach."

While she waited for Amy and Dylan's return, Beckie sunned herself in the surprisingly pleasant air, and worked on the look she wanted for the Brewster house, once it was hers.

At five past three, her phone rang; the display read Amy.

"Hello. You guys—"

"Hi!" Amy's voice sounded full of happiness. "We're gonna take a ten minute side trip to the Coast Guard Beach. Dylan wants to show it off. Okay?"

"Sure. Ten minutes is fine. Have fun."

Fifteen minutes later, Amy called again. This time, Beckie barely got "Hello" out before she heard a squeal and a gasp, cut off. "We're being chased!" Amy screamed. "Help!"

"Okay. Stay with me, okay?" She tried to keep her voice calm; Amy needed no more reason to stress. "Where—"

Another squeal. Crashing, thumping sounds… Silence.

Beckie pushed the speaker icon, then grabbed her laptop and clicked the Find My Phone app, all the while shouting at the phone in case Amy, or Dylan, picked it up. A few seconds was all it took; the phone was in Eastham, along Doane Road near Ocean View Drive. Close to the Coast Guard Beach. While it meant nothing to her, she loaded the coordinates in her GPS and ran out the door, still listening.

Beckie followed the GPS voice with half an ear, focusing on the road and other traffic while hoping to hear something from the phone. As she drove east on Doane Road, flashing lights atop a police car stopped her. Bet that's it, she thought as she pulled off the road.

"You'll have to go back, Miss. Take the first—"

"You have an accident up there, right? And a girl with blue hair? She's mine and I've come to collect her. Please." Beckie was hurrying toward the officer.

"How'd—"

"She called me as it was happening." Beckie looked at the phone. "Twenty-six minutes ago, now. May I go on?"

He made a notation on his clipboard, nodding. "Yes. Talk to Officer Westen. She can help you."

Beckie ran toward the ocean until she saw in quick succession, a police car across the road ahead, a car in a ditch to her right, a tow truck maneuvering toward the car, and as it backed, a police officer and Amy. Amy was sitting on the road with the officer kneeling beside her. No blood, but where's Dylan?

The woman officer heard the slapping of Beckie's shoes on the asphalt and stood and faced her as she slid to a stop, panting.

"What are you—"

"Amy! Are you okay?" Damn, I didn't want to sound so fear-struck. A little more calmly, she continued past the policewoman, "Where's Dylan? Is he—"

"Just a minute! What are you doing here?"

Beckie pushed the woman's arm aside to reach for Amy. As she did, she turned her head toward the officer. "Sorry. You're Officer Westen? I've come to collect my ward, Amy Arden." She pulled Amy to stand and then into a hug. With her other hand, Beckie dug in her pants pocket for the letter awarding Amy's short-term guardianship. "That should be sufficient, I think."

Closer, Amy's pale blue shirt had several buttons missing and Beckie observed splashes of drying blood decorating it. Beckie clutched the shaking girl close again and whispered, "It'll be okay, Amy. Just relax."

"This does look to be in order, Miss—"

"Sverdupe," Beckie completed while the officer was searching the letter.

"Sverdupe, yes. Thank you." She returned the document. "Do you have one for the young man, too?"

"No. I can get him home, since he's a friend of the family, but he's not my responsibility in that sense." Beckie turned to survey the scene. "Where is he, anyway?"

"Sitting in the squad." Westen pointed toward the cruiser. "He was dazed when I got on scene, so I had him sit down while I talked to him. The girl, Amy, she was out of the car and I saw her trying to use a piece of glass to hurt herself." She gingerly unwrapped Amy's left arm and held it where Beckie could see shallow cuts along the wrist.

"She said they were after her, trying to snatch her again?"

"Amy had a bad experience about a month ago. She's not fully over it yet. You sound like you doubt either Amy or Dylan was a target?"

With a wave, Westen led them to her car. Dylan gave her a weak salute as they approached. She smiled back.

Westen opened her door but remained outside. The radio provided an undercurrent of calls and signals, but she didn't pay them much attention. "Dylan made them a target by pulling out of the Coast Guard Beach road onto Doane Road." She pointed toward the coastline. "He saw them coming down Ocean View Drive, but misjudged their speed. As something near the speed limit," she said dryly. "Anyway, he was directly ahead of them, and he said she…" pointing to Amy, "… screamed about them being after her, so he took off instead of slowing to let them by. Their car forced him off the road…" She gestured at two ruts across the road from Dylan's car. "… and his car crossed the road and ended up where it is.

"I'm pretty sure the guys in that car weren't interested in two kids on their way home, since I was chasing them from the scene of an armed robbery up toward P-town. I wasn't in high speed pursuit, because there are too many driveways, and I didn't want this to happen. But I'm sure…"

"Yeah. Thanks for the background. I appreciate it." Amy was still quaking, but not as much as she had been. "Hey. You feeling better, now?"

Amy nodded, little jerky motions up and down.

"Can I take them both home? And…" Beckie lifted Amy's head to talk to her. "… what happened to your phone? Still in the car?"

"I think it got thrown when we hit. I'm sorry." She began to cry.

"Hey, no big deal. Stay here while I go talk to the tow truck driver and see if I can find it."

In seven minutes, Beckie returned to the police car holding Amy's sandy, pine needle covered phone. "Victory. At least, we won't have to load everything in a new one."

Amy and Dylan were both inside the cruiser, holding each other more or less vertical.

Westen put down her own phone. "Dylan's mother would be happy if you could bring him back. She's making an appointment to see his doctor to check for concussion, and that would be the other direction. The car will be at the impound yard." She handed Beckie a card. "Address and phone number's there. It'll be a couple of days since it looks like Dylan didn't lose control so much as he was pushed. We'll be taking paint samples off the fresh dent in the left quarter panel." She looked around. "How far back is your car?"

"Back where…" She waved. "I'll run back and get it."

In another hour, they had dropped Dylan off, after telling him to come over when he got back from the doctor's. On their arrival, Beckie had pushed Amy toward the bathroom, saying, "Get a shower and relax, okay?" While Amy was washing her fears down the drain, or trying to, Beckie confiscated Amy's ceramic knives, the ones she had kept from Abby's bag. No need to give her the implements, if she's still unsure about what life had in store.

Amy'd had no resistance to offer when Beckie pushed her toward the bathroom, saying, "Get a shower and relax, okay?"

Sure. Relax. Easy for her to say. Amy stripped and stepped into the shower. She turned the water as hot as she could stand and leaned against the wall, letting the spray beat her skin. As she turned pink, she thought about Dylan and the kiss they'd shared on the beach, before… Before those bastards came after her again. No, no, no! Not going to think about that.

She grabbed the bottle of shampoo and squeezed a handful out. When she worked it into her now far shorter hair, the bubbles almost smothered her. Quickly she rinsed, then used the bar of soap to scrub the rest of her body. One towel took care of her hair, with enough dry spots to dry herself, too. She had pitched her clothes where the shower had soaked them; with a mumbled curse about open doors and clothes and what will I wear, she bundled them to drop in the sink.

On the towel rack next to the door, she found the terry cloth robe she'd been using; with a silent "thank you" to Beckie, she pulled it on and belted it. Covered, she pushed the sleeve up to look at the cuts. A little blood showed, but she was sure it was from being rubbed. In the medicine chest, she found a bottle of antiseptic and daubed the broken skin. She drew both sleeves down to cover her hands and opened the door.

She stared at Beckie, waiting a foot away. With an arm around her waist, Beckie led her to a chair under the skylight. No, Amy thought, I don't want…

Beckie tolerated her resistance, token as it was, for barely a minute. Then she snorted and snatched the neck of the robe to yank it off. Nude, Amy squealed as she tried to grab it back, but Beckie threw it out of reach. Thwarted, Amy held her hands where Beckie could hold them for examination. The cuts weren't deep enough to worry her, though the symbolism surely did. "Stay there while I get some… stuff."

"I put antiseptic on them already."

Beckie sat down, hard. If she's trying to kill herself… why's she taking care—

"I know, stupid, right? Maybe you should check, make sure I did it right?"

That sounds like a plea for help. "Just to make sure you got all of them." In a few seconds, Beckie reseated herself. "Put the robe on." Once Amy had done so, Beckie slid the sleeves up to expose the injuries and with a will, daubed the disinfectant every place the skin had been broken. She set the plastic bottle on the table and checked the wrists again. "I don't think you'll need bandages."

"No, they stopped bleeding before I got in the shower. I think washing opened them up."

Beckie kept Amy's hands in hers. "Want to tell me about it?"

"Can we wait… wait till Dylan gets here?"

"For the things he can talk about, sure. I'd like to hear… God, Amy, I'm becoming my mother! But I want to help. I can guess why you might think those guys were after you. It's a reach, but you're pretty sensitive to things. What we need to work on is why you thought… cutting yourself would help."

Amy sagged inside her robe, head down. She brushed at her short hair, trying to pull it over her face, forgetting, Beckie guessed, about the new shorter do she sported. "I told you I was stupid—"

"Damn, girl, you're about as far from stupid as it's possible to get! *Never* use that excuse with me!" Beckie took several deep breaths before realizing Amy had shied away. "No, I'm not going to… anything. Start again, please."

Amy straightened herself, pulling the robe back together. "So, okay. Maybe I'm not stupid, but… I can sure do stupid things."

"Don't expect me to argue about that." She gave a short humorless bark of a laugh. "I've got you beat all to hell and gone with stupid things I've done."

Amy looked up into Beckie's face. "Well, I was sure it was what's his name, you know, Flores, come back." She stared at her hands, worrying at the injuries as if they belonged to someone else. "And then the car… there was a Thump and the car went sideways. I could see Dylan trying to save it, but it shot off the road and landed with a Thud before it hit the trees." She lifted her head. "There was a bump and then a bang when we hit. I was holding the phone up to my ear, you know, and something slammed my arm. That's when I dropped it, I guess. And my head bounced off something. I saw stars for a second."

She let her head sag again. "When I could see straight, I shoved the airbag away and looked. Dylan was lying against the wheel with the airbag between. He wasn't moving. I thought he was dead… and while I watched, he slumped down onto the console. I was sure he was dead.

"I opened the door and fell out. My shirt caught on something; hit my head again. There was a piece of glass right in my hand, and I thought… I thought, first, I like Abby and she's dead, and now I like Dylan, and he's dead… I don't want anyone else to die, Beckie!" She broke down.

It was easiest for Beckie to sit on Amy's lap; she did, hugging the girl and trying to comfort her. When the sobbing had slowed to an occasional hiccup, she used her thumb to rub the tear tracks away. Amy soon took over, using her knuckle to shut the tears off.

Beckie returned to her chair, and Amy took up her story. "So I had this sharp glass and I heard their car stop and I started to dig with the glass 'cause they'd killed Dylan—"

"Stop!" Amy's words had been getting faster and faster as she relived the experience, and Beckie knew the ending, "their car" was Officer Westen's and a major part of her fears were self-induced. Not that that made them less real, thinking of her own journey after Ian had told her to leave. She grabbed the robe and dragged Amy forward, clutching her to her shoulder. "It's okay, girl. You know that was the cop, coming to help. You're okay. We'll keep you safe. Trust me." Now I just hav'ta keep that promise.

"I do… mostly. Just… sometimes, you know, that shack comes back all black and hot and… an' those guys…"

"I know. We'll keep you safe." She sat up. "Go over, sit on the sofa. I'll throw a couple bags of dinner on and we'll eat."

"Where's Dylan? You think he's… okay?"

Beckie hurried back to Amy. "I think he's okay. I expect he's so okay the doctor's making him wait his turn." She slapped at Amy's rump. "Now go sit down."

Amy and Dylan's story hadn't made the evening news. "No video," Beckie said with a laugh. "Without video, there's no reason to waste time on a couple kids." Amy gave her a look, but then chuckled in agreement. They finished the ready-to-cook dinners and the newscast played, just loud enough to hear.

A knock interrupted the forecast that the morning rain would clear in time for their drive back to Brewster for the closing on Thursday. Amy waved Beckie back to watch the rest of the weather.

Beckie watched as the girl checked the peephole, and then out of the corner of her eye as Dylan came through the door and into Amy's arms. "Beckie doesn't want us to bother her. We'll go…" Amy's voice faded away.

Beckie laughed to herself. I wonder if she's—

A little scuffle grabbed her attention. Amy and Dylan were whispering in obvious disagreement; she was pulling him toward the bedroom door, he was standing firm. As Beckie was about to stand and insert her assuredly unwelcome guardian voice, Dylan stepped closer to Amy. Between his motion, and hers, her robe fell open. Damn, Beckie thought, we had plenty of time… Dylan stared, which didn't surprise Beckie. However, his next move dropped her back on the sofa in amazement. He blushed as he drew Amy to him, enough to tug her robe closed. "Let's go this way." With his arm around her waist, he walked her toward Beckie and the sofa. Good move, young man!

"I don't think that's what you really want," he said, "ending a day where, well, it was going pretty good until we started back."

"You have nothing to prove, Amy," Beckie whispered. To Dylan, she said, "She's had some bad experiences. No," she answered his look, "I'm not gonna say anymore. When she's ready, she'll tell you. And thanks."

"Do I get a say?"

Both Beckie and Dylan stared at her for a long minute. Amy returned their gaze but grasped Dylan's hand. "Well, do I?"

"I don't know. Are you going to change into something more revealing but less likely to fall off?"

She blushed almost as much as Dylan. "Hard to get more revealing. I'll keep the belt tight."

"Good. Dylan's had enough… whatever." Beckie slid to the far end of the sofa. "No kissing, or hugging, or—"

"Okay, Beckie," Dylan said with a laugh. "I think we can figure that out."

Amy nodded, still blushing.

Beckie watched the TV with half her mind; the other half kept track of the teens. Dylan was in the opposite corner of the couch which put Amy between him and Beckie. He was facing her, and she was a little more than quarter-turned toward him. Beckie exerted no effort to hear anything they said until…

"… not unattractive, even compared to, what was her name? Jenny?"

Beckie grinned internally and thought, I'll have to warn her about asking questions like that.

He'd leaned a little closer. "Even without… you know, you're awesome good looking. Just, you looked like it wasn't me you wanted… Looked like anyone might have done. Felt, I don't know, like *I* wasn't important, you were trying to… prove something, and that, that wasn't… I don't know. Maybe I shoulda not fought."

Yes, you should have! Beckie thought. That's not right for either man or woman.

Amy's voice was barely loud enough to overhear. "I hope… No, dammit! You're right. I'm sorry. That's not what I want from… whatever we could have." Keeping good control of the robe, she twisted around and worked herself onto his lap, leaning back against his chest. She allowed her head to rest next to his, but opened her eyes to smile at Beckie as she took his hands and placed them on her chest, but not where Beckie had to intervene. As long as I can see them!

Amy took a deep breath before she said any more. "Two months ago, Labor Day, I went on vacation." She heaved another immense sigh. "No." She turned her head into his neck. "I owe you honesty. Not vacation. I ran away to visit my girlfriend… to make her… my… lover." She sighed, but Dylan hadn't reacted at all. "Except it didn't turn out quite that way." Now, he squeezed her gently. She used her soft voice to describe the looking forward to seeing Abby, the pleasure of the blue water sail to Providenciales, taking care of *Guppy* and the flight to Miami.

When she told him about the limo and the needle in her shoulder, her voice became ragged. Dylan's grip around her chest tightened and she turned her head to him. "It's okay. But… I want to explain. You need to know." She caressed his cheek with hers. "I woke up, but I wasn't in the limo." Inside the robe, she shivered. She made a pushing motion when Beckie moved to slide closer; she stayed back.

"In a little shack is where I woke up. Beckie can tell you where; I didn't care. Still don't. I was naked, tied hand and foot to a bed. One at a time, five men raped me, over and over." Dylan slid a hand to cover her mouth, cut off the words, but she twisted her head away. "No! Don't stop me. I won't be able to do it again and… and I need to tell you." She forced his hand back to lay on her chest. "You need to know."

She sighed. "That went on for four or five days. Time didn't… I couldn't tell time except when the sun came up. One of the men brought a bucket of water in once or twice a day. You know, since I was tied down, I couldn't… move… It got pretty rank in there.

"A couple times I tried to drown myself when they poured water or some food drink in my mouth, but the first time, I couldn't do it and the second, they stopped me." She pressed Dylan's hand against her breast. "They grabbed my nipple and…" Her voice trailed off into choked sobs; she removed Dylan's hands and stood up.

After a stretch to relieve her tension, she sat on the table facing him, but where she could still see Beckie. "No, it's not your fault I got up," she told him. Though I did feel you. Her smile at the thought… Oops, that probably confused him. "Okay. So I couldn't kill myself. Or make them kill me. I was kinda upset about that. But I was disappointed in… Well, in the team, Mom and Mr. Jamse and all. But the one I was really mad at was Beckie. I'd left her a note explaining it all, so that made it her fault I was there, being slapped and kicked and… raped." She brought her arms in front of her chest, then reached down to her knees and leaned on her arms.

"The men stopped coming so often, then hardly at all. I guess the smell put them off. It did me! Then, they left. Just…" She began to shake, then looked up, glaring at Dylan. "When the hurricane came, they left me there, tied to the fucking bed." She stood again and walked to the window. "Beckie can tell you. She finally found me. I was so scared and sure I would die I couldn't do anything. She got me out. I lived." She came back to sit on the table, focused on Dylan. "Now you know. Am I damaged goods? Should I have given myself to you? Or was that slutty?"

Dylan had not been completely shocked, not into silence, anyway. "There is no way I can make that up to you. Even if—"

"It's not your fault!"

He smiled and continued, "Even if it's not my fault, I feel like it is. We've spent, what, thirty, forty hours together? Not long. Not long enough. I don't want those hours to end." He reached for her hands. "You aren't damaged, no way. I don't know what I have to do to convince you of that, but I'll do it, whatever it is. Will you come here; sit with me again?"

She nodded, then returned to his lap, leaning against his chest. "Thank you, Dylan." His lips against her neck were delicious.

Several minutes later, Beckie roused herself. "You know, Amy, I was gonna talk about tomorrow—"

Dylan's phone rang, which brought a flurry of activity while he dug it out of a pocket. "Hi, Mom... I'm feeling fine. Not even the headache he said I might have..." He glanced at Beckie, and shrugged. "I know. We're just sitting, talking. That's all... She wants to know when I'll be home."

Beckie smiled and said, "You have to leave when one of the two of you falls asleep. But wait! Let me talk, ok?" He gave her a look that said I don't think I deserve that, but handed her the phone. "Hello, Mrs. Rees. He's not going to stay the night. Since he's got school, and Amy and I have to leave tomorrow, I'll send him off before midnight, if that sounds okay?"

"That's fine," Mrs. Rees replied. "Thanks."

"No problem. He's a great kid. So good, in fact, that subject to pre-existing plans he might have..." Beckie had to stop to stifle her giggles at the expressions on both Amy and Dylan's face. Mrs. Rees was patient. "Well, if he's not already promised for family things and if our time visiting and sharing coffee has left you with a good feeling about us, I'd like to invite him to spend as much of Thanksgiving week with us as he can."

"But you're in..."

"We're in the Bahamas, yes. We'll pick up and deliver. He has a passport?"

Before she handed the phone back to Dylan, she and Mrs. Rees covered mundane topics related to the trip, if it happened. Dylan's mom wanted to have a word with Mr. Rees; Dylan would after all miss the family get-together. Beckie grinned inside; he seemed to be okay with that.

Before the eleven o'clock news was over, Beckie forced herself to admit Amy'd been asleep in Dylan's arms for several minutes, perhaps as many as fifteen. She roused them, chivying them toward the door. "Two kisses. One for good-night, and one for goodbye till you meet again."

Beckie watched Dylan into a car—his mom's, she guessed. When she turned around, Amy was standing with a confused expression on her face.

"What?" Beckie said.

"Why'd you invite him?"

"You don't want him there?"

"Of course I do. Just, I don't know…"

"You want some time to get used to your power? Don't worry, I'm gonna ask Mike and Lissa to come over, too. With Sandy, Marla and Greg, we'll have a ball." She grinned. "I'll bet we'll have to use the hangar. No one'll want our hollering and all anywhere near."

Amy's expression went from a grin to somber. "I'm sorry about…" She gripped her robe. "I didn't mean to show off everything."

"Not all at once, you mean." Beckie pushed the girl toward the bedroom. "Even dumb old me could see where you were headed."

"Yeah." She stopped and stared Beckie down. "Why didn't he want to go?"

"I think he explained it. You weren't taking *him* there. You were taking any guy there. Acting male. He didn't like that."

"I never thought a guy would turn down—"

"Your past experiences notwithstanding, most guys aren't entirely insensitive. Still, I'd have thought he would have waited. Well, goes to show, I guess." If she can't figure he's a keeper, I'm not gonna tell her.

"Would we have any chance?"

Beckie followed her into the bedroom and shoved her butt so she'd land on the bed. "You gonna sleep nude, or wrapped up in that robe?" She laughed at the girl's angry expression. "I'll bet whatever you want being dressed will serve you well in the morning." She threw an obvious glance at the clock. "About six-fifteen, mark my words."

Amy stopped shedding the robe long enough to gape at her, but dropped it and found underwear and a heavy tee shirt. "Shower?" Beckie said.

"Morning, if we have time?"

"Even if you run."

"So, why should I be dressed?"

"You should have dressed before Dylan showed up. My bad, I should have mentioned it. I don't want to make that mistake again." She pulled her night-shirt over her head and settled it. As she fluffed her hair, she said, "Because I suspect Dylan will want another goodbye kiss in the morning." Her smile went through a grin to a smirk. "And I'll bet he's regretting some of his recent actions!"

Amy pulled the comforter down and slid her long legs between the sheets, laughing all the while. "Maybe I could give him a second—"

Beckie stuffed a pillow over Amy's face, just enough to smother her words. "I see I was too quick to invite him into your backyard. How will I ever preserve his innocence?"

"You won't," Amy replied with a grimace, "unless he wants you to." She rolled over and pulled the pillow tight against her ears. "But I'm okay with him being the one."

Beckie woke a few minutes before six. Rather than disturb Amy, she unwound herself and rolled off the mattress. Her first action was to close the window; the rain had dampened the floor, so the next move was for towels. She found her sweats and was on the way to the kitchen when a rap on the door brought a smile to her lips.

"Dylan, good morning! But since you're not here to see me…" She pointed toward the bedroom. "You have five minutes to wake her up and kiss her goodbye again. At five minutes and one second, I'll be on you like… Well you won't be happy. I may even rescind my invite."

"I'll be back, I promise!" Both his hands were spread in a gesture of acceptance. "Please don't. Dad agreed I could leave Friday or Saturday and stay till the following Sunday, if that's okay?"

"God, yes." She put her hand in the small of his back and pushed."Five minutes starts… Now!"

She turned away toward the coffee maker.

"Ten… Nine… Eight—"

"We're here, we're here!" came in unison from Amy and Dylan.

Beckie laughed at them. She was sure their heavy breathing and bright cheeks were not entirely due to the short run from the bedroom. "Okay! You've got school, Dylan, so get moving. Amy, if we're going to run, get into your togs and let's go. I want to be on the road by ten."

"Don't you remember being a kid?" Amy groused.

She snorted in derision. "Better than you do, believe me."

The rain was barely a drizzle as Amy threw the last bag into the back of the MINI and dropped into the passenger seat. Beckie smiled as she turned the key. On their way to New York, they merged onto the two lane section of Route 6. Clear blue sky peeked over the trees to the west as if to welcome them. She wriggled her rear end to be comfortable in the seat and glimpsed Amy plugging the 4G interface into her laptop. The girl noticed. "Gonna get some research for that paper done, so Mom doesn't go ballistic on me when I get home." Beckie smiled at her quizzical expression. "When'll that be?"

Beckie had considered this question herself after telling Ian about Amy's misadventures, before throwing the last clothes in her bag and folding the clean sheets to return to the bedroom. "A week and a half, more or less. Closing's tomorrow, and after that, I should have the keys. We'll stay there. I want to spend the weekend going through everything."

"Not only to see what to keep, I'll bet."

Beckie glanced at her. "That's part of it, yeah. But not all, you're right." Amy was trying to balance the laptop on her knees. "So next week, we'll drive to Orlando and party for a day or two, then go on to Coral Gables. Sandy won't delay us much, so, like, Sunday week."

"Only two days at Disney?"

"Yeah. You should plan our visit." She waved at the computer. "Also, figure out where to go when you and your mom come back."

"Ooo! You think?"

"I think you could give her an unexpected Christmas present. Ian would be glad to fire her for that week. Or some week if the crowds get too big."

"Only if he'll take her back!"

Beckie's laugh was a snort. "Get to work and let me drive."

The closing began at nine the next morning, and by ten forty-five, with the assistance of a lawyer friend of Eilís,' Beckie had the house keys in one hand and Amy's fist in the other. Simmons suggested her agency also dealt in property management, and agreed to handle taxes, utility payments, security and similar functions once Beckie left.

At the house, Beckie unlocked the back door and went in alone. Amy hunkered down in the car holding her cell phone.

The precaution was unnecessary; Beckie waved her in.

With her camera, Beckie recorded every piece of furniture, then she and Amy examined each one to decide if it should be saved. Beckie wanted to make her choices early, because next, they would rip everything apart, looking for anything. They'd be more careful with pieces they wanted to keep.

The decision process took them until mid-afternoon, when Amy threw herself on the sofa in the living room and whimpered, "I'm dying of hunger…"

Beckie laughed before admitting she too was ready to eat. Amy directed them to the Red Rooster. After finishing, Beckie turned right out of the parking lot and less than a mile north, found a mall to the right which promised a hardware store. She bought flashlights, thinking of the safes, one in the tunnel and one behind the painting that had hung over the sofa, and a few tools. The tools would allow disassembly of the cabinets and wardrobes.

Back at the house, Amy stood for a minute at the spot on the lawn; Beckie waited until she saw the little shake of the girl's shoulders. With an arm, she guided them both to the house.

"Where to begin?"

Amy brightened at the prospect of something to do. "Well, it'll be dark soon." She danced through the four downstairs rooms and stopped in front of Beckie. "The kitchen's got too many hidey-holes, especially with two pantries and that huge refrigerator."

Beckie grinned in agreement. "Tomorrow, then."

"Yeah, in the morning when the sun's coming through the windows. Afternoon for the living room. Slicing open those sofas… Ugh!" She wiped her hands together. "So let's do the dining room. I love that clock!"

Beckie made a shooing motion toward the open archway between the kitchen and dining room. She turned toward the china cupboard.

Beckie'd been turning cups over and rifling through stacks of Royal Doulton china, wondering if she could sell it on eBay when she heard Amy crow, "Hey, great minds think alike!"

She carefully replaced the dishes and hurried to see what Amy thought was a treasure, but the girl was empty-handed. "What?"

"Look there, between the movement and the back of the cabinet."

Beckie scrooched over in front of Amy and peered into the case. While the lower section, where the weights and pendulum hung, was glass enclosed, the sides around the movement were wood; they opened to expose the works. With a small Allen wrench, Amy pointed to the back of the chamber.

"The plate back there isn't flat against the case, see? And when I held the light…" She demonstrated, then handed Beckie the small LED flashlight she was using. "… I could see something stuffed between the plate and the case."

No need for extended examination. "It's probably the receipt or instructions or something. Too far in to be anything we'd care about." When she handed the light back, Amy'd wilted. "But that's not to say we shouldn't check it out. There were small needle-nose pliers in the stuff we bought. See if you can… Or maybe," she said as she stuck her finger against the space, trying to judge its size, "try the tweezers in my kit, upstairs." Amy ran toward the steps.

Beckie went back to leafing through a stack of old instruction manuals in the bottom of the china cupboard until Amy thundered down the stairs. "Careful! No running with scissors," she hollered.

"Tweezers!" Amy rejoined, with a laugh. "Seriously, I'm being careful. I so don't want to break this thing apart!"

Beckie watched for a few seconds as the teen started to ease the tweezers into place, but went back to flipping the pages of dishwasher instructions from eight years earlier.

She'd pitched the pamphlets back and was peering into the next space—full of aperitif glasses—when Amy said, "Yes!" As Beckie rose from her crouch, Amy waved a folded square of yellowed paper at her.

"The age looks right," Beckie said with a laugh, then recalled she hadn't yet mentioned the underground tunnel or its safe.

On the well-lit island in the kitchen, she watched as Amy carefully unfolded the ready to crumble paper. Beckie placed a glass coaster on it to hold it flat, then snapped a couple of photos. "20-55-70," read the top line, followed by "50-35-90-15."

Amy copied the sets of numbers to a scrap of newer paper, then when they'd both finished, she folded the paper up and returned it to the clock.

"Well," Beckie said, "there are two safes."

"I only saw the one over the sofa. Where's the other one?"

"Under the yard. Want to save that one for Halloween? I'm sure no ghosts will be there!"

Amy shrieked at the thought of being underground on Halloween, but then smacked Beckie's arm before stomping into the living room.

"What? You found the entrance to the tunnel. That big hatch in the basement."

Amy gave her another look before reaching to the knob on the wall safe.

After fifteen minutes playing with the two combinations, Beckie read from her laptop. "Try the three-number one first. Six or seven spins to the right. Stop at the first number. Left three turns, then right two. On the last one back to the left till the dial stops. Says here that'll be about eighty."

The hinges had been well oiled, but the container was empty. "Not even any dust," Amy complained.

"Com'on, let's try the other one." Beckie started toward the kitchen. "Want to go through the basement, or the shed?" She stopped. "No, have to use the basement. I locked the entrance at the shed from underneath." She looked at Amy standing by the sofa. "Well, let's go. Don't you want to see what's there?"

"How far under the yard?"

Beckie pursed her lips in thought. "It was twelve steps, but the rungs were lower than I expected. Maybe fifteen, sixteen feet. No water, then at least." She came back and took Amy's hand. "Doing it now has the advantage of leaving the daylight for looking above ground! Bring your light."

In ten minutes they were in the tunnel standing in front of an olive drab box with Diebold Safe and Lock Company of Canton, Ohio inscribed on the top of the door in gilt and black.

"Wow," Amy breathed.

"Yeah. Okay, try your magic fingers. Use the four number combination, turning to the right." She consulted the paper she'd carried with her. "This time, you'll end going to the right till the dial stops."

The dial was stiff. Yeah. It's been a couple years since Talos went to jail, so maybe no one else knew this was here. The fourth time, Amy yanked hard and fell, almost knocking Beckie's legs out from under her as the door swung open. "Oof. Sorry."

Beckie was already kneeling, leaning over Amy's legs to see into the container. "Well, well. Good job, Amy Rose. Gloves."

Amy held the light as Beckie picked up a black book.

"Holy Bible," she read aloud. "Guess maybe this is the one Emidio thought wasn't here."

"Well, it isn't *in* the house."

Beckie snorted as she carefully opened it. "Inscribed with the Talos family name. Take it and we'll look it over later."

Amy pulled thin gloves over her hands and took the book.

Beckie delved into the safe again. "Small box of jewelry, and a stack of cash. And…" Her voice trailed off in wonder.

"What?"

"Okay, that's the lot." She pushed the door to and turned, still squatting. She held a couple of video cassettes. "It's almost time to call Ian."

The day of searching ended, they turned the front lights out and stayed upstairs in the former child's bedroom they'd commandeered. Beckie stared at the cassettes while Amy leafed page by page through the Talos Bible. For whatever reason, the room held a king-size bed; it allowed plenty of room for them to sprawl.

One at a time, Amy slipped three pieces of paper in front of Beckie. When Amy told her there were no more, she smiled as she reached for her phone, selected Ian's number and called.

After greetings that sent Amy, shaking her head, to the bathroom to don her nightclothes, Beckie laughed and said, "Whoever hid things for Donato thinks the same way Amy does." She grinned at Amy, who was now pulling the covers up. "She started with the grandfather clock in the dining room… I sent you the photo… and behind the mechanism, they'd hidden a slip of paper with the combinations for the two safes. The safe in the living room was empty, and I don't think there'll be anything else in the house. Well, nothing interesting, anyway."

"You have saved the best for last, then?"

"Yeah." She laughed. "Amy wasn't real excited about the tunnel, but the safe was something! It took a couple of tries after we read about how those safes worked, but inside, we found the Talos family Bible and what

I think are the videos Mamani is looking for. A couple small cassettes. Should I send them to Shen, or direct to you guys?"

"To Shen. Include a note that he should ask Else to copy them, then contact me. Good work! What about the Bible?"

"Amy's gone through it. I can guess why Emidio wants it. A birth certificate, an adoption certificate and a deed to property in Chautauqua County. I don't think we have any interest in anything there, so I was going to hand it all to Emidio."

"I agree, certainly if those are the only things within."

"Also, in the safe there's a little bit of jewelry and some cash. We left those there for now since no one's mentioned them. I'll tell Emidio, but not now."

"Again, I agree."

"Okay. I'll drop the stuff at FedEx tomorrow morning before we come back and finish." She thought for a moment. "I'll see if they'll accept Saturday delivery."

"Do not bother. It will require three days to get to Nassau, to the drop. Shen will have to pick it up."

"Yeah. That'd be a waste of money."

"I am relieved you believe so."

She laughed. "Okay, I'd spend another hour saying goodbye, but Amy's pillow's already shredded where she's holding it over her head."

Amy roused and slung the pillow at Beckie's head.

"And now she's attacking me with it. Gotta go, love, gonna teach the hellion a lesson!"

The next day, Beckie extended the trip to FedEx by fifteen minutes to hand Emidio the Bible. While he still shied away from Amy—Beckie was certain he believed Amy and her knives responsible for the massacre earlier—he allowed Beckie to catch his arm and support him as he took the leather-bound book and opened it. His eyes were shining as he thanked her and shook her hand.

While the girls sliced open the other furniture, marking it for disposal of one sort or other, as Beckie had predicted, nothing rewarded the search. They packed for the drive south. Once away from Brewster, their trip to Orlando was long and unexciting; Beckie drew it out to three days, with stops in North Carolina and then Georgia. As Beckie walked into the Savannah Riverfront Marriott, she wished she'd just kept going. Except their reservation at the Contemporary Resort was for tomorrow. The next morning, she was even more sure; all the nightlife she'd found was twenty-one and up!

Amy had done her work and the Land of the Mouse was great fun. They'd arrived at the Resort early enough to have dinner at the Coral Reef in Epcot. Beckie knew it'd be a success as soon as the cute waiter served the souvenir Ariel cup of lemonade. Amy's "Squeee!" settled it.

The next day, Thursday, was Magic Kingdom; Friday they started at Animal Kingdom and ended at Epcot once more. Saturday, they drove to Coral Gables, arriving before two in the afternoon. Traffic was heavy; the Hurricanes were at home, but Beckie avoided the worst of it.

She and Amy had a few minutes to relax before Sandy, Marla and Greg bounded through the door to greet them. Primed by Beckie, Amy professed eternal gratitude for Greg's help in getting her out of the Keys; he blushed and avoided telling her what she'd looked like the last time he'd seen her—as Dan and Kevin carried her aboard the plane for the trip to the Nest.

Beckie laughed at Greg's reticence, but pushed Amy toward him. "You can see she's alive."

"Yeah—"

"And a lot of that is due to you. Don't forget that!"

He smiled, but his twinge of embarrassment was apparent. Amy, however, took charge, stepping to him, enveloping him in a hug that used all of her body to express. "Thanks," she whispered just loud enough for Beckie to hear. "I'll be doing my best to live up to your… your willingness to help me."

"Well…" He stopped to give Beckie a look like please help me.

She patted Amy's shoulder. "I think he understands, Amy."

The other girls joined Beckie in a group hug, surrounding Greg in a way he didn't expect, and didn't know how to accept. After a moment, Beckie made the first move away, followed by Sandy. Amy was next, leaving Marla enfolding him.

"Whoa," Sandy said. "I didn't think it'd be that intense." She went to sit on the sofa. "Thanks."

Beckie shrugged, then took Amy by the arm and drew her to sit on the love seat across from Sandy while Marla and Greg disengaged and sat beside Sandy.

"You know," Greg said, "I didn't do anything special. But I'm glad you're doing so well—"

"Better than I was, but Beckie could tell you, not as good as I should be." Amy rubbed her wrists. "But knowing people like you… you! are willing to risk, like, everything…" She glanced at Marla. "… you've got to help me… Well, it makes up for what happened, some, anyway." She slid far enough from Beckie that she could face her. "That goes for you, too, Mom."

Beckie laughed and chucked the girl on her upper arm. "Okay! That's enough of the mutual admiration." She saw Greg's head move in agreement.

"Well, okay. It's just…"

Beckie took Amy's hand while she addressed Sandy. "What do you have to drink? Anything left?"

The next hour they filled with arranging the trip to the Nest and damaging the soft drink supplies. Derisive laughter met the news of Beckie's status change at school, especially when they realized why she'd been absent.

A call to the air taxi arranged for the flight from Fort Lauderdale to the Nest in the morning; a trip to a local underage saloon to celebrate the Hurricane's win with other students followed. At midnight, Beckie wrassled them all back home for some rest before the raucous alarm sounded to start the next day.

With Shen, Shalin met them at the Nest. After a quick stop to assure them both all was well, Beckie led Amy home to be welcomed by Boynton, who confirmed Ian would arrive before Thanksgiving. With fresh coffee, Beckie set up on the lanai and Skyped Millie, giving her the welcome news Amy was home, substantially unbroken. After a sip of her coffee, Amy agreed. "For now, Mom, I'm sure glad to be home. We had some, interesting experiences. Mostly good!" she hurried to add. "But I learned a couple of things, too. We'll talk about it once… once I understand it all, okay?"

Chapter Thirteen
Piero: Candidate, Father

"I APOLOGIZE FOR MY TARDINESS," Piero Salvadore told the group. "My daughter's soccer game ran late."

"We understand," Emil said. "Your attention to your family has always impressed me, and I'm sure the others. It will be a major benefit in the campaign."

Piero laughed. "I'm not sure Carmen will be so happy about that! But Sara can entice her if not. Now, it's the second week of *noviembre*. How are we doing?"

He looked around as the others gathered notes or placed their phones aside. Fernando, his personal assistant, was there as usual. Emil Gonzales, who, as campaign manager, was responsible for their actions. The financial wizard and the attorney would be quiet; their presence would ensure the campaign made no costly errors.

From behind the others, Fernando gave him an agreeable smile. In his hand, a glass of pisco sparkled in the light. "Thank you. Place the bottle on the table, if you will." Once he had his glass, he sipped. "Ah. Excellent! Thank you. Now." He set the glass down. "Emil, an accounting, please."

"Accounting, Piero? I don't—"

"A review, then. Where do we stand?" He noticed a hand motion from Fernando. What does he want now? Ah. He surely means calm down. Yes, I was too sharp. "Sorry, Emil. I'm a little nervous. Please."

The expression on Emil's face went from devastated to ingratiating in the space of Piero's seven words. "The polling, early though it is, isolates the race between you and Mamani. Your record as Minister balances hers in the Congress. Both of us have solid financial reserves, though yours are arguably larger. So far, our followers are greater in number than hers, but we have seen increases for her, especially in the southern districts."

The group spent the next three hours discussing Piero's concern: the campaign workers who would bring success to one or the other of them. As they wrapped up—as best we can now, Piero thought—he asked, "Can we be certain we have a two candidate race?"

This led to another half hour considering and rejecting the other known candidates, and some who Piero hadn't considered.

"I don't wish to sound patronizing, but the thrust for advertising should center on my—"

"Your family, certainly," Emil said.

"Of course, of course. But that's expected. And while Mamani has no children to parade about, her extended family has always been supportive."

"I would like to see us highlight your love of our country," Fernando offered. When Piero looked at him, the man was almost apologetic, leaning toward the door. "Even more than Emil has been doing."

"Thank you, Nando," Piero said. "Exactly what I was thinking. My actions always seek to benefit our country."

Emil shot up out of his chair. "That's perfect, Piero! And true, too. The writers have created two ads with that emphasis already. I'll have them continue their effort tomorrow."

"Yes, I've seen them and I like them. One of the next ones should stress securing our borders from the inside. I can talk with whomever you assign. Let me know."

Emil gave every appearance of having found the surprise in the candy. "I will, and thank you." He sipped his own drink, the first he'd had, Piero noted. "Have you had any luck with the other thing we talked about? The problem for Mamani?"

"Not yet, but I remain confident."

The next morning, Piero dismissed his driver. "I will drive myself this morning. After taking the children to school, I will arrive at the office before ten and be ready to depart for Lima after lunch."

At breakfast, he teased Carmen about the role she could play in his campaign, reminding himself not to be too forceful. After all, he thought, a thirteen year-old girl has little interest in being on a stage with adults! His son wasn't quite so negative, but Piero brought the conversation back to soccer after Sara gave him 'that look.'

The drive was pleasant, and he always enjoyed the time he could spend with his children. "But I must go to the capital today," he told them.

"Oh," Carmen said. "That's why you drove us."

"Right, little miss smarty. You know I hate to go away without you."

"When do you return?"

"On Friday. I'll be at your game unless the weather is terrible."

"We'll be looking for you!"

With hugs, he bundled them into the building and then headed for his Arequipa office. Outside the building, he parked and took out his phone. He scrolled to a nondescript entry and pushed Send.

When the ringing went on for the third ring, he glanced at the car's clock. No, he thought, not too early. So why—

"Hello, Samuel Goldfarb's office. May I help you?"

"Indeed you may. Is this Colleen? This is Piero Salvadore."

"Of course! I can connect Mr. Goldfarb instantly."

"Goldfarb here. How may I help you, Piero?"

"I require an update on the topic we discussed *en agosto.* What can you tell me?"

"Ah…" Piero felt no relief when he heard Goldfarb sigh. "We are diligently working to secure Mr. Talos' release." He has nothing, Piero thought. Goldfarb continued, "He has agreed to provide you the videos the very day of his departure from—"

"May I remind you, señor Goldfarb, time is of the essence. I have little interest in *how* you achieve our goal, but if I do not have the videos before Christmas, their value will diminish rapidly, as will Talos' revenue stream. Are we clear?"

"Perfectly, Piero. We shall have news after our Thanksgiving."

"That is?"

"The end of November."

"Good. See that you do. All the shipments from Peru are on hold until—"

"I understand your position, but that delay will severely damage my… our reputation."

"As I understand it, Thanksgiving is barely two weeks away. Hardly an inordinate period of time."

After listening to another five minutes of whining and complaining, Piero said, "I will permit one half of the scheduled delivery to depart next week, as planned. Then nothing until I have the recordings." He stroked his upper lip. "Others are willing to receive our goods, señor. Good day." He chuckled, imagining Goldfarb blathering into a dead phone.

Chapter Fourteen
The Nest

Thursday (Thanksgiving)

BECKIE WOKE TO THE DISSONANT ringtone she'd programmed Ian's phone with to signal a team member's call. At the same time, a chill where she'd been warm and snuggly told her Ian was up and going to answer it. She opened an eye to see him pick the phone up and answer it. He listened for ten seconds, no more; Beckie caught her breath as he set the phone down and tapped the face.

"… Shalin believes there are invaders on Port Cay, headed for the hangar."

Beckie was already out of the bed scrambling for clothes. "What—"

"They have cut off the cell station at the airfield. Satellite phones will work, but not everyone has one."

"What else is vulnerable? And what about Shalin?"

"Shalin was shot. She is at home. Perhaps…"

Beckie grabbed the first shirt she saw, a bright yellow polo. "I'm going to her. I can make sure the kids are in the safe room and free up Kevin." From the hallway, she finished, "I'll catch up with you. I love you!"

As the door slammed behind her, she heard Ian's "Be careful!"

Boynton met her in the entry way. "Ian's on the way out; he'll explain," she said as she slammed the door open. Outside, she stopped short to make sure she saw no one on the island. The delay frustrated her, but not as much as getting injured would, she admitted. After two sweeps of the area, she ran.

There's no need to be panic-struck. Still, her heart was pounding, and not simply from the hundred yard dash from her house to the cottage where her five guests were sleeping. What's going on? she thought, a snarl twisting her lip.

She burst through the first bedroom door; Mike's white hair showed beside Lissa's blonde.

No, she thought, I won't pull the sheet offa them!

She grabbed a lump that, based on location, had to be a foot and shook.

Lissa grumbled as she pulled her foot away all the while clutching the sheet to her chest. Mike responded to his partner's motion by rolling his back to her.

"Okay, I will pull the sheet, then."

Whipping the sheet away revealed both Lissa and Mike. The chill reached them; Lissa sat up with one arm across her breasts, the other hitting Mike's shoulder.

Mike needed another second to react to Beckie's scowling at them. "What the hell is going on, Beckie?" He glanced at the clock. "Our wake-up call is for later."

"Probably. But whoever shot Shalin didn't wait. Get your butts outta bed and into clothes; we're gonna see how bad she is." She glowered at their joint lack of motion. "Come on!"

They finally stood and moved, Lissa to the bathroom and Mike to the dresser.

"I'll be right back. Don't leave without me."

Across the hall, Beckie blasted into Marla and Greg's room. The only difference: the window was open and Marla had kicked off the sheet. The couple lay with limbs tangled together, breathing quietly.

"Sorry 'bout this." Beckie walked to the foot of the bed where she selected two feet, one each, and yanked hard enough to be felt.

Marla, like Lissa, woke first, but in keeping with her incendiary nature, wasn't as polite. Greg took the risk of covering her mouth while his look demanded an explanation.

"Shalin's been shot. We have no clue why, or who, or where else attackers might be. We're going to her, see what we can do. You're coming so I know where you guys are! Get dressed; I'll be back with Mike and Lissa, so if you want to be… clothed…"

Marla had shoved Greg's hand away as she listened. "Yeah, we want to be clothed." She rolled off the far side of the bed and tossed a towel to Greg.

He shook his head. "What's left to hide?"

Beckie gave him a weak smile before she went out. Sandy occupied the small room; a brief explanation had her up and moving faster than the two couples. Beckie hurried to the entry door and peeked out at Port Cay, across the channel. No motion, no color that didn't belong. She spared another glance for Bon Secours Cay, thinking of Amy, but nothing moved there either.

Com'on, com'on, com'on! "You ready yet?" she hollered as she turned toward Mike and Lissa's room.

Lissa had just shoved an arm into her green blouse when Beckie pushed through the door.

"Ready?" Lissa nodded as she buttoned the first button. "Wow, Mike, that's bright," Beckie said, holding her hand up as if to block the glare from his blue shirt and matching shorts.

"Seemed to go with your shirt."

"Oh. Yeah, I guess." She forced herself to stop bouncing on her toes. "Okay, let's go."

Sandy pulled Marla and Greg with her.

The spots of blood on the steps to the deVeel's home implied to Beckie any danger was outside; she kept her crew to the side while she reached the button.

She waited almost long enough to stab at it again but the door opened; Kevin peered out.

"What are you doing?" he spoke in an excited undertone.

"I'm here to help with Shalin and the kids. Ian's headed to Shen's office; there's a problem with the control room, I think he said."

She pushed her five through the door. "Marla, you and Sandy do First Aid. Go see about Shalin. Mike, Lissa, if the kids aren't in the safe room, get them there, then help get Shalin there, too, if Marla says she can be moved. Only open the door for one of us! Greg, see if Marla can use any help." She turned to Kevin and spread her hand on his chest. "Go and see if you can help Ian figure out what's going on. We'll keep everything safe here." When he hesitated, she said, "Go!"

Once she'd locked the door behind Kevin, she ran to the safe room. Her plosive sigh of relief, brought on by everyone having done what she'd asked, was louder than she wished.

Marla was kneeling beside Shalin, who was lying on the futon in the secure room. The twins were sitting, quiet in their discomfort and shock at seeing their mother lying before them. Melissa was comforting them as best she could. Blood-soaked bandages lay near Shalin as Marla and Sandy did their best to clean the wound.

Someone had thrown a towel over Shalin's bare chest; Beckie could see the wound in the woman's upper thigh.

"I guess it's a good thing I got over having people see me," Shalin said through clenched teeth, her eyes flitting around the small room, lighting on each of the eight people. "At least, most are female." Her laugh turned into a grunt of pain as Marla swabbed the back of her leg.

"Sorry 'bout that," Beckie said. "But you're mostly covered, now. I can't imagine they gawked—"

"Besides, Mommy," one of the twins said, "they're helping. Really."

"I know, sweetie, and I'm grateful." She reached her hand to him.

Marla dropped the rag she'd been wiping with and rubbed her forehead. Beckie knelt down beside her. "How's it look?"

"I got a pressure bandage on both sides and the bleeding's slowed way down. If she's still…" Marla pushed Shalin's chest to force her to lie back. "*If* she lies still…" She glared at the patient. "I think she'll be ok."

Beckie nodded, "Thanks, all of you." She looked into Shalin's gaze. "So, what happened?"

Shalin gave her a look to kill. Her glance in her kids' direction told Beckie why.

"Oh. Okay. Did Kevin take all the sat phones?"

"No, I wouldn't think so. Check in the desk off the kitchen. Before you go out."

Beckie nodded and rose. As she moved toward the door, Mike and Greg both followed. She decided not to have that discussion in front of the others. "If we leave the house, Marla, you're in charge." She waited until the others nodded. "I'll tell you what the plan is, and Shalin can fill you in if you need more info."

She opened the door and climbed the steps. In the desk she found two sat phones and handed one to Mike. "Take this to Shalin. Or Marla. They can't use it down there, but…" He was already gone.

While she waited for him to return, sure he would, she grabbed a glass of orange juice and pointed Greg at the bottle. He joined her as she poured a glass for Mike.

When Mike finished his, Beckie waved the men into the dining room. "Okay. Is it sensible for you two to be following me? And Lissa and Marla? How will they feel if you get hurt?"

Neither man responded. Beckie saw familiar determination in their eyes. Mike had done well in Arizona, and Greg in the Keys, and she knew neither had an answer for their girl-friends' reaction in the worst case. Still, she had to ask. "Are you sure? We know someone's out there with a rifle at least, and I can't imagine any scenario where guys on Port Cay are the only ones here." They nodded, and Beckie smiled inside to see the look they shared before turning their gaze to her. Well, they're sure. I don't know of what any more than they do, but they're certain of it.

"Okay. Last question. Can you take orders from me?" This was boilerplate; neither had been a problem in the past, but it needed to be clear.

They agreed.

"Of course, I'll be talking to Ian, too. As long as the phone works, anyway." She picked it up and dialed, then while waiting, she set it on the table in speaker mode.

His voice brusque, Ian answered, "Yes?"

"Can you talk?"

"Are you all safe? If so, attempt to see if Home has been trespassed upon, and call back in… four minutes."

Beckie heaved a sigh of relief as he hung up, then she said, "Mike, tell the others we'll be leaving the house. When you're back—" He was gone.

Greg was at the window, peeking around the storm shutters someone had closed. "Nothing I can see."

Beckie joined him but she too found nothing out of the ordinary.

Mike ran into the room. "Okay, they're locked in and waiting. What's next?"

Beckie pointed to the lanai. "Go check the south side. Shouldn't be anyone there, but keep your head down. There's enough cover for bad guys. Meet back here in… two minutes." She turned away but then quickly added, "Maurice could be out there, too. Be careful!" She waved him away and took Greg by the arm. "You go to the rooftop, up those steps…" She pointed along the hallway. "… and take a good look around that end of the house, down to the water. I'll check the front." As he moved, she grabbed his arm again. "Keep under cover, just in case. They have awnings up there, for lying outta the sun. Use them. Two minutes!" She released his arm and headed to the front door.

She slipped out of the house and quartered the area between the house and the dock, keeping an eye out any unexplained motion.

Her watch signaled time to return just as she finished the second sweep. Beckie hurried inside the house with the door closed. She caught her breath, then hurried to fetch Mike.

Greg met them in the kitchen. She sat at the island and said, "Anything?"

Their negative reports didn't surprise her. Ian was next. Her fingers were steadier than she expected; for the second time, she dialed with no errors.

Ian sounded a little calmer when he answered, and allowed her to report the lack of activity. She ended with, "But we didn't go back to the house."

"Boynton has that under control. Do not worry."

"Okay. I have Mike and Greg. We're okay; considering our next move."

Beckie heard, "Ian! Over here!" before Ian said, "You are certain Shalin and the twins are safe?"

"As they can be."

"Then, do nothing foolish. I love you."

Beckie waved to Mike and Greg. By the time they'd reached the front door, she'd crafted a plan. Of sorts, she thought. Lots to be determined by opportunity, still.

"When we get outside, we need to stay under cover best we can. I'd like to get over to Bon Secours to check on Amy and Dylan, but with the sun coming up, even swimming will be like holding up a sign. But the boats don't have any protection either."

In two minutes they were at the dock. Even with no activity in sight, they were cautious. Until Mike looked in the boat. "Shalin was out getting groceries?" His voice was incredulous, rising more than a simple question would account for.

"Well, it is Thanksgiving." She noticed Mike's look, now of surprise. "Yeah, I know. She's Kashmiri, and Kevin's South African. Not a holiday in those places. Nor here, even. But remember, she's invited all of us for dinner. And you know Shalin, she never does anything to do with food or holidays halfway."

Greg had already picked up a bag and handed it to Mike. He now grabbed the second one and handed it to Beckie, saving the third for himself. "Ooof! I got the heavy one, I guess."

They spent five minutes carrying the food to the kitchen and fitting the chilled items in the fridge and freezer. Back at the dock, Beckie looked around before stepping into the boat.

"Hop in. Let's head to Port." She pointed to the island with the hangar and airfield.

"Isn't that where you said Shalin got shot from?"

"Yeah." Beckie stared across the water, eyeing the distance. "Less than a thousand yards. I couldn't make the shot, but Ian? Kevin? Pieter, certainly. And he missed his target, probably, hitting her leg." She shook her head.

"Okay," Mike said. "If we go there, what's the plan? We're not so heavily armed, you know. Unless this thing has torpedoes or something." Beckie shot him a glance before seeing the snarky humor; she giggled at his smirk.

"Well, it's not all laid out like in stories or movies, but..." Since they had boarded, she untied the line and waved to Greg, sitting aft by the engine. "Yeah," she said to his querying gaze, "might as well use the outboard."

She waited while he started it and steered around the end of the dock toward Port Cay. "Don't head for the dock. Let's land... there." She pointed to the section of shore closest to the back corner of the hangar. "We can see what damage they did to the generators and maybe the cell tower."

"The plan?" Mike prompted.

"The plan is to get ashore and, without getting caught or killed, find out how many there are and if any of the team are there. I can get the report to Ian." She tapped the sat phone.

"No details on how we avoid getting caught or killed?"

She gave him a look she instantly wanted to take back. Mike wasn't the cause of all this and of the three, she was the professional. "Sorry. No, no details. Keep your heads down and know the situation before you break cover. Follow me, and watch out for the other guy, too."

The sun had been up for almost an hour when Greg nosed the boat to the shore and Beckie splashed to the beach to find a place to secure the boat's painter. She glanced at the sat phone: seven thirty. Damn. We're moving too slow.

Mike investigated the beach away from the hangar, toward the one hill on the cay. While he slunk toward the peak, Beckie grabbed Greg's shoulder and pointed him at the small steel building that housed the Nest's diesel generators, used for Port's equipment as well as for emergencies when the solar and geo-thermal units on the individual islands were insufficient.

He nodded and, crouching, stole the twenty feet to the open door. Beckie watched him all the way in, then looked for Mike.

The bright blue shirt and shorts Mike'd grabbed showed up against the sand like a beacon. For the second time, she made a full circle survey of the area. Nothing out of place. Mike was now lying with his head at the peak, under a stray bougainvillea growing next to the tower. As she watched, he wriggled back down the small slope. She did another circuit waiting.

However, Mike didn't return. Instead, he made his way to the beach and a few feet into the water. Beckie stopped herself shouting at him to get back. He waded further away from her, not even gracing her with a look so she could wave him back. Damn! What the fuck's he doing?

She could feel her tension increase as Mike kept on, disappearing behind the slope of the beach and the hill. Impotent, Beckie stamped her foot. Though it didn't help, she did it again.

The second time, Greg walked up and scared the life out of her when he touched her arm. The reaction took her five feet sideways in a single bound; if she'd been closer, she would have slugged him once she recognized him.

"Sorry," he said.

"No, no." She took a deep breath. "My bad. Mike walked outta sight over there..." She waved indiscriminately. "... and I was a little tense, I guess." She shook herself. "What'd you find? Anything?"

"My experience as a senior EE major tells me indisputably someone beat the shit out of the switch box connecting the generator to the rest of the system. It looks like they tried to whale on the fuel lines, but those are better protected. I doubt it'll take long to fix, so most likely, they wanted to cut it off while they were here."

"Makes sense," Beckie agreed. She spun to make another survey, but stopped when a boat appeared in the water headed toward them.

She didn't recognize it, which meant it wasn't one of the team's inter-island skiffs. As she dropped to the sand, pulling Greg with her, she wanted to scream for Mike, "What happened—"

When it got within five-hundred feet, it was obvious it was running at low speed, not what she'd have expected from invaders, who would want to clean up as quickly as possible. And then, as she lifted her head, she saw the bright blue of Mike's shirt under the white of his hair.

"I'll kill him," she muttered.

"After me," Greg responded. "He ruined my news!"

Beckie rolled over to gape at him; together they broke into smothered laughter. As they recovered, Mike ran the hijacked boat gently onto the sand beside the skiff.

"I found it up there, round the point. It was all lonely—" He ducked as Beckie threw a mock punch at his arm. "What? Not good?"

"It's fine as long as you're safe," she admitted. "What's it got we might use?"

"A radio, but it's built-in, so we'd be stuck here to listen. Mostly it's about pictures of the hangar and the airstrip. And the two islands to the north."

"Nord and Cottage."

"I guess. They aren't using names. The cables up the tower have been cut, accounting for cell phones and WIFI. Radar, too, if I remember what Kevin said." He reached into the cockpit and came up with a handgun. "One of you would be better with this."

Beckie glanced at Greg, who gave a little nod. "You," he said. "My limited experience is with long guns."

Mike leaned over the rail to hand it to Beckie. She smiled when he turned it butt first. "Good job. Maybe I can forgive you for running off by yourself."

As he clambered out, he said, "It was just there, waiting."

Beckie looked at the weapon more closely. "Glock 30S. Nice feel. I wonder why…" she mused.

"Huh?"

She looked into Greg's eyes. "Why'd they leave it?" Holding it pointed out toward the ocean, she released the magazine. "Full," She handed the magazine to Greg and pulled the slide back to make sure the chamber was empty. After releasing the slide, she checked the trigger and then with a look down range, dry fired it. "Feels okay and the safeties all clicked." She took the magazine and inserted it. "Well, I'll hope it's okay if I need it, until I can get Pieter to check it out." She slid it into a back pocket. "Did you see anything else?"

"Three sets of footprints, headed up toward the end of the runway. I didn't follow them."

"Thank you!"

While Beckie was examining the weapon, Greg had grabbed the boat's bow line. "Do we want to tie it up, or turn it on and let it go?"

She looked up. "Tie it up. Can you find the fuses for the radio? I'm gonna head up toward the runway."

When both men's attention snapped to her, she pointed to the space between the hangar and the shack. Greg finished tying the boat off while Mike dropped back below the rail. She made her way away from the beach, then turned back.

Mike brandished something at her; she smiled, guessing it was part of the boat's electrical system. With a wave, she drew them up beside her and with a shushing motion, led them toward the expanse of runway just ahead.

She kept them against the metal wall of the building as she approached the front. Across the runway and a little to her left, something moved. Trillian? After a gesture to Greg, directly behind her, she took a step past the building to survey the field and surrounding area.

She swept the arc from her left, lit by the rising sun, around to her right, backlit and difficult to differentiate things against the bright solar disk. She took another small step, turning toward the motion she'd seen before when simultaneously she realized she was now perfectly highlighted in her bright yellow shirt and the hardest blow she'd ever felt hammered her left arm, flinging it back and pitching her off her feet.

Screaming something unintelligible, she fell, but her head bouncing off the pavement cut it off. "Damn! This'll hurt!" A moment later, someone moved. "Stay back!" she commanded Greg and Mike, both leaping forward into the kill zone. "Get the fuck back!"

At least they dropped, she thought, but the pain now took all her attention. She reached for her arm, but when her hand touched it, she only felt it in her right hand. She pulled it back to see more blood than she thought she had covering it. This time, she reached and tried to clasp the wound, but her arm felt really funny, like it was all wobbly. Fuck, she thought, I've seen that. It's broken. Ian will be so mad. She felt herself drifting into blackness and bit her lip to stay conscious.

She felt a tug on her leg and opened her eyes to see Mike pulling. As she watched, Greg grabbed her other leg and helped. Between them, they got her behind the wall.

Gasping with the pain, she choked out a thanks, then, "My shirt. Rip it up for a bandage. I think it's broke, so try not to wiggle it too much." She closed her eyes, but when she felt them trying to lift her, she opened them again. "Cut it off. Hurts too much to pull it over." Another session of panting and whining. "Greg, keep your head down. I saw someone over there…" She rolled her eyes back toward the runway. "Not where the shot came from. See if you can see anything, okay?" As Mike bared her torso, she let go the arm and made a gesture to Greg. "Head down, hear!" She forced the words out between gasps. "I don't want to explain anything to Marla. Or Lissa."

Mike had cut her shirtsleeve off and slid it to expose the injury. Beckie forced her eyes open again; the dismay in his expression was disheartening. She gasped again as he made pads from the shirt and wrapped them on either side of her arm with the last piece of fabric. Her eyes closed again.

This time she tasted blood when she came out of the dark; she could almost feel pain in her lip.

"… get something for a splint," Mike said as he scurried back the way they'd come.

She rolled her eyes when Greg skittered back beside her head. "There was a scuffle over there. Two people. Looked like one had a rifle, but he was getting the worst of it. Then two others running this way. Do you think they're friends?" He took off his shirt and laid it over her bare chest.

"Thanks. I'll be right pissed if they're not friends," she gasped. "Don't feel much like fighting, right now." The pain is so intense. But what about Amy… Her mind closed again.

FRIDAY

Beckie opened her eyes. If she'd felt better, she'd have thought she felt like crap. The deep, dull ache in her arm, a twitchy uncomfortable feeling, and an unwelcome smell that, in a moment, she realized was her.

Events seeped in from memory: Ian's wild look from she didn't know when, concern on Mike's face, the tense, focused stare in Shakti's eyes, but they weren't focused on Beckie's look. She figured she was completely back when the memory of being spun by the blow on her arm resurfaced.

She tried to look around without moving her head, since it was connected to her neck, and thus to the ache that was her shoulder and arm. Well, if I want to see the clean white ceiling, I'm okay. She tried to rock her head; it didn't move. The pressure on her ears was more substantial than she'd thought. Before she could attempt to raise her head, a hand reached in and as it touched her forehead, she saw a nurse's face at her side.

"Hello. Don't move, please. I've called Doctor Krishna."

"Okay, thanks." The nurse was one she'd met while sitting with Ian. Mid to late forties, Beckie thought. She tried to dredge the woman's name from her head. "I'm sorry, but I don't remember…"

"Josie," the nurse said. "Don't worry about it. The sedatives haven't worn off, yet."

Beckie heard the door click, and people scuffling, moving.

"Good job," Beckie heard Millie say. She rolled her eyes around to see what the doctor meant, but nothing seemed different. Wait, Shakti's right there.

"What?" she mumbled.

"You be still." That was Shakti. Her voice was softer than Beckie'd expected; it was a welcome surprise. Maybe I'll be able to move.

She felt the restraints slide away at the same time the sheet lifted away from her chest. "Hey—"

"Be still! Just a couple of minutes while Shakti checks your arm. Hush!" Millie commanded as Beckie took a breath.

"I don't feel much," Beckie said. "What's that mean?" She rolled her head so she could see her hand, proving her arm was still attached.

Shakti was again not interested in Beckie's question; her eyes and hands were both at Beckie's biceps. However, as she worked, Beckie heard her soft voice, "Good. The anesthetic is still blocking most of the pain. Don't worry..." She gave Beckie the briefest of quick glances. "... you'll miss it when it's gone."

In another few minutes, Shakti asked Josie to help her help Beckie sit up while she examined the back of the arm. "Well." She came around to stand beside Beckie's hip. Millie was across the bed. Beckie smiled at them and at Josie, at the foot. Shakti returned the smile. "Everything seems just as we wish. The incisions are healing, well, for twelve hours old, at least." She faced Josie. "If you roll the portable X-ray in, we'll make sure the bones haven't moved."

As the nurse left, Shakti said, "I remember how much detail you like with your treatment..." Beckie blushed at the big grin both the doctors gave her. "... so I'll keep this low tech. Since the wound went through, the tissue damage isn't as bad as it would have been with a soft-nose bullet. I can't tell if the bullet hit the bone, or it broke when you hit the ground, but Millie thinks the fragments argue the bone was hit. By the bullet," she answered Beckie's look of confusion. "We cleaned everything up as best we could and put an external fixator on it. That will allow me to make sure the wound heals while still supporting the arm."

"What's an ext... what did you call it?"

"External fixator. This." Shakti lifted the sheet covering Beckie's arm from shoulder to forearm.

Beckie gasped. She wanted to cry. She wanted to scream. A piece of metal like an i-beam stood about an inch and a half from the skin of her arm. Where the skin showed, at least. But the part that turned her stomach was the half-dozen pins driven into her to hold the beam. Or really, I guess, she thought, fighting the nausea, it's holding them.

"Oh." She gagged once before Millie waved and Shakti dropped the covering green cloth. Millie placed a hand behind her head and offered a cup with a mouthful of water. She sipped and swirled the cool feeling before swallowing. "Thanks. Seriously. How long will I have to be a Transformer? And will it heal right?"

"Being a Transformer has some advantages. So far, we haven't put any plates or rods inside, because when we got everything lined up, the fragments moved into place, except for a couple we removed, and with Mathilde getting the splint on quick and Jan being careful, well, my expectation is you'll heal just fine. Several weeks for the fixator, though. Another thing. With it, you'll be able to move more. That'll help the rehabilitation."

"Wow." Beckie took a deep breath, which reminded her she wanted to smell better, and soon. "Can I lie back now, for a second? Then—"

Josie opened the door and rolled a portable X-ray machine in.

"In a minute," Shakti said. "This will be faster while you're sitting up."

"Okay." She sighed. "I guess I won't be sleeping on that side for a while."

The doctors snapped several pictures before leaving Beckie in Josie's care.

"You know there are a bunch of people waiting to see you?"

"And I'm waiting to see them, too! But, can I get cleaned up some, first?"

The nurse laughed. "The women, it's always their first question. However, no, *you* can't. I will take you in and wash you top to bottom, keeping the arm dry."

"But…"

"No buts, Miss. Doctor Ardan would hand me my head if I let you do anything more strenuous than breathe today."

"Tomorrow?"

The nurse pulled the lovely green sheet off, exposing the shorts she'd dragged on when…

"What day is it?" Beckie asked.

"Com'on, slide into the chair." As Josie settled her in the wheelchair, she said, "Friday. About lunch time. Which reminds me, After we get you presentable, you need to eat."

Beckie had never been an invalid; she was thoroughly embarrassed for the whole of the next forty-five minutes. She was stripped, allowed to relieve herself—about the only thing I *could* do, she admitted later—helped to the seat in the shower and washed. That required perhaps twenty-five minutes; washing dried blood from her hair took the rest. That and dressing in one of the ugly pajama tops. The bottoms were pull-on drawstring pants, but the top went over her head and then around her belly. Velcro closures held it together, and Josie stuck one sleeve on her right arm. The bandaged left arm, mechanical contraption and all, hung out for everyone, including Beckie, to see.

"How shall we do your hair?"

Beckie snorted; she almost spit the mouthful of water she'd just taken. Here I'm worried about the Tin Man being jealous and Josie wants to put up my hair! "Can you pull it into a ponytail? We did get it all clean, right?"

"I'm sure we did." She quickly pulled the long chestnut tresses back and captured them in the elastic Beckie had worn before. She dropped it over Beckie's shoulder. "Here. You can check."

Beckie blushed. That's what Mom would have done, too. "I'm sorry, Josie. I didn't mean it that way."

"Good thing I didn't take it that way, then." She stepped back and cast a discerning eye at her charge. "You all covered up and ready to meet your public?" Beckie smoothed her pajamas and nodded. "Let's go."

As Josie pushed her out of the bathroom, Beckie noticed the bed had been remade with clean, though still green, linens and had been cranked up so she could sit. It took a minute and heavy breathing on Beckie's part to install her and pull the sheet over her legs.

As she relaxed, eyes closed, the door snicked and she heard people enter. She opened her eyes to see Ian's face. And Mike coming up on her other side. Lissa peered in behind him; Beckie felt her lips curve automatically in response to Lissa's faint grin. Her eyes swung back to Ian. "Sorry I screwed up, love."

Ian said nothing. She allowed her eyes to close, to keep her tears inside. With them closed, she felt something brush her lips; she peeked to see Ian kissing her. The hand on her forehead kept her from joining as forcefully as she wanted, but her tongue wasn't restricted. After a moment, Ian pulled back. There's the smile I love!

"Okay, you've all seen her." Josie said. "Back up a little. She's hungry and lunch is here."

After Beckie had forced as much lunch in as she felt likely to stay, she gave Ian a Can-you-get-rid-of-this look. He smiled and pulled the over-bed table away.

"Thanks. It was good, but that's enough for now." She used her good arm to sit up a little straighter. "Okay, I know my situation. What about Shalin? And Amy? And… and everyone. I noticed bruises on Millie's face; what's that about?" She sighed and reached for her ponytail. "Sure hope everyone's okay."

Ian's expression wasn't as rueful as she'd expected. Hope that's a good thing. If I'm the only one…

"Your injury is the worst the team suffered, and Doctor Krishna believes you will recover fully."

"But there are other injuries?"

"Indeed. You are aware of Shalin; she also will recover fully. Her wound did not affect her bones or major blood vessels. Amy Rose… Amy Rose and her young man assisted Bethany and Elena in keeping Millie from worse than cuts and bruises. Dylan? Is that his name?" She nodded, wondering what might have happened to him. "He and Amy

Rose both suffered beatings, he more than she although according to Millie and Josie, the results damaged her more than him."

"What… what do you mean? Did my getting shot—"

"No, not at all. Our best estimate, based on what everyone recalls, is that the men on Bon Secours had been directed to avoid the hospital and the Administration building, and seek individuals who could inform them of the location of the gold and the video tapes. Failing that, where Ms Rochambeau might be found."

Beckie's gasp echoed in her ears. "They're *still* looking for her? Com'on! They can't be that stupid."

"No, but the men attacking certainly believed she could be found and questioned. Perhaps…"

"Perhaps what?"

"I thought for a moment the principals might expect she had died, but wish us to believe, as you said, they are foolish. I do not believe that, however. They were unaware."

"Were?"

"Shen exclaimed she was dead when one of the men told him of their goal."

"Oh. Well, I guess I'd have done the same thing."

"Indeed." He paused to gaze out the window, then went to the small in-room refrigerator. "Would you like a juice or water?"

"I'm good," She said as she tipped her head at the bottle on the table beside her. "So I couldn't have had any effect?"

"I think that is accurate."

"So, Millie, then? Worse than the bruises I saw?"

"I think not. Doctor Krishna gave her first aid once she'd finished with you, and she indicated the only other concern was that Millie had lost consciousness briefly after a blow, but earlier today, her concern had been allayed.

"No one else of the team reported more than bumps and scuffs."

"How many were there?"

"One who had beguiled Shen and Rou into a position in the security force, and eleven or twelve more. We have ten in Shen's lock-up; they will be transferred to Nassau for processing by Customs and Immigration."

Beckie'd been counting as Ian spoke. "That leaves one, two or three?"

"The man who'd snuck into Shen's force hanged himself once he provided the attackers the information they required. Kevin, along with Mr. Daniels and Samuel, ran one and perhaps two others off in the direction of Matthew Town."

"Wow! Oh, and señor Gomez? Almost forgot him. Is he okay?"

"He is fine. Also, he is anxious to meet with us." I love that look of, interest? curiosity? on Ian's face. He threw a glance at Josie before refocusing on Beckie. "When… How long…"

Josie's gaze bounced from Ian to Beckie and back before she excused herself and left.

"I'll bet either Millie or Shakti will be here. Soon." Beckie snickered. "Not today, I'm afraid. The drugs haven't worn off if I think rousting either of them is funny."

"Indeed." However, Beckie noticed his lips curving slightly.

"Actually, I'll bet by tomorrow I'll need something to take my mind off the pain. If it's as much as Josie was warning me."

"We will—"

The door slammed open. Beckie's gasp died when she saw Millie's look of embarrassment. "Sorry. I didn't mean to make quite so audible an entrance. Josie tells me you were discussing Beckie going back to work?"

Both Beckie and Ian nodded, Ian more contritely than Beckie. A little scuffle drew Beckie's attention; Melissa and Mike were easing toward the door. She gave them a nod and mouthed "Come back later, please." Melissa nodded.

"We already decided today is not the day for me to do any thinking, Millie." She smoothed the sheet. "You'll let me go home tomorrow, right?"

"If this was a for-profit operation, probably. But it'd be better for you to stay here a couple more nights." She apparently correctly read Beckie's expression. "If you're careful, I'll let you out during the day, as long as the pain isn't too bad." She patted Beckie's leg under the sheet. "We'll reconsider Monday."

Beckie grimaced, then looked at Ian. No help there. "If you insist. A better question for me to ask might be when will I be able to think?"

Millie chuckled before saying, "You might be a little fuzzy this afternoon, but you should be okay tomorrow." She giggled. "No, I won't say that."

Beckie gave her a look she hoped would telegraph her confused feelings.

"However," Millie continued, "no matter how you feel about medicine, you will be better off if you take the pain killers Shakti prescribed. Before the pain gets a foothold." She picked up the bottle of tablets on the bedside table and read the label. "Yeah." She turned to Ian. "Will you make sure she takes them? I don't want to see her doubled over vomiting because of pain."

"I will do my best," he said, squeezing Beckie's hand.

"These won't affect your mental processes. Josie will start you on them this evening when the blocks should begin to fade." She eyed both of them. "I'll be back later to check on you." She opened the door much more quietly than before and slipped out.

"Will Gomez be able to stay?"

"Yes. We planned to return mid next week. I know—"

"I still don't trust him. He rubs me the wrong way, laughing all the time. And wiping his face." She stared at her hands, right holding the left in her lap. "I know that's a lousy reason to judge a person, but he…" She trembled. "Yeah, he makes me feel like that."

"I have some sympathy for that opinion." But your face doesn't show it, Beckie thought. I'd better base my likes and dislikes on actual, you know, facts and actions. "We can meet tomorrow morning. Rather than take extraordinary measures to move you for a few hours, we will talk to Gomez in Shen's conference room."

Beckie smiled. "That's not my choice, but in my medicated state, it's probably for the best." She grimaced as she reached for his hand. "Probably I shouldn't be swimming anytime too soon."

The door opened and Josie returned. With a smile, she walked over to Beckie's bedside. "While we have a minute, I'll explain to you both about the fixator. First, you'll have it until the external wounds heal, three or four weeks, probably, unless you're particularly quick or slow healing. We'll take pictures to see how the bone is doing, and Doctor Krishna will decide when she wants to take the fixator off and replace it with a normal cast. So that's what's coming up.

"Now, keeping the pins clean."

For the next fifteen minutes, Josie instructed both Beckie and Ian in the care of her arm.

When she finished, she looked at Beckie's face, now drawn more than it had been. "One of these with water."

Beckie made a rude gesture, but immediately took it back. "I apologize. Uncalled for and… I don't know what else." Her gaze dropped to her hands again. "Sorry."

The nurse waved the words away as she had the gesture. She handed Beckie the pill and a small cup of water. "I think it's a good sign you're getting feisty."

Beckie swallowed, but Josie was already out the door.

"Thank you for making the effort to… ask pardon," Ian said softly. When Beckie looked up, his eyes wanted to say more.

"It was uncalled for, especially after all she's done. All the whole of Millie's crew have done for me. When I was stupid enough to step out there."

"What happened?"

She leaned on her good arm, rolling away from him, just a little. "I saw movement across the runway, and I stepped out from the shadow to see what it was. I did a short sweep, west to east, but there seemed to be nothing." She rolled back and raised her hand to rub her forehead. "I thought the danger would be from the buildings. Never the bush across the way. I actually thought it might be Trillian."

"Trillian was on Port, if we accept the evidence of one of the invaders. He suffered slashes which Millie ascribed to her claws."

"I'll thank her myself. Has anyone seen her?"

"Boynton took it upon himself to walk Port, through all the underbrush she loves. He found her, uninjured and, if I may use Josie's word, feisty."

"Cool! And how is Shalin?"

"You and Shalin are both lucky—"

"Lucky!" She swung her legs off the bed and grabbed his arm with hers. "I damn sure don't feel lucky with this piece of ironwork sticking out of my arm!" She dropped her hand. "I'll bet Shalin doesn't feel lucky either."

"Indeed. The word is relative. Had it been one of our shooters, your arm would be gone."

"Huh?"

"When Elena went to check yesterday, she found the rifle was loaded for, 'paper punching,' she said. Targets," he said responding to Beckie's incredulous look. "Fully jacketed rounds. While the shooter was a marksman, he was obviously unaware those cause far less damage in flesh."

"So, we don't use them?"

"No. When we use weapons, the goal is to bring the enemy down with no casualties to our side." He ran a finger along her chin. "You were down but not disabled. Had no one been available to assist you, you would have used the weapon you were carrying."

"I don't know, Ian. It hurt like hell."

"If the attacker was running at you and Michael had no weapon? Or Amy Rose?"

"Or you," she whispered. "Even if it killed me."

He pressed her head back and kissed her. "Rest now. I will be here."

Her sleep was fitful, but each time she opened her eyes, Ian was sitting beside her. Once, she recalled, he'd given her another tablet and helped her sip enough water to gulp it down.

SUNDAY

Beckie awoke Sunday morning to find Ian waiting patiently. A shower, and dressing, and she was ready for the day's meetings. Ian drove her wheelchair to the Admin building, but Beckie stood and walked in and to the conference room. "Woof," she whooshed her breath out. "Harder than I thought. And that's only two days lying on my back!"

Ian smiled sympathetically as he brought her a bottle of water, then seated himself beside her.

"So, what's the agenda?"

"Wide and varied, as suits you," he replied, his smile morphing into a large grin.

Beckie felt her forehead wrinkle and forced a more neutral expression. "And that means?"

"Ms Ardan and her friend asked to visit with you. Millie says Amy Rose views you as the 'big sister she never had,' and... Well, I will allow her to speak for herself. Elena will join us to discuss the recordings you sent from Brewster, and finally, señor Gomez. He wishes to speak with us about Mamani, and we agree you should be included."

Beckie took the bottle and drank several swallows. "I hope you brought the meds."

He nodded. "It is not yet time, however. If this is too much—"

"No! No, that's not a problem." She reached across to take his hand. "Yet, at least. Just making sure. Thanks."

She had barely finished when Shen opened the door and ushered Millie in, followed by Amy and Dylan.

It took only moments for Amy and Dylan to ask for Beckie's help in remaining together under more acceptable terms than she just moving to Chatham or he to the Nest, which options the parents had dismissed out of hand. But it took past lunch for Beckie to describe and then convince first Amy, then Dylan and finally Millie, of their joint best option. "Amy, you move to my place in Coral Gables. Where you'll attend public high school. One weekend out of four, you two will spend in Coral Gables. With me. Holidays, you both will spend in Chatham with Dylan's family or here at the Nest, alternating."

"But… Why?" Amy straightened in her chair, then sagged as Beckie watched. Dylan clutched her hand, but he looked lost, too. "Why?" Amy said. "I mean, it's great and wonderful of you and all, but… what'll it do to Mom?"

Beckie flashed a glance at Millie, whose astonishment was clear. At Amy's concern? "To be brutally honest, I think it will relieve her." Millie nodded, slowly at first and more firmly as Beckie continued. "That'll make her feel even more inadequate, so we'll have to work on that. That's the reason you'll come back home here every weekend except when Dylan visits."

"But… No, I don't get it. Am I stupid?"

"No. It's simple to me. The only reason not to let you and Dylan live together or get married or whatever is because we all think you both need more life experience first. Especially you. I have no idea how you could get peer experience if you stay here. This is the best way I can think to have you learn and still have time together."

"But… How?"

Beckie looked around the room. Yeah, I guess it makes more sense to me than everyone else. Except Ian. He's got that little I-know-what-you're-doing smile. That's good! She grabbed Amy's hand—the one Dylan wasn't clutching— and drew her closer. "By putting you in high school there. Socializing you. Same thing Dylan will be doing in Chatham."

"But… But what if I find someone else? Or he does?"

"Then you will. The whole point of kids growing up is they learn things, and they meet people. They figure out what they want to do, and who they want to do it with. And who they don't want to do it with."

Amy stood and came around behind Beckie's chair. "Okay. So how do we keep Mom from feeling like she's being replaced?"

Beckie reached her good hand up to take Amy's again. "You tell me."

She fidgeted for a minute or more, then wandered around the room without making any eye contact Beckie could see. Looking out the window, she said, "By keeping her a part of what's going on." She turned back to face her mother. "That's why I come back weekends." She snorted a little laugh. "I think I'll need a new computer just for Skype."

Beckie laughed. "If that's all you need…"

"Yeah. Now you can tell me why you're doing this."

"I told you before. You're my sister."

"Hmm."

"You'll do it for someone else." Beckie turned the sternest look she could manage on Dylan. "This applies to you, too, Dylan. It'll be easier, I hope, since you'll be with your family more, but don't forget them while you're all-the-time calling and messaging and Skyping with Amy. And studying, too, I hope." Internally, she grinned, but kept her unrelenting expression facing the two teens. "Grades *will* be reported. Minimum standards apply. Got it?" Dylan nodded, carefully enough that Beckie could believe he meant it. Amy's face had gone from lips curved up, though compressed and ended slightly down-turned at the warning. Beckie was about to respond when Amy's face flashed into a smile. "That's right, girl. Benefits accrue to those who earn them."

Amy turned her smile to Dylan. "We've got a chance, Dylan. We won't screw it up, right?"

His answer involved a warmer, somewhat longer embrace and kiss than some adults felt appropriate. When she thought it sufficient, Beckie laughed and said, "Okay. Sit back down. Your parents, Dylan. Can you ring them up?"

In twenty more minutes his parents, like Millie, had decided Beckie's plan improved the odds the couple wouldn't do a bunk and declared Amy would be welcome in their home on the holiday plan Beckie laid out. They had pressed for a one-in-five week schedule for visiting weekends in Coral Gables, but relented when Beckie proposed the one-in-four be moved to include special occasions, dances for example, instead of being in addition to them. Neither Amy nor Dylan were pleased with that compromise, but accepted it.

"Amy and I will bring Dylan home, probably tomorrow," Beckie told Dylan's parents, "if I'm cleared to travel. Amy's mom will come along, too, so everyone will at least have met. Tomorrow night, we'll stay at Eilís O'Bannon's house rather than fill your home with strangers."

"I'll call tomorrow morning with final details, Mom. Thanks from the bottom of my heart!" Dylan clicked the disconnect icon and Shen closed the laptop.

As Dylan offered a hand to Amy and Millie, Ian looked around, taking attendance, Beckie guessed. "Who should we invite for señor Gomez' session?"

"I doubt Millie or Dylan would add anything," Beckie said. "Or Amy, either."

Ian nodded, and from the doorway, Amy said, "If you change your mind, Mom will know where we are."

Beckie turned to Ian. "Can Elena go over the stuff I sent before he gets here? I'm still not comfortable with Gomez." He wrinkled his brow at her, adding a one-sided smile. "Yeah, I know," she replied, "I'm pushing because he makes me… I don't know. Uncomfortable?"

Ian nodded. "Perhaps due to his temperament? Not his heritage, I hope."

She nodded. "No! Not that. I don't know…" She closed her eyes and frowned. "I also remember thinking I need to get over that." With a toss of her head, she continued, "I'd still like to hear Elena's report first."

"Very well." He rose from the chair and went to find Elena.

"I did several translations," Elena said. "I have verified parts of them with others I trust, and the consensus is they are accurate, by which I mean it's the same as another reader would understand. First, the audio clip—"

"That's from the audio cassette Beckie sent, right?" Shen said.

She nodded. "Else concurs this is the long version of the tape Amy found in Abby's bag—"

"The one I gave O'Bannon, right?"

"Yes. It is a recording of a meeting between two men." She referred to her notes. "Señors Talos and Huamán. They discuss the weather and then a delivery. Huamán spends a long time trying to get Talos to tell him he has it, whatever 'it' is, before they come to terms on the payment. Huamán asks about the Argentum Dei, and Talos agrees it is quite satisfactory. They make arrangements to meet at 7:15 the next evening in a park off 42nd Street to consummate the transaction."

"Argentum Dei?" Beckie said. "What's that?"

"Earnest money," Ian said. "A deposit. From the discussion, Huamán had earlier sent Talos a sample of the gold."

"So," Elena continued, "that transcript is here..." She tapped a small pile of papers. "... if you want to read it."

Ian reached across and slid them to Beckie. "Our opinion is the recording, in and of itself, means nothing. However, since Talos' defense claimed Talos and Huamán were unknown to each other, this would put a strain on that claim, much more than the fragment you passed along to Ms O'Bannon."

"Uh-huh. So, since we found this in that safe deposit, seemingly connected to Goldfarb and Talos, and the key was sent from Peru... That might imply some one there supports him."

"It might also suggest a form of payment for services rendered," Ian said.

"Oh," Beckie said, her voice hushed. "Or to be rendered. That opens up a raft of choices, doesn't it?"

"Indeed it does."

"How about a drink of water and then Elena can go over the next batch."

With a smile, Elena reached into her case and withdrew a second stack of papers. Unlike the first, this stack looked to be an inch thick; Beckie then noticed it was clipped together with a metal binder strip. Elena slid it across to Beckie.

"Whoa!" She flipped the first few pages, then raised her head to stare at Elena. "How about the Cliff's Notes version? Please?"

Elena gaped for a second before she covered her mouth, laughing. "Okay." She composed herself. "This is the transcript of the video you sent, and the translation."

Beckie was on the edge of her chair, waiting. Ian moved his chair closer and gently nudged her away from the table. She glanced at him and smiled, then relaxed as he continued to rub her back. "Sorry. Little tense, I guess."

"That's okay," Elena said. "The combined video shows several meetings of a group consisting of at least Mamani and four men. The thrust of the meetings, until the last one, was how to force the Ministry of Justice to ignore campaign violations of one Jaime Lobera, one of their number. Unstated was the implication all of them might face similar charges. In the last meeting, Mamani and Mateo Huamán agreed—they'd disagreed earlier—the effort should be dropped, since the Justice Minister had publicized Lobera's upcoming arrest." Elena looked around at them all. "This is a real abbreviated version, since Ian told me it matches what Mamani told you when you met."

"Wow." Beckie faced Ian. "How much did you guys talk about this? And how'd you keep it quiet?"

"Ms Rios and I had a cryptic discussion before we left, and a more transparent one aboard the plane returning. We would have included you when we arrived, but—"

"But I was having too much fun entertaining everyone. Yeah. Okay. Hmm. Could I have another water, please?" Shen spun in his chair and took a bottle from the cooler. As Ian took it from him, Beckie continued, "Thanks. That was then. How'd it go?"

Elena shrugged. "As you say, that was at least five years ago, dating from some of the things they reference."

Ian continued, "You recall she gave us her word the attempt was abandoned. We have no evidence she lied. The member of the group they were protecting was tried and convicted, which argues their efforts bore no fruit."

"I thought I recalled that."

Elena tapped the binder. "Her plan… One of the supporters was Piero Salvadore—"

"He was in that meeting with Mamani, right? It is the same one?"

"It is," Elena agreed. "He is now the Minister of the Interior and probably Mamani's chief competition for the Presidency. He's a mining magnate with holdings in at least one gold operation. He pledged to siphon up to a thousand kilos of refined gold for the cause."

Beckie was trying to remember gold's price when Shen said, "Something north of 25 million euros. Or over a hundred-million *neuvos soles*, today, if I calculated correctly."

Beside Beckie, Ian nodded. Beckie tried to close her mouth. "Once?" she finally stammered.

"That was the initial investment, as Mamani described it. We haven't any idea if it was to continue, or even if any of the gold pledged was delivered."

"What about Huamán's bullion? The bars we have. Where'd those come from?"

"Not from this. Both Gomez and Mamani are adamant Huamán's gold actually came from her. Which may have come from the same source," Elena admitted, "but Huamán was opposed. He stomped out, according to the video."

Beckie reached for her hair and began twirling it one-handed. "Wait. Mamani's trying to buy justice for a friend, and someone stole the video of it. Huamán's against Mamani's idea. But later, he's killed in New York trying to buy the evidence back? Why am I confused?" She rubbed her eyes and forehead. "Is this supposed to make sense?"

"Well," Ian replied softly, "it makes little sense to us, either."

"Does Gomez know about this?"

"We're pretty sure he knows some of this," Elena said, "but not from us. That's the reason Ian and I spoke in code while we were in Peru. And it's the reason we brought him here. So we could broach it to him without any prying ears to contend with. But it seems like it's an urban legend in Peru, if you get what I mean?"

"Got it." She raised the water bottle and drank. "Could it be Huamán didn't know what Mamani was asking him to buy?"

"Can't tell for sure, though that's a possibility I like. Ian's not as happy with it, though."

Beckie turned to Ian. "Why not?"

"He is in the video, and Mamani told us he was one of the co-conspirators, until he 'stomped out.' The only way he would not know what the deal involved, I believe, is that he was unaware Mamani had sent him, that it was her gold. I believe he was using Mamani's gold to acquire the videos and present them to her to destroy. Or to reveal them himself, to discredit her."

"Could either of those have been a motive for Talos to kill him?"

"That seems less likely," Ian said. "Of course, if we uncover evidence Mamani feared Huamán might reveal them, all bets are off."

Beckie relaxed and gave him a big grin. "Indeed! Elena, how good are your translations? Not to impugn your work, but you're not a native Peruvian."

Elena waved off Beckie's explanation as she smiled. "Right, I'm not. And I wasn't going to have anyone down there be privy to the contents. So, there's a risk. I think it's small."

"Yeah, I knew that already, I guess. Thanks for tolerating me. What else is there?"

"Everything else is how the plan would be put together. Nothing else."

"Hmm. Do we have any idea how Talos got hold of that stuff?"

Ian got up and went to the cooler for a bottle of water. As he did, he said, "None. Of course, we would not expect it to be contemporaneous with the meeting described there, but I was hoping for a hint. Some contact, or…"

"Is that… Well, first, is that something we think Gomez might have an insight to? And second, does it matter? I mean, he got the stuff. Now, we have the stuff. And…" She turned sharply to face Ian, bumping her injured arm on the table "Oww! Damn! I really have to be more careful." When she recovered, she said, "What difference does any of this mean to us?"

Ian had reached when she'd cried out, but settled back. "If this subversion continues," he said after a brief pause, "I would terminate our contract. I can see no justification for supporting this kind of…

oppression? Not exactly, but still, not in the best interest of the Peruvian people."

"Yeah. I guess I have some reading to do on the plane." She touched the binder. "When I'm not refereeing Amy and Millie, anyway."

Ian almost chuckled. "Indeed," he said. "How long do you believe you will stay?"

"Overnight, unless something comes up." Beckie excused herself; when she returned, she said, "Is it time for one of my meds? Beginning to ache again."

Ian looked at his watch and nodded as he opened the bottle and spilled a capsule to the table.

Beckie swallowed it with the end of her water and sat down again. "If we give Gomez all this..." She patted the binders. "... he's gonna want some time to read and absorb it. So going to Chatham is probably a good plan from that perspective, too."

"I will ask Boynton to bring him over, then."

Beckie nodded.

In half an hour, a knock on the door heralded Boynton's arrival with Philip Gomez. They both entered and took seats across from Beckie and Ian, closest to Shen on the right and Elena on the left.

"Good afternoon, señor Gomez." Ian said. "I appreciate your patience while we resolved our issues with an invasion, then waiting for Rebecca to regain her faculties."

"It is my pleasure," he said. While he had still wiped his forehead twice since arriving, Beckie was happy he'd stifled his non-funny laughter. So far, anyway. "I appreciate the opportunity to visit this lovely place, and hope to assist you as you will assist me." His English was not quite perfect, but his accent was pleasant to hear now that Beckie wasn't focusing on his behavior. "I hope you and the other lady injured will soon recover completely. Have you discovered the motive behind the attack? I hope it was nothing to do with the work you prosecute for us."

"Thank you, señor." Beckie laughed softly. "I appreciate your wishes, and heartily second them."

"I suppose you do. But, please, call me Philip."

"Very well," Ian said. "Ms Saunders and I asked you to leave your home to visit us here, thinking it would be safe, for which I apologize, but more importantly, so we could speak with you on a matter of urgency which I did not wish anyone to overhear, either inadvertently or surreptitiously."

Gomez smiled. "Yes. Our police and Interior Ministry have some small capability of that sort."

Ian nodded, then continued, "Ms Rios has done yeoman service in transcribing and then translating a video from a meeting some five or six years ago." Elena slid a binder, twin of the one she'd given Beckie, over the table to Ian. "Our interpretation is that Nayra Mamani was then embarked on a mission to corrupt the enforcement of campaign financing laws in your country." Beckie watched Gomez carefully, but there was no shock in his expression. Ian had apparently noticed the same thing. "You do not appear surprised by this news."

"No, it has been rumored she sought recordings of a meeting like that."

"I have to assume you didn't raise this issue with, well, with anyone, I guess," Beckie said. "Why not? Is campaign financing too insignificant for the law to matter? And why not advise us when we were discussing whether or not we should support her efforts to be elected?"

"My conversations with my employer are my own, and hers. I would not reveal this to an outside party. It is an internal problem."

"Hmmf." Beckie forced herself to make a fist with her injured hand; to allow the pain to defuse her anger. Not worth telling us! She squeezed a little harder, but Ian noticed and stroked her good hand. The contact was enough; she relaxed and took a deep breath. "Thanks for your candor, señor. Which is not to say I approve or even understand." This time, she rose and went to the cooler, but Shen had a bottle of juice ready when she got there. She nodded and thanked him.

Ian watched her return before he said, "We are disappointed in your position, although I believe I understand it. It puts me in an uncomfortable position, as I have committed to señora Mamani I would return the videos if we recovered them."

From her seat behind the bottle of orange juice, Beckie watched Gomez' face collapse. He's scared to death of that. There's something going on we don't understand. Or me, at least, she thought as Ian continued, "Since you do not wish the recordings' existence, apocryphal until this moment, revealed to outsiders, what would you have me do with them?"

"Yeah," Beckie interjected. "If you don't want them revealed, why don't you want Mamani to have them? Seems like she'd be real happy to destroy them as soon as she could."

"The video must be revealed, but the circumstances must be opportune."

"And what would be 'opportune?'" Ian said. "Why would I not merely send it to, for example, the BBC, Al Jazeera, *Canal* N, *El Peruano, El Comercio* and *La República?*"

"What about your commitment to Mamani?"

"Come now, señor. It is unconscionably easy to create a copy of this material and send it to arrive the day after she and I complete our agreement."

Gomez nodded, but he didn't look any happier. "You want to be the one to reveal this," Beckie said. "Why? What do you gain by doing so?"

"She can do good, important work," Gomez said. "She leads the field. If she is forced to withdraw, who would be elected?" Ian shook his head and Beckie knew she had no clue about Peruvian politics. Gomez rubbed his hand over his hair. "That's always the case, isn't it? The devil you know or the devil you don't. While Ms Saunders and Mr Quinn are at loose ends, you might have them look into opposition leaders. While I have distaste for some things Mamani has done, I believe she is the lesser of several evils."

"So how would giving them to you differ from giving them to her?"

"Because I can hold them over her."

Beckie couldn't hold her guffaw in, although she smothered it quickly. "That's a short trip to pushing up daisies, as we say. You can't imagine after all this, once she knows where they are, she wouldn't move heaven and earth to get her hands on them. I didn't mark you as a stupid man, but this… this is just… it's beyond the ken." Beckie stopped for a breath. "In fact, except it was so poorly executed and I'm certain no one outside this room knows what we have here, I'd worry the attack on Thanksgiving was an effort to recover them." She looked at Ian and then Shen. "Does that seem reasonable?"

They nodded, though Shen less confidently than Ian.

"In fact," Ian said, "according to one of the participants, the raid was intended to achieve that as a primary goal." Oh! He never mentioned *that*. "As Rebecca intimated, they had no certainty the video was here, but had no other place to search."

Ian shrugged, then stretched. "Very well. Before we talk further, I ask you to study these translations so you can share your opinion of their accuracy. The possibility Ms Rios made a significant error is small but present. I would value your thoughts. I continue to request you not contact anyone other than one of us."

Elena took a cassette from her case and set it atop the binders, which Ian handed to Gomez. "A copy," Ian said. "Shen will bring a player—"

"Ms Meyer brought it over prior to your call," Boynton said. "We had a few moments of interesting repartee concerning its use, which has now been rendered obsolete."

Beckie chuckled. I know how *that* feels.

"Indeed. We will adjourn until Tuesday evening unless there is a pressing need to meet earlier. Rebecca is traveling and will return then. The Nest will be at full force later tonight, as vacationers return. Thank you all."

"Mr. Jamse, must we await Miss Rebecca's return?"

"I am uncertain of your meaning. The answer is no, we need not. However, unless something seems critical, my preference is to include her in these discussions." He nodded to Beckie. "Especially as she has gained a rapport with the señora. On the other hand, we can begin earlier if it makes you easy."

"Ah. I understand."

Beckie smiled. "Maurice has games in addition to chess. You might find them interesting if you find yourself bored. As Ian said, my plan is to be back Tuesday, but please don't let my absence stop you asking questions or proposing solutions when they occur to you. You and Ian can acquaint me with those on my return."

With a nod of thanks, and a smile from Boynton, he and Gomez left.

Beckie sagged in her chair, but straightened when Ian's discomfort became obvious. "I'm okay, love, really." She ran her hand through her hair. "I am so mad at him. Not wanting to tell us, or even hint to us. Damn!" She got up to throw the empty juice container in the trash, but it bounced off the rim. "Sorry," she said as she grabbed it and dropped it in. "I understand his reasoning, but I don't like it. We have people, good people, who might be at risk because he… he wants to be all the hero and get himself killed!"

"Our people were not at risk." He shot a quick glance at Elena; she was clearly in agreement.

TUESDAY

Taking Dylan home was completely uneventful; the thirty hours were even pleasant, Beckie reflected on the way home. Fortunately, Amy seemed to bond well with Dylan's family.

Back at the Nest, Ian took her to the lanai where Boynton, obviously alerted by Karen or perhaps Jannike, had laid a light dinner for her. "No wine?" she asked.

"I've been advised the interaction of alcohol and the pain relievers you are taking is not beneficial, so, no. You may have sparkling water."

She smiled and nodded. "That's fine. This all looks great." His specialty, a bright conch salad, tasted as good as it appeared and she did it justice.

About ten, she poured another glass of San Pellegrino and gazed across the table at Ian, watching all together too amusedly. "Are we ready?

I am. If we wait, I'll fall asleep after that dinner. Thank you, Maurice," she said as he removed the remaining dishes and utensils. "That hit the spot. Any coffee?"

She heard his "In a moment," as he left the lanai.

"He will invite Gomez to join us while the coffee is brewing."

Beckie nodded and took Ian's hand. "Anything I should know to start with?"

"Nothing. Our conversations were exceedingly mundane." He smiled. "I believe he took our request to involve you at its face. Perhaps I should have traveled with you."

"*Now* you say that! It would have been so nice with you there, too. Though I'm sure Millie would've had strong warnings about… things," she finished as Gomez and Boynton entered.

"Indeed," he said with a laugh, then invited Gomez to sit. Boynton laid out the coffee; Beckie immediately helped herself.

After all the little motions and greetings had settled, Beckie placed her cup on its saucer and gazed at Gomez. "Thanks for your patience, Philip. I appreciate it. I assume you've discussed the translation with Ian, and based on Elena not being here, it is accurate."

He nodded. "While there may be tiny discrepancies, there is nothing that affects the meaning Ms Rios ascribed."

"Good," Beckie said. "Correct me if I'm wrong. You wish to take control of these videos and, without making them public, hold them to convince Mamani to do as you wish? Or prevent her from doing as she wishes?" She chewed her lip for a second. "I guess those are the same, defining what you want her to do."

He sat quiet, stoical. She sneaked a glance at Ian; he was quiet, too. Boynton, however, was smiling at her. Is that because I'm doing well, or I'm so far off he wants to laugh?

She took a drink before fixing Gomez with her stare again. "You ask us not to reveal this, and I'm not sure I understand why. According to you, everyone in Peru already knows… well, not knows, I guess, but suspects. Suspects so strongly they believe it."

"While as you say, everyone believes this, a… a whisper campaign unsupported by hard evidence will be ineffective. But if the recording becomes public," Gomez replied, "the Justice minister must react, and in such a way as to end Mamani's opportunity to be elected and her seat in Congress, even if no other legal action is taken."

"And what you want is that we should trust you to know what's right for the people of Peru?"

Gomez nodded. "I have been involved with them more than you—"

"Of course!" Beckie felt herself going nuclear again; she made a fist to bring herself down. As she felt Ian's hand cover hers, calm flooded her. With a smile that began in her toes, she leaned over and brushed her lips against his cheek.

"I beg your pardon, Philip," she said. "I acknowledge your far greater familiarity with your country. What I don't like, greater knowledge or not, is you acting as proxy for thirty million people, more or less. What evidence is there your understanding actually matches the majority of the people better than Mamani's? Or another candidate? Leaving aside for the nonce the idea you could successfully pull off your plan."

"How do I convince you?" He laid his hands on the table, palms down. "I have no evidence, as you say, my opinions should have more weight than any others.' It is a difficult position I have put you in. I apologize."

Ian squeezed Beckie's hand as he faced Gomez. "We appreciate that. You said earlier Mamani is, I believe, the lesser of several evils, those being the potential replacements were she to be eliminated from the candidate pool? I suppose the primary one of these must be Minister Salvadore?" Gomez nodded. "If you can do without sleep a bit longer?" He nodded again. "I would like to add Ms Saunders via teleconference. She has been working, investigating the candidates who she believes may be viable, and we may benefit from her work."

Boynton had already left; he now returned with a laptop which he laid on the table before Ian. "Skype should be up—"

The sound of the connection being made filled the lanai, and Ian adjusted the volume.

"As we discussed earlier, Barbara, señor Gomez is going to review the several leading politicians who might be viable candidates, especially if Mamani does not run."

"Good," Barbara said. "I'll try to find things to add."

For the next twenty-five minutes, Gomez listed politicians and his opinions of them. When he finished, Barbara added her own observations.

The two reports had more similarity than Beckie'd expected. Even the men, and one woman, Barbara had dismissed as unable to muster sufficient support, had a similar assessment from Gomez. That's kinda scary, but maybe he does have a handle on the situation there. But still, to speak for the majority of Peruvians? I just don't know.

While Barbara and Gomez disagreed about the individuals' chances to make their campaigns successful, there were no arguments on their suitability: none would be preferable to Mamani. Only one man on Barbara's list was judged by the two of them to be preferable to Mamani, and he hadn't made Gomez' list because "He has no chance of being elected!" Unfortunately, Barbara agreed with his assessment.

"At the end of the day," Gomez said, "none of these matter, I think. Do you agree, Barbara?"

"I do, unfortunately. Señor Salvadore and señora Mamani will almost certainly be the two facing each other in the final election."

Gomez merely nodded.

"What is your opinion of Salvadore?" Beckie asked. "Neither you nor Barbara discussed him."

"I omitted him because, I suppose, he is a known quantity, compared with the others."

"And you, Barbara?"

"I ignored him because, from the scuttlebutt I've heard, he's about the same as Mamani. Different in some ways, but overall, as far as Peru is concerned, some things would be better and some worse, and in twenty years, no one would be able to tell which one had been elected."

"It's always nice to think you're backing the top horse," Beckie said, laughing. "Things could be worse, I suppose. They could be at the bottom of the heap instead of the top."

"I cannot disagree with Barbara's comments," Gomez said. "And while Ms Rios ascribed no additional significance to it, Salvadore appears in the videos, also."

"Which gives him some motivation to find them himself." Beckie thought for a second, twirling her ponytail. "Mamani could hold them over him."

"Correct," came from both Barbara and Gomez, but the Peruvian's response was accompanied by a yawn.

"We have kept everyone awake too long." Ian said. "Thank you all for your assistance and—"

"Hang on," came from the computer.

"… patience. What is it, Barbara?"

"Sue and Rich just came in. The demonstrations from up north seem to be moving down here. I'll call you back when I have better info." The call ended message followed.

Beckie didn't like the expression on Ian's face, but with the news, or lack thereof, from Barbara it wasn't surprising. It was her turn; she took his hand and squeezed. He snapped around like he'd forgotten she was there, but she could see concern had overridden his mien, and he calmed.

"Trust me," he told her, and she nodded, mouthing "Always." Now, he smiled. "Philip, I offer you this option: I will hold the recordings. I will neither publicize them nor make any comment about their existence, except to señora Mamani, when she and I have the discussion you intended. As long as you know where the videos are, you should be free to resume your chosen career."

"Hmm. And under what circumstances would you consider changing that position?"

Ian glanced at Boynton. "Would coffee keep you out for more than a moment?" Boynton shook his head and left, and Ian said, "When he returns…" In another minute Boynton brought a coffee service to the table. "Thank you." He poured; as he did, he said, "I would change my position if Mamani becomes not the lesser of the evils, but the greater."

"Or she supports someone like that!"

"As Rebecca says. This would seem to fit your professed motive, would it not?"

Gomez leaned forward, running his hand through his hair. "Yes," he finally said. "Additionally, it removes the temptation for me to raise money through unsavory means, which is probably just as well." He laughed before sitting back in the chair. Boynton offered him a fresh coffee, but Gomez held his hands up. "No, thank you. It will ruin what little sleep I will get. Two assumptions: You will not change your mind. We will leave for home in the morning."

"Yes, to the first at least." Ian sipped from his cup. "To the second, probably. I will make that decision once Ms Saunders has called back." He drank and set the cup down. "In case you or another might be tempted, you should know the videos are not kept here."

Gomez nodded as he rose. "Thank you for the hospitality. And the information." Boynton went out with him.

Once they'd left, Ian turned his chair to face Beckie. "Would you like some?" When she nodded, he slid the service across and poured her a cup, stirring in a lump of sugar. Her raised eyebrow brought a snort of laughter before he said, "A few extra calories to compensate for lack of sleep."

"Well okay, if the caffeine doesn't work. What's the plan?"

He spun a little further, so his back was to the table, and his chair and Beckie's were side by side. He moved a few more inches to take her hand and observe her. "It does depend on Barbara's report. I do not wish…" Beckie tipped her head to Boynton, who had just entered. "Thank you," Ian said to him. "Bring a seat around here and join us." When he had, Ian continued, "I do not wish to have you away from here again so soon…" He reached to touch her lips, blocking her objections. "… but I also greatly desire your presence when we speak to Mamani. Even in our brief meetings, you two came to a quick rapport, and that may tip the balance."

Boynton nodded, which surprised Beckie until she recalled their friend had spent the past four days with Gomez and probably knew more about Peru than Wikipedia. Certainly about current events there, she thought.

"So," Ian said, gazing first at her and then at Boynton, "warn either Mathilde or Jean-Luc we may need to fly to Peru on short notice, please."

"If Mathilde's available, she made the trip last time," Beckie reminded him.

Again alone, Ian said, "I'm hopeful we can delay until day after tomorrow. That way, you will be able to see Millie tomorrow. Would you prefer to rest now?"

"I'll stay with you. I feel better with you beside me. Just holding me." Don't know why I have to justify myself.

He nodded. "Your opinion?"

"Of your offer?" He nodded. "Well, it's not exactly what I hoped for, but it might do the job."

As they walked to their room, Ian tucked Beckie into his side. "I have been thinking of Willie and his family."

Beckie was sure this was going someplace she should have expected and hadn't. She squeezed even closer. "In what regard?"

"You and Amy Rose will set up in Coral Gables. He has asked for the opportunity to move to the mainland temporarily, and since you told me you planned to return to school…"

As they reached the door, she stopped and stepped in front of him. "What? As a guard?" She leaned into him, then backed and opened the door. "I know he'd do it, but do you think that's what he wants to do? I mean, watching out for two wild teenaged girls in addition to his own family?"

She heard him behind her as she walked around to open the curtains overlooking the water. The moon had set, or hadn't risen—she didn't know which and wasn't bothered—and it was dark out there. The slider was open and she stepped onto the balcony lanai.

"Are you planning to use Skype when Barbara calls?"

He joined her, slipping an arm under her sling to hug her gently. "I had not considered one way or the other. Do you have a suggestion?"

"Yeah," she said with a giggle. "It's so warm, even now, compared with Chatham, and I swear, Karen had the AC set to hang meat in the plane. Help me undress and then sit with me out here."

"Should I worry about the consequences?"

With a laugh, she said, "No! Absolutely not! Damn the consequences! Full ahead; ramming speed, Mr. Sulu!"

Ian's chuckle warmed Beckie all over, and his hands undoing the buttons of her shirt and working her arm—with the three inch pins and support bar still decorating it—free gave her little quivers. When he kissed her bare skin, she clutched him to her and, finding it hard to breathe, managed to squeak, "So the iron work doesn't diminish my appeal too much?"

He raised his head from her breast to smile. "Never. Believe me, never."

As she raised herself to slip her shorts down her legs, Ian's phone rang with the discordant tone they both knew. "That'll be Barbara. Sit at the small table and I'll take your lap. Unless that will be too distracting?"

"If I can watch the wall, I can avoid distraction. Most distraction," he said as Beckie took his hand and ran it across her chest. He tipped her head back to kiss her lips and touched the phone. Damn, he's good! Only three rings.

"Good evening, Barbara. What is the situation?" He placed the phone on the table and touched the speaker icon.

"… not as bad as I feared when Rich and Sue came in, but not good. Willie's investigating the opposition in Arequipa, and they seem to be organizing to protest against Mamani, but later this week. Maybe the weekend, or because she's doggedly secular, maybe the eighth, the Immaculate Conception feast day."

"Not here," Beckie whispered in Ian's ear.

He convulsed to keep from laughing out loud and answered Barbara when she asked if he was okay, "I am fine, thank you. Rebecca is testing my humor reflex. Go ahead."

"Well, Rich would like some backup, and I agree with him. We'll talk to Willie again in the morning, but he's for lying low so far."

"I have confidence in the four of you. I will talk with Mathilde in the morning, but I expect we will travel Thursday morning. Should we plan to arrive at Mamani's headquarters?"

"We'll make that decision when you land in Lima. I'll have transport lined up, so we can go anyway we need to."

"That will work well. Check in tomorrow afternoon, or earlier should it prove useful."

They signed off, and Beckie felt good about caressing Ian once more.

WEDNESDAY

Morning was heralded not by the sun, though the sky was lightening when Beckie opened her eyes. Rather, the chill on her bare back roused her. What's Ian doing? she pouted to herself as she noticed the ache in her arm. Only then did the musical notes of Boynton's ring tone penetrate.

"Good morning," she heard Ian whisper. She rolled over and attempted to raise her injured arm so he would know she was awake. She wanted to hear at least his side of the conversation.

Not that it did her any good. "Very well. Fifteen minutes. Rebecca will be down later, so just coffee, please."

He replaced the phone and came to sit on the bed beside her. "Your choice of attire is intended to lure me away from señor Gomez." He leaned over and began a series of kisses Beckie wanted him to continue. "Unfortunately," he said as he straightened, "Boynton understands the pitfalls of a lovely, intelligent and sensual partner. If I do not appear, he will." With a final kiss, he drew the sheet up to her nose and went to find his clothes.

Beckie threw the sheet off with a laugh. "You can't get away that easily! What did you mean, 'Rebecca will be down later'?"

She could see he was doing his best to ignore her, but once he'd tucked in his shirt, he spun on the ball of his foot to… He's admiring me! That feels good!

"I must advise Gomez of Barbara's message, and our plans to leave. That should require less than twenty minutes." He glanced at his watch.

"I will return then, with coffee, and assist with your morning ablutions." He smiled as he approached. "If you permit?"

She used her good arm to grab his shirt front and drag him down to her lips. When she allowed him to rise, she said, "Of course I permit. But, may I have one pill before you go?"

"I didn't bump it?" She smiled at the barely disguised tinge of fear in his voice.

"No, silly. The last one's worn off, that's all."

Ian's word was good; twenty minutes after he left, he came through the door after knocking gently. When she made a quizzical face at him, he said "What?"

"It's *your* room. Why knock?" She giggled. "You don't expect I'd be in here in flagrant whatever that phrase is?"

He laughed with her. "No. Long ingrained courtesy, which has obviously left you in its dust." He sat on the bed beside her again. "I see you have not been motivated to don public attire."

"Didn't seem to make much sense, since you were the only one coming by and I need a shower. Besides, I like your eyes when you look at me. Well, except for my ironwork." She lifted the sling. "Besides, it covers this breast, and…"

He lifted her arm gently to expose her for a gentle kiss.

However, much to Beckie's regret, he then replaced the sling and stood, offering her a hand.

After breakfast, Beckie followed Ian's lead to Millie's office, where the doctor set to work prodding and poking her arm. When Shakti came in, they took an X-ray and amused Beckie with the professional 'hmm's' and 'm-huh's' they made while examining it. "Well, whatever you two did last night doesn't seem to have damaged anything," Shakti said with a chuckle. "The bone is still in place and while it's too soon to see any regrowth, everything looks good. And the wounds are healing as we hoped as well."

Beckie drew herself up and suggested they find another victim, "since I'll be gone for the next week. Don't want you to get out of practice," she teased.

"Will a trip to high altitude be a problem?"

Shakti and Millie exchanged glances before they both focused on the couple. "No. As long as you get enough rest and keep the wounds and pin sites clean, and you're not gone too long, the healing will not stop."

"How long do you expect to be gone?"

"I expect a week to ten days. However…"

Millie made a face. "Yeah. We understand the nature of the business."

Beckie's next stop was Millie's home, to roust Amy. They spent the rest of the morning past lunchtime Skyping Sandy and then determining what Amy would need to enroll in Coral Gables High School. That at least seemed to go as Beckie hoped.

As Beckie, Ian and Boynton pushed back from their delayed lunch, Boynton said, "I believe the Ardan family is approaching."

Beckie put off her packing to shoot him a glance, then looked at Ian. "Do you have any idea…"

He shook his head as Boynton opened the door and ushered Millie and Amy in. A moment's exchange for them to refuse any refreshment —"We just finished, thanks."—and Beckie sat up, keeping her arm out of Millie's view.

The doctor said, "Did you do something, Beckie?"

Of course she'd notice that, Beckie thought. "No, Millie. I guess I'm a little nervous when you show up unexpectedly." With a grin, she stood and walked to exhibit the arm. "See? Just like this morning." As she returned to her chair, she said, "So, what does bring you out this fine day?"

"Sam. Or maybe Amy."

Beckie grunted in confusion as she looked from Millie to Amy. Amy's eyes, wide and bright, looked hopeful. Millie's had more of a plea in them. This is funny, Beckie thought as she looked at Ian, but he was impassive as usual.

"Well, you've got me confused."

"No matter," Ian said. He faced Millie. "Samuel is due to return to Syria, I believe? And he mentioned it to you? You believe you should travel with his team."

Millie nodded. "I left when you were injured and they've been extraordinarily lucky. I should be there if their luck runs short. Of course, the clinic has been without overall guidance, too."

"Which leaves Amy at loose ends, so to speak." Before anyone else spoke, Beckie continued, "Normally, I guess Shalin would host her, but with her injury… You're looking for us to take her?"

Both Ardan's nodded with varying degrees of enthusiasm.

Beckie looked at Ian; he was neither obviously opposed nor in favor. Boynton had his small smile, but when she caught his eye, he dipped his head enough to be noticed.

"I hear no plaintive refusals. Is the laptop handy, Maurice? And is Barbara likely to answer?"

Ian glanced at his watch. "We should call her phone. She may not be at her computer."

"Maurice, never mind. Sorry."

His hand waved through the door as Ian finished dialing and set the phone on the table.

"Barbara, hello. How are things going there?"

"No different than earlier, Mr. Jamse. And you?"

He waved to Beckie. "I shall turn you over to Rebecca. She has questions."

"What questions, Beckie? And how's the arm?"

"Healing, thanks. I'm contemplating bringing a minor with me. She could pretend she's my nurse, I suppose, but that's nothing to do with you."

"No, surely not, as long as you have her papers. Shall I guess?"

Her continued, "Is it Amy Ardan?" overlapped Beckie's "Yeah, of course I—" but Barbara said, "Go on," and waited.

"Yeah, it's Amy. If I bring her, the trouble you're seeing? Is it likely to get violent?"

There was a pause. As it went on, Beckie watched Amy's face fall. Before the disappointment took over, however, Barbara said, "No. There's no hint it will even be as much as the protests up north. But, before it gets even that bad, Mamani asked Minister Salvadore to set up a, safe house, I guess you'd call it. Under the Guardia's protection."

"You think it'll be safe for her?"

"I do. So safe, that… Well, we arranged it for you, after we heard about the arm. If we needed it."

Beckie looked at Ian; this sounded like his idea. The look of surprise as he stared at the phone: she decided it couldn't be faked. And who had told Barbara didn't matter anyway.

"Is that okay?" Barbara sounded concerned.

"It's fine." Beckie looked at Millie. When the mother nodded, Beckie said, "We'll see you tomorrow."

Chapter Fifteen
Peru

Wednesday

PIERO HAD SPENT MUCH OF Tuesday evening wondering about the request Mamani and her contractor had made of his ministry: a safe house for an injured staff member in the unlikely event of unrest or protests. The contractor, a woman named Barbara Saunders working for Ian Jamse, LLC, had offered the information that another woman planned to arrive in the next day. The woman had been injured Thanksgiving Day, and Mamani wished her to be protected should the need arise.

During the meeting, he had of course agreed—even if he and Mamani were opponents, the contractor was benefitting both of them, and filling the request was good politics as well, costing as it would, almost nothing—but he'd spent the evening thinking about the ramifications, if there was an advantage to be gained, and if so, how best to achieve it.

He recalled an earlier visit by the contractor to Mamani; a check of immigration records gave him a possible name: Rebecca Sverdupe. Ah, yes. I recall meeting her. *Una hada*. A pixie with long brown hair.

Wednesday during lunch, the thought of Thanksgiving reminded him Goldfarb was to have made progress toward freeing Talos and delivering the video cassettes. This call he would make from outside. He walked out of the squat green Ministry building. The sky was clear, and the temperature comfortable this late spring day.

In the car park in front of the building, Piero waved to one of the security guards on patrol, then dug in his pocket for his personal cell phone. Again, he scrolled to the nondescript number.

"Is señor Goldfarb available?"

In a moment, Goldfarb's voice, not as calm as Piero had hoped, responded. "Goldfarb here."

"Salvadore. May I know how your Thanksgiving went?"

"Well, thank— No, that's not what you meant," as Piero interrupted him with a snort of disgust. "Not as well as we hoped. The videos are still missing; it is even odds they are in the hands of the group the woman Rochambeau worked for."

"Are they aware of what they hold? And if it is even odds, where else might the videos be?" Piero paused. In the earpiece, Goldfarb's heavy breathing comforted him even less. The man is incompetent! Either himself, or in surrounding himself…

"Since your former mistress tells me the same group has been contracted by your rival, Nayra Mamani, for her campaign security, it would beggar belief they do not know what the cassettes contain. I suppose… No. While they may not know, we should proceed as if they do."

I should think so. Mamani told them what the videos were. "I agree. If not them, who has the recordings?"

"They would remain under our control… Well, under Talos' control. I will see him on Monday and make your case once more."

"Please do so. Let me think a moment."

Piero dropped the hand with the phone to his side and looked over the traffic outside the fence. He didn't really notice it, however; he thought about Barbara Saunders' request.

In less than a minute, he raised the phone and spoke. "Why do you believe that group may hold the videos?"

"Our attorneys in Nassau have been assisting the men we had searching the group's headquarters. I understand from one of them Talos' gold is certainly under their control, and the videos, he was nearly as certain they were actually there. In addition, we found no other work to justify such security."

Piero scoffed at the idea Goldfarb's research would be all-encompassing, but he kept the opinion internal. The connection with Mamani is too strong. I wonder when she will release the tapes to discredit me. The editing to remove *her* appearances… that would require time. Perhaps I can still act quickly enough to prevent embarrassment. He took a deep breath and said, "I will arrange for one of the contractor's staff members to meet you at the airport in Arequipa on Friday. Send someone to collect her. That should give you the leverage you need to recover the videos." He paused. "Send your people to Lima; one of my planes will ferry them to Arequipa and back. We will ease the exit process for you and the… guest.

"I remind you no product will move from this day until the recordings are in my hands. I have already spoken with other dealers; they are more than willing to accommodate my surplus."

"But—"

"But nothing, señor. I told you the requirements. I will call you… Saturday to make sure everything has arrived as we wish. From then, it shall be up to you and Talos."

He stabbed the disconnect button and turned the phone off.

As he started back to the Ministry building's entry, he realized Ms Sverdupe would recognize him; thus, he would not be able to pick up the 'injured' staffer. However, the fewer people involved at this end, the better. A couple of junior recruits at the hotel… That will work fine. And Fernando! He will be an excellent choice.

He smiled. Time to back up my threats. He took the phone again. "Señor Koslov? Pedro Gonzales here. I would like to make an introductory shipment to confirm the discussion we had last month. If you agree, my aide will contact you tomorrow."

"Excellent news! I will alert my people. Adios until tomorrow."

"Adios indeed."

THURSDAY

Mathilde had again planned for a 2AM departure for the flight to Lima, so Beckie did her best to get some sleep before Ian's alarm went off. Amy was down the hall; when Beckie knocked, she was already dressed, sitting on the edge of the bed.

"You okay?"

"Yeah. Just… just nervous." Beckie watched the girl pull herself vertical. "I'll be fine."

Mathilde landed at Lima after she told them Barbara had elected to have them fly on to Arequipa. "Getting used to the altitude should start earlier; the crowds won't wait till you're ready." They went through the entry process while the plane was refueled; by half past one, they were in rental cars at Rodriguez Ballon Airport, on the way to the Libertador Arequipa, the same hotel the last meeting with Mamani had been in, so Beckie was relaxed.

By three, the trip was over and Beckie was again finding it hard to breathe in the 2300 meter thin air. Not as bad as Mamani's headquarters, she thought, as she sipped a *mate de coca* while curled up to Ian. Amy had come in with them, but was now in the adjoining room. She'd said she would nap and read before dinner.

After dinner, Barbara told them Mamani would meet them at nine. Amy said she'd lock the doors and hide rather than tag along. "I don't know how good I'd be with a future president," she admitted.

Entering the suite converted to conference room gave Beckie other concerns: How do we broach our decision to hold the original videos? What does Ian really need me to do here?

As she thought of him, Ian touched her shoulder and offered her a pain pill. "Before we begin," he suggested in a soft voice.

In agreement, she swallowed it with a gulp of water. "Thanks. How long before they arrive?"

"Barbara told me Mamani is in the hotel; she expects her…" They both heard the rustle of people approaching. "Now, I believe."

Mamani entered leading her staff, proceeding directly to Beckie and, until she noticed Beckie's arm 'jewelry,' reaching both hands to her. When she saw the fixator, however, both hands flew to her mouth, attempting to cover her gasp.

"*¡Santo dios!*" she said from behind her hands. "What has happened?" She extended a hand as if to touch, to confirm the stainless steel's reality.

Beckie smiled. "It's nothing, really. The doctors are pleased with my progress so far, and it could have been much worse." She shuddered at the thought. She stepped back to look at the woman. "Your dress is most attractive."

Mamani had chosen another peasant colored shirt which, though it seemed out of place with her tailored suit, wasn't. Beckie colored, thinking of her more casual shirt over jeans.

"Thank you. Philip told me some of your misadventures. I'm happy to see you have survived. He also told me you have information?"

"Indeed," Ian said. "Before we begin, who should be present? What has Philip shared with you?"

"I believe Philip and I will be sufficient. As for what he has shared… Let us pretend he has shared nothing." She glanced at him, and he nodded.

"Very well. We have recovered and secreted the recordings which we believe you seek. Of course, unless you see them, that remains uncertain. I have transcripts of selected portions, portions which might arouse minor questioning if discovered, but nothing significant, and will turn those over to you for your confirmation.

"We will maintain control over the original tapes unless circumstances change."

Mamani's eyes were large until Ian's last statement, when they slitted in what had to be anger.

"And what 'circumstances' might change?"

Beckie sat forward to catch Mamani's attention. "First, may I acquaint you with the history? The stories?"

Mamani snapped around; she forgot I'm here. Her expression softened—slightly. "I will not forget my question."

"Good. Neither will I."

About ten minutes after Beckie began, Mamani stopped her. "May the señorita Ardan join us?"

Beckie shot her a glance after one at Ian. "She was… uncomfortable with such… rarified company as you, señora. However, if you feel…"

Both Mamani and Gomez were laughing; their amusement had started small, but had become full-bodied as Beckie continued.

"I hope," Mamani said as her chuckles faded, "I am not so rarified a capable young woman need feel… uncomfortable around me. However, I understand she played a part, apparently small but important, in finding the cassettes. I wish to acknowledge her, as well as…" She chortled once more. "Well, perhaps I may calm her, showing I am not a fire-breathing dragon set out to devour innocent villagers."

Beckie felt her eyebrows rising as she listened to Mamani. With a grin to Ian, she went to the door and asked Sue, waiting there, to ask Amy to join them. In a few minutes, the sheepish girl shuffled in, Rich and Sue behind but not pushing. When Beckie patted the seat next to her, Amy inched over to drop into the chair, looking down between her knees to the floor.

"You've been invited," Beckie said, "so the señora may give evidence even potential future presidents are real people first. Señora Mamani was first amused you felt yourself… inadequate, I guess, to meet with her, and then dismayed at the idea. She wished an opportunity to change that opinion."

"Also, to hear your telling of the story and thank you for your help," Mamani finished.

Amy had raised her head, in disbelief, Beckie was sure, but the girl took a breath and looked Mamani in the eye. "Thank you, señora. My part mostly consisted of getting angry at my mentor…" She snapped her gaze to Beckie and back. "… falling in love, and stumbling on… Well, given Beckie's reaction, I suppose she might *not* have found it. The clue."

Beckie smiled, thinking back to the slip of paper she'd dismissed as the receipt for the clock. She's right. I might never have looked there, or seen the possibility.

Between them, the account was finished in less than an hour; Mamani called for refreshments. Then, she slid her chair back and addressed Beckie. "I understand your actions. Whether I agree… I must reflect for a little time." She settled herself again, then examined her fingers. "One of your questions, felt but not heard: as I told you, the attempt to… influence…" She's having a tough time pulling the words together, I guess, Beckie thought, and offered Mamani a small smile. "… affairs of justice failed and has not been reanimated. Once Jaime Lobera was charged, Mateo, Minister Huamán, and I could no longer agree the benefit initially perceived still existed. And once Mateo died…"

Ian stood. "Thank you, señora. That was a concern we did share. However—"

"However," Mamani said with a chuckle, "how shall I prove it? That is your new question, as it would be mine. It is difficult to prove the absence of a thing." She paused, glancing first at Beckie, then at Ian. "I offer my word."

Ian dipped his head in acknowledgment. "That will do. Now, I believe Rebecca should rest, so if you will excuse us?"

"I apologize, señora, but Ian is right; I'm about to fall over." Beckie stifled a giggle.

"Of course." She turned to Beckie. "Perhaps you and señorita Ardan could join me for lunch tomorrow?" She looked over to Philip, who was studying a large notebook. "At…"

"You have ninety minutes free from 1320."

"Will that be suitable?"

"Eminently. Amy and I will be…"

"I will meet you in the lobby," Gomez said, "at 1305."

"Excellent. Thank you."

Back in their room, Beckie pulled Amy through the connecting door to go over the conversation with Ian. "We didn't say anything troublesome, did we?"

"I think not. You maneuvered around the history carefully enough neither of them will be dissatisfied."

"I may ask her tomorrow. And why would she invite just Amy and me for lunch? Not even Barbara or Sue. Or Elena?"

"I suspect she wishes to discuss the changing circumstances I alluded to earlier. Also, she may well have additional questions bearing on Talos or on Ms Rochambeau, and may attempt to breach your defenses."

"Well," Beckie said when she calmed her laughter, "to 'breach my defenses' she only has to grab my arm, I'm afraid. Amy will be better than me!"

"I don't know," Amy retorted. "Grabbing your arm would get to me, too!"

"I doubt she will resort to measures that crude. Cajolery seems more her métier. You made significant inroads on her anger with me, and once her questions are answered, that may be her next offensive move."

"But there's nothing there we'd do differently… if I understood?" Amy asked with a look to Beckie.

Ian's voice took their attention. "I am always amenable to reasoned argument, but as it stands today—"

"Nope, not gonna give anything away," Beckie finished. She pushed Amy toward the door. "Sleep."

FRIDAY

Beckie felt the chill when Ian rose and began his preparations for the day. She rolled over, watching as he selected his uniform for the day, a white short-sleeved shirt over khaki slacks. "You look wonderful," she said with a lilt in her voice. God, I love him!

"I appreciate your confidence. Shall I return in an hour to assist you in the shower?"

"I'd like that, but, no. Amy can do some of the work she's along for. And I want to quiz her on the reading she's supposed to be doing."

He came to kiss her lips before departing. She lay still for another five minutes before a quiet tap on the connecting door brought another smile to her lips. "Com'on in, Amy. I'm ready."

Forty-five minutes later, Amy put the brush down. "You're done. And I'm hungry!"

With a laugh, Beckie said, "Good! If I recall—"

The loud rap on the door to the outside shocked her. A glance through the peephole revealed a man in the Guardia uniform she recalled seeing on her last visit. She didn't recall having seen the man before, though like the ones she did remember, he appeared to be solidly built. She couldn't see his hair or eyes under his helmet's brim. As he raised his hand, she opened the door to find two Guardia there.

The closer man stepped into the doorway and looked around. "Please, señorita… señoritas, you must come with me."

"Why? Where?" Beckie pushed back on her concern. "What's going on?"

"I have been ordered to move you… and the other señorita to a…" He paused again, as if searching for a word. "… protected place. Please come with me."

"What about Ian and the rest of the team? Mr. Jamse?"

"They are being moved also. Please hurry!"

The man's anxiety and, Beckie had to admit, his near panic, led her to grab Amy's arm and follow the man out the door. Amy shot her a questioning look, but Beckie pushed her along in the guard's wake. The guard, clumsy in his obvious nervousness, escorted them down the back stairwell to a door marked la salida. "Exit," Amy whispered. Outside, an olive-drab car waited.

As he hustled them in, Beckie held Amy's hand tight; she looked around the car's interior. All the windows had been blacked out. Amy started to speak, but Beckie shushed her while she investigated.

The blacked out windows hinted perhaps this wasn't the trip she expected. The lack of handles on the doors seconded it. And finally, a steel plate separated them from the driver's compartment.

She took Amy's head and laid her lips beside the girl's ears. "Be quiet," she whispered. "I have a concern about this." She stopped as Amy moved in agreement, then continued, "This is a cop car, I think, and maybe that's okay. But I'm… We'll see what happens when we stop."

Amy reached to hug Beckie's arm, then fell back against the plastic seat. But she didn't let go of Beckie's hand.

The car had been stopping and starting frequently. Beckie pulled her phone out of her pocket; she wasn't even disappointed to see "No service" in the display. The clock, however, showed they'd been on the move for less than half an hour when not only did the car stop, but the engine did also, and the body rocked as someone exited.

She hadn't slipped the phone into her pocket when both doors opened and she and Amy were grabbed by the arm. Beckie shrieked as the hand gripped her left shoulder above the fixator, and Amy swung around, throwing a fist at the man's face. "*¡Dejarla ir!*" "Let her go!"

By the time Beckie's right hand reached her shoulder, the man had not only let go but fallen away from the open door. Amy hadn't hit him; her captor had dragged her out of the vehicle and stood her up against the door, arms hanging over the top.

"Hey, leave her alone!" Beckie's voice was shrill; she forced herself to breathe. "And don't fuck with my arm! Tell us what you want, and why. Now!"

"Señorita," the man holding Amy said as he allowed her to stand on her own, "we are told to bring you to *la casa segura*, *el refugio*. A fight has started. Please, you must go inside!"

"Safe house," Amy said across the backseat.

Beckie nodded before looking around. They were in a garage with room for three or more cars in addition to the one they'd arrived in. It didn't appear to be a working garage, merely one for storage. A few boxes stood against the far wall, but the block walls were otherwise unrelieved. Not even a damn window! "Okay. When will the others arrive?"

"They do not share with us," the man who'd grabbed at her said.

Beckie crawled out of the car and waited for direction.

The man beside her gave her an apologetic look. "Your phone, please."

It was no good trying to hide it; she'd had it in her hand since he opened the door. Expecting the answer would be "Orders," she didn't even ask why; she handed it to him. I will be ecstatic when this arm is healed and I can argue with people again.

In three more minutes, they had been shown to a room three flights of stairs above the garage and the men had closed the door and departed.

The room was fifteen by eighteen or so, based on pacing the walls off. The window and the door were the only openings except for a skylight in the ceiling ten feet overhead. The walls were white plaster, the floor, tile. Beckie kicked at a seemingly loose tile, to no effect. Then, while she walked one direction around the small room; Amy walked the other.

"Not very much to see," Beckie groused, "inside, at least." They met facing a floor to ceiling window Beckie estimated to be five feet wide. It was a single light; there was no obvious way to open it.

Amy spun slowly and agreed. "Besides, look at the glass. Gotta be an inch thick."

Beckie looking at the frame and nodded.

The view was pastoral, since the walled roof the window looked out on blocked any view down. El Misti stood off to their right, still snow-covered, but with a white plume rising from the summit.

"I don't think we'll be here all that long," she said.

Amy said nothing but gave her an inquisitive look.

"No bathroom. No… chamber pot. No drain in the floor."

Amy nodded, then slid down the wall to sit on the floor. Beckie joined her. "Your phone?"

"In my room. Didn't think I'd need it."

Beckie shrugged. No worse than me, showing it off.

Amy rolled her head to Beckie's shoulder. "Any ideas what's going on?"

"No. I mean, you were there when Barbara told us about the safe house. That is what that guy said, right?" Amy tipped her head, but didn't pick it up. "But I have no idea why they'd lock us in, or even take us without anyone else from the team. If they're trying to protect us."

"Yeah, but those guys, they were scared of something."

"That's the thing that bothers me. If we've been moved for our safety… Why were they so nervous? And if we weren't, again…"

"Maybe he was honest when he said they didn't really know what was going on?"

"It's probably the best answer. Just, it's not all that satisfying, you know?"

Beckie'd watched a few clouds drift past the window, a long enough trip that Amy's head drooped when the girl dozed off. Wow! She's relaxed! Or really zonked.

The cloud watching reverie was destroyed by a clatter outside the door, followed by its opening. A Hispanic man came through, followed by a similar woman, though she wasn't as dark-skinned as he. They both had straight black hair. In alpaca sweaters over jeans, it was difficult to guess their weights. Beckie forced a calm expression; she recognized the man from Mamani's meeting in September. He'd been outside, waiting at Salvadore's car, I think. What…

Amy had roused at their entry and was giving first them and then Beckie, a long look. Beckie couldn't figure how to share her discovery; she shrugged again before pulling herself to her feet. She reached to give Amy a hand, but the man was there first.

"Hello," Beckie said as Amy and the man straightened. "Welcome to our cell. I hope you have as wonderful a time as we."

Amy goggled at her, as did the man, but the English must have been too… esoteric for the woman; she maintained her stolid expression.

"I don't understand," the man said when he recovered. "This is not a, 'cell,' if I understood your meaning."

"I think you did. Door has no handle on the inside. Window has a great view but won't open and is likely bulletproof and unbreakable. No furniture. No food or water. My phone is taken and not returned. How would you characterize it?"

He smiled. "Minor inconveniences." He waved them away. "I hope your visit here was explained?"

Beckie turned and walked away. This is unbelievable. Inconveniences? Can he really be that stupid? She stood gazing out the window. This puts paid to the story this is for our safety, doesn't it? One of the candidates' drivers? But could he really be on the up and up? She shook her head. I don't believe it. Something else is going on… Mamani's videos? But I better get back to here and now. She turned to lean against the glass, glaring back at him. "A reason was given; however, it lacks… substance, depth… A fight. How about *you* explain exactly what we're doing here, on top of the world?"

"We keep you safe," he said. "And you are. We will move, now, to —"

"Where's the rest of the team? And señora Mamani?"

He made what could have been an attempt to sooth her, both his hands out pressing down. Beckie sloughed it off waiting for a response. He settled back and said, "You will meet them all, soon."

"Even Mamani?" Amy interjected.

"Even Mamani," he agreed. "Now…" He waved at the woman. "… she will accompany you to the… *baño*, so you may wash up, and then we will move."

The window in the bathroom was too small and too high, even if her arm hadn't been damaged. The woman stayed close, although she did allow them the privacy of closing the stall door.

The drive took longer than Beckie had expected before she admitted to herself she had no clue. She, Amy and the woman were all sharing the back seat of a large black car, one that looked like it should have a driver who would chauffeur someone around. Or maybe he *is* the chauffeur.

Amy sat beside her, holding the Transformer arm; the woman had taken the window on the other side leaving Beckie in the middle. She'd bitten her lip hard enough to draw a little blood; Amy finally noticed and leaned over to wipe the blood away.

Will we get another chance? Beckie decided, probably not. She allowed her head to loll on Amy's shoulder and whispered, "Cover my mouth." She almost giggled as Amy started, then turned it into an overall motion that left her arm as close to Beckie's mouth as Beckie could have hoped. "The guy… works for Salvadore. Repeat it." When Amy twisted around as if to look out the back window, she repeated the words before the woman told her to sit facing front. The man caught her eye in the mirror, Beckie held it with as harsh a stare as she could work up until he turned back to the road ahead.

The darkened windows did not prevent her from observing the city as the drive continued. Eventually, the car stopped and the man killed the engine. When the woman opened her door, Beckie saw the facade of a two story adobe house. The drive was crushed stone and the walkway to the door less than ten feet away was the same. She glanced around to see Amy exiting the far side. Behind her, Beckie saw a tall fence beyond which either tundra or low, not yet green, grass grew. In the distance, a few alpacas grazed.

A phone rang and the man grabbed for his pocket. He answered the phone in a spate of Spanish, then disconnected and told the woman something, also in Spanish. Beckie's language skills did not keep up at all. He slammed the door Amy had used, pushed her away from the car and got in. In a flurry of dust and small stones, he sped away.

He's been called to a meeting! Amy grabbed at the car's rear fender as he shoved her out of his way and got in. She stood flat-footed until he slammed the door. A glance in the mirror showed he wasn't looking at her. The car roared and slewed into motion, spraying dirt and stones at

Beckie and the woman. Amy took a couple of steps toward the gate. He's gone! I can do this came to her in a rush of excitement; Beckie can't.

The car missed the post; as soon as it was clear, Amy ran.

She slithered between the moving barrier and the post with barely a hand's breadth to spare. The car turned right, headed down the slight hill and she raced after it, sure he was headed to the civilization where she needed to be. As she ran, red brake lights flashed. She desperately searched for a place to hide, but there was nothing. With another glance at the car, she dove into the ditch alongside the road. When she raised her head, the brake lights went out, and the car turned on a cross-street.

Her excitement had faded, a lot. She picked herself up and spit out several blades of grass. Before she took a few seconds to brush herself down, she stared behind her, waiting for the woman to appear, but nothing. A quick assessment of the scrape on her elbow where it had uncovered a rock: not as bad as it could be. I'm glad Sue found these peasant skirts!

Once she began moving again, running in her long easy stride, the skirt wasn't as useful. She finally hitched it up so the hem fell above her knees, tying it with the scarf, and adjusted her stride. Her breath wasn't as easy as she expected. Oh, yeah. Seventy-five hundred feet, Mathilde said. She made more adjustments. Tears rolled down her cheeks, but she swiped them away, looking for the big black car to return. She had no way to tell time, or where she was, or, really, as she thought about it, anything at all. Great move, girl! Here you are in a foreign country, no clue where you are, no way to find out. At least I speak a little Spanish. If I can find someone who's not out to kill me!

As she ran, she took time from fearing the man's return to observe the landscape she ran through. The road looked like about a lane and a half wide, with ten or twelve foot high walls marking individual lots, or maybe buildings, based on the large tire tracks in the gravel and dust. Where no walls stood, the fields ran to nearby hills, green, though Amy had no idea what the plants were. Or why low stone walls divided the fields. Almost random, she thought. She focused on making sure she didn't turn an ankle while simultaneously watching for traffic.

As she reached the corner where the car had turned, she surveyed the opportunities. Ahead, she could see buildings. That was also true to the right, where the black car had turned. But straight ahead, in the distance a bus, a city bus, trundled by; she chose that path.

As she approached the street her road intersected, she dropped the skirt into its normal place and used the scarf to cover the blue in her hair. He'll remember that. Rather than running, she walked, but hastily, watching for any sign of undue interest.

Of course, she thought, I have no money to ride a bus. But maybe a taxi'd be willing to take me to the hotel? If I can find one.

When she crossed the street, there were gas stations on both sides, each with small shops, and she headed toward the busiest one, planning to ask for the use of their telephone. As she reached the doorway, a taxi, obvious by the signboard perched atop the roof, stopped to allow a fare to exit. She slipped up behind the man as he paid. He gave her a dirty look as he bumped into her on his way to the building's entrance.

"*¡Hola!*" She continued in Spanish, "To the Libertador Arequipa, please." The driver gaped. I guess my Spanish isn't as good… "*¿Hablas Inglés?*"

He gave her another glance and said in Spanish, "I understood you. I was surprised one would wish to go there, from here." He waved at the depressed industrial area Amy'd run to.

"I did a tourist thing and got lost," she said. "Please tell me if you don't understand my street-Spanish. Can you take me to the hotel?"

"Sí. We are going."

Amy collapsed against the seat back and heaved a sigh. She looked up to see the driver's eyes in the rear view mirror. "Are you all right, señorita?"

She nodded her head, pulled the scarf off and fluffed her hair before retying it. She asked what she thought might be acceptable turista questions: Why was the hotel in the middle of a park? What were the main churches in the city? How did people earn their living? He relaxed as he drove, answering her for the twenty-five minutes it took to reach the hotel's entry.

Both Beckie and the woman turned their heads to avoid the dirt kicked up by the car; before the woman did anything but cough, Beckie saw Amy racing toward the still open gate. She made it through before it closed and continued downhill. With her heart pounding, Beckie whispered "You go, girl!" and pretended to trip, falling against the woman's legs. "Ooof! Sorry, I tripped on something."

The woman picked herself up and began to brush herself off before realizing Amy wan't standing there with Beckie.

"*¿Dónde está ella?*" The woman shouted her question, but Beckie just splayed her hands before her. "Where is the other girl?"

"I don't know." And it's an honest answer, Beckie thought. I have no fucking clue where she is! Muttering in Spanish, the woman grabbed at Beckie's good arm and pulled her through the door to the house. The door slammed after she'd been shoved into a small dark room on the first floor; she heard the lock go home before footsteps stomped away.

Beckie surveyed her new accommodations. Nothing to brag about, she thought, as she tested the door again, then the windows, closed by wooden shutters outside the glass. But the sashes didn't open, whether because they were painted shut or locked or something else, she couldn't tell.

There was a sofa and a straight chair, clearly part of a set with the table it sat under. The floor was wood, and covered by a rug to within a couple feet of the walls. It was soft under her feet. She dropped to the sofa and worried about Amy. Damn kid shouldn't be running off, all save the world! But I'm glad she did! Could be her damaged feelings are healing. At least she speaks better Spanish than I do. Everyone does. At the thought, she giggled. And maybe she'll remember…

She allowed her head to fall back on the sofa, eyes closed. There was nothing she could do for Amy right now. "Not much I can do for me," she muttered, but even before she stopped feeling sorry, the door rattled open.

The woman peered in, as if to make sure Beckie wasn't lurking with a knife or other weapon. "Don't worry," she said to her, "with my arm, I'm little threat."

"I shall return." She closed the door.

"Hmmf."

By dead reckoning, it was ten or more minutes before the door rattled again. This time, her keeper, as she now thought of the woman, scuttled through and backed herself against the wall. She held a bottle of water. "Would you like?"

Beckie nodded and rose from her seat. The sofa was low, making the process awkward especially since she could push off with only one arm. Clumsily she managed, and continued the sluggish trip to take the bottle. "Thank you very much."

"*De nada.*" Beckie could guess what she meant, and the woman continued in passable English. "Would you like the baño… bathroom?"

"No, I'm okay for now. But, do you have a scarf or towel I could borrow? The Guardia hustled us out so fast I didn't grab my sling." She raised her iron arm a few inches and mimed putting a sling around it.

The woman nodded and scurried out the door. Beckie watched the door close before sipping from the bottle. The water tasted good. She thought back to the plane ride to Egypt and the water she'd been offered there. But this bottle had been sealed!

As she sipped, she wondered what Salvadore's driver, or aide, could possibly be doing, and whether it made sense to admit to this woman she'd seen him before. The cons still outweighed the pros when the woman opened the door again, bringing a bright scarf with her. "Do you need help?"

"No, thanks." As she worked, she asked, "Why am I here? The Guardia told us fighting had begun, and we'd meet the rest of the team —"

"Where did the other girl go?"

Beckie finished tying the knot to support her arm. "No, I asked first.

Why am I here?" She stared at the woman until it was obvious even to her she would not answer. I'll try a different tack. "How long till I'm freed?"

"Not long, I hope." The woman left her alone again.

Damn, Beckie thought. Amy has the pain meds.

Becky sat, not bothering to move about the room. Through slits in the window shutters, she could follow the sun's movement. It was all pretty boring, she reflected.

A rattle at the door took her attention; this time she watched Salvadore enter, closing the door behind him.

"It is time to leave, Miss." His voice was quiet; Beckie heard no hidden message. Knowing she was leaving was nice, but knowing where she was going, that would be great. And what was going on. Well, nothing ventured…

"That's nice. Where are we going? To meet Ian, I hope?"

His face tightened. "Your friend's untimely departure has made that impossible, I fear. However, you will not be injured if you follow directions."

She decided to glare at him but he focused on her arm; she turned away from him instead.

"I can carry you," he said, "but with your… splint, I guess, it will be difficult—"

"Never mind." She hoped the venom in her voice made her feelings clear. "I'll walk."

He waved her to stand and used a short piece of line to tie her wrists together. While the cord was tight around the wrists, he left some freedom for her to protect the fixator.

Beckie followed the tall man through the house out to the big car again. When a guard came up behind her, she was both relieved and disappointed. Relieved that she hadn't broken free simply to run into him; disappointed there now would be even fewer opportunities for escape.

The last was confirmed when Salvadore opened the car's trunk and the guard wordlessly urged her in its direction.

"I apologize, Miss, but..."

Not for the first time did Beckie regret her diminutive stature. Piero scooped her up and with some direction to the guard, the two men placed her on the floor. The guard pushed a rolled up blanket against her back, between her and the car's body, and adjusted her arm to keep her iron work from coming in contact with the body or the lid. Beckie watched, hopeful for an opportunity.

Ian had received the information that Beckie had been taken from Eilís O'Bannon, who attributed the particulars to Goldfarb. His lack of previous response to the lawyer rankled in a most grievous fashion; however, correcting the problem would now have to wait, certainly until Beckie and Amy were recovered. His planned retribution would be determined by any damage the two girls had received.

He and the rest of the team had been busy, but since Beckie's phone had been turned off, they had little to go by. Contact with Mamani had led to the police, both National and Arequipa forces, becoming involved, but they had had little time to effect any results.

With no further ability to affect his own destiny, or Beckie's, Ian took a seat at the table outside the hotel and said, "Now, Ms Rios, we sit, waiting for the other shoe to fall." He chose not to respond to her sharp glance, staring instead at the hotel.

Behind him, the sounds of children playing gave an unrealistic sense of normality to the scene. Or perhaps, he thought, theirs is the normal reality.

Three hours after Beckie and Amy had disappeared, Ian was still watching the hotel when several Guardia came out the entryway. Behind them, Mamani hurried across the drive and up to him. She reached to take his hand as she greeted him.

Their brief words of commiseration and welcome done, Ian said, "Have you any news?"

"None. Barbara provided pictures of both women; they will be in police hands in thirty minutes or less. Perhaps someone will see them."

"There was no reaction to the observation a Guardia vehicle was seen behind the hotel?"

"None out of the ordinary. Piero, Minister Salvadore, has charge of the Guardia; he will investigate why a car was present. He will report when he has information."

"Minister?"

"Interior Minister. You may recall meeting him."

As Ian nodded his agreement, he watched a taxi roar up the drive and stop. Both doors on the driver's side opened and the driver and a woman alighted and turned toward the hotel. The woman's hair was covered by a scarf, but her carriage appeared familiar. "Excuse me, señora, for a moment. Elena, will you please see who that woman is?" He pointed as the driver disappeared.

She nodded and hurried up the slight hill.

"Who is it?"

"I am unsure, señora, but she appeared familiar."

"It is not Rebecca?"

"No."

Elena appeared in the doorway, waving to him.

"Excuse me for another moment, please."

As he broke into a trot, he heard her, "Certainly."

Elena had returned to the lobby when Ian pushed through the door. Pleased his breathing felt normal, his heart jumped when Amy stepped from behind the taxi driver. As soon as she saw him, she ran across the space to hug him.

"Mr. Jamse, I am so glad to see you and Elena!" She gripped his shirt. "I need some money, then we have to go find Beckie!"

Careful not to break contact, he brushed his lips across her forehead. "Calm, Amy Rose. Relax."

Elena's voice intruded on his attempt to sooth the girl. "I have no cash, Mr. Jamse, nor does Amy, and the taxi driver needs to be paid."

"Of course." He dug in his pocket, bringing out his wallet and handing it to her. "Take what is necessary. Add a gratuity of 50 soles, and..." He looked at the driver. "... another 50 soles should he be willing to return to the location he found Amy Rose.

"Now," he said to Amy, hoping to bring a twinkle to her eye, "what brings you out all alone this clear sunny day?"

She gasped and pulled back from her hug to gape at him. In a moment, she must have recognized the humor in his eyes; she pulled herself against his chest again. "I truly get why Beckie loves you!" She reached up to touch his cheek. "No. Beckie's captured. A couple of cops grabbed us and took us in a police car.

"They said we should go to a safe house, because there was a fight beginning, and we'd meet you guys..." Her eyes flashed from Elena to Mamani to Ian, then returned to Mamani. "Even you, señora.

"They left us in a, house? I think it was. On the fourth floor. Nice view. After we'd been there maybe fifteen, twenty minutes, a man and woman showed up and moved us again. To a place that looked out on tundra, I think, to the west. In the car, Beckie whispered the guy who took us worked for Salvadore, or something like that... I might have gotten it wrong—"

"Excuse me, please!" Mamani pushed Elena and the taxi driver aside to stand staring at Amy. "Did I hear you correctly, Amy? Rebecca said the man worked for Salvadore?"

"Yes, señora. If I got it right."

"Of course. Please, go on."

She paused. "When we got to wherever it was, he got a phone call. When he drove off, I ran out the gate." She paused, her lips pursed for a second. "I think that's all."

Ian squeezed Amy. "Thank you from the bottom of my heart. Can you direct us there? Or close by?"

"Sure." She released her embrace. "Well, Tomás can, can't he?" She called to the cab driver, "¡Hola, Tomás! Can you take us back where you picked me up?" she said in Spanish.

"Sí, señorita. It will be a pleasure."

Elena turned to Ian. "I'll call Barbara and Rich; see how long till they're back."

Ian nodded and turned to Amy again. "Was any reason given beyond taking you to the safe house?"

"No, Mr. Jamse. Beckie didn't have any ideas either, except she was pretty sure we were being captured. The car doors being locked and all."

"May I ask how you…"

She grinned. "It was my turn, you know. Beckie's helped me, so… They took us to this, ranch, it looked like. While they unloaded us, like I said, he got a phone call and told the woman he had to leave right now; she should take care of us. Beckie and me. He pushed me away from the car and jumped in without a glance. I ran out the gate before it closed. Then I ran for a half hour or a little more, before stopping where I found the cab."

"Barbara will be here in… There she is," Elena said, pointing to the elevator.

Mamani took his attention by touching his arm. "You may recall, Mr. Jamse," she said, "The minister named Salvadore. The Minister of the Interior. He was just here, at our meeting. As we broke up, he placed a phone call." She shifted uneasily, swinging her bag from her right arm to her left. "I hope and believe it is a coincidence."

Elena caught her breath before saying, "Who could benefit by involving him?"

"I do not know. *I* probably have the most to gain… But it is not I!" Mamani said. "If it is not *una estratagema, una trampa para incriminar*, then I have been mistaken. Sadly mistaken. And not only I."

Elena's brow wrinkled, then she said, "Ah. Yes, perhaps a frame-up." She shook her head as Mamani nodded. "But again, who?"

Mamani had no response.

As Ian shuffled the party to the parking area, Amy asked, "But how would the Minister have known about the safe house? I only heard about it in Barbara's call the other night."

Mamani gave Barbara a quick look.

Barbara sighed. "You heard the call, right?" Amy nodded, but her confusion was obvious. "The Minister made the arrangements. At our request."

Amy's "Oh. Of course," was almost quiet enough to be unheard.

"Of course," Mamani said, "I also knew of the plan, having assisted Barbara in the making of it." She took Amy's hand and continued, "I hope you can take my word I did not set the Guardia on you. I was looking forward to our luncheon."

"Beckie and I were, as well." Amy pulled her skirt away from her legs. "We'd even selected compatible outfits."

Mamani gave the girl what Ian considered an encouraging smile. "I think you'll be able to use them. Both of you, even if not today."

They had reached the parking area. Ian and Barbara sorted the team into cars, and Mamani's escort arrived with her vehicle.

"Please follow the taxi," Ian said. "Amy Rose and I will ride with him."

With the four vehicle entourage, Tomás needed forty-five minutes to make the trip back to the gas station where Amy'd flagged him. She popped out of the back seat and after a quick survey, pointed out the street she'd run in on. Ian waved, then waited until the others had crossed behind them. The three-plus miles it had taken Amy forty minutes to run flew by; in another six minutes, she had pointed out the turn and then the gated home with alpacas still grazing in the distance to their left.

Beckie heard rustling noises from the front of the car. Wonder where the woman went. Okay, I need to give Amy a chance. She hiked her long peasant skirt almost to her hips and bent her knees. She picked her feet up to make sure they wouldn't be encumbered if an opportunity arose.

Since my hands are tied and my goddam arm is…

She didn't finish the thought; the two men were speaking. Beckie's twelve words of Spanish did not begin to explain what they were planning. However, their actions gave her a hint.

The guard—she hadn't noticed before, but he was the taller one from the morning—appeared around the trunk lid and the rear fender. He stopped, apparently agog at the sight of her bare legs. This is it, she thought as he began to bend over. Showtime!

She recalled every exercise Sam and Elena had put her through, and the experiences she'd had using her feet on offense. Bracing against the blanket, she pulled her legs to her chest and uncurled her feet at his face. The sound of the heels bending flesh and bone wasn't pleasant, exactly, but the sound of him hitting the gravel was. She hooked the back of her knees over the trunk opening; her good arm sought purchase to lift her up, but Salvadore followed the guard; he stopped directly behind the car.

He's going to… She eyed the distance, slid forward an inch or so and kicked her right foot into his groin.

She wasn't happy with the kick—not strong enough and not quite on target, not to mention her left arm hit something when the reaction shifted her—but it was close enough, she guessed, as Salvadore bent clutching his crotch. She grinned as she tried again to lift herself to the rear bumper.

The next few seconds felt otherworldly, like she was in an alternate timeline. She balanced herself on the lip of the trunk/bumper. Salvadore, still holding himself, began to fight his way to stand. A taxi swerved through the open gate to the street. Three more vehicles followed the taxi, one of which she'd seen: the rental Ian had picked up at the airport.

Salvadore had reached his feet, but wasn't quite vertical. He took a look at the train of cars and bolted around the driver's side of his. Beckie heard the door open and slam; just as she realized it would, the car jumped out from beneath her. She managed to twist to land on her right shoulder and arm. Her "Oof!" could probably be heard at the Nest. She protected her face from the dirt and stones, then rolled onto her back to watch Salvadore's car swerve through the gate and after bouncing off the rental car, shoot down the hill, just as it had earlier.

The car's departure had masked the shouts now approaching; Beckie heard Amy's squeal and another couple of voices, but in an instant, the one she wanted to hear: "Rebecca, are you—"

"I'm fine, now you're here." She reached her bound hands to him. "Maybe you would help me up? Then I could kiss you!"

SATURDAY

Beckie's Saturday started with aches when Ian moved enough to chill her back. He smiled and pulled the covers back up. "I will instruct Amy Rose to wake you in an hour. Rest." He opened the door and peered out. "Mr. Quinn has accepted the challenge of making sure we are safe."

She waved her good arm at him and closed her eyes. She was still tired from yesterday's events. Her thought as she drifted away was simple: Why'd he take me? Us?

Amy came along mid-morning to rouse Beckie; they were ready for the rescheduled lunch with Mamani in good time. Outside the room, Amy almost tripped over Rich Quinn, who admitted to stationing himself there as defense against unfriendly activity. "Though we expect none," he quickly added.

"Well, thank you for making sure," Amy said, and Beckie echoed the sentiment as they stepped into the elevator.

"Ian's there," Rich said as the doors opened on the lobby.

"Yeah." Amy stepped out then stopped short. "But who's that, do you think?" A man in a Guardia uniform, not as tall as Ian, was talking with him near the front entry. As the girls watched, he tipped his cap and exited.

"No idea," Beckie said. "As long as he doesn't say something about safe houses, I don't care, either."

Rich laughed. "I'll see you in a couple minutes."

Amy waved, but Beckie headed toward the buffet and the coffee urns.

She poured; when she turned back, Ian and Amy were seating themselves at a table. She headed in their direction.

"Will you be okay?" Beckie asked Ian as she placed her coffee cup at her seat.

"Of course. We will spend our time consulting with the general about the several candidates' security and the information Willie learned last night. No," he said in response to her query, "he added no clarity to to Minister Salvadore's actions." They stood together and Ian kissed her. "You and Amy Rose enjoy your luncheon."

She nodded and took Amy's hand; they walked to the lobby where Rich was waiting with the car.

Rich dropped the girls at the restaurant with Sue just as Mamani's car pulled to a stop; the four women entered the building together. Sue detached from the group to wait for Rich; they would keep watch for Beckie and Amy. Mamani smiled as she pointed to her own guards. "They will work together, I'm certain," she told Beckie.

At their table, Mamani, Beckie and Amy enjoyed small talk over glasses of wine—Amy being teased by both women about her age; Beckie cut her off after one glass, but refrained herself, too.

Mamani began by toasting Beckie's successful recovery the afternoon before, then said, "I have some news…"

When the pause grew too long, Beckie said, "Is there something we should *not* know?"

Mamani gave her a forced smile. "Not really, as long as you do not publicize my foolishness." She waved away Beckie's protest and continued, "I don't know if you were told Minister Salvadore remains, at large, I think you say."

"He hasn't been arrested?"

"He has not. His car was found, but as yet, there have been no sightings of him. However, a different event may provide us insights.

"One of Salvadore's Ministry aircraft arrived yesterday, in time to meet him, had he arrived. Under his direction, it brought two Americans from Lima. One identified herself as Salvadore's ex-mistress while the other claimed to be a… friend, I suppose is the way he thought we would accept.” She sipped more wine. “After some… interrogation, their stories began to come together. We must do more investigation to verify the truth, but…

“Both of them agree. Since Mateo Huamán was stabbed in New York, Salvadore has been working with, or possibly for, the man who killed Huamán, Donato Talos. He has made illicit export of both counterfeit currency and cocaine easier for Talos. Actually, for his organization, since Talos himself—”

“He’s in jail!”

Beckie grabbed Amy’s hand and squeezed. “Yeah.” She stared at Mamani. “But that doesn’t stop his organization, does it?” She turned to Amy. “We know that.”

Amy nodded. “It wasn’t… Flores, was it? On the plane? Silvio Flores?” Beckie squeezed Amy’s hand again.

Mamani eyes went wide, but she kept her mouth closed. After a moment, she said, “No. That is not his name.” Beckie waited, but Mamani said no more about the man.

“Salvadore has been working with Talos, the woman told us, in the hope of regaining the videos you…” She nodded to Beckie. “… hold; the ones concerning our scandal. He was party to that, providing financing, but while we believed he agreed with the… wisdom of dropping our effort, apparently he did not. Or…” She pursed her lips, then rubbed her forehead. “Or he now has a different plan.” She sighed. “We believe he has been acting alone, at least until he could obtain the videos and have me arrested or banned.”

“Wow,” Beckie said. “Besides the smuggling, what else would Talos’ organization get? They told Ian they made the raid on the Nest to find the videos; that plays well with your information. But they suffered a pretty big expense, especially the way it worked out. I’m just not sure it’s enough.”

“We haven’t any information, at least yet. But his gold resources are undiminished.”

“Seems like his efforts and the group working against your campaign are unrelated."

"I'm not convinced. Some of my advisors do believe the conjunction is coincidental, that Salvadore was taking advantage of an unrelated incident that would take my attention. Still, I have asked for the investigation to continue."

Mamani sipped the last of her wine. After the server refilled her glass and left, she said, "I was undecided whether or not to tell you the last thing we have learned. However, I feel it imperative. Salvadore was to turn you, Rebecca, over to the two; they would return you to New York. They do not know, or perhaps, refuse to say, what purpose that would serve."

Beckie threw herself back in the chair. Fuck! I didn't need this! Not now. Amy… she was almost over this.

"Be careful!" Amy's squeal broke through Beckie's frustration and she smiled, though more sheepishly than she wanted.

"I apologize—"

"No!" Beckie felt her smile wash away. "It's not you, señora. God, no, it's not you. It's just, how do we get them to stop?" She raised her hand and scrubbed her forehead before pulling her ponytail around in front of her. "But that's not your job, it's ours." She flipped the hair back again.

"You may have some help; the United States embassy person who was present was dismayed at what he heard. He said something about the District Attorney in New York being interested." She caught the eye of the server. "Now, let us enjoy our lunch. We will talk only pleasant things."

The savory meal filled Beckie's belly, meeting her expectations. She sipped her coffee, then said, "If I am not too forward, we are both…" She glanced at Amy, who favored her with a curious look. "… intrigued by your invitation to lunch."

Mamani chuckled. "I'm sure, given your backgrounds and training, you must have made some interesting suppositions. The truth is likely quite far from anything you may have speculated. Even before yesterday's events, I wished to understand your relationship better. One of my *sobrinas...*"

"Nieces," Amy said.

"Ah, thank you. Yes, nieces. One, Lia, approaches your age, Amy, and I hoped understanding you might also assist in understanding her."

"I hope she's not as, hard-headed's probably a good term, as I am," Amy said.

Beckie snickered as politely as she could, then said, "The only advice I'm willing to offer is expect her to act her age and beyond, not less. And... and if she's half as intelligent as you, make sure there's a good reason every time you tell her she *can't* do something. And explain what that reason is."

"Act her age?"

Beckie smiled. "Yeah. Well, a better way to say it... Expect her to act the age she wants to be treated as. Let her know that's your expectation. Then treat her the age she acts."

Amy said, "Beckie's good at that. Me, not so much." Her little laugh made both women chuckle.

"Does that give you any ideas?"

"I will begin with those," Mamani said. "Thank you."

"Thank you, señora," Beckie replied. "One last thing I wanted to bring up... if we have a little more time?"

"As much as we need."

Beckie dipped her head in thanks as she picked up her tea and brought up the videos again. "Now that we hold them, rather than Talos..." She sipped, unsure exactly how to broach the next. "I am almost convinced destroying them would be better, though it would go counter to our promise to Philip. Mr. Gomez," she said in answer to Mamani's unspoken question. "Did he not mention that to you?"

"No, that must have slipped his mind," she replied with a wry smile.

"You know he supports you..."

"I do, but I also know it is because he is a political animal. If he believes I am going to fall, he will seek the best alternative at the time."

"He didn't put it quite that way, as I recall."

"Nonetheless, that is his position. I accept it." She sipped her own coffee, then leaned back. "Allow me to guess. He wished the tapes also." Beckie tried to keep still, placid. "Ah! But he did not wish to reveal them, at least for now, which is why you and Mr. Jamse still hold them. Or rather, why Philip returned with you." She smiled. "If I thought for a second Philip's interest did not serve our country… But I believe he does."

Beckie smiled. "We felt the same. Anyway, Ian offered to hold the tapes."

"Until?"

"You should discuss that with him directly, but the short answer is forever, unless we believe your country will be better served by their release."

"Hmm. I trust that will not be a unilateral decision?"

"That was our agreement."

"I would like another tea, I think." She signaled the server.

The next event only added to Amy's cachet, Beckie told Ian later.

As the waiter approached pushing the service cart, Amy slapped at Beckie's hand; behind the waiter, a man with a revolver was drawing a bead on Mamani.

Rich and Sue wouldn't make it in time, and Mamani's guards were farther away. Beckie had no time to even gasp before she followed Amy's lead and grabbed at Mamani's arm. She yanked Mamani's arm so hard she fell off her own chair, dragging the woman to the table, into the empty dessert dishes.

Over the clatter of scattering and breaking china, the gunshot rang in her ears; she kept her head down, waiting for another shot. Mamani's amazed exclamation ended with a scream of pain, quickly covered by the sounds of a heavy scuffle.

Damn. I hope the fight means the Guardia's neutralized him! As the noises faded, she felt a hand grasping at her side; when she opened her eyes, Amy was also lying on the floor. "You okay?"

Amy took a quick inventory. "Yeah. You?" Beckie followed her gaze, focusing on the fixator. "Your arm? Is it—"

"Fine," Beckie said. "I landed on my hip. Mamani?"

Rich's face appeared behind Amy and Beckie felt hands lifting; as she twisted, Sue helped her to an upright chair.

Amy said, "Thanks—"

Rich's smile morphed into a wide grin. "No, Amy, you and Beckie get the thanks!"

Because the girls had pulled Mamani flat across the table, the bullet merely grazed her, leaving a furrow from midway up her back to her shoulder. Rich made sure they were fine, then assisted the Guardia. Sue allowed Mamani to thank both Beckie and Amy from her stretcher before leading them out and whisking them back to the hotel.

Ian had heard the report before they arrived; after he opened the car door, Amy took his hand, but as soon as she'd emerged she pushed him around the back of the vehicle so Beckie wouldn't have to scramble through.

After a reasonable stint of hugging and kissing, Mr. Jamse stepped away from Beckie and turned toward her. "Amy Rose—"

She stepped into his embrace. After a single kiss, she leaned back to smile at Beckie. Attempting to work her single good arm about the two of them, Beckie said, "Amy reacted perfectly."

"But he was ready to fire!" Amy said. "What happened?"

"He took extra time to avoid the waiter," Beckie said. "That gave us the second we needed to drag Mamani out of the line of fire. Almost, anyway."

"I was so scared! But it looked like she would be okay, didn't it?"

"Indeed. Philip reports she is on the way to hospital with a flesh wound. He sends his strongest appreciations."

In the hotel bar, sharing well-deserved glasses of wine, Beckie said, "I'm really happy about the way Amy's reacted down here." Amy made a fake swing at her before smiling a huge smile.

"I am also," Ian said. "She has earned our high respect. What do you think would be a suitable reward?"

Beckie paused, to give the girl the impression she had to think about it. Then, she said, "If it's all right with you, I think I'll take her home. She's been at risk twice in two days; I can't see how we can justify keeping her here. Besides, it's only a couple weeks till school."

"I believe that to be a perfect payment."

"Thank you, Mr. Jamse. And you, Beckie, for being willing to—"

Beckie touched her arm. No need to go into that. I have to trust Ian.

Amy kissed them both on the cheek and asked Rich to escort her to her room.

SUNDAY

Beckie followed Ian out of bed the next morning when the alarm went off at seven. She dug through her bag while he was in the shower, then accepted his assistance as she showered and made herself ready for the trip home.

Amy knocked on the door at quarter of eight; she dragged her rolling suitcase behind her. "Mathilde did say she wanted to leave about half-past ten, right?"

"Yeah. She figured that would put us home about five or six tonight."

"Well, we better get down there, then."

"Not to worry," Ian said cheerfully. "You have time for a light breakfast."

They walked onto the tarmac from the non-commercial side of the terminal, and looked for the Gulfstream. "There," Amy said. "At least, I think that's ours."

"Yeah. The official one beside it… I guess that's the Minister's plane señora Mamani was telling us about."

"I guess. Look! Is that Mathilde waving to us?"

Beckie stopped short, then turned back toward the terminal, as if she'd forgotten something. "Have you ever seen Mathilde wave from the plane when she's piloting? Ever?"

Amy had stopped when Beckie turned. She came back to grab Beckie's bag. "No. So… What's going on?"

"Bet they still haven't caught Salvadore."

"Not gonna take that bet," Amy scoffed. "But you don't think…"

"I do, actually." She turned back after making a wave-it-off gesture toward the building. Speaking softly, she said, "The entry's narrow, between the cockpit and that closet forward. From the angle, I'm guessing he's… Well, him or some one of his crew, anyway… they're in the door to the cockpit forcing Mathilde to make pretty for us."

Amy spun around the suitcases like she was dancing. "So, okay. You think your Ruger is still in the galley?"

"Hope so. Bottom right cubby. Don't hole the plane, okay?"

"Okay. You go up the stairs first—"

"Cool! I'll pretend to trip into Mathilde and push her toward the flight deck—"

"Excellent! I'll barrel on behind you, throwing my weight around, and see if he has any troops with him." With a stern expression, she said, "Be careful with your arm, hear?" before she glanced up at Mathilde, still half-heartedly waving. "Anyway, what's the worst that can happen?"

"We could die, is all. No one'd be very happy about—"

"I certainly wouldn't! So, let's cause someone else to… Well, not die, maybe, but… you know."

"Yeah, I do."

They were now twenty feet or so from the stairs. Beckie made a come-closer gesture with her hand. As she quickened her steps, she heard Amy following behind her to the right.

"Ready?" Beckie whispered.

She felt Amy brush her hand.

Mathilde was leaning out the hatch. She might be a little off balance, which would be good. *I've gotta twist to hit her with my right shoulder… I wonder how strong the Transformer arm is.* She hit the first step and allowed the slight recoil of the ladder to pitch her into the steel railing at the aft side of the stairs. It rebounded just as she'd hoped and threw her into Mathilde. She felt the woman collapse under the blow, and the stairs jounced again. Amy.

Amy'll take care of herself. Beckie's right foot slipped, but she caught the hatch coaming with her left, and drove her right shoulder into Mathilde's solar plexus. The woman's breath blew out, but her motion stopped as she ran into something. Beckie felt like a miniature tackle; she kept pushing and shoving, thrusting, but keeping Mathilde between her and whatever was impeding them.

Over the sound of her breath and Mathilde's, she heard a clatter and then three Pop's. The middle one she thought she recognized—her Ruger, chambered for .22 LR, but the other two—Heavier. A .45, I'll bet. She kept her head down and thrust again, but whatever had been resisting Mathilde's backward progress vanished. Wow! She did a little free-form dance to keep her balance, and tried to catch Mathilde, but failed. The woman fell atop an unmoving man, then wriggled her way off and up into a crouch. Beckie ducked down beside her to survey the cabin.

Thank God!

Amy sat, draped across the first chair in the cabin, smiling like the Cheshire cat. "I got this one." She stood and handed Beckie her Ruger. "Clean out the cockpit." She held a M1911. When Beckie raised her eyebrow, Amy nodded toward a man in anguish sitting on the sofa and said, "He understood the wisdom of allowing me to hold it once he'd shot at me and hit what's his name there."

Before Amy finished speaking, Beckie heard the engines spin up and gave Mathilde a look. Without a word, they dragged the man into the galley. It was Salvadore, with blood leaking from at least two holes. Mathilde looked out the open hatch at the passing scenery and punched the entry door control, closing it.

"Hey, what's going on? Who's driving?" Amy's voice was a little more frazzled than it just had been. Beckie glanced in that direction, then waved her back. "Take care of him. I'll be there in just a second." She turned and looked toward the flight deck.

"Knocked out Janice, huh?"

Mathilde nodded. "She's aft. What do we do now?"

"We take the plane back… but I think we'll wait until there's some air under us, since this guy is ready to rotate."

"You don't think he wants to kill us all?" Mathilde's voice was a bare whisper.

"Naw. He's gotta be too smart to be that committed to a drug dealer." She nudged Salvadore with her toe. Since he hadn't moved except in response to the plane's actions, she didn't expect a reaction.

The plane had rotated and was well into the climb-out. Beckie glanced back at Amy, and signed to her, "Watch this guy," pointing to Salvadore.

When she nodded, Beckie grabbed Mathilde's arm and eased her to the right. "Any idea which seat he's in?"

"He's in the right hand seat."

"Naturally." The plane dipped and then rose; Beckie grabbed the door frame to keep from falling. "Okay. Here's the plan. I go first, and introduce him to the folly of flying uninvited with Air Jamse. Hang here until I call or you feel the plane's outta control. You can take the left seat, right?"

Mathilde nodded. Beckie reached for the sliding accordion door and shoved it open. She brought the Ruger around before the man in the seat looked back. Bouncing it off his skull fazed him just enough for her to slip in behind him and point the open end of the barrel at his eye from about four inches away.

"¿Hablas Inglés?"

He nodded until Beckie tapped his ear with her sling. "Good. Mathilde, come on in and be careful." When she reached the seat, Beckie said, "Take the wheel and head due west. I want to get past the two hundred mile limit. Then turn north. You got enough gas to get us home?"

"We'll talk in a few minutes."

"Okay. This gentleman is going to get out of his seat now, and I'd like you to be ready in case he tries something stupid and his lifeless body falls into your lap. Okay?"

The man's shudder echoed Mathilde's grimace. "Okay, you." She wiggled the gun just enough to show him the way. "Up and back into the cabin." I wonder just how we're gonna be able to get these guys secure with just the two of us. And if there's anything to tie 'em up with. "Sit there beside your buddy."

"Everything okay?"

Yeah, Amy sounds a little better now. "Fine. You see any rope or—"

"You got these guys?" When Beckie nodded in agreement, Amy said, "Here, take the Colt." She handed the M1911 over. "Mom leaves a kit everywhere she goes. There'll be tape, good unremovable adhesive tape. You know the kind." She smirked as she stood and went aft. "Hey, what'd they do to Janice?"

"We'll see to her in a minute. Right now…"

Amy ran back up the aisle. "How's best?"

"Hang on." She handed Amy the Ruger so she could check the M1911. "Okay, four rounds left. Good." She took the Ruger and shoved it into her back pocket. When she looked at the men this time, she recognized the not-pilot from the car ride to Salvadore's ranch. A glance at Amy with her head cocked toward him. Amy twisted her lip and nodded, then shrugged. Beckie matched it, then focused. "First both you guys, put your seat belts on." The M1911 helped enforce her words. When the belts clicked, she scurried around to the end of the sofa. "If you so much as twitch, the round will go through both your heads. Even if it doesn't, there's more behind it. Should you feel the need to even sneeze, holler out first, without moving. Got it?" When they didn't respond, she racked the slide.

"Yes!" and "¡Si!" rang out loud and clear.

"Okay, Amy, start with the guy farthest away. Since I can get them both with a single shot… Four turns of tape around the seat belt buckles, then pull them as tight as you can." When that was done, she said, "Now, they're gonna hold hands and you're gonna tape their wrists together. And their hands. Then, tape their other hands to the… to the outside seatbelt, I guess."

Amy showed a welcome flash of ingenuity; instead of the outside seatbelts, she taped their free hands to the other's opposite knee, which looked awkward, but since they were settled in for a nice seven hour voyage, Beckie was okay with it.

"Hope you got my meds, Amy." Beckie had just freed Janice. The co-pilot had a headache and a slight cut above her ear, but her pupils were the same size and reacted to light, so based on her lack of experience, Beckie hoped any concussion was light.

Amy pitched a plastic bottle over the seat back; Beckie caught it and found a water bottle. Fortified, she went forward to talk to Mathilde.

Their discussion covered the several problems Mathilde listed: leaving Peru without clearing Customs and Immigration, not allowing Peruvian citizens to leave the plane before departure, carrying a dead citizen around, not following the flight plan, and running closer to maximum range than Mathilde was comfortable with.

"We'd probably make it, but if weather comes up—"

Beckie's sat phone rang with the team members' ring tone. She and Mathilde shared a questioning look before she touched Accept.

"Beckie?" Shen's voice came out of the instrument.

"Yes? Shen? What—"

"Else was right. She was monitoring the surveillance system on the Gulfstream—"

"Our Gulfstream? The one I'm... the one I'm sitting in right now?"

"That very one. She spent several minutes trying to reach Ian once the attackers made their move on Janice and Mathilde. I thought I saw Janice up and about?"

"Right. So all our exploits are captured on video, huh?" Mathilde was very focused on the uninteresting view out the cockpit windscreen. "Hold on a second, Shen." She touched Mathilde's shoulder. "Did you know that?"

"Not till the phone rang. Or... I guess I knew, but didn't think about it. We never turn it off, since your experience going to Egypt. But I'd never have thought Else would be watching it..."

"Oh. Yeah, of course. I guess if I'd thought about it..." She spoke to the phone again. "So, Shen, did she get hold of Ian? Or anyone?"

"We did. The message, which he'll convey directly as soon as we finish, is that you should proceed directly to Lima per Mathilde's flight plan. The police will board and remove the two men and the body. They've already seen the video; they will not be interested in you beyond routine questioning."

The plane was already in a turn back to the east.

"Good news, Shen. Thank Else for us, please! And did she say *why* she happened to be watching us this morning?"

"She had nothing else to do, she says. And she may have been testing some minor enhancements to the system."

"Hmm." She muted the phone and laughed. "Serves us right, I guess, giving a brilliant engineer near complete freedom!" Mathilde chuckled along with her as she unmuted the phone. "Okay, Shen, we're headed back to Lima. As if you didn't know that already. Thanks again, to everyone! See you soon."

Ian's call came seconds after she disconnected; she had great pleasure in the conversation even though it contained no new information.

The stop in Lima took three hours instead of one, but once they'd pointed out Amy's single shot from the Ruger had ended in one of the tables in the plane rather than a person, the small revolver's existence seemed to fade away. Mathilde landed them safely on the Nest before ten that night.

Chapter Sixteen
Coral Gables

FRIDAY AFTER NEW YEAR'S, AMY grabbed her bag and Beckie's from the cab that had brought them from Fort Lauderdale airport to Beckie's house in Coral Gables. While Beckie had had the metal thing removed from her arm—"A wonderful Christmas present," she'd admitted—it had been replaced by a fiberglass cast, so carrying things was still problematic.

Amy said, "I can get all this stuff. You go open the door."

The house was empty; the others hadn't returned from their holidays yet, since the University's classes began on the twentieth.

Unlike mine, she thought. I have till Monday. She shivered a little, but when Beckie asked if she was okay, she lied, "Just the air in here. Maybe I'll open the window in my room." The expression on Beckie's face argued she'd been seen through. Do I want to get better at lying? Probably be convenient.

Still, she was scared. I haven't been in public school since second grade.

She dropped Beckie's bag on her bed and went on down the hall to the room she would live in for the next couple years, maybe. If she lasted that long. She fell to the bed, face up, staring at nothing. "Hey," she heard Beckie call, "in an hour or so, we'll go get pizza, okay?"

"Fine, Mom." She heard Beckie's answering laugh and closed her eyes.

The past week had been great fun; if it hadn't been she wasn't sure she could go through with this… whatever it was Beckie was promoting. She and Dylan had talked, a lot, even his sister had talked to her about schools and such.

But second only to Dylan was the talk Eilís had had with her and Beckie, who, since Mr. Jamse was still in Peru, had flown up from the Nest for New Year's and the trip back to Fort Lauderdale. Lying on the bed with eyes closed, she could see and hear it all again.

"I've talked to a friend in New York," Eilís had told them. "After Pella's testimony—"

"Who's Pella?" Amy asked.

"Frankie Pella. One of Goldfarb's minions. The one picked up in Peru with Salvadore's mistress. Anyway, after he talked down there and then in New York, Talos' sentence is being reviewed. But wait," she said as Amy clutched at Dylan and Beckie smiled, "that's not the good part. Well, maybe good's not the right thing to say. Goldfarb was being investigated enroute to being disbarred, but he was run over outside his office. Hit and run." She gave Beckie a long stare; so did Amy. That's kind of a contented look. I wonder… No. Not going to go there. "He died at the hospital. It was a stolen car, and the driver hasn't been found." Eilís got a thoughtful look on her face. "I suppose it could have been Talos…"

"Why's that?" Beckie asked.

Amy sat up in Dylan's arms. Wait! Why's Beckie surprised?

"I was reviewing the sale documents from Brewster, getting ready to add the deed restriction for Jo's marker. Anyway, turns out Goldfarb executed all of the documents transferring the Brewster property to Maria Talos' sole ownership. Given what you found, I can't imagine Talos would have agreed if he'd been asked.

"Anyway, with that, and the arrests of Talos' other men, well, we'll keep watch, but it looks like you don't need to worry about them." She raised her flute. "Here's to that!"

Amy glanced at Beckie, who was now gazing at her. "How about…" Amy choked on the name.

"Flores," Beckie finished, patting her on the arm. "Silvio—"

"Yeah. Mr. Flores remains in Nassau. When the Bahamian proceedings against him are complete, my friend in the DA's office in New York says they've already filed papers to bring him back."

"Excellent!" Amy said as she high-fived with Beckie.

An hour later, Beckie'd finished unpacking and walked down to Amy's room. She gave the sleeping girl a glance, then picked the footie sock off the bed. A little yank on the bare foot roused sleeping beauty. "Here," she said. "Supposed to rain later; you might want this." She tossed the sock over.

"Yeah, I guess." Amy rubbed sleep from her eyes. "Everything okay?"

"Everything's wonderful!"

Amy laughed as she sat up. "That's your I-just-talked-to-Ian smile. Is he headed back?"

Beckie's smiled faded a little. "No, not yet." Her face brightened again, and Amy smiled. "But maybe in a couple months. Time to get some education in!" She reached with her right hand to pull Amy off the bed. "Let's go. It's time to meet Willie and his family for dinner."

Amy followed Beckie down to the garage. "Miata or MINI?" Beckie said.

Amy studied them both; she took a deep breath. "Miata." From the door, she finished, "With the top down, of course!"

Beckie laughed. "Of course!"

She dropped into the driver's seat; as she reached for the shifter, Amy reached over the console to touch her hand. "Thanks, sister."

Yeah. Ian'll be back soon. And Willie's just down the road a bit.

"Thank *you*, sister."

Time to get on with my life. And Amy'll do the same.

End Of Connections

Beckie and Ian will return in Coda?

APPENDICES

TEXT OF NOTES

LEÓN'S FAKED ABBY EMAIL TO begin Amy's lark:

> Amy, can't wait to see you again! The work's going well here, and I can get away for a week or maybe ten days. If you want to get away too, well, I set it up. If you miss the flight, the whole thing will fall apart by itself, so you don't have to worry if you can't for whatever reason. Like your mom or Mr. Jamse object.
>
> You can be my sister, Amy Rochambeau, 'cause then you can be eighteen, and ok to be traveling by yourself. That passport's in the care package I sent a day ago—I hope you got it!
>
> I remembered about your open-water sailing, and figured Shen might have less influence in the Turks and Caicos than at Mayaguana, so if you can sail there and park your boat someplace, you'll be booked on American Airlines from Providenciales to Miami at 3:30 the afternoon of September 3.
>
> When you get to Miami, clear Customs as a citizen Miss Rochambeau! and wait outside the exit from arrivals in the North Terminal. I'll send a big white limo for you; it'll meet you there and I'll see you later, down at Key West.
>
> Hope you can do it! Love, Abby

Abby's note to Ian, in the package with her passport:

~~Dewey, Cheatum and Howe~~ JD
Samuel Goldfarb

León's email to Abby:

> Jolene, you haven't answered any of your mail. That's very naughty of you, and we need to find an adequate punishment. While we consider what that should be, enjoy the show at our favorite file-sharing site. You know what to do to free this girl and make us go away forever. If your memory needs jogged, just watch it again. I'm sure something will occur to you.

Amy's note to Beckie:

Hi, Beckie! I don't really expect you'll ever read this unless I tell you about it first, but just in case. Mom'll never look in my room, so something'll have to really be wrong for you to see it, in which case, I want you to know what's happened.

I got a little package from Abby the other day, but it said wait to open it, so I tucked it away in my underwear drawer. Then early today, Monday, I got an email from Abby.

She said she was able to take a week off, and if I wanted to join her, I should open the package. If I didn't, or couldn't, just leave the package alone. Ha-ha! You know I wasn't going to pass up the chance!

You were flying, I guess, so I couldn't talk to you. I ripped the package open and in it was a passport with my picture in it, and Amy Rochambeau's name. She's eighteen, or I am, I guess, with it! Inside the passport, there's a plane ticket from Providenciales, that's in the Turks and Caicos you know. She said she remembered when I told her about sailing there a couple years ago. My butt's still sore from that ha-ha!

The ticket is from Providenciales to Miami, where she's gonna send a limo to pick me up! A big white one, she said!

This will be such fun! I can't wait!

Anyway, I expect I'll be back in about a week, and then we can laugh about this letter before I burn it ha-ha.

Hope you and Mr. Jamse work your thing out. Thanks for helping out Shalin with Alisha; I really like both of them.

Your friend, ARA.

Abby's letter to Amy:

A Rose,

I figure you'll never see this, so whatever I write is safe. And, better safe than sorry.

I've really missed you the past few days. First, finding out you were being rap... [unreadable; smeared] *account of me. Then I hear you're dead, drowned somewhere. You'll have to tell me about getting out of that; I am so happy! I was really happy to get your message that you were back home! I jumped up and about hit Eilís, I was so happy!*

Eilís and I—I want you to meet her, she's great! Anyway, we talked about me going home, but I decided, just me! that I'd keep on after those guys. From the instant I saw what they were doing to you, I promised myself that if they were gonna punish you because I was in the wrong place, I was gonna punish them for attacking the girl I love instead of me directly.

You're smart enough to know better, so that's all I'll say. When I get back, it won't matter. If I don't get back, it won't matter, except I'll have tried to make sure those guys will <u>*never*</u> *do that again.*

Gotta get going now. This'll be my last stop before I head home, probably with Mr. Jamse and anyone he brings to help me fight my fight. Not sure I want the help, but I finally accepted that I shouldn't turn help down when it's offered.

No matter what, I love you—finally figured <u>*that*</u> *out! Can't wait to see you again, hold you and kiss you—and make sure all your good parts are still in working order!*

Bye till tomorrow, Jolene.

PS: It's cool I'll be able to use my name again! JAR

PPS: In the event, everything is yours. This is my will: it's all yours. Signed Sep 16, Jolene Abigail Rochambeau.

Love you, girl!

THE NEST

THE NEST IS A FICTITIOUS archipelago sited in the Commonwealth of the Bahamas. It is described by the map in the front matter, as well as here.

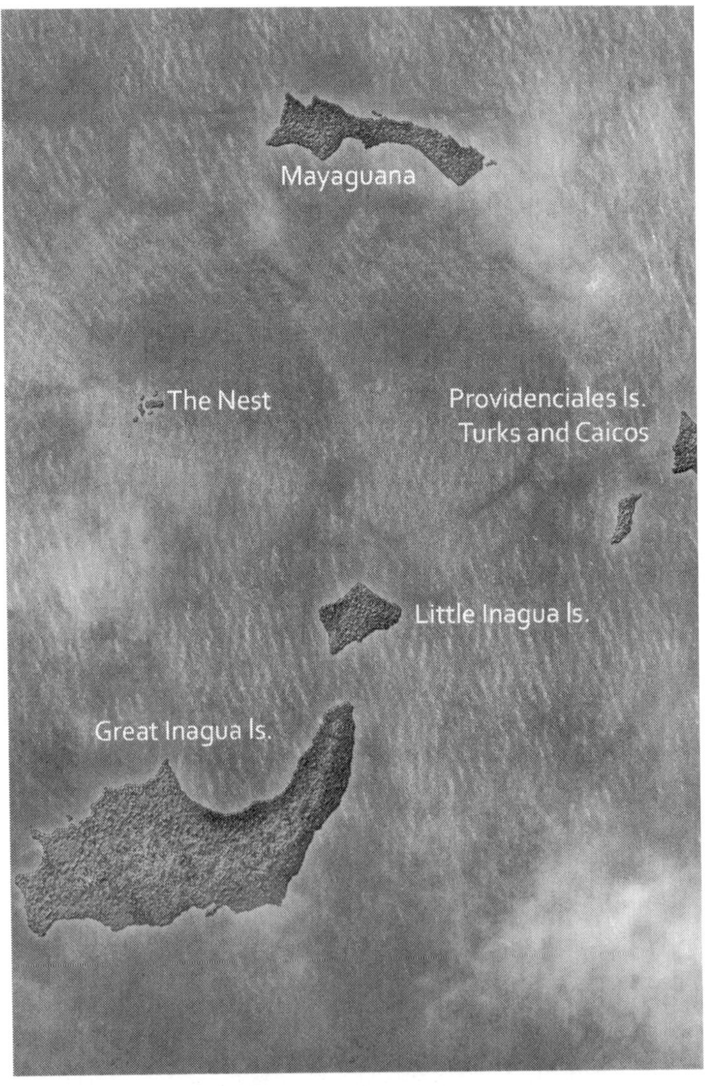

Cartography based on "Eastern Caribbean." 21.680164° N and 73.463645° W. Google Earth. Image date not given. Accessed April 7, 2013.

There are seven islands, listed in order of decreasing size.

Port Cay: 11050 feet by 4050 feet (largest dimensions in two orthogonal directions). Average elevation is 15 feet, and the maximum elevation is 50 feet, both above mean high water (mhw). Port Cay houses the team's airfield (8000' by 200' asphalt runway, heading east-west, east end is 18' elevation, dropping to 12' at the west end.). The island was artificially extended to accommodate the runway. To support aircraft operations, the island also has a hangar. The Nest's communication and radar facilities are adjacent to the hangar.

Bon Secours Cay: 7000' x 2000', avg. ele., 15'; max. ele., 40' mhw. The name denotes the home of the team's hospital. The camp's administration and security offices are adjacent to the hospital. Homes occupy most of the other area.

Nord Cay: 4100' x 1940'; avg. ele., 15'; max. ele., 25' mhw. Northernmost island. Team member homes.

Sud Cay: 2000' x 3000'; avg. ele., 18'; max. ele., 40' mhw. Southernmost occupied island. Sud Cay has the only deep draft dock on its eastern shore. More homes and storage facilities.

Home Cay: 3200' x 1580'; avg. ele., 13'; max. ele., 20' mhw. First island settled; Ian Jamse and Kevin deVeel's homes are there.

Cottage Cay: 2600' x 1200'; avg. ele., 10'; max. ele., 30' mhw. A community of cottages for single or unattached team members. The southwest shore has a protected lagoon; the team's small boat anchorage is there.

Tiny Cay: 2000' x 1000'; avg. ele., 8'; max. ele., 10' mhw. Uninhabited with only brush, Tiny Cay lies about two miles south and slightly west of Sud Cay. It is used for training.

All islands except Tiny Cay have a dock with boats capable of navigating between islands. Bon Secours has three of them due to its relatively central location.

Cell phone and WiFi service are provided, with a connection to BTC. Security monitors all coastlines for intrusions as well as passing traffic.

The team's aircraft are leased, including two Gulfstream g150's, a B737-700C and a Piper Mirage. The team owns outright a Lockheed C130 retired from US Air Force service. The hangar is capable of protecting these as well as a Eurocopter EC-135.

Cast

IN ORDER OF APPEARANCE

PIERO Salvadore:	Sub-Minister of Interior - under Mateo Huamán. Later Minister, running for President
Mateo Huamán:	Minister of Interior, Salvadore's superior
Donato Talos (Donny):	New York crime boss with wide interests
León:	One of Talos' men - Talos' third-in-command
Camila:	One of Talos' women; Piero's mistress
Jolene Abigail Rochambeau (Abby, Jo):	Columbia student, later one of Jamse's team, infatuated with Amy Ardan
Detective O'Keefe:	NYC police detective
Frankie Pella:	One of Talos' men - Talos' second-in-command - boat driver
Samuel Goldfarb (Sam):	Donato Talos' lawyer
Sara Salvadore:	Piero's wife
Colleen:	Goldfarb's assistant
Rebecca Sverdupe (Beckie):	Ian Jamse's fiancée and apprentice teammate
Go Shen:	One of Jamse's team, handles security for the Nest; Rou's husband
Millie Ardan:	Jamse's Chief Doctor, Amy's mother
Ian Jamse:	Beckie's fiancé, the team's leader and her mentor
Jean-Luc Fereré:	Pilot, one of Jamse's team
Kevin deVeel:	Jamse's co-leader, Shalin's husband
Barbara Saunders:	One of Jamse's team; working in Peru with Nayra Mamani
Maurice Boynton:	Jamse's factotum, team member
Derek Hamilton:	One of Jamse's team, married to Emily
Elena Rios (Lena):	One of Jamse's team, trainer; Pieter Nijs' wife
Sandy Daniels:	Beckie's roommate at Univ. of Miami, Greg's sister
Greg Daniels:	Beckie's roommate at Miami, Sandy's brother, Marla's lover
Marla Suarez:	Beckie's roommate at Miami, Greg's lover
Amy Rose Ardan:	Millie's 15 YO daughter, infatuated with Abby Rochambeau
Eilís O'Bannon:	Abby's attorney, friend and former lover
Go Rou:	One of Jamse's team, Shen's wife, handles finances and legal issues for the team
Else Meyer:	One of Jamse's team, a boffin who handles IT and intelligence; Jannike's partner
Philip Gomez:	Mamani's Campaign Manager

Cast

Nayra Mamani:	Peruvian politician, running for President, contracting with the team
Jannike Meyer:	One of Jamse's team, airside manager; Else's partner
Rich Quinn:	One of Jamse's team; Sue Jinet's significant other
Mathilde Moreau:	One of Jamse's team, a pilot
Sue Jinet:	One of Jamse's team, Rich Quinn's significant other
Willie Llorens:	One of Jamse's team
Jaime Lobera:	One of Mamani's group, arrested after recording their meetings
Dean of Students:	Beckie's school contact
Dan Wu:	One of Jamse's team
Bethany Stadd (Beth):	One of Jamse's team
Shalin deVeel:	Kevin deVeel's wife, Beckie's friend
Silvio Flores (Goldfarb Junior):	Talos' youngest son
Paulo Estevez:	Talos' man, working for Shen in the Nest's security
Dylan Rees:	Resident of Chatham, becomes Amy's boyfriend
Rosa Simmons:	Real estate broker in Brewster, NY
Three bad guys:	In the SUV in Brewster; all Talos' men
Emidio Talos:	Donato's brother
Judith Weston:	Police officer on outer Cape
Mrs. Rees:	Dylan's Mom
Emil Gonzales:	Piero's campaign manager
Fernando (Nando):	Piero's assistant
Carmen Salvadore:	Piero's thirteen-year-old daughter
Three bad guys:	On Port Cay; attacking the Nest
Melissa Durst (Lissa):	Beckie's friend, Mike's girlfriend
Michael Sverdupe (Mike):	Beckie's brother, Lissa's boyfriend
Pieter Nijs:	One of Jamse's team, armorer and chief mechanic; Elena Rios' husband
Shakti Krishna:	One of Jamse's team; trauma surgeon
Josie:	One of Millie's nurses
Karen Wilson:	One of Jamse's team, a pilot
Two Guardia:	In the hotel in Arequipa
(unnamed woman):	Fernando's girl-friend
Tomás:	Cab driver in Arequipa
Janice:	One of Jamse's team, Mathilde's co-pilot

Also

Trillian:	Jamse's ocelot

ACKNOWLEDGMENTS

Great thanks to my wife and family for their support!

Thanks to Amy Rose Davis, one of the *Twelve Worlds* contributors, who graciously lent her name to Amy Rose Ardan. I hope she's not dismayed with the way her namesake character turned out. Find her excellent work at http://www.amazon.com/Amy-Rose-Davis/e/B004GG38AI/

Also, to Critters.org and the several critters who provided suggestions and comments to improve my work. Among them are Martin, Peter, willisouth and especially Andrea, Carol, Charles and Phil. Without their efforts, I can't imagine the problems this story would have.

In Chapter 18, Beckie misremembers the title of "Cancun" by John Forster, from which she does remember the last line of the chorus.

Like all budget constrained authors, I draw heavily on Google Earth for scenes set in lands not local to me. Any discrepancies in fictionalization are my failure, not Google's.

About the Author

Tony Lavely lives with his lovely, compassionate wife in Massachusetts, in reasonable proximity to their children and grandchildren. Retirement has provided ample time for him to pursue writing as well as other mundane pleasures. *Connections* is his third novel. One of the Mercenaries stories, it is a thriller in an approximation to the real world.

He was privileged to be a part of the Twelve Worlds Anthology for Charity, still available at on-line outlets. This collection of short stories benefits Reading Is Fundamental, and meeting (in an on-linely way) the other authors was great fun and excellent experience. Those guys are great! ('Guys' used in the best The Electric Company tradition: "Hey, you guys!")

The Mercenaries series has grown to three volumes with the release of *Connections.* Coming up next is *Coda?*, now the subject of heated debate with beta readers. At present, it seems likely that at least one more volume will follow; it is tentatively named *Served Cold.*

He reads fantasy and adventure, confidently believes that *The Muppet Movie* is one of the best movies ever made, and his iPod playlist includes works from Beethoven to Twisted Sister.

He blogs at http://www.tonylavely.com/

You can also scan this code to arrive there painlessly.

On Twitter: twitter.com/tlavely

Email: atl.for.writing at gmail.com.

If you find a typo in this book and report it with this number (CS150501.5), you can score a coupon for *Coda?* as well as Tony's thanks.

Excerpt From Coda?

This story follows *Connections* by a year and a half. Beckie and Ian have settled most of their troubles; their marriage took place in Stonehenge, just as Beckie wished. The planned release date is fall 2015; watch for it or follow my blog or Twitter. This excerpt is from the draft; you could end up with words that don't make it into the final version!

Chapter One
The Error

Testing Amy

LOUNGING ON THE LANAI AT her home on the Nest, Beckie Jamse had her feet up, contemplating the blue sky and water, and sipping an iced coffee.

She started when Elena's ring tone blared from her phone, and again when Sam Dabron greeted her, "Morning, Beckie. Are you—"

"Sam? What's going on? Is Elena—"

"Nothing, Mrs. Jamse. Lena's fine. I left my phone and she offered me hers. Now…"

His pause allowed her to respond, but she mumbled something unintelligible.

She heard the amusement as he continued, "We were about to have a work-out session with Amy Ardan, until she reminded us *you* were her mentor."

Beckie took the phone from her ear and stared at it. Could Amy be pulling that to avoid Sam and Elena's training? Not likely. So why… Chattering from the phone drew her attention; she put it to her ear and listened.

"You there, Mrs. Jamse? Hello—"

"Yeah, Sam, I'm here."

"With an invitation like that, we'll pick you up at the dock in… in ten minutes, Lena says." Beckie heard someone mumble in the background before Sam laughed. "Unless you want to call it off?"

"See you in ten." She smiled at her husband's factotum, Maurice Boynton, as he placed fresh coffee on the table. "Thanks, Maurice, but I've just been summoned to save Amy from a whupping. Sam's on the way."

He smiled and wished her well.

She hurried to the dock to wait. The sun had been up almost two hours; the water surrounding Home Cay where she and Ian lived—when they were not off being soldiers of fortune or skilled bodyguards or even thieves—was blue and calm.

The boat hove into view around the west end of Port Cay, which housed the team's airstrip. She could see three figures in the boat; Sam, the tall black man, was lounging on the far side rail, allowing Amy to drive. Must have picked up Elena at Nord, Beckie thought.

Beckie greeted the others, then leaned against the rail opposite Sam. The skiff needed a half-hour to run south to Tiny Cay.

On the almost twenty-five acres of sand and brush they called Tiny, the hand-to-hand with Amy was too amiable, Beckie thought, though not sloppy! Neither Sam nor Elena would have permitted that. Beckie's irritation finally took control: she ripped Amy's shirt and screamed in her face, "This is how you fight!" while picking her up and throwing her down. She almost missed the practice area, but Elena, laughing almost too hard to help, hip-checked Amy's torso to land safely.

Beckie sat on Amy's belly as hard as her hundred pounds would and yanked her face up. "It isn't a useful practice if you don't go full-bore! You won't get what you need from this if you keep pulling punches and don't use all your assets." She looked at the girl's stricken expression and sat back, pulling her into an embrace made slightly more awkward by Amy's missing shirt and both Elena and Sam's amusement at her 'attack.'

As Beckie considered Sam's motivation in inviting her, Amy grabbed the remnants of her shirt and flipped it up and over Beckie's head, around her neck. Further consolidating her position, she flipped Beckie to her back and dropped flat against Beckie's chest, driving the wind from her lungs. Before she could catch her breath, Amy had turned her face down and made the shirt into a garrote. Not wire thin, to be sure, Beckie thought as she gasped, but that only means it'll hurt more!

She heard the slap and guessed that Sam had smacked Amy's butt, since the pressure at her throat relaxed and the girl rolled away. It took a few seconds for her breath to steady; seconds while she and Amy glared at each other.

When she could, Beckie rose and reached a hand to her partner. She helped her up and into a friendly hug. "That's what I mean, girl! Well done!" She let go the hug and draped the shirt around Amy's neck, almost covering her. "What's your rating?" she said to Sam and then Elena.

"I wondered just what you were playing at," Sam said. "She was doing ok, I thought, when you grabbed her. But you're right, she brought a whole other thing to it when she fought back."

"You thought she wasn't going too easy before?"

"Not really."

"We try not to kill sparring partners," Elena added with a laugh. "Too hard to get new ones."

Beckie felt her flush brighten. She pulled Amy close again and pressed their cheeks together. "Sorry."

"Not a problem. Dylan will enjoy the story."

"Unfair!" She took her turn smacking Amy's camo covered butt. "Are we done, then?"

"Yeah," Sam said. "For now. This afternoon, I want you three and Beth over to Port, to do some shooting. Tomorrow, you and Amy will do this again, but you'll take me on, since you both seem to have hidden reserves. I want you to learn how to bring them out before you're at death's door. You available, Lena?"

"Wouldn't miss it!"

On the boat ride back to Home, Amy said, "Sam, thanks for that." But Beckie popped her eyes open when Amy continued, "What is it you do?"

Sam chuckled. "I'm not sure what the bosses want me to say to that. Mrs. Jamse, can you enlighten… your protégée, I guess would be right?"

"We've been saying apprentice, but you're right, too. As for the other, Ian or Kevin would be better, I think, but…" She thought a moment. "Sam… Well, right now, he's assisting Elena in training, making sure that she puts everyone through the right wringer. But his primary job is soldier. Mercenary. He's heading a team of eight protecting… Protecting an asset in Syria that our customer didn't want to see damaged." She leaned back and looked up at the blue sky, a frown wrinkling her forehead. "At least, that was the motivation a couple years ago when we took the job. About a year ago, the customer raised the ante by asking us to sometimes join rebel forces fighting both the Assad regime and the Islamic State."

"Whatever for?"

"When Ian came back from the negotiations, he said their goal was to continue protecting the… asset, and bring a secular government into power."

"They've been trying that for years! I know Sam's good, but—"

"I told you she was bright, Sam." Elena was doing her best not to laugh aloud.

"Right you are, Amy," he said. "That's why they put the protection above the rebellion. There will be a political solution, eventually, and whether Assad or the rebels or the IS survive, they'll need the infrastructure." He glanced at Beckie. "Does Ian really feel that we should protect the… identity?"

"No. That was me, being too coy by half." She turned her head to Amy and gave her a wry smile. "They're protecting a thirty-six inch natural gas pipeline running from Deir Ali to Al Rayyan. Roughly Damascus to Homs. We, Ian and I, think the customer is supplying gas and wants to keep it flowing."

"Yeah, that makes sense. And no matter who wins, they'll need energy, like you said."

They'd reached the dock at Home Cay. With a promise to return in an hour or so, Amy left on her way to Cottage Cay, where she and Dylan were staying.

KEVIN

Beckie had showered and warned Boynton that Amy and Dylan would probably appear for lunch; now, as she relaxed in the warmth of the Bahamian August, her eyes drifted shut.

She started, then was embarrassed when she found not only Boynton, but Amy, Dylan and Beth standing at the foot of her chair, all except Boynton grinning like crazy people.

Boynton, however… "What's wrong, Maurice? Did the lunch not work out?"

"Much more serious than that, I fear." He held his phone out. "Barbara has advised me that Kevin has been injured in an… incident near his parents' home. Seriously."

"Oh, no! What about Shalin? Who's with her? And is it worth us commandeering Jean-Luc or Patrice—"

"Patrice is preparing to leave as we speak. He is filing a flight plan to Durban with a stop in Paris for fuel. Mathilde will be able to join you in Paris, coming up from Riyadh, and fly on while Patrice rests."

"And Ian…"

"Suggested, according to Barbara, that you be prepared for rural… encounters. No," he said in response to her look, "I don't know what that means either. However, the deVeel's home is near the Jamse's, about 55 kilometers west of PMB."

"PMB?"

"Ah. Pietermaritzburg."

"Of course," Beckie said. "I knew that. Sorry."

"And both homes are near the Drakensberg Wilderness Area, which certainly qualifies as rural. But I have no information about why Kevin would be there, or how he was injured. Barbara said they are still seeking answers."

"Call Sam and let him know. I think this is higher priority than target practice, though…" She giggled. "… I'll miss sparring with him if we can't get to do that soon."

Amy blanched slightly. "I suppose 'miss' is one way to say it."

"I don't think you and—"

The look on Amy's face warned Beckie. "I'm not sitting on my ass while Kevin's hurt and something's going on with his parents. Shalin's been too good to me to flake out on her!"

Well, that's not a surprise. Shalin'll probably need support, too. "Not Dylan, though. I don't think this is…"

Amy's expression wasn't as definitive as a second ago, but Beckie thought she read it correctly before Amy slid her arm around Dylan's waist and walked him to the far end of the lanai, out of earshot.

Boynton hurried back to the lanai. "Sam says to tell you you can't get out of his training session that easily; he'll join you." His glance took in the couple talking at the end of the lanai.

Beckie followed his look. "I suspect Dylan will… Well, let's see."

Holding each other tightly, Amy and Dylan returned to the group. "Dylan allows me to go, and he will fly back to Chatham—"

"Holding my sat phone close to my heart for whatever updates come along." He brushed a kiss along Amy's cheek before fixing her with a stern gaze. "There *will* be updates, or my promise is off."

Amy nodded with quick firm motions.

"I'm in," Beth said. "I'll head over to get my gear. Who's calling Elena? And Willie? He won't want to be left out."

The 737-700ER was not crowded, though everyone seemed to congregate near Shalin's seat. The deVeel twins were back at the Nest, staying with Josie, one of Millie's nurses.

Patrice came out of the cockpit about five hours out of the Nest. He walked Beckie and Willie toward the back of the plane, away from the others. "Barbara just called. Kevin didn't make it."

"Damn!" escaped both Beckie and Willie together.

Beckie gave the two men a quick embrace; they'd both known Kevin longer than she had, but her memory turned back to the sleeping bag in Arizona, when Kevin had given her the support she hadn't known she'd needed. And all the help and camaraderie the two of them had shared since then.

"I guess we better talk to Shalin," she said. Willie nodded and Patrice preceded them up the aisle. However, when they reached the others, he kept going, back to the cockpit.

"What is it? What did Patrice want?" Beckie was pretty sure Elena was just curious, but both Beth and Shalin seemed more… prescient.

"News," she said, adopting Ian's laconic approach. Willie worked his way to the seat behind Shalin, and Beckie took one of her hands.

"It's Kevin," Shalin said, her voice catching on the name.

Beckie dipped her head. "Barbara said he… he didn't make it."

Over the murmured expressions of shock and sympathy, Beckie heard, "Any other details?"

She can't take it this well, Beckie thought. "Patrice didn't say." She squeezed Shalin's hand. "You gonna be… okay?"

The look of surprise on Shalin's face threw Beckie for a loop, until she recalled the stabilizing influence the woman had had on everyone at the Nest. "Of course. We had good years together, Kevin and I, and of course, the twins. I will mourn him, and remember him, and forever love him, but he always warned me that his career choice, as he put it, might end badly." She looked around, meeting each of the other's eyes. "But I would like some time alone, I think."

Willie offered his hand over the seat back, and led her to the last row of seats. When he gave her a quick hug and whispered to her, she reached up to brush his cheek with her fingers, then dropped gracefully to sit. Willie came forward a few seats and made himself comfortable—if anything in this situation could be comfortable, Beckie mused.

"Patrice said nothing else?" Beth asked.

"No. Guess we'll find out soon enough."

Elena stretched in her seat. "We're going straight to Durban, right?"

"Yeah. Well, except for the fuel stop in Paris. Mathilde will take us the last ten hours, Patrice said. Maurice made reservations at some resort between King Shakta Airport and the city. I didn't want to head into the scene until we talked to Ian, and he wasn't available before we left."

"Why a resort?" Beth asked. "Not gonna be a lot of playing around."

"That's for damn sure. But we figured sleep would be necessary after eighteen or nineteen hours flying. And the six hour time change, too, like Cairo."

Beth grimaced, then curled into her seat.

Good idea, Beckie thought. She dropped next to the seat where Amy was still asleep. Like Sam, the girl hadn't roused during the exchanges with Patrice or Shalin. However, the impact of Beckie in the adjacent seat opened her eyes and brought her head up. "What?"

Beckie told her, and after Amy's trip back to whisper condolences to Shalin, they curled up together and by turns, cried and dozed.

Patrice woke her before they started the descent into King Shakta, teasing her with an offer to join Mathilde in the cockpit, "to see how it could be done," but she declined with a half-laugh, seeking out a container of orange juice and a cup of coffee instead.

Her phone told her the time in Durban was seven and a bit, a look out the window said it was evening. She walked the cabin, rousing the others, ending with Shalin, now sitting with Elena. Looks like she hasn't slept much.

In two hours, they'd cleared customs and immigration, at least with the baggage they intended to carry. As they looked for the hotel shuttle, her phone buzzed.

"Ian!" Her voice broke and she stepped away from the others. "Ian, I'm so sorry! How—"

"As well as can be expected, love. I will meet you at the hotel in about…" A pause, maybe looking at a clock? "… in about an hour. I hope you will be able to remain awake."

"If I'm asleep, wake me with a kiss!" She caught her breath. "Shalin's with us; we told her what Barbara said, and she wants more detail. So do we all, but her need is… exigent."

"I understand. I will share with all of you, and her especially."

"Do we need a car? I think Maurice arranged the shuttle to pick us up, but we could also get a car or two. There's like eight or nine of us, including Patrice and Mathilde."

"We can arrange that in the morning. We will need off-road vehicles, so the airport rentals would not suit."

Beckie felt a hand on her arm; Amy was pulling her toward the now arrived shuttle. "Bus is here, love. We'll see you at the hotel in a bit."

During the twenty minute ride, Beckie told the others that Ian was on the way, and that he'd shared nothing else with her.

Beckie started out of a strange dream when something touched her shoulder. She shook off the fading memory of… whatever it was, to find Sam waiting for her to come to. "Ian's out front," he said.

That cleared her head better than anything she could imagine; she ran ahead to the front room. They embraced, crying into each others' neck, then shared a hard, fervent kiss. "God, I'm happy to see you," Beckie breathed into his ear.

"Believe me, no happier than I am you!"

Wow, never heard that kind of feeling from him. I love him… "I love you, Ian. Never forget that!"

She leaned away to see his face; his eyes were alight as well as somber. "I never shall. I love you."

Sam cleared his throat and in another moment, they separated—slightly. "Sorry, Sam. But first things first," Beckie said.

Ian gave them his wry smile, then stepped back. For the first time since entering, Beckie noticed that all the others were in the room with them. Makes no difference, she thought. "Well, let's sit down and get started, okay?" She took Ian's arm and headed toward the empty love seat.

For an hour, Ian explained as much as he knew about Kevin's trip and the action that had eventually claimed his life. "For several weeks, his parents had dealt with transients on the back edge of their property. He was convinced they were smuggling *dagga* from Lesotho."

"Dagga?"

"Marijuana. It is illegal in South Africa, and the smugglers are well-compensated, at least, in comparison to farming, say." He waited another second. "My parents have experienced similar incursions, though not as close to their home. In any event, he and I, with Barbara of course, decided to pay a visit to his family, and determine if the police should be involved, or what steps might be appropriate or prudent."

He stopped and caught Shalin in his gaze. "Would you prefer… waiting before…"

"No, Ian, thank you. As I said to Beckie, the two of us kept the possibility of sudden death in mind… Recall how we met, after all."

Beckie thought back to Kevin's description of his introduction to Shalin: she'd been blown into him by a suicide bomber—her brother—in Tel Aviv.

Ian bowed his head in acknowledgement. "He and Barbara went to his parents while I visited mine.

"Barbara called soon after I arrived. The intruders came to the house and in the guise of insurance, demanded first, money and valuables, and second, that everyone depart for the next two weeks."

"I'll bet Kevin didn't take that well," Shalin said.

"He did not. He signaled Barbara to keep the family members safe and slipped out the back door. She believes he intended to flank them, possibly taking them out one or two at a time. Five or six were all she saw.

"As soon as the first shot was fired, Barbara got all five of the family down into the basement where—"

"Five, Ian?"

"His parents and sister, and her two daughters. They were visiting from Johannesburg."

"Oh, okay. Thanks."

"Barbara held her position where she could defend the entry to the basement and still monitor the front doorway. A minute or so after the shooting ended, several more shots destroyed the locks. The two men who kicked the door open afterward were not as cautious as they should have been; Barbara terminated them.

"She waited several minutes before moving. One of the intruder's weapons she gave to Kevin's sister before using the back door. Light from the house was sufficient to find Kevin; he was near the front door. During an admittedly cursory examination, she found three bullet wounds in his torso. She applied pressure bandages and continued to investigate. He had eliminated four, and with the two in the house, she believed the entire force had been neutralized.

"She called me; we brought my parents after advising the police."

"Where's… Oh, Millie's still with Jimmy, right? In Syria?"

"Indeed."

"Hmm. And the police?"

"Since moving Kevin to hospital, they have been investigating the events, with no resolution so far except that Barbara has been 'asked' to remain available for questioning."

"They aren't charging—"

"While they will not commit, the sense is that they agree she acted in self-defense, since the door was damaged from outside."

"Okay, I guess."

"Very well," Ian said. "The hour is late and I do not wish to leave either the deVeels or our parents alone longer than necessary. Though the police are watching them both tonight," he finished, to forestall Beckie's obvious complaint.

Beckie waited until the others had dispersed to their individual rooms before leading Ian to hers. No, I won't tell him just yet, she decided of her own news. He has enough to worry about for now. They gave each other great pleasure, then slept the sleep of the just.

Beckie woke when her back chilled. Ian had risen; he was looking at his phone. "What's the news?"

"Nothing to concern yourself with, Rebecca. Mother would like Shalin at our home early, for Kevin's family, and for settling how the service will be held."

"Should the twins be here?"

He finished dressing before speaking. "They are old enough to understand what has happened. However, arranging their transport… We should allow Shalin to decide how best to handle it."

"Yeah. But I think Patrice and Mathilde between them could make the trip back to get them, so that shouldn't be the issue."

"Indeed. You should sleep for another two or three hours. I will drop Shalin off and return—"

"No!" Beckie rolled out of the bed and ran toward the bath. "Give me five, six minutes. I can go with. If I need to sleep, I'll do it in the car." She knew the closing door cut her words off.

In four minutes, she threw open the door and ran to her bag. The towel went in the direction of the chair as she snatched underwear and garments, then raced to dress.

Three minutes later, Ian said, "An entrancing several minutes. I expected you would need another two minutes, but…" He opened the door and with a hand on her back, bade her lead.

On the terrace, the buffet was in full swing and with her glance, Beckie pleaded with Ian for coffee. He nodded and while she went there, he continued to the table where Shalin and Elena waited.

"… hope you have not waited long," Ian was saying as Beckie approached. She tipped her head to acknowledge the women, then sipped from her cup.

"We're fine," Shalin said. "After I speak with Kevin's mum and dad, I will likely ask about how we might arrange for the twins to be here."

"Certainly. Rebecca suggests that Patrice and Mathilde should be able to make the return flight, then with some time off, bring them here. However, are you certain that… that the interment should be here?"

"No, but I suspect the deVeel's will press for that. We can place a marker at the Nest, as we did for Abby, so the kids will have something tangible to focus on. But, we'll see. There's no need to launch Patrice just yet."

She's way too calm about this. I could never even think if I lost Ian, let alone be rational. I'll ask Elena to see if she's really okay. Or Millie; she should be arriving soon.

"That seems a good plan. Now, if you are ready, we should leave. You have visited the deVeel's, I believe?"

"Yes, before the twins. And they visited the Nest just a year ago."

Beckie rode with Ian, along with Shalin and Elena. Since Beckie chose not to sleep in, Sam thought they all should follow Ian; he quickly arranged another rental and trailed Ian's car. "We'll get whatever we need later today," he said, waving away Ian's half-hearted protest.

Ian drove; he gave no travelogue. The hotel about split the thirty-five kilometers between the airport north of Durban and the city, and Beckie recalled that his parents' home was another hundred or so kilometers west of the city. Since the deVeels were staying with Ian's parents while the police and repair work was completed, that was their destination. The hundred and twenty-five kilometers passed quickly enough, and the green of the countryside was repeated on the farm where Ian had grown up. Trees still outlined the fields, which remained fallow.

Beckie followed close on Ian's heels once they arrived. Hardly surprising, she thought, that the atmosphere's kinda tense. Not only is everyone dealing with the emotions from Kevin's death, but we've brought people no one here knows—a bunch of them—and none of us knew Kevin's sister Tamryn and her girls, Mikeala and Courtney, before Kevin's parents introduced them.

To the volatile mix, we've added six obvious combatants. Well, Amy might not qualify yet, but Sam and Willie—their presence will cast an implication on all of us even if Ian and Kevin's profession isn't known. The trick would be, she thought, keeping the police from a) recognizing their profession and b) guessing accurately just what they were all doing there once Kevin had been mourned. I'll talk with Ian later; he must have thought it out.

In short order, however, Carys' gracious welcome reduced the tension. She gave Shalin a firm hug, then sent her to the front room with Kevin's parents, Pieter and Natalie. The others went through introductions and before Beckie had even a chance to give her a hint, Amy had scooped Kevin's nieces up and taken them out front where the police were still watching.

Sam, Willie and Elena faded into the background. Before much time passed, Pieter returned and asked for Barbara, to give her account of Kevin's last minutes, Beckie guessed, and decided Barbara knew as well as she what to include and what to leave out.

Beckie tried to engage Tamryn, Kevin's sister, but the woman, as might be expected, was worried about her girls, especially since Amy'd taken them out of her view. With a glance to Ian as he moved in Sam and Willie's direction, she took the woman to the front door, so she could watch as Amy sat with the girls, describing something that took their entire attention. More comfortable, Tamryn responded to Beckie's questions about her life and her husband and, with almost a literal glow, her girls. Beckie recognized the symptoms: two more spoiled young ladies were about to be inflicted on the world.

With a twinkle in her eyes, Beckie described the Nest, and some of Amy's past, adding the twins' exploits, since Tamryn's life was certainly not going revolve around whatever would happen here in the next few days once her husband, Marc, joined them.

They watched both the kids and the policeman watching them and the house until Carys came out the door and announced dinner, "Early today, since everyone seems to have a different schedule. Rebecca, I think Ian's looking for you."

With a quick "Thanks," she turned toward the door as Carys joined Tamryn in hailing Amy and the youngsters.

Seeking Smugglers

Inside, Ian was next to the small table holding the Frederic Remington piece, *Polo*. Sam stood beside him, and Beckie saw Elena there, too. Wonder where Willie is? And Beth? as she counted up in her head.

"Hi, love! What's the plan?"

"After dinner, I plan to do a recce; I wish to see what the surrounding area looks like."

"Can we do any of that from the air? And who will get the 4x4s for us?"

"I prefer to do an initial survey from horseback; depending on what we find, I will ask Patrice and possibly Mathilde to charter either helicopters or light planes." He raised his hand to his mother. "We will be just a moment." He lowered his voice again. "I wish for you to join me in the survey, while… If Amy Rose is willing… where is she?"

"She took the two girls out to take their minds off death and other distractions. She seems to be doing fine."

He nodded. "If they are willing, she and Bethany should stay at the house, because I believe the police will withdraw before the evening. Willie is seeking rentals for us." He gestured as Willie entered the room. "Elena and Samuel will accompany him."

"You want three then?" Elena asked.

"Indeed. We will use them tomorrow, I suspect, depending on what we discover tonight."

"Good," Beckie said. "And I was worried about the police and their reaction to… to all of us, moving in on them."

"Since we have taken no action, they have no concerns to act upon," he said with a small laugh. Elena wasn't so reserved. "We will take our horses; it will be not quite a thirty kilometer ride to the area I wish to investigate."

That'll be fun! Nice to be in the saddle again. They both turned as Carys gently repeated her call to dinner.

The meal was excellent, and everyone seemed calm and relaxed. Beckie collected Amy and Beth, and the two girls who had seemingly attached themselves to Amy. "It's okay," Amy said. "We're teaching each other about things."

"Cool. Ian would like to ride out to do some recon, and he'd like you guys to keep watch here." Before either could voice a protest, she continued, "He thinks the police will remove the guard tonight, and so you…" Her glance took in both of them. "… will be the protection."

"We can help, too!" one of the girls said.

Beckie thought about dropping to her knee, but she was short enough already. She leaned over so her face aligned with the girl's. "Let me guess. You're Mikeala, age fourteen, and in grade eight, I hear."

The girl blushed. "Grade nine. I'll be fifteen soon."

"Excellent," Beckie said. "Amy will put you to work as soon as we're ready. In the meantime, you make sure your mom is okay while you wait for your dad to get here. Okay?" She twisted to face Courtney. "You too, okay? Please?"

They nodded in unison, and ran to find Tamryn. "Good work," Amy said with a snicker. "Just like Elena and Beth…" She waved in her direction. "… handled me and Dylan, back then."

"Well," Beth said, "I don't think we'll be giving them weapons. I hope!"

"That's for damn sure!" Beckie covered her mouth. "Sorry," but no one seemed to have noticed. "Anyway, we'd appreciate it. I think Willie's coming back, too, with Elena and Sam once he finds some off-road trucks for us. While Ian didn't say, we'll probably be out till morning. I have my phone, if anything happens… No, I have no clue what might turn up, here. Beth, your phone has all the contacts, too, right?"

"Yeah. We'll be fine. Just, when you go for a little touchy-feely, watch for the poison ivy like tree we have round here. Hard to treat when you get it all up —"

Beckie and Amy both exploded in laughter; their merriment brought chastising looks from two of the adults, and questioning ones from all the others. "Sorry," Beckie muttered in their direction. "Good thing the girls left, yeah?"

Now Beth and Amy had to muffle their mirth. Beckie pulled them out the front door to avoid bothering the others, but in a few minutes, Ian appeared and said, "It is time to go. Will you two maintain the… peace?"

Beth giggled, but Amy said they'd be fine.

In the barn, Beckie backed Ian against the stall wall for a lingering kiss, then told him about Beth's warning. For the first time since they'd arrived, he laughed before saying, "You will have no difficulty. I have great familiarity with the area. Still," he said with a smile—the smile I love! Beckie thought—"my strong preference is the bed. At the least, a blanket!"

"So, you're saying no fooling around this evening?"

"I fear not. But that is not why—"

"It sure isn't! I never thought of it till Beth said."

"Indeed. She hails from Pretoria, and the plant is as prevalent there as here." He pulled her in for a final kiss, then took her to select tack for the ride.

"What time's sunset?"

"About quarter to six," Ian replied. "Not quite two hours."

"And the horses? In good shape?"

"Probably over-coddled. We should arrive… just before sundown, given that the trees will bring darkness on earlier. The area I wish to investigate… I plan to reach it by nine or half-past."

"Hmm. Okay. How's Kevin's family doing?"

He rode several yards before answering. "I suspect Shalin is the most stable of them, though Tamryn's concern about her husband may be her greatest issue. You did well, suggesting that her girls help her." He rode a little further. "I believe they will all recover, sooner or later. Shalin asked that Patrice and Mathilde return and collect the twins before the service. I agreed."

"Good!" She twisted in the saddle to catch his eye. "When will the service be, then?"

"They are still discussing that, but I expect very soon after the twins arrive." He looked at his watch. "That will put it Monday morning, I think."

"What day's today? Sorry, just confused."

"Friday evening. Now, when we enter the undergrowth ahead, take care for your horse's footing. If I remember, he is not as adept as you might wish."

"You've ridden him before?"

"Your astonishment cuts me to the quick!" His laugh belied his words. "I put you on him intentionally. He's just over thirty, and it has been twelve or fifteen years since I last rode him."

"That was… before you met me."

"That note of astonishment again. I did have something of a life prior to our engagement."

"I guess you must have," she said. "Sorry I missed it. Well, some of it, anyway."

The canopy closed over them and Beckie followed Ian's lead between the trees and bushes.

With an hour to go, they broke out of the trees into a clear area. The moon, though waxing, was about an hour from setting, and three or four days from first quarter, so dimly lit best described the scene as Beckie reined up beside Ian.

"What?"

"Checking the waypoint."

When he finished and took the reins again, she took advantage of the relatively easier riding to ask, "Where are we headed? And more important, what do you expect we'll find there? Unarmed, as we are."

"Ah, yes. I suppose this would now be appropriate." He turned in his saddle and wrangled his pack around in front.

After a minute's digging, he drew a… Beckie couldn't tell what it was. It looked like a… "A web belt, Ian? What's that for?"

"Patience, love." He spurred his horse close to hers and handed her the belt, wound tightly on itself.

"Damn," she said as she fumbled and nearly dropped the lump. Finally it was clear and she could see. "My God, Ian, thanks! I meant to complain about Amy's P229, but, but this should be awesome! A…" She held the pistol to catch the light in the engraving: SIG P238. "I was looking at their website the other day, and this… this feels as awesome as it looked." She hefted it. 'Yeah, it's a lot lighter than the P229." She checked for the empty magazine and chamber, then sniffed the end of the barrel. "Have you fired it?"

"One box, just to verify it. Tomorrow, we shall visit a range just outside PMB where you may test it yourself."

"So we won't need it tonight?"

"Indeed. Due to its size and caliber, that is a defensive weapon, not an offensive one. However, I expect to see no one tonight." He slapped his mount carefully.

And that's all you're going to say about that, I guess. She buckled the belt with the holster, and followed, pushing her pique away.

Before they moved back under the trees again, Ian raised his hand to signal a stop, and swung down. He pulled the pack off and as Beckie watched, he spread a blanket and with a wave, invited her to sit.

She took the invitation, grabbing her own pack to lay beside her. "What's all this, love?"

"We are enough early that we can pause for some refreshment."

"Champagne and caviar?" she said with a giggle.

His snicker confirmed her guess; he held up a handful of energy bars and two bottles of water, one still, the other sparkling. "Your pleasure, Madame?"

She took the effervescent one along with two bars and set to them. While they enjoyed the repast, the moonlight faded as clouds moved in from the escarpment twenty kilometers to the west. When Beckie pointed behind him, Ian said, "I believe we should don our waterproofs."

Beckie's astonishment returned until, watching him, she opened her own pack and found a neatly folded poncho. By the time she had it over her head, Ian had fitted his own, and a light rain had begun. "Will the rain be enough that the horses will need covered, too?" Beckie asked as she fitted her pack to the saddle in preparation for leaving.

"No. We will be under the trees until we return here on the way back, and the temperature, while chilly, will remain above freezing."

"You're sure of that report?"

He turned to look back, and Beckie pretended a huge shiver was racking her body. He did a double take, then laughed with her. "We will be fine."

"Sure! And… Oh, never mind." Better to focus on the riding.

In another couple of hours, Beckie was sure that snow was falling above them, covering the treetops. However, only water was dripping down on her; no ice so far. She'd just wiped her face and neck when Ian's hand went up in a quiet-stop warning. She reined the horse in and rubbed his neck in case he wanted a calming touch. He seemed fine, not even blowing in frustration.

Ian swung down and tied his mount's reins to a branch. Beckie did the same, then sidled up beside him.

"I heard something ahead; perhaps a donkey?"

"I must have been sleeping," Beckie said. "Heard nothing."

"It was not loud. Move off to the left about five meters, and we will see."

Beckie was always pleased when Ian assigned her a full role, even though it had been that way since before the wedding. She slipped in the direction he'd said and, finding a couple of landmarks, started away from the horses.

Only a couple of steps out, she stopped and worked her way out of the wet poncho. Be easier to move, and I can pick it up on the way back. She was happy she'd pulled on black for their jaunt. The tracker would allow Ian to find her, as his would her.

She'd heard the quiet braying a couple of times when Ian's mini-flash lit in her direction. She stopped and waited while he made his way to her. Waiting, she took another few steps and through a break in the branches, saw a clearing with a rope corral holding a half-dozen small pack animals. Yup, donkeys.

"You have seen?" She nodded in response. "My plan is to circle around. I neither see nor hear anyone, just the animals, and I wish to verify that."

"Hmm. Who would leave them here?"

"Smugglers. As they move the product on, the animals wait here. They have food. The smugglers will return, but probably not tonight."

"You sure?"

"Relatively. The trip back up the escarpment is not easy, and in rain, it is even worse. At night in the rain… I believe they will await daybreak, at least."

"So what are we looking for? Besides the donkeys, anyway, which I guess prove that something's going on. We are on the deVeel's property, right?"

Ian reached for his GPS. "Yes, by almost a hundred meters."

"And we can be sure the deVeels wouldn't have left animals out while they're staying with Carys and Nigel. So something's going on. What are we going to find?"

"Indeed. I hope to discover their camp close by, and that they may have left useful clues there, thinking themselves safe for the time being."

"Okay. I'll park here, and keep watch from this side. Signal if you find anything. If you want me to join you, flash the light."

He pulled her into a damp embrace, ended it with a kiss, and walked off.

Wish I'd kept that poncho now! Against one of the evergreens that filled the forest, Beckie made herself as small a target for the raindrops as she could. She waited for twenty minutes before a slight noise sharpened her attention. Reaching for the butt of her new pistol, she waited for Ian to pop out of the bushes. He did, but cautiously; stepping well clear of a bush perhaps ten meters from her, he made sure she could see and recognize him before joining her.

"Come." As they walked, he said, "They left a rudimentary camp, with nothing of value. However, I did discover five roaches. Hardly sufficient, to be sure, but it seems likely these are our smugglers."

"Roaches?"

"The butt of a smoked Marijuana cigarette."

"Oh. I missed that in the D.A.R.E. class, I guess."

Beckie looked around the space that Ian had led them to. "How many guys? And with six donkeys? How much can they carry, anyway?"

"Until we know more, it is all conjecture. However, dagga prepared for shipment to the United States, for example, can be sold for R1000 a kilo. The animals can carry perhaps fifty kilos each, though half that might be a better estimate, given the terrain between here and Lesothos. This dagga would not be ready for shipment, so would be worth less. Perhaps R100-R150 per kilo. So, if they carry—"

"If they carry 25 Kilos each, that's..." She worked the problem out. "That's over R20 000 for them all."

"For less than two week's work. And they can repeat every two weeks. R20 000 twenty or twenty-five times a year. R400 000 per year. With per annum poverty level income at R10 000 or less... You can see the attraction."

"Yeah! If it's two guys, they've beat the game in one trip."

"Indeed." Ian began a survey of the area, and Beckie did the same, going in the opposite direction. When they finished, Beckie posited that they'd learned only that the campers had used two or three tents, of a size that made two occupants likely.

"Well, are these the guys that raided the deVeel's home, do you think? 'Cause *they* won't be coming back."

"While it is certainly possible, I doubt it. It seems more likely that the purchasers here were attempting to acquire a spot for the smugglers to use, perhaps as a way to sweeten the deal, or because the smugglers asked for or demanded the facility." He tipped his head. "I am uncertain which is more likely."

"Well, I don't think we're gonna gain any more insights tonight. Unless you have another idea?"

"I do not. We should return and determine our next move."

Beckie walked through the undergrowth a few steps before taking Ian's arm. "No. I'll stay here and wait for them. I can keep back far enough to not get noticed, and I can let you know how many there are and where they head. That way you can start with the police or whomever looks after these kinds of things. You'll be better at that than me."

Ian's surprise was short-lived, but his concern was not. Beckie watched his expressions change until he finally said, "Your suggestion has several merits, but as many cogent reasons to argue against it. Before deciding, shall we check our supplies?"

"Yeah, including my phone's battery!"

Ian could find no reason to ask Beckie not to stay, based on their provisions. Beckie's phone was at sixty percent charge, sufficient for another day in the woods.

"Very well. Stay clear of any activity and I will return in the morning with Samuel and probably Willie and Elena to relieve you. Call if anything happens." He took her chin in his hand and gazed into her eyes. "You will do this, will you not?"

"I will, love. Too many things I still want to do with you." She pulled him close and kissed him. "Now, go! It's too wet to spread a blanket here, much as I want to!"

He returned her kiss, then chuckled. "Very well. Look for us by…" He glanced at the GPS. "… no later than nine-thirty, if we leave before sunrise."

She pushed him gently before saying, "I'll go with you to the horses. I can bring mine back here to wait." She looked around. "This should be far enough that they won't hear each other."

The wait was cold and since the rain continued, wet as well.

She started. Guess I dropped off to sleep… now, what…

Voices were approaching from her right. The men—it sounded like men only—were speaking loudly enough to cover any noise they made pushing through the wet bushes and ground cover. The sounds indicated that they were headed toward the campsite Ian had found earlier. She glanced at her phone: one-thirty. Ian's been gone… three hours, not long enough to make the house. While Beckie could hear words, she didn't understand the language; she decided to move a little closer.

A vantage point behind a shorter yellowwood bush gave on the campsite, probably twenty-five feet away. Five men had just thrown down packs and looked to be ready to set up their tents when one of them shouted, pointing at the ground. Beckie couldn't see what had attracted his attention, but it was in the area where she and Ian had examined the remnants of the discarded cigarettes. Whether his concern was shared, or merely his authority, the others wasted no time in grabbing their packs; they all rushed to the donkey pen.

She expected that the noise they made opening the gate and getting the donkeys ready to travel would cover any she and the horse would make; she edged her way back. After a pat on the nose, she looked at the overhanging branches and decided to walk. "You'll be fine here," she muttered in his ear, and eased back to where she could see the corral.

It was empty, and the last donkey's butt disappeared around another yellowwood bush. She glanced at her phone, and pushed the button to save her location. Still too early to call Ian.

While she was sure the men had been spooked by something she and Ian had left, they gave no evidence of worrying about being followed. The pace was good, considering nighttime and the rain, with no attempt at quiet. Occasionally, one of the donkeys would bray, calling for food or rest, Beckie thought with a chuckle, but by and large, she trailed by listening to the sounds of tramping ahead.

In deference to Ian's wishes, she made sure the donkey at the group's tail end was out of sight, not wishing to be caught. The men had all appeared to be dark, though in the rain and night, it was hard to be sure. Their clothes were heavy, the type that her web-based investigations of Lesothos and the Drakensberg Mountains suggested were common to the people who lived and worked in the near-alpine ranges above the cliffs.

The cliffs. In short order, she thought, they'd be bound to hit open grassland, and then the face of the escarpment itself. I guess I'll stop there and mark the point. Unless… She didn't want them to get away, but unless some way to cover herself showed… That'll be the end for today, I guess.

Her expectation was met in another fifteen minutes. While the sky hadn't lightened perceptibly, the sound from ahead changed, and she slowed, stopping just short of the plain that stretched off into the dark.

As she observed the field and the line of donkeys and men marching away from her, something hit her in the middle of the back. Her foot caught; as she fell she heard a shout followed by a burst of pain and a flash of light in her head.

Made in the USA
Charleston, SC
18 May 2015